Foreword

May 2022

From Ashlyn Kane:

MORGAN AND I wrote *Winging It* in the spring of 2014, two years before Auston Matthews was drafted. There had been a handful of Latinx professional hockey players before, but none with Matthews's star power. There had never been an openly gay or bisexual NHL player. As I'm writing this, there still hasn't, though current prospect Luke Prokop could be the first. Fingers crossed and knock on wood.

By the time we decided to turn *Winging It* into the first book in a series, it was already six years old. A facelift seemed to be in order.

That facelift turned into reconstructive surgery when we realized not only how much we'd grown as writers, but how much the league had changed. So if you're picking up this book and wondering what's different between this version and the original, here's a primer.

Characters. We've tried to trim down the number of characters and to keep the nicknames to a minimum to avoid confusion, at least as much as possible in a book about hockey players. For simplicity, Chef became Olie, a nickname derived from his last name. After a moment of horrified Googling, we decided to rename Fifi to Flash.

Point of view. It turns out Dante has a lot to say, and he's got such a way with words, so we let him talk this time.

Fictionalization. It would be impossible to keep up with which players are on what team in real life, so we didn't try. In this version, all the professional teams and players are fictional—no cameos. (We could not, however, bring ourselves to rename Mario Lemew.)

Focus. The original Winging It was a love story to hockey. Don't get us wrong. We still love hockey. But this is a romance about hockey players. This version has a little less hockey and a lot more romance.

Tone. When you're going into year three of a global pandemic, it turns out the only thing you want to write is romcoms. So this version has all the fun, energy, and humor, and less of the darker, nastier, less pleasant side.

If you're brand-new to *Winging It*, then welcome! We hope you like disaster adults with ice in their veins, fire in their hearts, and knives on their feet. You won't need any knowledge of Version 1 to enjoy Gabe and Dante's story.

From Morgan James:

THIS BOOK wouldn't exist if Ashlyn hadn't taken "Do you think you can edit this book in time for a rerelease in 2022?" as a challenge. The demands of life had me hopping to a different tune during the early months of the year, and I couldn't have given the book the attention it needed. So Ashlyn took the lead and whipped this baby into shape. I'm forever grateful to her patience with me as I was unable to match her time commitment to the project this go around.

By Ashlyn Kane

American Love Songs
A Good Vintage
Hang a Shining Star
The Inside Edge
The Rock Star's Guide to Getting Your Man

DREAMSPUN BEYOND
Hex and Candy

DREAMSPUN DESIRES
His Leading Man
Fake Dating the Prince

With Claudia Mayrant & CJ Burke:
Babe in the Woodshop

With Morgan James
Hair of the Dog
Hard Feelings
Return to Sender
String Theory

HOCKEY EVER AFTER
Winging It
Scoring Position

Published by DREAMSPINNER PRESS
www.dreamspinnerpress.com

By MORGAN JAMES

Purls of Wisdom

DREAMSPUN DESIRES
Love Conventions

With Ashlyn Kane
Hair of the Dog
Hard Feelings
Return to Sender
String Theory

HOCKEY EVER AFTER
Winging It
Scoring Position

Published by DREAMSPINNER PRESS
www.dreamspinnerpress.com

WINGING IT

ASHLYN KANE
MORGAN JAMES

DREAMSPINNER PRESS

Published by
DREAMSPINNER PRESS

5032 Capital Circle SW, Suite 2, PMB# 279,
Tallahassee, FL 32305-7886 USA
www.dreamspinnerpress.com

This is a work of fiction. Names, characters, places, and incidents either are the product of author imagination or are used fictitiously, and any resemblance to actual persons, living or dead, business establishments, events, or locales is entirely coincidental.

Winging It
© 2022 Ashlyn Kane and Morgan James

Cover Art
© 2022 L.C. Chase
http://www.lcchase.com
Cover content is for illustrative purposes only and any person depicted on the cover is a model.

Mass Market Paperback ISBN: 978-1-64108-425-3
Trade Paperback ISBN: 978-1-64108-424-6
Digital ISBN: 978-1-64108-423-9
Mass Market Paperback published October 2022
v. 1.0
First Edition published by Dreamspinner Press, February 2015.

Printed in the United States of America
∞
This paper meets the requirements of
ANSI/NISO Z39.48-1992 (Permanence of Paper).

Dekes Training Camp: Who's Who in the New Season
By Kevin McIntyre

Happy hockey season, Dekes fans!

With October just a few weeks away, training camp is starting, and there's lots to be excited about—so here's a primer on players to watch.

<u>Established Players</u>

Jacques Fillion, center, #96. Captain Jacques "Flash" Fillion is thirty-four this season and showing signs of slowing down. But with age comes wisdom, and Fillion has plenty left in the tank.

Gabriel Martin, right wing, #53. Martin has been the team's undisputed superstar since he was traded here three years ago. At twenty-eight, he's never won a Cup and has to be itching for a deep playoff run.

Isak Olofsson, goaltender, #33. At six foot four, Olofsson is a giant in the net in more ways than one. He's been nominated for the Vezina goaltending trophy twice but hasn't taken it home yet. Is this his year?

Emerging Talents

Mikhail Kipriyanov, defense, #7. Kipriyanov is young, talented, and a big body on
the ice, but he hasn't proven himself as a
top-line defenseman yet.

Dante Baltierra, left wing, #68. After a middling first season playing up and down
the lineup, Baltierra had a fantastic soph-
omore year until a concussion knocked
him out. It will be interesting to see
whether he can reclaim his spot next to
Fillion.

Unknown Quantities

Expect most of this year's draft class to
start the season with their juniors teams or in
the AHL. Two prospects we might see in the
pros are forward Tom Yorkshire and defenseman Dave Symons.

Conclusions

So what does all this mean? On paper, the
Dekes are a team that's primed to win and win
now. Fillion's window is closing if he wants to
take home the Cup before retirement. Martin's
in his prime and hungry. In Olofsson, the team
has a goaltender I'd pit against anyone in the
league. Look for the Dekes to be a strong contender this year, and don't be surprised by big
moves come the trade deadline as they look to
capitalize on their prime players' best years.

WARMUP

A TWO-STORY-TALL image of Gabriel Martin's face stared fiercely down at the man himself as he approached his team's arena.

Gabe wasn't normally that broody-looking off the ice—at least he hoped not. Today, though, he had a feeling it wouldn't matter if he was having the best hair day ever. Not even his signature blond curls could make anyone call him the press-given nickname "Anglo Angel" when he was glowering hard enough to peel paint.

In the locker room, he tried to put the morning behind him and focus on his job… but he could still hear the mental echo of the front door closing.

Unfortunately he could also hear the shrill note of Olie's catcall. "Holy shit. Would you look at the size of that thing!"

Gabe grabbed his trainers from the bench and fussed with the laces. He needed a few seconds to brace himself before he turned around. It had been bad enough to break up with his… whatever Pierre was… the day before training camp started *and* subject himself to a restless night's non-sleep. Now he had to face the ass of one Dante "Baller" Baltierra, a specimen large enough to have its own gravitational pull.

In seven years in the NHL and several more in the closet, Gabe had learned how not to look. But if there was a trick to not noticing, he hadn't discovered it.

There was nothing for it now, though. With all the attention the rest of the locker room was giving Baller—high fives and the occasional wolf whistle—Gabe would be more conspicuous if he *didn't* look.

He raised his head and wished he hadn't. Hockey ass was a documented phenomenon, but no one had it like Baller. Gabe had never seen an ass so perfect. And now it was even bigger and rounder.

"That's no moon—it's a space station!" a defenseman piped up from across the room.

Baller took it all with the grace of someone who'd spent his rookie season getting ragged on for the size of his butt. He bowed, then went in for a hug from Flash, who took advantage of his rights as captain and Baller's previous landlord and ruffled his black hair as he pulled away. Baller fussed with it as though he could push the longer strands on top back into order. "You're all just jealous because my milkshake brings all the girls to the yard."

"Your milkshake spent a lot of time on internet gossip sites this summer," Gabe added as Baller parked it in the stall next to his.

"Why, Gabriel, have you been keeping tabs?" Baller fluttered his eyelashes and faked a swoon. "Don't worry. There's plenty of Dante Baltierra to go around."

One more reason for him not to come out, as if Gabe needed one—it would make it so much more obnoxious when guys flirted with him in an attempt to chirp. Breaking things off with Pierre when he couldn't accept that Gabe wasn't going to be his boyfriend *or* his sugar daddy had been the right thing to do.

He wasn't the first guy to try it. He probably wouldn't be the last either.

"We know exactly how much of you there is to go around, you nudist." Flash swooped to Gabe's rescue just as he finished tying his shoes. He snapped a towel in Baller's general direction. "Put it away. Coach will make you do extra suicides tomorrow if she finds out you're fucking around in here. Two minute," he said to the rest of the locker room—his accent was always thicker after a long summer without English. Then Flash and Gabe headed to the training area to warm up.

"Think she'll put him on our line?" Gabe asked in French as they climbed on neighboring treadmills.

"If she doesn't, it's a waste of talent." Flash shot him a sideways look, giving Gabe a glimpse of the ragged, almost lightning-bolt-shaped scar at the corner of his eye. "You going to be okay with that?"

Only Flash and Olie knew Gabe was gay. And while Flash was always supportive and pretty good at nipping homophobic trash talk in the bud, Gabe wasn't taking chances with the rest of the guys. His own mother hadn't stuck around once he came out. The truth certainly wouldn't endear him to a professional hockey team. He could think about a rainbow parade once the Stanley Cup had his name on it.

"I never should've told you I thought he was hot." Fortunately Baller was such a caricature of himself that Gabe didn't have to worry about catching feelings. He deflected the conversation back to hockey. "He played well on our line last year."

"Yes, I remember," Flash said dryly. He stopped the treadmill for a minute to adjust the compression bandage around his right knee. "I was there. I also watched the game tape. Then I reviewed the statistics—"

"Oh my God, okay, point made." Gabe laughed and shook his head. "I'll stop back seat captaining." But Flash was still looking at him like he expected more. Like he was still thinking about—ugh. Gabe's stomach squirmed. He hated that look. It made him feel like a bug under a microscope. "Seriously, though. It's fine. Baller's… whatever. It won't affect my play."

"Yeah," Flash said, in English this time as the other players started trickling out of the locker room. "I know."

Famous last words.

"What?" Gabe finally asked when he couldn't take Flash side-eyeing him anymore.

"You could tell them," he said quietly. "They're not going to care. They're good guys and they like you."

Gabe took a deep breath and concentrated on not punching the treadmill. He didn't say what he was thinking: *They don't even know me.* And that was how it had to be. "No." He wasn't ashamed of being gay, but he didn't want to be Gabriel Martin, gay hockey player. He wanted to be Gabriel Martin, star Nordiques forward and Stanley Cup winner.

He couldn't do that if he got traded because suddenly his teammates didn't want to pass to him.

Besides, he practically grew up in locker rooms. He didn't have any illusions about universal acceptance.

Flash sighed. "Have it your way."

That was the idea.

DANTE LOVED media day.

That was probably vain of him, but whatever. Dante refused to pretend he was anything other than his whole self. Sure, there was something ridiculous about standing around in gear and running shoes and making sexy faces at the camera, but Dante was a ridiculous guy. Making the camera crew laugh kept him entertained, and with any luck they'd respond by not using the ugliest shots on the team's social media.

Admittedly, the makeup was not his favorite part. He felt shellacked, which the techs had definitely done to his hair. But the point was to minimize the glare from the lights and not to make his brown skin look whiter, so Dante sucked it up and did his best Mexican American version of Blue Steel until Tricia from PR threatened him with a water bottle.

"You love me!" he shouted over his shoulder as he jogged down the hall toward the locker room.

"You're trying too hard!" she shouted back, but he could hear the laugh in her voice.

Dante grinned. He could already see his face on the Jumbotron screen at Quebec City Amphitheatre, the stats beside his name ticking up with every point he scored.

Last year he'd taken a flukey hit to the head and only played a third of the season. This year he needed to do better. A point per game sounded pretty good. A little lofty maybe, but shoot for the stars and all that.

All he had to do was convince his coach that the open slot on the first line belonged to him.

Good thing Dante thrived under pressure.

He chucked his gear in his stall and ducked into the showers to melt the crap from his face and hair. Then he dried off and slung the towel over his shoulder. Time for phase one of his master plan—ingratiate himself with his teammates.

The locker room was a little over half full when he returned. Most guys were changing into street clothes, and a handful of prospects were talking in the corner, heads bent. Dante couldn't make out the words, but their body language said *I can't believe we're finally here*. Adorable. And relatable.

Olie was smirking to himself as he checked over his goalie gear. The locker-room lights glinting off his shiny brown head gave him a kind of halo, but Dante wasn't fooled. The gear-checking was part of his ritual, but the smirk wasn't. Someone was getting pranked today.

No Flash yet, but the captain always had extra media time. Gabe Martin, his right winger, was here, grimacing at his phone. As Dante watched, he silenced the thing and shoved it farther into the pile of stuff at the back of his stall. Dante knew that expression. That meant girl problems.

And *that* gave Dante a perfect opening.

He chucked his towel in the laundry and clapped once. "Can I have your attention please!" It wasn't a question.

When the volume in the locker room dropped, he realized he was naked. Whoops. Oh well. "I know you jerks missed me over the summer. Dinner and drinks at O'Ryan's?"

The prospies whooped. Olie looked up from his gear, met Dante's eyes, shook his head in fond exasperation, and went back to it, so Dante assumed he was in as well.

Now for his real target. Dante grabbed his underwear from the stall next to Gabe's and shimmied into them. Shit, his ass really had gotten huge. He might need to upgrade his boxers to accommodate. "You're coming, right?"

Gabe came out to the bar after games some nights, but he was always the first to leave, just like he was always the first guy in the dressing room or on the ice for practice. He didn't make small talk, which was annoying, because Dante was dying to pick his brain. Gabe could do things on the ice that made goalies cry for their mothers.

Gabe blinked, almost like he was looking through Dante, then shook himself and met his eyes. "Sorry?"

Woof. Whatever was going on in his head, a night out with the boys would do him good. "To the pub? To drown your sorrows?" Dante suggested. "I saw you looking at your phone. I know that look, man. Forget about her and come have fun."

Finally realization dawned in ice-blue eyes. Gabe's cheeks went slightly pink, which made him look every bit like his stupid media nickname—the Anglo Angel. The blond curls did kind of remind Dante of a fresco he'd seen once. "You've got me pegged, eh?"

Heh. *Pegged.* Dante clapped him on the shoulder and reached for his T-shirt. "Not yet," he said cheerfully. "But I bet we can find you a girl who's into that at O'Ryan's."

When he popped his head through the neck hole of the shirt, Flash was staring at him, judgment written all over his face.

Please. Dante had lived with the man, his wife, and their four kids. If Yvette got half a mind to whip out a strap-on, Flash would be on all fours in no time. But Dante wasn't going to say that out loud. He had *some* sense. Probably better to pretend he hadn't noticed the gimlet eye. "Cap! Tell Gabe he should come to O'Ryan's tonight and turn that frown upside down."

Flash's judgmental stare continued for another few seconds. Then he turned to Gabe. "Ouais," he agreed. "Captain's orders."

Dante fist-pumped. "Victory!" Now he could proceed to phase two—charming Gabe into agreeing Dante should play first line.

He reached for the jeans hanging at the back of his stall, but when he bent over to put them on, there was an ominous tearing sound from his boxers.

Son of a bitch. He paused with one foot in his pants.

Finally the snickers reached his ears and he straightened up and pulled his pants off again. "All right, Olofsson. You got me." Switching his boxers for the same brand in a smaller size. That took planning. Dante threw his jeans at Olie's head. Olie caught them, laughing, and Dante and the rest of the room joined in. "Yeah, yeah, my ass is so big it's normal that my boxers don't fit. You're hilarious. Now where'd you hide my underpants?"

O'RYAN'S PUB served food in hockey-player-sized portions and the owner had been a Dekes fan the first time around, so it was a perennial favorite among Gabe's teammates. Gabe liked it well enough—more social than a restaurant and lower-key than a club.

And the sweet potato fries were excellent.

When Gabe walked in, half the team was already sprawled over a few of the larger tables, laughing over beers. Gabe reminded himself that he belonged here as much as any of them and that any weirdness was in his own head.

"Gabe!" Baller waved him over.

Gabe mentally resigned himself to an exhausting evening. Baller had a personality that matched his ass. He was loud, exuberant, larger-than-life. He'd been the Dekes' first-round draft pick a few years back, but the coaches had deemed him unready for the NHL, so he spent a few seasons in the minors until he got called up two years ago. He played most of that first season up and down the lineup, and then last year, he started with Gabe and Flash… until he took a hit to the head and got sidelined for the second half of the season.

He slid into the seat next to Baller. "Are you corrupting the prospies?" It was the same every year.

Baller grinned his crooked grin. "Who, me? It's not my fault your country's drinking laws are so lax."

Next to him in the booth, Olie nudged his shoulder. "Flash's gonna make you babysit on our first road trip in the US. You know that, right?" Gabe caught his gaze behind Baller's back, and they exchanged smirks. It wasn't that rookies couldn't get into bars, but making them believe they couldn't was fun.

Baller was twenty-two—plenty old enough to participate in bar shenanigans in any country—but he shrugged and waved it off. "My liver will need a break by then anyway." That was probably true. "But for right now…." Baller lifted a shot glass of yellow liquid in each hand and offered one to Gabe.

He might as well get it over with. He just hoped it wasn't tequila.

Around the table, Flash, Olie, and a handful of prospies, most of whom probably wouldn't make the end of camp, raised shot glasses of their own. Nobody said *to the season*, because that would jinx it. You didn't talk about winning streaks for fear of breaking them, you didn't talk about playoffs in case you didn't make them, and God forbid anyone utter the word *shutout* before the clock ran out.

They touched glasses and swallowed the alcohol.

Fucking tequila. Gabe made a face. "You're the worst."

Baller patted him none too gently on the shoulder. "Admit it—you love me and Jose Cuervo really."

The tables filled up, and the servers took their orders. Gabe worried he and Baller would have nothing to talk about or that Baller would take the lull as an opportunity to offer him more tequila.

Instead Flash sucked him into a breakdown of the merits and weaknesses of power-play and penalty-kill units in last season's Cup final that lasted until their plates were cleared.

Baller looked on in bemusement. "You know, we're gonna have like eight months of nothing but hockey talk."

Flash snorted. "You'll learn. Gabe is very… focused."

He said it like it might be an innuendo. Gabe bristled. "Sorry I like winning."

Baller laughed. "No, no, it's cool. I respect it."

So it was nice. Even if he wasn't going to make hanging out with the guys a habit, Gabe enjoyed himself. At least until his phone buzzed in his pocket.

Gabe should've ignored it, but he pulled it out to check. *Unknown caller.* Yeah, right. He'd had two other "unknown callers" since he blocked Pierre's number.

They had met last season in Ottawa, where Gabe grew up and where he'd spent his summers. Pierre had had no idea who Gabe was. Gabe had been attracted to his lack of interest in hockey, and they spent the first few months of their acquaintance fucking like crazy whenever Gabe was in town.

But the fantastic sex had obviously fried Gabe's brain, because it took him months to realize Pierre wasn't being understanding about being Gabe's secret fling. Instead, he was biding his time, hoping to convince Gabe to be his sugar daddy.

Gabe wished he'd figured that out before he invited Pierre up to Quebec before training camp, but it was better to break things off now than have to handle drama during the season. He put his phone back in his pocket only to find Baller watching him.

"Dude, whoever she is, I guarantee you can do better." Then he gave Gabe a not-so-gentle nudge toward the end of the booth. "You gotta get up, though, 'cause Coach scheduled practice for ass o'clock tomorrow, so I have to pick up early."

Gabe let Baller out. "Gentlemen," Baller said with a jaunty wave. Then he disappeared toward the crowd of bodies around the bar.

"Our little rookie, all grown up." Flash sighed dramatically and leaned his head on Olie's shoulder.

One of this year's crop—Tom something—shook his head and hunched his shoulders. "How does he even pick up girls here? He doesn't speak any French."

Gabe caught himself before he sprayed the kid with a mouthful of beer. Olie took it upon himself to answer instead. "He's a professional hockey player. He makes almost a million dollars a year. And he's cute."

"Dat ass," Flash added gravely.

Gabe rolled his eyes at the memory. "Last year he tortured me by singing 'Lady Marmalade' until I taught him some better French pickup lines." That was one of the few times Gabe had gone out with the team.

Brightening, the prospie beside Maybe-Tom leaned forward, all lanky teenage earnestness. "Can you teach me?"

"You should get a native speaker to teach you." Gabe learned basic French in school, and he'd improved drastically since moving to Quebec, but he wasn't going to fool anyone into thinking it was his mother tongue.

"Why didn't Baller?"

"Baller *did*, but Flash was unhelpful," said Baller himself as he reappeared at the table with a beautiful girl under each arm. Gabe made a note to check his watch next time, because that was *fast*. Baller unwrapped his arm from the girl on his left, who had sharp cheekbones and full lips and was blushing shyly. "This is Fleur"—he gestured to the girl on the right— "and Elise. She wanted to meet you," he added to Gabe in an undertone. Then he winked. "Thought she could cheer you up."

Oh fuck. Gabe should've told Baller he was getting spam calls or something. He'd been stupid to hope Baller would forget about it.

"You have your phone?" he asked Elise in French to cover his discomfort.

Elise nodded and produced an iPhone in a pink case with the Nordiques logo. Gabe stood long enough to put his arm around her shoulders while Baller snapped a photo, then shook her hand. "It was nice to meet you, Elise." Now to steer her back to someone who was actually interested. He tilted his head at Baller. "Be careful with this guy, he's fragile. Still sleeps with his teddy bear. Leaves the hall light on." He winked at Flash and added, "François's wife used to tuck him in at night until he finally got his own place."

"What are you telling her?" Baller squawked as Fleur laughed out loud.

"Nothing that isn't true," Gabe said in English. "Have a good night, kids."

Baller didn't look at all reluctant as the girls dragged him toward the door.

Gabe turned back to the table to find the prospies staring at him. He sighed. "What?"

"You just—" Tom gestured emphatically.

"She was *so hot*," the prospie whose name Gabe had forgotten said mournfully. "Is Baller seriously going to go home with both of them?"

Gabe shrugged. "Probably."

"But *why didn't you…?*"

"Superstitious," Flash said, proving he wasn't Gabe's best friend for nothing. "One time he picks up on the road, pulls a muscle in his back doing too much athletic sex. Missed three games."

It was a true story. It just didn't involve a woman and had nothing to do with why Gabe never picked up when they went out.

"But it's still training camp."

"And a bunch of prospies are gunning for spots on the team—including mine, if I'm not careful," Gabe said. "Though if you keep drinking, I don't know about your chances."

Tom looked at the plethora of empty shot glasses littering the table and turned a little green. Gabe smirked and passed over a couple bills. "I'm out for the night. See you kids bright and early."

In his pocket, his phone buzzed again. Gabe took it out and turned it off as he walked out of the pub. For some reason, he had a powerful urge to spend some time in his garage, swinging a club at his golf simulator.

Maybe the satisfying *thwack* of the ball would ease the tension in his shoulders.

ON THE third day of training camp, Dante walked to the rink so deep in consideration of The Plan that he ran into Olie outside the locker room.

"Really, dude?" Olie's tone held a definite note of judgment.

Normally Dante had better spatial awareness. "Shit. Sorry." He paused and shook his head in wonder. "How are you this big even without your pads on?" Like, Dante wasn't the tallest guy on the team, but he was *solid.* Colliding with Olie almost made him fall backward on his ass.

Olie flicked him between the eyes, which was when Dante realized he was still wearing his sunglasses. "How bad did you overdo it last night?"

Dante *tsk*ed. "You know I don't kiss and tell." He enjoyed casual sex with interested women, but he was respectful about it. Besides, he had a Plan to see through; he hadn't stayed out all that late. He took off the sunglasses to prove he wasn't hungover. "I was just thinking."

"Don't hurt yourself!" someone chirped as they passed him in the hallway.

Dante sighed dramatically. "Everyone's a comedian." But he grinned anyway. The scrimmages that would help Coach St. Louis decide who to put on that empty first-line slot would start today.

Time to lace up.

Half the team was already on the ice when Dante finished in the locker room, but the coaches were still talking with each other, not running a formal practice, so he wasn't late. For a minute he let himself soak it in. An adopted Latino kid from a Southern state, he'd made it to the NHL. Two years of grinding it out in the AHL, hoping the big show would call his number, and then a frustrating injury that cut his rookie season short.

Now's my chance.

Coach St. Louis blew the whistle, and Dante hit the ice. He wouldn't let his opportunity slip away this time.

Not if he could help it.

Practice started out promising. St. Louis put him on the red-jersey practice squad with Flash and Gabe.

Dante knew he wouldn't pick up right where he left off—he'd been out for a while with a concussion at the end of last season, so he expected to be a little rusty. Of course, Flash and Gabe had played with each other for years and seemed to read each other's minds with every stride or minute movement of a stick. It was awesome to watch and hair-raising to be a part of.

Which only made it chafe that much more when Dante couldn't match them.

Oh, he kept up fine, speedwise. He didn't have any trouble getting where he thought he should be, and not even hulking defenseman Kitty Kipriyanov could knock him off the puck. He got the puck on Flash's tape often enough.

But Gabe was never where Dante expected him to be, and vice versa. It was like they saw totally different angles of attack. They dropped as many passes as connected.

By the time they broke for lunch, Dante was re-evaluating stage two of the Plan. It wouldn't be enough to simply get the coach to put him on first line with Flash and Gabe if they played like this. Their possession numbers would swan dive right into the toilet, and everyone would blame the new guy.

And Dante wasn't entirely sure it *wasn't* his fault. His ego would not allow him to be responsible for that kind of catastrophe. So first, he had to fix... whatever was keeping him from connecting with Gabe on ice.

No pressure or anything. Just the fact that he had zero chemistry with the team's top scorer. Like, that shouldn't even be possible.

Maybe Dante just hadn't given it enough time. But he didn't have much more time to give. There was no guarantee St. Louis would put him on the same practice unit again tomorrow. And sure, maybe he'd get lucky and hit it off with another center... but maybe not.

Lunch was catered, because afterward they had the annual sexual harassment/financial literacy/mental health seminar. Dante snagged the seat next to Gabe and started loading his plate with carbs and protein. "So listen." Was that some kind of white wine sauce on the chicken? It smelled incredible. He added a breast to his plate and then offered the tongs to Gabe, still holding the platter. "I wanted to ask a favor."

Gabe side-eyed him carefully, as though he was expecting Dante to dump the chicken in his lap. Obviously Gabe didn't know him very well yet; Dante would never waste food.

"I'm listening." He took a chicken breast, and Dante passed the platter down.

Fantastic. What was in that bowl of orange stuff? Roasted sweet potatoes? Interesting. He served himself a scoop and then glanced at Gabe again.

Gabe's suspicion had evidently been transferred to a dish of steaming creamed spinach. Yikes. Dante didn't blame him; he was passing on that too.

"We can't read each other on the ice."

Gabe went for the pasta instead, then wordlessly offered it to Dante, who nodded his thanks. "Yeah, I noticed. I was there for practice." When Dante said nothing, Gabe prompted, "So…?"

Finally Dante had to accept that, at the moment, his plate simply could not accommodate anything else. He picked up his knife and fork and sliced off a piece of chicken. "So I think I'm still the best fit for the spot on your line"—he wasn't going to pretend he didn't think he was hot shit; that fake humility BS wasn't for him—"but obviously we have to fix that. So will you stay late with me so we can work on it?"

Gabe blinked. "Who's to say I don't have plans?"

"You and the girl whose calls you've been dodging, you mean?"

"You don't know what you're talking about." He rolled his eyes.

"C'mon," Dante wheedled. "I'll buy you dinner after. Steak, even! And maybe we won't suck this year."

That earned him a flat look. Oops. Maybe that was a little insensitive. Gabe stared at him.

"I'll throw in dessert," he offered, desperate. "Beer. Wine. Look, I will fucking cook you a three-course meal if that's what it takes. Just say yes."

"Okay."

"Seriously. I will break out the risotto and—oh son of a bitch." Baller deflated and his shoulders slumped. "You were going to say yes the whole time, weren't you?"

Gabe glanced at him slyly out of the corners of his eyes. He was smirking.

Mierda.

"I think you're the best skater for the job." He shrugged while Dante fought not to bristle at the faint praise. "And it worked last year. I don't know why it's not working now. So yeah, I'm down for extra practice. But I'll definitely need dinner after… what are we calling this?" He jerked his head toward the conference room doors, where a large sign reminded them of the afternoon's agenda.

Dante quirked his lips. "Social-responsibility community theater?"

Gabe buried a snort in his dinner roll.

A COUPLE hours later, Gabe regretted his choice. Yes, Baller was fast. Yes, he had a great shot.

He was also vibrating at a frequency that felt like it would knock Gabe's fillings out. Shifting from foot to foot, tapping his stick relentlessly against the boards, squeezing all the air out of his water bottle and then letting it slowly wheeze back in, all while Gabe was tying his skates. "Did you drink an entire case of Rockstar during that meeting? You've got the fucking jitters."

"I had three cups of coffee," Baller admitted sheepishly. "Haven't had any all summer. Maybe not the best idea."

You think? Gabe shoved him toward the ice. "Go work it off. We can't practice like this." Forget getting their passes to connect. They'd be lucky if they accomplished more than learning to hate each other.

While Baller did laps, Gabe stretched out on the ice. It was weird. Hockey gear stank like nothing else in every context except when you were on the ice, and then it was… good. *Right.*

"What is this, yoga hour?" Baller called from the other end of the ice, bouncing a puck in the air as he skated. "Come on, let's go."

One day Baller wouldn't be twenty-one anymore, and then he would understand. "Who begged who for this practice session again?"

Baller sprayed to a stop beside him. The snow he kicked up fell just short of Gabe's face. At first he looked like he might laugh. Then he grimaced, and the mask of cocksure exhibitionist slipped just a little, revealing something real underneath. "Sorry. I guess I'm kind of anxious."

Gabe took a deep breath and let it out as he finished stretching out his hamstrings. His irritation eased as the muscle relaxed. He'd been anxious too when he was new in the league and eager to prove himself. He'd just reacted differently. "I get it." Then he jerked his head toward the bench, where one of the equipment guys had left some stickhandling trainers. Not as good as live opponents, but they could make do for now. "Come on, let's get these set up."

They started out running standard plays from the previous season, using the stickhandling trainers as opponents—set right side up to indicate their foot placement, with the obstacle flat to the ice in an arc around them, showing where their sticks would get in the way.

The set plays at low speed went fine. But when they moved the "players" around and started improvising, it fell apart. Gabe would see a shooting lane open and put the puck there for Baller, only to find Baller had gone somewhere completely different.

"All right, what are we doing wrong?" Baller said finally. "One of us is seeing something the other isn't."

They went over the passes that hadn't connected. "... and you're a left-handed shot," Gabe said. "This guy and this guy"—he gestured to the obstacles and their phantom sticks—"one of each, and they're covering more of the middle between them than you think. But if you skate a little farther—"

"I'll be around the defending lefty with a sharp angle at the net," Baller filled in.

"Or you can backhand pass around him to a cherry-picker in front."

It didn't always work, but they got better. To Gabe's surprise, for every two corrections he made, Baller came up with an equally valid one, pointing out something Gabe had overlooked—that they weren't taking advantage of how fast Baller was, or that he *could* actually deke through a narrow opening without losing the puck.

And his shot wasn't just good. It was *filthy*.

Gabe couldn't wait for the season to start.

They were still having trouble improvising, though. Sometimes things on the ice didn't go according to plan. They would still need to be able to anticipate each other's movements. Having a centerman would probably help, but Gabe wasn't going to ask Flash to stay late at training camp. He barely saw his kids during the season. Besides, Flash wouldn't always be there to bridge the gap.

"Maybe we just need to feel each other out a bit more," Baller suggested. "One-touch? With the trainers set up down the ice?"

It was a pretty simple drill—skating down the ice together and bouncing the puck back and forth. They'd both been doing it since before they were three feet high. But it did require them to work together, since the point was to ping-pong the puck and not keep it.

They skated the length of the rink a few times, slow and then at full speed, and it worked. But as soon as they tried to do it the way they'd need to in a game, without looking….

Baller swore in Spanish, obviously frustrated.

"We keep losing the rhythm," Gabe said unhappily.

Baller froze for a moment before a mischievous smile lit his face. "I've got an idea." He skated over to the bench, and a minute later the tinny sounds of music piped through a portable speaker filtered into the air. He gestured as if to say "ta-da." "If we keep losing our rhythm, then let's make sure it sticks."

At first Gabe didn't recognize the song Baller had picked, but he could appreciate the appropriateness of the first line about shooting for the stars.

Gabe started moving, skating down the ice to the beat, dribbling the puck. When Baller joined him, it was easy enough to pass to him on the downbeat. Even without looking, he knew it was going to connect. Baller caught the puck and passed it back on the next.

At the end of the rink, they curved around and headed back up in the other direction, slipping into one of their plays without discussing it. Gabe still had no idea what they were listening to. After another length, he lifted the puck and fired it into the net. He'd just resolved to ask when the chorus started.

"'Moves Like Jagger'? Really?"

Baller laughed. "What, you didn't recognize my man Adam until now?"

Who? Gabe considered asking but didn't want to look more ridiculous. "'Moves like Jagger' isn't exactly high up on my list of favorite songs," he said dryly.

"Your loss," Baller said as he singled out another puck from the pile. "You go behind the net with it this time and I'll come up the boards."

Eventually the song ended. And then started back up again.

"Really?"

Baller grinned. "It's got a good beat." He wiggled his butt a bit to demonstrate, but he still managed to catch the puck Gabe shot at him. Apparently the rhythm was just what they needed. He toe-dragged to the net and dumped it in.

"So do a lot of other songs. New ones, even." Gabe wasn't sure how old the song was, but he had the vague sense its inescapable airplay had coincided with his rookie years.

"Don't be a hater! I'll have you know this song was totally cool at my first middle school dance." And there was another reminder that Dante was barely more than a babe and Gabe shouldn't want to bang that ass like a screen door in a hurricane.

"Besides, it's good for running! Don't you run?"

"Yeah." Shaking away those thoughts, Gabe picked up another puck as they turned around again and made for the other end of the ice, weaving in and out of the obstacles. Baller caught his pass, no problem.

Okay. So maybe the music thing wasn't a terrible idea. Gabe was even starting to like the damn whistling since he was quickly associating it with the rhythm they were sharing and the satisfying swish of vulcanized rubber hitting the net.

Despite his thawing toward the song itself, Gabe didn't find Baller any less annoying when they packed up and he started singing to fill the void left by his phone—obnoxiously and off-key.

This was definitely a "look at your life, look at your choices" moment. This was *not* cute.

Gabe whacked Baller's still-wiggling butt with his stick. "Put that damn thing away before you hurt something. Or someone."

"Oh, fuck you." Baller smirked. "My ass is magnificent."

Unfortunately Gabe agreed. "You're a magnificent ass, you mean."

"Ouch." He put a hand to his chest as though wounded.

"Hit the showers," Gabe told him with a roll of his eyes. "You stink. And for the love of God, find something else to sing while you're in there."

Of course, that led to a rousing shower-room serenade of "Lady Marmalade," which was particularly entertaining when Baller gave up on the actual lyrics and started making up his own.

When he'd dressed again—Baller was still warbling "he starred in a porno that wasn't fresh enough"—Gabe bit the bullet and checked his phone.

Two missed calls. Four new messages. It could've been worse.

His voicemail inbox was empty. Though his phone indicated they originated from a blocked number, the texts were both obviously from Pierre. Gabe deleted them without reading them and headed home before Baller got out of the shower.

DANTE WOKE with a "Moves Like Jagger" earworm and didn't care one bit. In fact, the lyrics on repeat sent him grinning into his morning routine even as he chugged down the protein shake the team nutritionist had put him on last spring. He and Gabe had a rhythm—they had chemistry. Last year wasn't the fluke, yesterday's practice was, and Dante intended to prove it.

He kept the bounce in his step all the way to the locker room and only smirked when some of the guys asked what he'd been up to last night. No one needed to know that he'd gone to bed early after some quality time with Disney+, or that Gabe Martin was the one responsible for his pep. Not that Dante cared what the team thought—they could rag him for a hockey crush all they wanted—but he doubted Gabe would be pleased if teammates started joking about them having an affair.

On the ice, the morning passed with more drills, more scrimmages. Coach got them moving, trying different pairs, and she seemed pretty pleased at the rhythm Dante and Gabe had built up the night before. Dante shamelessly hummed the tune under his breath to get the rhythm, but whatever, Gabe was totally doing the same. The point was that it was working.

Coach kept putting Dante back on Gabe's line, and every time, Dante curbed the urge to fist-pump in victory. Coach had tolerated him last year—he liked to think she had the same fondness for him as she might have for a puppy that sometimes knocked over the furniture—but she was all business on the ice and didn't put up with shit.

Considering she was the only female coach in the league, Dante figured she'd played "my balls are bigger" more than any other coach just to get here. She wasn't about to let any dumb dog get in her way, no matter how cute.

Still, if Dante gave some happy shimmies while lining up for the next drill, no one had to know why.

"Oh my God," Gabe muttered. "Did you mainline coffee again today?"

"What?" Dante blinked, projecting innocence.

"You keep shaking like you have to pee."

"I promise not to piddle on the carpets, dude," he laughed just as Flash reached them. The captain just shook his head and muttered darkly in French, so Dante didn't bother to explain.

After practice, Dante followed the team back to the locker room, but he didn't rush for the showers. He took his time, enjoying the atmosphere, the energy. As a kid, before he fell in love with the sport, Dante had loved his team first. There was something about knowing that you were part of the group, that these were your guys, you were in it together. And every summer, Dante missed that. So he lounged in his stall, shooting the shit, calling out jokes, and teasing the boys. It wasn't until the room was half empty that he noticed Gabe's bag was still in his stall and the man was conspicuously absent.

He found Gabe on the ice, gliding aimlessly around the rink. Yeah, Dante wasn't passing on this.

Gabe took his time gliding over. "What's up?"

Dante shrugged, all casual, like his inner thirteen-year-old girl wasn't squeeing her damn head off. "Thinking about practicing shooting. You in?"

"Sure."

Grinning, Dante grabbed the pucks.

They kept staying late. They'd mess around on the ice, playing keep-away and having dumbass competitions about who could shoot better or skate fastest, and it was awesome.

Until Coach found them on the fourth day and kicked him out.

"Tabarnak!" she swore. "What are you, crazy? You trying to burn yourselves out before the season even starts?" She gazed up at them with righteous fury. Her brown hair was loose around her face for once, instead of the tight neat ponytail she wore during practices and games, and it made her look wilder. Dante hurried off the ice, tail between his legs, with Gabe hot on his heels.

The next day Dante arrived home earlier than usual and sat on his couch for a few moments, at something of a loss. It was too early for dinner and he had to fill the hours somehow, so he called his *abuela*.

"Mijo," she greeted with delight. "How are you? Are you happy to be back in the cold?"

Abuela always said there was too much Mexico in her blood to enjoy the snow, and she'd never understood Dante's love for a sport played on ice. Dante liked to joke back that maybe his bio parents were northerners who had embraced the cold. But she only tsked at him. "You were found in a house of God, mijo, bundled in a Mexican blanket with a *mal de ojo* bracelet. You are Mexican."

Dante figured his dad being Mexican mattered more in the grand scheme of things—growing up in the culture meant something—but Abuela was convinced it was in his blood. And though he could take one of those DNA tests, he didn't want to risk shattering his abuela's deep-rooted belief.

"Very happy," he laughed. "It's good to be back on the ice. I think I'm going to be first line."

"First line! How wonderful." Abuela might not have a natural love for hockey, but she'd learned for her grandson. "Tell me everything."

So he did—about the terrible first practice, about he and Gabe staying late, about their developing chemistry.

"What a good boy, that Gabriel." She said his name in Spanish. "I am glad you have such men looking out for you. You are young, and young men are foolish."

"Thanks, Abuela."

"Tsk. You know what I mean. Only a young man gets his trysts documented on the internet."

Even Dante blushed when he found out that his grandmother had read something about his sex life. "Okay, yes, I'm young and foolish, and I'm very lucky to have older, wiser Gabe looking out for me and my irresponsible ass."

Abuela laughed.

The rest of training camp passed in a blur. Before Dante knew it, he was pulling his truck up at the Fillion residence for the start-of-preseason barbecue. Tomorrow they'd have their first exhibition game. Dante couldn't wait.

But in the meantime, there was phase three of the Plan.

"There you are, Coco!" Flash's wife, Yvette, embraced him almost as soon as he opened the door. "You've been away too long."

"I'm back now." He swung her around and then set her feet back on the floor and offered up his bounty—a bottle of Glenlivet. "And I brought your favorite."

Yvette kissed his cheek. "And the kids' favorite too."

"Uncle Dante!"

"Baz!" He swooped down and scooped up the second-youngest Fillion child. "Ooof. You got heavy. How much growing did you do this summer, huh? How'm I going to throw you in the pool now?"

Baz giggled. "Practice. Like we do with English."

Flash's kids were abominably cute. Dante had never been around children much. He'd grown up an only child—an adopted one. His mother's family didn't live close, and his dad didn't have any siblings. Last season, he lived with Flash and Yvette and three—four, after Dominique was born—small humans, and got a taste of life in a big family. It tasted like chaos—warm, loving, occasionally very shrill chaos. Practically Dante's natural habitat.

He propped Baz on his hip, ready to create some chaos of his own. "Good idea. Should we start now?"

"*Non*—I have to take my—" He looked at Yvette and said something in French.

"Bathing suit," she supplied.

Dante winked at her and carried Baz through the house toward the back door. "Are you *sure*? I think I could throw you in just like this." He pushed the slider open.

"Noooo," Baz squealed dramatically as he tried to squirm away. Dante adjusted his grip to make sure he wouldn't fall or hurt himself. "I need my bathing suit! Put me down!"

"Oh, well." Dante stepped outside onto the grass. "If you say so." He pretended to drop Baz, caught him before he could fall more than a few inches, and then lowered him to the grass, where he laughed like a hyena for ten seconds and then scampered off, presumably to get changed.

Mission accomplished.

Though Dante was early—early*ish*—the yard was already full of people. Flash had invited all fifty or so players who'd participated in training camp, though half of them had already left to go back to the Dekes'

AHL affiliate. Partners, offspring, and staff were invited too. Flash said he didn't want his *own* wife and kids to be bored.

No danger of that today, Dante thought. But apparently the two call-ups who'd come out with them the other night were not so easily engaged, because they were skulking around the drinks table, jostling each other's shoulders.

Rookies. What were their names again? Tom something... Yorkshire? Yes. And... Simmons? Stevens? Something like that.

Either way they were up to something, and it didn't look like anyone else had noticed. Fine. Dante could deal with it. Perfect opportunity to develop his off-ice leadership skills. He walked up behind the pair and draped his arms around their shoulders. "Rookies!" He injected the word with artificial relish. "Who are you again? Yorkshire, right? And... Simmons?"

"Symons," the kid on Dante's right corrected. Shit, had he had them mixed up in his head this whole time? Oops.

"Symons," Dante repeated. "Yorkie and... Symzy? That's terrible. We'll workshop it." He glanced down. Symons was holding a bottle of Jack Daniel's, which proved that he was two kinds of idiot. "I can't help but notice that you're lurking in front of the drinks table. That's shady, kids. You're not thinking about spiking the punch like a fourteen-year-old at homecoming, are you?"

Yorkie's ears went scarlet. Not his idea, Dante guessed, especially since he wasn't the one holding the bottle.

Symons handed it over, shamefaced. "We just wanted to make sure it was a good party."

Dante set the bottle on the table, at the back, where no kids would be able to reach it. "Did you fall asleep in class this week and miss some important information?"

Yorkshire squirmed. "I told you it was a dumb idea," he muttered.

Dante wondered what it said about him that the rookie's willingness to sell out the instigator warmed his heart. "I know you weren't thinking about spiking the punch, 'cause that would be illegal, unethical, and also a real juniors-level stunt. Take a look around, *gilis*. There are kids here, and *someone is always pregnant*."

Seriously. There were forty guys between the ages of eighteen and thirty-five here, as well as their partners. Morons.

"Sorry," Yorkie said quickly. He'd gone white-boy pale. "You're right. This was really stupid." He stepped on Symons's foot.

Symons grimaced. "Yeah. Uh, obviously we won't be doing that again. Thanks for stopping us before we fucked up."

Dante took a step backward and gently knocked their heads together. "You're welcome."

They moved away from the drinks table, and Symons shook his head. "I can't believe internet playboy Dante Baltierra called me on a party foul."

Fuck, now Dante needed a drink. He grabbed one of Flash's fancy microbrews from a cooler. "Yeah, well. Don't go telling anyone."

FLASH WOULDN'T let Gabe skip out on the barbecue, and Gabe wouldn't have tried. He kept his distance out of necessity, not because he liked it, and there were enough people here today that he could fly under the radar.

When he first arrived, he left a bottle of eighteen-year-old Bowmore on the liquor cabinet for Yvette—it was only for her and she shouldn't have to share—and let himself out into the backyard.

It was a good thing Flash had a big lot. Besides the pool, he'd set up a volleyball net in the far back corner, along with a tent and folding tables. Gabe had plenty of places to disappear to.

He picked the volleyball game first, because it was sociable but not intimate and it looked like fun.

"Need an alternate?"

Kitty turned and beamed at him. "Gabe! You're tall. You can be on my team."

"Wow, glad I meet your high standards."

"Hah! High standards." The laugh came from Baller, who was standing on the other side of the net with one of the rookies. "C'mon, old guys. I bet we can take you."

"Old guys?" Gabe looked at Kitty. "You see any old guys?"

"I am twenty-four," Kitty said. "You see children?"

"Lots of 'em," Gabe confirmed. "And I bet they'll cry like babies when we're finished with them too."

With a laugh, Kitty passed him the volleyball. "You serve first."

When the game ended—in a tidy win for Gabe and Kitty, who had a height advantage, even if Gabe did get distracted once or twice after Baller took his shirt off—he retreated to find a drink. In the time they'd been playing, the yard had filled up the rest of the way, largely with couples and children. Now the volleyball court had two defensemen and their girlfriends facing off, with Baller and Yorkie each bolstering one side. The pool was awash in children climbing on parents and honorary aunts and uncles, the young ones in floaties and the older ones decked out with goggles or snorkels. Kitty and Flash's oldest were having a pool-noodle battle on the diving board. Opposite the volleyball court, a bunch of primary-age kids were embroiled in a water-balloon fight.

Gabe shoved down whatever emotion was trying to surface at the scene, acquired a second beer to be polite, and meandered to the back of the yard, where an ominous cloud was rising from Flash's grill. He waved a hand through the smoky air. "Tout va bien ici?" Jeez. He blinked hard to clear the sting from his eyes.

"Everything is under control," Flash informed him with a cough. His apron read *Kiss the Cook*.

Gabe pried off a bottle cap and thrust the beer at Flash, who reached for it automatically. While he was distracted, Gabe grabbed the tongs from his other hand. "Everything is on fire."

He lifted the lid of the barbecue and inhaled a lungful of carbon. Healthy. With a mental shrug, he poured some of his own beer onto the grill in an attempt to douse the flames. "Your wife says raising four children is hungry work and she doesn't want to starve, so she's lucky she has me to provide for her." Lies. Gabe was useless in the kitchen, but at least he didn't burn meat on a grill.

Flash scowled. "She did not say that." Then he looked at the barbecue, and his lips twitched. "Fine. You can take over, but you have to wear the apron."

Gabe would hand the tongs over to the first competent person to make a comment about his grilling technique. It shouldn't take long. "Fine." He fiddled with the barbecue knobs. Finally he could see the alleged "meat"—now charcoal briquettes. He scraped them into a corner.

"Olie's bringing a date."

Gabe blinked. "Oh?" Olie hadn't said anything about meeting someone new. Then again, Gabe didn't talk to most of his teammates about relationship stuff since it was awkward when he couldn't reciprocate. "You think it's serious?"

"I guess we'll find out." Flash nudged him. "Her name is Adele. If she can put up with us, he should marry her."

That would officially make Gabe the team's oldest bachelor. "True." He placed a bunch of raw burgers on the grill. Surely some unsuspecting dad would wander by, tell Gabe he was doing it wrong, and insist on demonstrating. He peered around the lid.

He didn't see any obvious suckers, but he did see Olie and the woman who must be Adele standing together on the back patio. She was beautiful, of course—tall, glossy brown hair, wide smile. She wore a pink-checkered sundress with bright lime-green sneakers and somehow made it work.

Yeah. Olie was definitely going to marry her.

"Another one bites the dust, eh?" Baller said, approaching with five-month-old Dominique on his shoulder. He kept her well clear of the barbecue smoke and had tucked her yellow sun hat under his chin so she couldn't dislodge it. When he got a look at the apron, his eyes lit up. "Don't worry, Gabe, I'm sure you're next."

Flash coughed indiscreetly.

Baller met gazes with Gabe, his eyes dancing with laughter. "Wow. What a vote of confidence from the captain." He *tsk*ed and turned Dominique around so Gabe could see her face, then took her right hand in his and waved it at Gabe. "Nikki believes in you."

Dominique reached her chubby arms toward Gabe, and he put his out. "Here, trade me."

"What?"

But Baller was too slow to react. Now Gabe had the baby and Baller had the barbecue tongs.

Gabe kissed Dominique's cheek and backed away from the grill. "Thanks, Baller! Don't let Flash take over if you want to eat today. His nickname is a little too accurate. He already made a kilogram of charcoal."

While Baller sputtered, Gabe made a beeline for the shaded patio. Dominique might throw up on him, but at least she wouldn't comment on his relationship status. And baby cuddles made for an excellent distraction.

FOR THEIR first preseason game in Ottawa, Dante got assigned Tom Yorkshire as his road roomie.

"Nice!" He bumped shoulders with Yorkie and plopped down next to him on the team bus. Symons had been sent back to his junior team, but Yorkie might crack the roster come the regular season. It would be nice to have someone closer to his age to bond with. "That's a good sign for you. And I'm an awesome roommate, obviously."

"I'm not," Yorkie said. "I snore and I'm messy and I never put down the toilet seat." He waited a beat, then grinned. "Just kidding."

Dante snorted. He wasn't exactly the world's neatest person himself. "You had me going. Hey, what video games do you like?"

Normally he'd have slept on the bus ride, but he was too keyed up. Maybe it was only preseason, but Dante was itching to play real hockey again. Besides, if

Yorkie was going to be sticking around, chances were they'd be roommates in the regular season too. Time to make friends.

So he told Yorkie all about growing up in the southern US. He was adopted in Louisiana, but his parents had also lived in Kentucky, North Carolina, and Tennessee. He was an only child and really close to his parents, which Yorkie would figure out pretty quickly since Dante called them for a few minutes almost every night when he was on the road.

In turn, Yorkie regaled him with stories of the pranks he and his two older sisters used to play on each other and the shenanigans he'd gotten up to in boarding school.

"… but it worked out okay because Jenna agreed to go out with me."

Dante cackled. Maybe Gabe wouldn't be the next one to get married off after all. "That's adorable. And you said she goes to school here now?"

"Yeah! She's a junior. She took extra courses even though she's also got a hockey scholarship, 'cause she's so smart."

This was adorable. "Are you gonna meet up with her tonight?" Dante waggled his eyebrows.

"She's gonna come to the game."

Even better. "You gonna go back to her place after? I could cover for you."

He sighed. "I wish. She's in the dorms. Like, archaic dorms where your roommate is in a bed four feet away from you."

Dante snorted. "Like ours will be tonight?" Although really, who was Dante to stand in the way of true love? Surely someone else on the team would be willing to take him in so Yorkie could have some quality time with his girl. Half of the guys on standard contracts—unlike Dante and Yorkie, who were still on entry-level ones that meant they had to share hotel rooms—would probably end up with an extra bed they wouldn't use anyway.

So it was just a matter of picking his target—somebody who owed him a favor or wouldn't mind exchanging one, like Flash, who sometimes needed a sitter last-minute so he could get alone time with his wife... or maybe somebody who'd already done Dante a favor. Someone who had proven he was soft and would probably do it again.

He'd wait until Gabe said yes to mention it to Yorkie, though. No sense getting his hopes up.

Since it was a preseason game, the roster was mostly young guys and newer team members, the better to test them in game scenarios. It made for a fun team dinner. Dante always loved a captive audience, and the wide-eyed kids listening attentively to his pearls of wisdom—and the eye-rolling veterans scattered between them—were nothing if not captivated.

Once he'd lulled everyone into a false sense of security, Dante turned brown puppy eyes to Gabe. "So, as you may be aware, I'm sharing a room with Yorkie."

Gabe arched a brow as though to say, *And?*

Dante already knew he had him. "His girlfriend is in college here, and she's living in res just a couple minutes away from our hotel—"

"So she's in university," Gabe cut in.

Derailed, Dante blinked. "What?"

"If she's downtown, she's probably at university." Gabe patted Dante's shoulder, a gesture of exaggerated condescension. "You're in Canada still."

Dante rolled his eyes. "Whatever, dude. Where she's studying is not relevant to the story. What is relevant is universally tiny dorm beds and roommates. Yorkie wants to be a gentleman and bring her back to the hotel, but...."

"But he also has a roommate?"

Dante knew Gabe had a brain under all those curls. "You have a double anyway, right?" He might've arranged to peek in a couple rooms when they were all dropping off their bags. "Let me crash in the other bed. I promise to be the quietest roommate ever."

Obviously Gabe was a sucker for young love and puppy-dog eyes, because he caved. "We can move your stuff to my room when you go back to change before drinks."

Baller grinned and punched his shoulder. "Awesome. Hey, Yorkie. Guess what!"

The game that night wasn't perfect. Dante and Gabe played top line, but Flash was home in Quebec City, so their center was a guy Dante had played with in the AHL. Still, when he got the puck to Gabe in the neutral zone, Dante knew it didn't matter. He knew exactly where he needed to be—where Gabe was going to put the puck. It came sliding perfectly through traffic, right onto Dante's tape.

Dante faked a shot at the far side of the net and went bar down instead. The ring of puck on metal—sweet music. He whooped, and his teammates slammed into him to celebrate.

It didn't last, unfortunately. The game ended 3–2 in Ottawa's favor. But Dante was still full of adrenaline, high on having hockey back and on being one step closer to his goal of a permanent spot on first line. "I am going out tonight," he announced to the locker room after the game. "Who's in?"

Not Yorkie, obviously, but maybe Dante's new liney would want to celebrate their hard-won chemistry. He fluttered his eyelashes at Gabe. "I'll be your wingman."

"Pass," Gabe said, deadpan.

The locker room broke out in laughter.

"Ouch." Dante put a hand over his heart as though he'd been shot. Of course Gabe didn't want to come out with him. Hockey aside, they didn't have all that much in common, and Gabe didn't exactly go out to pick up anyway.

Dante had made sure Gabe knew who he was. That was the whole point of Dante's what-you-see-is-what-you-get philosophy of life—to weed out people who wouldn't accept all of him. There was no reason for the rejection to hurt, so Dante told himself it didn't.

"I go," Kitty offered. "You buy."

Dante pasted on a grin. "Yeah, okay. First round's on me."

From the sudden chorus of enthusiastic responses, he should've opened with that.

He was just buttoning his suit pants when Gabe said, "I'm meeting my dad."

Oh. Dante raised his head. "I didn't realize you were from Ottawa." That made sense, though. No wonder he knew so much about the college and university situation here.

"Born and raised." He shrugged into his suit jacket. "I try to visit whenever I'm in town."

"Must be nice. My parents live in Louisiana. No chance of scheduling dinner with them while I'm on a road trip."

As they made their way out of the room, Gabe glanced at him sideways. "You don't have an accent."

Dante snorted. "Yeah, I do." He let the vowels drag out, then quirked a half smile when Gabe stared at him. "But it made it harder to have a conversation with guys who speak English as a second language, so I learned how to fake Midwest." Mostly true. He'd mastered it as a kid in juniors, tired of being the butt of jokes. By the time he realized other people were the problem, he really did find communicating with his foreign team-mates easier.

"Should've picked something cooler." Gabe nudged his shoulder. "Californian. Scottish. Australian."

Completely logical suggestions all. Dante nudged him back. "The idea was to be *more* understandable."

That earned a self-deprecating laugh. "Fair." Dante followed him onto the bus, then thought, *Why not?* and sat down next to him.

"Are you going to be out late? Should I send a search party if you're not in the hotel by midnight?"

"I'm not going to turn into a pumpkin," Dante promised with a grin. "But, like, it's gonna be close. I might be slightly orange."

"So you're saying I shouldn't wait up."

"That's what I'm saying."

The bar Dante and Kitty and company found them-selves at that night was full of college—or university, *whatever*—students celebrating the return of freedom from their parents. Dante dutifully waded up to the bar to take care of a round of drinks, then slipped into the sea of writhing bodies on the dance floor.

He slipped back out twenty minutes later holding the hand of a short, curvy girl with brown skin and a pink streak in her tightly curled hair. "I'm Tessa," she said when they were far enough from the speakers to hear each other talk. "You wanna get out of here?"

Dante loved college bars. "Absolutely."

LESS THAN two hours later, Dante thanked his Uber driver and headed into the hotel. The evening had definitely not gone to plan—heartbreak was a bitch and Dante never wanted to be That Guy—but there would be other nights for Dante to make a connection. Besides, he had hockey back, and nothing could bring him down.

He whistled to himself as he strolled down the deserted corridor. Gabe was probably still out with his dad, and Dante could have a nice hot shower with the company of Mrs. Palm and her five lovely daughters.

He held his key card up to the door and pushed it open.

And froze.

Gabe and a man he didn't know were sitting on the bed farthest from the door, shirtless, kissing.

Or they were, until they heard the door open, and—

"Actually, this explains a lot," Dante said after a moment of excruciating, mortified silence. "I'm gonna—uh—"

He closed the door and fled.

GABE PULLED away from Nick and buried his face in his hands. "Fuck."

Served him right for being too lazy to cab downtown to meet Nick at the condo Gabe kept in Ottawa—but it was a half hour from the hotel, and Nick had already been in Kanata, just a few minutes away.

Nick cleared his throat. "Well. That was kind of a mood-killer. But at least he didn't walk in ten minutes later."

This was not how Gabe had intended to come out to a teammate. Not that he'd *ever* intended to do that, but at least he'd have preferred to be fully clothed.

Would Baller tell the team? Worse, would he tell people who *weren't* on the team? Would the whole world find out Gabe's secret?

"Hey," Nick said gently. He ran his warm palm over Gabe's back. "Breathe. I take it you're not out to your teammates."

"Not all of them," Gabe confirmed.

At least this had happened with Nick, a friend-with-benefits Gabe had known for years, instead of Pierre, who would have been insufferable.

Nick reached into the mini fridge between the beds and pulled out a couple bottles of water. He handed one to Gabe. "First time being outed to a coworker?"

Finally Gabe cracked open the bottle and took a drink. "No, but it's definitely the most embarrassing."

Nick drained half of his own water and set it aside. "He seemed to take it okay." He gave Gabe a winning smile. "Look on the bright side. At least I'm hot."

God damn it. That actually would probably help, with Baller. But the problem was that he knew at all. Being okay with someone being gay wasn't the same as being okay with another man being attracted to you.

Gabe would just have to make sure Baller never found out about the second part. At least he'd probably stop wiggling his ass in Gabe's face in the locker room now.

He sighed, feeling vaguely sick. "I should probably talk to him. Sorry. He was supposed to go home with some girl tonight."

"Maybe he struck out?"

Gabe snorted. He knew he was sort of biased, but… "Maybe pigs'll grow wings and learn to fly."

Nick laughed. "Okay, fair. Help me find my shirt and I'll get out of your hair so you and Mr. Learn to Knock can have an adult conversation. But you totally owe me dinner next time we're both in town."

"I'll text you the schedule," Gabe promised.

"I'll keep an eye on GameCenter," Nick shot back, rolling his eyes. Which, okay, so Gabe wasn't the best at staying in touch. Sue him.

Ten minutes later, it was time to face the music. Gabe pulled on a T-shirt and a pair of jeans, then shoved his phone and keycard into his pocket. With any luck, he wouldn't run into anyone else from the team.

DANTE WAITED in the lobby, curled into a chair that wasn't quite big enough for him to be comfortable. He kept his back to the flow of people and his nose buried in his phone, just in case. Any other night, sure, he would be happy to sign autographs. Tonight… his brain was going to endlessly replay the scene he'd just walked in on.

How had he not known Gabe was into men? It seemed so obvious now. Of course he never picked women up in bars or brought a girlfriend to a team event. Dante might have only been around the team for a short time, but he felt stupid for not noticing. Did anyone else on the team know? *Someone* must have guessed; Gabe had been on the team long enough.

Flash must know, Dante decided. With the way he ruthlessly squashed anything homophobic in the locker room…. He could just be a good guy with a functioning brain, but Dante didn't think so. No one was that vigilant unless they had a personal stake.

But if he still had to remind their teammates, probably no one else knew, which meant Dante had inadvertently stumbled onto a huge secret.

And now he had to work out what to do about it.

First, though, apparently he was going to think about Gabe's broad palm on his partner's chest. Gabe was a big guy—two inches taller than Dante, even if Dante was more solidly built. His partner had been clinging to Gabe's muscular shoulder.

He should stop thinking about it, but now his brain was trying to fill in details. Where had Gabe's other hand been? Dante didn't think he'd seen it. Had it been placed on his partner's thigh? Had he been putting his weight on it to steady himself? Or maybe he'd used it to tilt the man's face to the right angle.

Dante curled his hand around his phone and exhaled sharply. This was really, *really* not his business. Dwelling on it would not do him any favors. He needed to be able to pretend everything was normal. And obsessing about your teammate feeling up some guy— and kissing, can't forget the kissing—was not that.

So. Normal. He'd been sexiled by a roommate. That was fine! It had happened before. Today, actually. He hoped Yorkie was having a better night than Gabe.

Most importantly, sexiling was normal.

Was it hot in here?

Footsteps jarred him out of his spiral, and he looked up to see Gabe walking toward him. His head was down, shoulders hunched. He didn't exactly have the look of the freshly laid about him.

Fuck.

Or, like, probably not.

Gabe dropped into the chair across from him. He looked as awkward as Dante felt and was loudly projecting that he would rather stand in front of about fifty of Kitty's slap shots than have this conversation.

At least they were on even footing in that respect.

Dante put his phone away and tried to square his shoulders. Conscious of the quiet—but not completely deserted—lobby, he kept his voice low. "So, uh, sorry for cockblocking you." *Even if it's kind of your fault. Who doesn't use the Do Not Disturb sign? Why didn't you tell me to pound rocks when I asked to share?*

Considering the circumstances, he kept a lid on these very valid criticisms. He could bring them up again later, when Gabe didn't look like he was about to puke all over the hotel lobby.

"I wasn't exactly expecting it to be a problem," Gabe said. He slumped a little farther, but Dante thought his shoulders were relaxing too. Maybe he'd thought Dante would come out swinging. "Did you strike out or something?"

"Ehhh." Dante waggled his hand in a seesaw motion. "Sort of. We passed her ex on the way back to her place and she made it like ten more feet before she burst into tears. So we stopped at Dairy Queen for ice cream, and then she went to the bathroom and fixed her makeup and we took a selfie for her Instagram, and I came back here."

The color returned to Gabe's face and he met Dante's gaze for the first time since that hideously awkward moment upstairs. "Guess neither of us is getting laid tonight," he said, a little tentatively, like he wasn't sure Dante would laugh.

"I won't tell if you won't," Dante offered. He meant it lightly—Gabe wouldn't tarnish Dante's ladies'-man reputation and Dante wouldn't mention Gabe had struck out too—but then he realized the underlying promise, which also applied. He wasn't going to blab about Gabe's sexuality.

"Deal," Gabe said immediately. The lines of tension in his face disappeared under a relieved half smile.

Good. Dante was glad they'd settled that. "Great." He yawned. "So can we go upstairs now? I've had just enough booze and ice cream to make me sleepy."

The conversation wasn't over, but it couldn't continue until they had some privacy. He waited until the hotel room door closed behind them. "I wish you'd told me you liked guys," Dante said as he kicked his shoes off. They *thunk*ed dully against the wall. "I wouldn't have tried so hard to hook you up with chicks last season." Or last week.

Gabe stared at Dante's shoes as though they'd insulted his mother. Then he lined his own up neatly under the desk. "It's not exactly something I advertise."

"No fucking shit." Dante shimmied out of his jeans. He had too much ass and thigh to be able to get them off any other way. "Does anybody else on the team know? I mean, I'm guessing Flash, and that's why he plays whack-a-mole with shitty comments in the locker room."

A snort of a laugh. "I told him when I got traded here. I was really drunk." He sat on the bed he'd been on earlier. The covers were still wrinkled. Dante decided not to think about it and went to his suitcase to look for his shower kit. "Olie guessed."

"And that's it?" Gabe was twenty-eight years old. He'd been drafted at eighteen. Had he been keeping this part of himself hidden for ten years? Fuck, that sounded lonely. Dante tossed the kit onto the bathroom counter.

"And now you." Gabe paused. Something about it made Dante stop before he turned the shower on. Instead, he poked his head back out into the hotel room and waited. After a beat, Gabe said, "You're being really cool about this."

Dante turned the bathroom light off and sat in the desk chair. He had a habit of saying the first thing that came to mind, and right now that was *Actually, I'm kind of freaking out*. He needed to take his time instead. "I really think I'm… I mean, obviously I'm not mad or upset or whatever. I'm—accepting, maybe? Ugh, that's a garbage word." He huffed, frustrated with himself. "Look, you're… gay?"

The muscle at the hinge of Gabe's jaw bunched. "Yeah," he said quietly.

"Cool." He drummed the fingers of his left hand on the desktop, realized he was doing it, and then forced himself to stop. "And obviously if you haven't told most of the team, you're expecting at least some of them to be assholes about it, and some of them probably will. And that sucks. Because as far as I'm concerned, my reaction? Is, like, a pretty low bar."

Gabe rubbed the back of his neck. "I mean, it's not like you could come in and introduce yourself."

If you can't beat 'em, join 'em, Dante thought, feeling like he was losing his grip on reality. He bit his lip so he wouldn't say it out loud. "Yeah, maybe not." He chewed on his thoughts a little more and then blurted, "When I was a kid, I thought Phil Esposito was Latino."

Off Gabe's nonplussed expression, Dante backtracked. He could feel himself going red, but he needed to get his point across. "It's relevant, just bear with
me. I wasn't on the internet all the time, all right? And
Esposito can be a Spanish last name if you put an accent on it. Jerseys never have accents anyway, right?"
Sometimes they did in Quebec, if the players had
French names, but not usually. "So when I started to
get into travel hockey, all my teammates were white.
But a Latino guy was in the Hockey Hall of Fame, so
it didn't matter."

Gabe cleared his throat. "So when you found out
Phil Esposito is Italian Canadian...."

"Oh, I was crushed." He smiled slightly, the hurt of
the memory having long faded. One of his teammates
had tormented him about his misconception for weeks.
"But by then I was the best player on the team, and I
was pretty sure I'd make it to the NHL. Someone had
to be first, and I figured it might as well be me. And
after I got in, no one would ever say Latinos can't play
hockey."

From the wrinkled caterpillars of Gabe's eyebrows,
he still didn't quite get what Dante was trying to say.

"It's not exactly the same." Dante shrugged. It
hadn't been easy for either one of them and it didn't
matter which of them had had it worse. Neither of them
should've had to struggle. "But you didn't even have a
Phil Esposito, you know? That would've sucked."

Now he got it. "Yeah, well." Gabe glanced down,
then back up again, the corner of his mouth tilted up.
"That's life as a pro athlete. Sucks if you like to suck
dick."

Dante laughed because he knew he had to, but the
image struck him low in the gut, deep down where he'd

shoved the images from earlier. "I guess. Just promise me one thing."

Gabe stopped laughing and inclined his chin, as if maybe he was still expecting Dante to drop the gloves.

Nope. He was just being a shithead. "Promise me that guy wasn't your dad."

"Augh!" Gabe's mouth dropped open, and he buried his face in his hands as he got it. After all, he was the one who'd told Dante that he'd planned to see his father tonight. "No, he isn't my—that's so gross. But I deserved that."

"Eh." Dante waggled his hand again. "Maybe not. But it was funny. I'm gonna go shower now, though, if it's cool with you. I stink like dance club."

"Sure. I'm just gonna...." He picked up the television remote.

"'Kay."

The television came on, and a moment later Dante closed the bathroom door behind him and started the water in the shower. Mechanically, he removed his clothes and stepped under the spray. The hot water sluiced over him, washing away the sweat and club grime and what had maybe been just a little too much hair gel.

But the image of Gabe kissing another man on the bed in their hotel room stuck with him, and now, in relative privacy and naked, alone with his thoughts, Dante was forced to confront the truth of his own semi.

"I did not see this coming," he muttered as he reached for his shampoo.

IF ANY of his other teammates had walked in on him, Gabe probably would have spent the rest of the preseason on tenterhooks, waiting for the inevitable fallout. But it hadn't been any other teammate, it had been Baller, who didn't give enough of a shit what people thought about him to bother being anything other than genuine.

And more importantly, he kept Gabe's secret. He never even *hinted* at slipping. For the first few days, Gabe overanalyzed his every action, but when he didn't come up with any differences, he had no choice but to relax and go on with his life.

And life was good. The Dekes closed out the preseason with three wins in a row. Gabe only played one of them, with Baller on the opposite wing, but they scored two goals against the Voyageurs.

And now the season opener was upon them.

They were playing the Vancouver Orcas in QC, which was great for the Nordiques—the Orcas had jet lag. They didn't.

"Try not to fidget like a toddler who needs a potty break," Coach told Baller as they filed onto the ice for the anthem.

Baller grinned back. "Yes, Coach."

Flash rolled his eyes and shoved him out the gate.

Standing on the ice as the music rose, Gabe felt the hockey season settle on his shoulders like a cloak. Now was the time for *serious* hockey. The regular season always seemed like a kind of bubble—from early October through mid-April, the world narrowed to this insular community. Gabe never had time to be bored or worry about anything besides the game. Major mid-season trades were fairly rare, so once the roster was set, he could just buckle down and concentrate on the things that mattered most to him. He'd done the training. Now all he had to do was win hockey games.

It felt safe.

The music faded. The lights came up. The puck dropped.

Flash got his stick on the puck and flipped it back to Gabe, and he streaked up the ice.

The roar of the crowd at his back, Gabe pushed on. He didn't need to look to know where to send the puck for Baller—he knew exactly where he'd be and when he'd be there. The biscuit landed right on his tape. Before the opposing defender could close in on him, he snapped the puck up to Flash, who shot.

The goalie stopped it, but Gabe got his stick on the rebound. It didn't go in, and the goalie scrambled to cover the puck.

Their shift ended without a goal, but Gabe's heart was pounding in anticipation. He knew it was only a matter of time.

The goalie didn't deny them on the next shift.

Dante took the puck into the zone and sent it to Flash, who tipped it to Gabe. But he didn't have an angle, so they tic-tac-toed it back the other way. Baller sniped the puck over the goaltender's left shoulder. Fuck, that was sexy. Gabe careened into Baller for a celebratory hug. "Fucking right!" he yelled.

The cheers of the crowd sent his mood even higher. On the bench, Baller jostled his shoulder against Gabe's and laughed in delight. "That's what I'm talking about!"

The energy carried them through all three periods, and they finished the game outstripping Vancouver 5–1.

The locker room afterward was buzzing with their shared high. It felt so damn good, Gabe didn't think twice about joining the team's celebration.

In high spirits, they piled into the booths at O'Ryan's. "Vodka!" Kitty called toward the bar.

Their favorite server waved her hand at him in acknowledgment.

"Tequila!" Baller argued.

"No," Gabe said.

Baller huffed. "Come on! I scored the first goal of the season and I don't get to pick the booze?"

"*You* can have tequila," Gabe said magnanimously. "I'll have something less vile, thanks. Beer for me, please, Avril."

"Got it!"

The drinks came quickly, and Flash stood and raised his glass. "All right. Tonight we feast!"

Gabe thought that was kind of dramatic, but he lifted his beer anyway.

"To eighty-one more games just like it!"

And he'd *definitely* drink to that. "Hell yeah."

Gabe was two beers into his evening and feeling relaxed. The win of the first game of the season was a high that no alcohol could depress. Next to him, Baller was nursing something neon in color—it was probably about fifty-fifty sugar and alcohol, but Baller was clearly not put off in the slightest.

Gabe had expected him to wander off ages ago and find himself someone pretty to spend the night with, but Baller didn't seem interested in leaving his boys tonight. Instead, he spent the evening shouting a mixture of praise, harassment, and terrible advice at one of the rookies.

Shaking his head, Gabe stood.

"Gabe!" Baller whipped around with surprisingly sharp reflexes and eyed Gabe with suspicion. "You

can't leave yet! We're celebrating our collective awe-
someness! Where are you going?"

"The john," he said drily. "That okay with you?"

"Hm, okay. But I'm watching you!" Baller pointed
two fingers at his own eyes, then at Gabe. He looked
slightly less threatening than a drunken bunny.

"Sure." Gabe patted his shoulder on his way past.

On his way back from the bathroom, he detoured
for the bar—a third beer wouldn't hurt—which was
where Kitty found him.

"Beer?" He made a face. "Vodka is better." He lifted his glass in a toast and downed his drink.

"I'd like to be able to see straight tomorrow." For
once, the paranoid and slightly bitter part of his brain
didn't point out that it was dangerous to get too drunk
around the team—around straight guys who didn't
know about him.

"Americans. Don't know how to drink," Kitty
lamented. Then, before Gabe could protest—he was
Canadian, after all, damn it—Kitty clapped a large hand
on his shoulder and pushed. "Come. We play darts."

"You sure that's a good idea?" Pointy things and
alcohol seemed like a bad mix.

"Da. You only little drink." Considering some of
the wilder drunk-Russian internet videos out there, Gabe
was probably lucky nothing would be on fire. Kitty
grabbed the projectiles and handed Gabe the set with red
fletching. "You first. We see how bad you are."

Gabe hadn't spent much time with Kitty. Hockey
culture wasn't exactly progressive no matter where you
were from, but Gabe was extra leery of teammates who
grew up in places less gay friendly, and always gave
them more space.

Kitty, though, had come by his nickname honestly, as far as Gabe could tell. He was a mountain of a man and a tiger on the ice, a fierce and effective defenseman, but off the ice, he was kind of like a friendly stray—he'd rub himself all over you for affection.

Gabe squinted at the dartboard. "How does this work again?"

Kitty snorted. "We play easy game. Around World, you hit one, then two, then all the way to twenty. Da?"

Gabe shrugged and took aim.

Well, at least he hit the actual dartboard. More than once, even.

Kitty shook his head. "How you so good at hockey and so bad at this?"

"I'm drunk?" Gabe offered. After all, he couldn't exactly say, *I never really had much opportunity to play before, since my career in hockey and my desire to stay closeted has kept me out of bars and away from bro time.*

"You not drunk," Kitty said firmly. His eyes twinkled with mischief. "Yet."

Baller found them in the second match, after Kitty had closed out the first when Gabe was barely on the board. Gabe wanted to think he'd get better at the game, but three beers and a glass of whiskey—courtesy of Kitty—was more alcohol than he'd consumed since winning a gold medal. And it wasn't helping his aim.

Gabe's next dart barely hit the board, and on nine, Gabe was pretty sure he couldn't have gotten farther from his current target if he tried.

"Wow," Baller said behind him, then flung his arms around Gabe's shoulders and rested his chin on his shoulder. "You're really bad at this."

Gabe ignored the warm breath ghosting over his ear, jaw, and neck, and focused on less appealing things. "How much have you had? I think your breath is flammable." He put a hand on Baller's face and pushed him away. Baller grinned.

Having retrieved the darts from the board, Kitty held them in Baller's direction. "You know how to play? Gabe is…." He cocked his head and said something in Russian.

Baller grinned. "Terrible? Awful? Painful to watch?"

"He getting worse. No hope he get better."

"He's definitely hopeless." Baller swiped the darts.

Gabe ceded the floor and watched from the sidelines, nursing the new glass of whiskey that had found its way into his hand. "You know," he said to Baller after Kitty hit double fifteen and ended the game, "you're almost as bad at this as I am."

"At least I know a more thrilling game than Around the World!" Baller looked way too happy for someone who still had over 100 written on the board. They'd switched to 301. Gabe had considered being insulted when he realized Kitty thought the rule of "subtract your round's total from 301 until you reach 0" too complicated to explain to him, but he felt too charitable, what with the whiskey.

Besides, who wanted to do math while drunk?

"You both terrible." Kitty shook his head sadly.

"Hey! I am way better than Gabe over here," Baller whined. He narrowed his eyes. "I bet a hundred bucks I can beat you next game."

Kitty snorted. "No chance."

They shook on it.

Baller strode to the scoreboard and cleaned it.

"You so bad at this game," Kitty said, "I even give you advantage. You go first." He waved toward the wall.

With a stubborn lift to his chin, Baller said, "Thank you. I accept." He situated himself at the line and lifted his arm for the first throw.

Suddenly the drunken looseness of his limbs disappeared, and he narrowed his eyes. He hit double 20, the required opening move. Then he landed the next two, both clustered in the bull's eye.

Kitty cursed; Baller smirked.

Gabe downed the last of his whiskey and told himself that level of confidence was not scorching hot.

DANTE WOKE up feeling like he could fight God and win. A 5–1 victory at home to start the season, followed by a night out with the boys? He had buns of steel and a titanium liver. He was invincible.

Or at least, that was what he thought... until he rolled out of bed and tripped on last night's pants, which he'd left in the middle of the floor. He managed to catch himself before he fell, but he stubbed his toe on the corner of his dresser.

Maybe his mother was right and he should've looked for a place with one of the other guys on the team so he'd be more motivated to pick up after himself. It also would've prevented this whole weird loneliness thing he had going on. He should've been used to it—he was an only child—but he'd spent his adolescent years with billet families and then last year he'd had Flash's whole family around whenever he was home.

He might've felt kind of weird about his gay-porn experiment if he had a roommate, though.

Practice was optional this morning, so Dante took his time waking up. He limped into the kitchen for coffee, flexed his toes to make sure he hadn't broken anything, and considered the results of the experiment.

Conclusively, he was bi. The day they got home from Ottawa, he sat in his living room and watched the highest-rated gay blow job video he could find. He picked it because he figured he liked *getting* blow jobs, so it wouldn't be bad either way, but he ended up looking at the guy enjoying himself on his knees and thinking, *I want to do that.* For a few minutes after the revelation, he sort of stared at his dick in shock, wondering what had taken it so long to clue in his brain. Dante had seen a lot of naked guys in his life.

Then he remembered what the locker room smelled like. Anyone who could think about sex despite the olfactory assault of twenty-three dudes competing to create the world's rankest hockey-gear stench should have their brain studied for science.

Now that he'd made up his mind, he wanted to tell his parents. It wasn't that he didn't have secrets from them—he had boundaries, even if they were flimsier than a lot of people's. He just didn't like the thought of them not knowing. He wanted them to have a clear picture of their son.

And, okay, he also wanted some advice. Dante was not accustomed to discretion, and the idea of living in the closet made him feel like he was going to break out in hives. But coming out would be a pain in the ass.

Also, Abuela was going to flip her shit.

Dante pulled his coffee toward himself and hunched his shoulders as he thought about it. His grandmother loved him, had doted on him as a child. They'd always been close. He'd looked forward to long weekends at her house, just the two of them making *flautas*, or working in her garden and occasionally watching one of the milder *telenovelas*.

Of course, she'd also insisted on dragging him to Mass. Dante had a hard time sitting still as an adult—it had been torture as a child.

Dante hadn't been to church with her since he was old enough to play travel hockey. Maybe things had changed. Or maybe Abuela still nodded in approval at everything the priest said.

He wouldn't know until he talked to his dad. And since he wasn't planning to attend practice, he had time this morning.

But when he picked up his phone to make the call, he found it littered with notifications from the team group chat, news sites, missed calls, and a text from his former billet sister. *Madre de Dios*. Did he get traded?

He opened the text first. Rina was a straight shooter; he could trust her to get right to the point.

She'd sent a link, along with the message *Hope your friend is ok. Send him my best.*

Dante clicked.

NHL Superstar Gabriel Martin's Secret Gay Love Affair

There was a picture of two men together, taken in a bed. They were both shirtless. Dante didn't recognize the man on the left, but the one on the right was obviously Gabe. His eyes were closed.

Oh mother*fucker*. Had the guy taken a picture while Gabe was sleeping? What a fucking scumbag. Who did that?

Dante stared at his phone for another three seconds.

Then he cursed, scrambled up from the table, and ran back to the bedroom for his pants, all while dialing his phone. Gabe's phone rang and rang, but he didn't pick up.

Last night's jeans smelled like vodka, but he wasn't going to waste time looking for clean ones. He pulled on the first clean T-shirt on the top of his laundry pile and struggled into it. Keys, keys, keys—why wasn't Gabe picking up?

Dante didn't have his address. He had no idea if Gabe would be at home. Where was Dante even going to go? Practice?

Maybe Gabe wouldn't be there—he was hardly out to his closest friends; Dante doubted he wanted to face the whole team—but Dante could go nip any asshole comments in the bud. He could… he didn't know. Make it clear to everyone that Dante had Gabe's back, for whatever that was worth. He was already late, but better late than never, right?

Fuck, he really hoped he didn't have to punch anybody. In the bigger picture, Gabe was an important player. He was one of the best wingers in the league. On the ice, he was irreplaceable. Anyone else with his skill would've been made captain years ago.

But he didn't want it. He kept to himself. He didn't let his teammates get close.

Dante just hoped that didn't mean they'd be ready to turn on him.

He pulled into the players' lot driving way too fast and parked like an asshole. Gabe still wasn't picking up his phone. *Fuck.* Dante shoved his cell into his pocket and booked it for the locker room—

Only to skid to a halt before he could run into Coach St. Louis in the hallway. "Baltierra." She inclined her head, but her eyes were narrowed. "Don't you check your messages?"

Dante said, "Uh."

He couldn't get a read on her. There were rumors that she spent the off-seasons in Vegas, bluffing her way through the highest-stakes games and taking un-suspecting yuppies for all they were worth.

After a moment she softened a bit. "Practice is canceled today." She waved her hand vaguely. "Giv-en the… circumstances… front office wants to present a united front." Dante could practically hear the air quotes. "Which means they have to figure out how to do that."

Right. Of course front office hadn't known either. "Oh," he said. "So is there gonna be, like, a meeting…?"

"The details are in the email," she said evenly. Coach should've been a lawyer or something. "You ran in here pretty fast. Do you have something you need to say?"

Dante deflated. The urge to do something was still there, but he had nowhere to put all that energy. He couldn't do anything. "No, I just… I wanted to be here for Gabe. In case I could… help." Ugh. He hated how childish that sounded.

But Coach surprised him by smiling—a small, wry thing, but a real one. "You're a good kid, Dante. I'm sure he'd appreciate it if he was in any state to think about anything other than damage control."

"Wait, he's here?"

"You boys must've had quite a night after the game. He came in looking like he'd pledged a frat last night, said he forgot his phone on the dresser. He had no idea…."

Jesus. Dante hoped everyone else had gotten the message and stayed home. "Is he still here? Can I wait for him?"

She pursed her lips and looked him up and down. "You swear you're not here to give him a hard time?"

"Coach, I'm here to punch anyone who tries."

She let out a long breath, as though considering. "All right. He's up in the PR office talking to Tricia. I guess there's no harm if you wait outside. But for fuck's sake don't make this worse."

"I won't!" he promised, already backing away. "Thanks, Coach!"

FOR THE past ten years, Gabe had kept such tight control of himself that he'd never indulged in more than two drinks at a time, gold-medal victories excepted.

Unfortunately that meant his alcohol tolerance was for shit, and because Baller and Kitty were bad influences—and apparently Gabe really had been starving for social interaction outside of work—now he was very hungover.

He gulped down some coffee, put on his sunglasses, and swung through the McDonald's drive-through on the way to practice, hoping the caffeine and greasy food would fix his head and stomach.

By the time he pulled up at the arena, he was awake enough to realize he'd left his cell phone charging on his bedside table. He hoped Coach went easy on them at practice this morning. It was an optional practice or he wouldn't have indulged last night, but he didn't want to skip it. He wanted to keep their momentum going.

But the locker room was empty when he got there.

That was weird.

He wasn't late, yet there was nobody on the ice. Even the staff seemed sparser than usual. Gabe was striding down the hallway back toward the locker room, wondering if he'd woken up in some kind of weird parallel universe devoid of hockey players, when someone clapped him on the shoulder and he almost jumped out of his skin.

"Jesus *Christ*." He *hated* being startled like that. He turned around. "Flash. Where is everybody?"

Flash's face was serious, his brow furrowed in a way that puckered the scar at the corner of his eye. "Have you checked your phone this morning?"

"No. I was running late and I forgot to charge it." This whole situation was freaking him out. "Why? What's going on?"

Flash sighed. "I should let you see for yourself. But not here. Come on."

He herded Gabe into Brigitte's office.

Oh shit. This had to be bad if it warranted the general manager's intervention over Coach's.

Brigitte sat behind her desk, her graying hair in disarray. Across from her sat Coach, looking objectively terrible, with dark circles under her eyes. Empty Tim Hortons cups littered the desk's surface. From the looks of things, they'd been there a while. "He doesn't know," Flash said shortly.

Brigitte rubbed her hands over her face before placing them flat on the desk and looking at Coach.

"Okay," Coach said in English. "Gabe, you're going to want to sit down for this."

Gabe sat. Was he being traded this early in the season? He had a limited no-movement clause. They could be asking him for his list of teams. He didn't know what else could cause this level of gravity.

"I want to preface this by saying we're not angry you kept this from us," Brigitte said seriously. "I wish you'd been more open with me, with the team, so we could have gotten in front of this, but I understand you must have had your reasons."

Oh.

Fuck.

As bile rose in his throat, Gabe searched for words. "What…?"

Coach shook her head. "It's just as easy to show you." She nodded at Brigitte, who turned her computer monitor toward him.

GABRIEL MARTIN GAY: FORMER LOVER TELLS ALL

There was a picture. Gabe's hands started to shake, and his throat felt thick.

He was lying fast asleep in bed with Pierre, who had one arm outstretched to take a selfie. As usual, Gabe had wrapped himself around Pierre; he'd always been a sleep cuddler. His face was pressed into Pierre's neck, one arm thrown over his chest. Between the pose and their obviously shirtless bodies—and the prominent hickey on Pierre's collarbone—there was little doubt what they'd been up to.

Gabe thought he might be sick.

"Why would he take a picture?" was the first thing that came out of his mouth. Kind of stupid, but Gabe was caught up on it. He'd never let Pierre take any pictures of him. He wasn't stupid enough to let anyone get potentially compromising photos. All bitter exes started out as happy partners. No one ever expected a lover to share pictures after the fact.

He'd been right to be cautious, but it turned out he hadn't been cautious enough.

Flash laid a hand on his shoulder and squeezed. Gabe took a shuddering breath. How was this happening?

"PR's been fielding calls all morning. So far we're sticking with no comment, but we'd like to put out something official," Brigitte said.

Gabe nodded, even as his fight-or-flight response rebelled. It made sense from the team's perspective, but he wanted nothing more than to go hide in his own basement until the press forgot his face.

His fond, sleeping face, attached to a man who was wrapped around another man, naked.

"I should call my agent," he said numbly. He reached for his phone, then remembered he'd left it at home. "I don't have...." He felt lost. He looked at Flash.

"Hey. It's going to be okay. Tout sera bien." And fuck, that was his comforting-dad voice. Knowing that Flash felt the need to bust it out made Gabe feel even worse.

"He ruined my life," he croaked. Why couldn't he just be angry? Anger would be better than this bitter helplessness, than feeling like everything he'd worked for was slipping through his fingers.

"Hey, no talk like that," Coach cut in. "He's just thrown a few obstacles in your path. You're too good a player to let this break your stride."

Right now Gabe wasn't sure he believed that, but he wanted to.

Brigitte took over again. "We want to get on this right away, so I'm going to call Trish from PR in to work out a statement. We have options—threaten a lawsuit, claim it's Photoshop or a lookalike, whatever. That's Trish's department. We'll call up your agent— Erika Orrick, right?—and get her in on this too." She grimaced. "I'm not thrilled about how all this came out, but I'm not going to hold it against *you*. We're on your side. Just keep playing your game and it'll be fine."

Just keep playing your game. How was Gabe supposed to do that when the whole world had seen something he never wanted to show them?

But he went to see Tricia anyway. There wasn't much else he could do.

Tricia's office was on the second floor of the arena, in a cheerful room with a south-facing window and soothing pale sage walls. Knitted tchotchkes dotted a few of the surfaces—one of them, a snowman with hockey gear, had Gabe's number 53 stitched onto his back—which contributed to the welcoming atmosphere.

Tricia sat behind her desk, her long dark hair pulled back in a braid. She offered a toned-down version of her signature friendly smile as she pushed a plate of Girl Guide cookies toward him. "Hi, Gabe. I'd say good morning, but it looks like that ship has sailed."

That ship had exploded in the harbor. He tried to smile back, but it felt sickly. "Hey. Sorry for making your job harder."

"Oh, are you kidding? As far as PR crises go, this is a dream scenario. No cheating, no law-breaking, no public intoxication…. You didn't do anything wrong."

"I got caught," Gabe blurted.

"You… got caught," Tricia echoed. She frowned.

Gabe's defenses went up. "What?"

She shook her head. "Nothing, just… can someone 'get caught' being gay?" Then she backtracked. "Uh, assuming you're gay and not bi." He nodded. "Right. So, you know, like I said. Can you 'get caught' being gay? You're gay all the time. What you got caught at is lying by omission."

Oh. Gabe swallowed. That put the situation in a different perspective. Gabe knew there was nothing immoral or wrong about his sexuality. So why had he always felt guilty? Why had his stomach turned when he thought about people finding out?

He hadn't felt ashamed because he was gay. He felt ashamed because he was lying.

Maybe he was quiet for too long, because Trish said, "Jeez, sorry, there I go. You wouldn't believe how much psychology is involved in PR work. You want me to get your agent on the line? She's been in touch a couple times already today; I'm sure she's just waiting for my call. Or we can talk about what you want to do first. I don't know if you and she have talked about a contingency plan?"

They had, but back then Gabe had been heavily in favor of denying everything and hoping it blew over. What if he didn't do that? What if he stopped hiding?

Sure, it would suck. But at this point, suckage seemed inevitable. Some guys on the team would probably not be cool about it. But some of them might be like Baller and Flash and Olie—the only three guys on the team Gabe could really call friends. If he stopped hiding, he could have more of them. He could stop worrying about slipping.

He could be himself in public.

But if he was going to do that—if he was going to leave the closet behind him once and for all—then he owed it to his teammates to talk to them first. The press was going to chew this story down to the bone. They were all going to be asked to comment. And that meant they should hear it from him, not from a canned PR statement.

He cleared his throat. "Can you excuse me for a second?"

She nodded. "Of course."

Gabe stood up and went to the door.

Flash was sitting in the hallway, playing on his phone, right where Gabe had left him.

Next to him sat Baller, uncharacteristically still, head tilted back as he stared at the ceiling. He snapped his gaze to Gabe when he heard the door open. "Gabe! Hey. Uh. Coach said I could wait here for you in case you wanted some moral support."

Flash tucked his phone away. He didn't say anything to Baller, but his expression spoke of pride. "What do you need?"

He took a deep breath. "Can you call a team meeting?" He glanced back into Tricia's office. "But, like… maybe not 'til lunch."

Flash and Baller looked at each other. "I'll book the conference room and text the guys," Baller offered.

Flash said, "I'll call Catering." He took a few steps down the hallway, already holding his phone to his ear.

Baller fired off a few quick messages on his phone and then looked up. "Hey, um. How are you doing? Do you want company in there? I can just sit quietly."

The whole situation was completely fucked, but that made Gabe want to laugh. Sitting quietly wasn't Baller's strong suit. "Can you?"

Baller grinned, and Gabe suddenly remembered how good-looking he was, with his lively dark eyes and thick eyelashes and roguish smile. But right now the support meant more to him than anything. "Probably not! But I mean, I have no horse in this race. It might be good for you to have a somewhat objective opinion, you know? If you want."

For a moment Gabe thought about it. It *would* be nice not to face this meeting alone, to be able to articulate his thoughts out loud to a coworker instead of a professional. But if he was going to do that, why Baller and not Flash? He'd known Flash longer. Flash was his best friend.

Flash always tried to offer advice—*You could tell them. They're good guys, and they like you.* And maybe he was right.

But Baller had said, *You didn't even have a Phil Esposito. That sucks.* Right now, that was the kind of friend Gabe wanted with him.

He stepped backward into Tricia's office and held the door for Baller to follow him in. "That would be… yeah. Come on in."

Whatever happened next was absolutely going to suck for a while. But for the first time in a long time, Gabe wouldn't be facing it alone.

DANTE KEPT his word and sat quietly in Tricia's office, slightly behind Gabe so he wouldn't disturb him. Tricia put Gabe's agent on speakerphone, though she occasionally stabbed the mute button so she could discuss things with Gabe. If Gabe wanted to speak to his agent in private, he never gave an indication of it. For the most part, Dante was only window dressing, so he listened while texting as calmly as he could that yes, everyone really did need to be there and no, Yorkie didn't need to wear the rainbow T-shirt. If everyone showed up in rainbow T-shirts, Gabe would cry. Hell, *Dante* would cry, and the ink wasn't even dry on his bisexuality card.

He did message Flash about getting some You Can Play shirts, though. The You Can Play organization supported LGBT athletes in all sports, and their gear was a little more subtle. Dante wouldn't mind having one or two in his closet for the foreseeable future, specifically to wear every time he suspected the media was about to ask a dumb question.

Once he had the whole team's RSVPs, he shut his phone off and tucked it in his pocket. Even if he was mostly here for moral support, he could be respectful.

He didn't actually expect Gabe to ask his opinion on anything, so it surprised him when Gabe handed him the printed draft statement he, Trish, and his agent had worked out and asked, "What do you think?"

The press release was pretty bland. Everyone agreed that denying the story was the wrong way to go, so they simply acknowledged the truth of the article, stated Gabe had the organization's unconditional support—despite the fact that he hadn't talked to the team yet; Dante got that there was some fudging involved in PR but that didn't sit right with him—and then made a firm request to respect Gabe's privacy. It finished with a formulaic assertion that he just wanted to play hockey.

Yawn. Boring.

"If it was me, there'd be more shade about your ex." Dante handed the paper back. "Selling a picture of your famous, closeted ex-boyfriend to a tabloid is pretty trashy." He paused. "Uh, no offense to your taste in men or whatever."

Trish coughed behind her hand. Gabe said, bemused, "None taken."

Dante tapped his foot restlessly on the floor as he searched for the right words. "Look, it's—fine, right? Objectively. There's nothing wrong with it. It's inoffensive."

When he didn't continue, Gabe prompted, "But…?"

"But is it *you*?" he asked. "I mean, you only get publicly outed once. I hope. And it's totally cool if now that it's happened, you just want to acknowledge it and move on with your life and wait for the shitstorm to blow over. But the thing is, you're out now whether you like it or not. You don't have to pretend to be just like everyone else anymore. You can, I don't know—" But then the right phrase came to him. He smiled crookedly, hoping Gabe would get it. "—be your own Phil Esposito."

Part of him expected Gabe to dismiss the suggestion out of hand, but instead he looked thoughtful. "I don't want to do it the way you'd do it," he said after a moment.

"So hiring a skywriter is out." Dante spread his hands, trying to silence the tiny voice that was a little sad his own plans needed to stay on hold for a while. "That leaves a lot on the table. Rainbow tattoo? Joke Grindr profile? *Real* Grindr profile? Full-page ad in the *Ottawa Sun*? The world is your oyster."

"The Grindr profile is a no," Trish said. Buzzkill.

Finally Gabe turned his attention back to her and handed her the press release. "Can we make it a little gayer?"

Hell yes, Dante thought. This could be the beginning of a beautiful friendship.

FIRST PERIOD

BY THE time the team meeting rolled around, Gabe had skated through *numb* and *determined* and had now sprayed to a stop in *stomach-churning dread.*

After his meeting with Trish, she let him use her office to call his dad, who'd been leaving frantic voice-mails on Gabe's phone all morning.

When he let himself out of her office, raw and shaken, Flash, Olie, and Baller were waiting for him.

"Uh—"

Before he could move, Olie hugged him. Startled, Gabe held still until he realized he was being awkward and hugged back.

Olie eventually released him with a spine-jarring slap to the back, and then the three of them flanked Gabe as they made their way to the conference room.

"What are you guys, my bodyguards?" He frowned. "And what are you wearing?" They'd all put on identical T-shirts, but he hadn't thought to read them. Baller's was distractingly tight around the… everything. It was doing great things for his shoulders.

"Clothes," Olie answered. But when he turned to check around the corner, Gabe recognized the T-shirt the Dekes had sold at last year's Pride Night. "Ready?"

No.

Flash nudged his shoulder. "Come on."

With no better option, Gabe let his friends and the momentum of his feet carry him forward.

The conference room was abuzz with activity when they entered. Tables covered with chafing dishes lined one wall. To Gabe's surprise, his stomach growled, reminding him he hadn't eaten since his insufficient McDonald's breakfast. Tricia's Girl Guide cookie bribe did not count.

Eventually Tips, their second-line center, noticed they'd walked in and whistled sharply.

The noise and movement stopped. All eyes turned toward them.

Gabe was suddenly glad to be sandwiched between Flash and Olie. "Uh," he said out of the corner of his mouth. "How exactly did you plan to work this?"

"We could set it up like a press conference," Baller suggested. "Table at the front for us, everybody else in the middle."

"Like the head table at a wedding?" Olie scoffed.

"More like a trial," Flash grumbled. Gabe couldn't help but agree. "I veto that."

"Thank you." Maybe Baller would enjoy fielding questions that way, but Gabe would rather take a stick to the nuts. "What's plan B?"

Flash clapped for attention. "Everybody get some food. We're gonna sit there." He gestured toward a table at the back, on the opposite side from the buffet. "Take turns visiting. Don't be an asshole."

Gabe's chest constricted a little when Bricks, a ruddy-haired defenseman with hands like shovels, spoke up. "So is this an announcement, then?"

Gabe didn't know if he'd be able to answer, but before he could stammer something out, Baller spoke up. "What, you thought there'd be a team meeting to keep the status quo? Have some lunch, Bricksy. Your IQ drops when you're hungry."

Hockey players could always be counted on to eat. Gabe was thankful for that as Flash and Olie installed themselves on either side of him while everyone else loaded their plates. He was wondering how he was going to manage to get his own food without leaving the safety zone when Baller set a plate in front of him, pulled a bottle of water from each pocket, and sat down opposite Flash with his own plate. "Buen provecho."

Swallowing against the lump in his throat, Gabe was suddenly powerfully grateful for his friends. From today forward, he was going to make a better effort to actually get to know them and spend time with them. "Thanks."

He couldn't decide if it would be worse if everyone wanted to talk and ask questions at once or if no one sat down, so he focused on eating. That way he wouldn't have to think about it.

But before he got more than three bites into his chicken, Bricksy sat down across from him. "Hey, Cap. Hey, Gabe."

"Bricksy." Olie nodded. "Thanks for coming."

Then he pulled a tiny plastic orange water gun from his pocket. "The rules are, say something dumb and I squirt you. Second offense is a five-hundred-dollar fine with money going to You Can Play."

"Nice." Bricks nodded approvingly. "I accept your terms." Digging a fork into his potato salad, he asked, "So did Trish give you a hard time?"

As first questions went, this one was kind of a softball. "No. She was great."

"Good. Always liked her." He speared a meatball. "So. Next game's in Toronto. What do you think of their new goaltender—just got called up from college level, can't think of the name…?" He looked at Olie.

Olie thought for a moment. "Vanderberg?"

"That's the one! Think they're going to start him much this year?"

And just like that, Bricks was done asking questions about Gabe's sexuality.

Something inside Gabe unclenched.

He didn't know if it was because word of Olie's threats had gotten around or if they were trying to be respectful since Gabe's whole life had been turned on its head, but Bricksy set the trend.

Tips sat down a few minutes later with "So you want us to put out a hit on this Pierre guy? What a twat."

Baller jumped on that. "Yes! We should at least, like, get someone to key his car."

"*No*," Gabe said. When Baller pouted, he sighed and explained. "If they get caught, I might have to see him again. In court. No."

"Ugh. Fine."

Some of the questions were more difficult, like their backup goaltender's "How long have you known you're gay?"

The guy didn't know that was a tough subject. Gabe's mom had left his father shortly afterward, and then she and her affair partner moved to the UK. Gabe's dad had tried to convince him it had nothing to do with Gabe coming out to them, but Gabe never bought it.

Olie reached for the water gun, but Gabe stopped him. If he didn't give people the benefit of the doubt, it would only make the whole situation more painful. "I was twelve when I came out to my parents. I guess I knew a little before then, but that's when I was sure."

The rest of the questions were a grab bag of good-natured teasing—"Are you seeing anyone now? Because I've got this cousin…" and "Is this why you never get drunk with us?"—and the sort of getting-to-know-you things Gabe probably should've exchanged with his teammates years ago but hadn't because he was afraid they might find out.

Yorkie wanted to know where he got his suits. Gabe promised to take him shopping next time they had a few days off, and the kid lit up like Wayne Gretzky had just told him he had a great slap shot.

"I keep telling you," Flash murmured when Baller had distracted Yorkie with talk about *Super Smash Bros*. "You're a big deal. The rookies look up to you. You teach them a few things, you make them feel like they're special, they'll love you forever."

For the first time, that felt like something Gabe could think about.

Not everyone stopped by the table. Some of them would need time to adjust, but their working relationship wouldn't suffer. He'd seen it before with guys who didn't see eye to eye on anything from football teams to politics. At the end of the day, winning games was more important.

But that didn't mean it didn't hurt, glancing at hunched shoulders across the room, knowing people had decided not to talk to him because of something he couldn't change.

"Hey." Baller nudged his foot under the table and gestured toward the bowl in front of him. "Are you gonna eat that?"

Flash had requested the catering team get in some ice cream, but Gabe had only managed a couple bites before he noticed Kitty stalking out of the conference room. He hadn't returned.

Today might not be a total disaster, all things considered, but his appetite had deserted him.

He smiled a little as he pushed the bowl across the table. "Help yourself."

DANTE HAD intended to have a lazy day around the house, work out a bit, recover from last night, and oh yeah, talk to his parents about his sexuality. Instead he'd done absolutely none of that, too busy trying to be there for Gabe.

It was kind of a mind fuck. Dante had always been a hockey fan as well as a player. Gabe got drafted when Dante was twelve. From his rookie season, he'd been a star, and he'd only gotten better.

Then, when Dante was eighteen, he got drafted to the same team that had just traded to acquire Gabe. He'd been so excited to play on the same team as one of his heroes… only to get stuck in the minors for years because his coaches didn't think he was ready. Finally he got called up for most of a season and proved himself enough that last year they'd let him play on first line. Then he whacked his head before he could get more than a handful of games.

It meant a lot to Dante that Gabe went out of his way to help with his game.

Dante would've wanted to be there for any teammate going through what Gabe was, but it wouldn't have been personal like this.

Or, shit, maybe it *would* have been, now that Dante could see himself being the one in Gabe's shoes.

There was still one thing from today's to-do list that he could tackle.

He kicked his shoes off by the door, grabbed a beer from the fridge, and flopped down on the couch.

Then he tilted his head back against the cushions, put his phone on speaker, and made the call.

"Hi, sweetheart!"

Dante smiled reflexively. "Hey, Mom. How was your day?" His mother was a social worker at a seniors' residence, so she was basically a saint.

"Oh, well, you know it was live music day today." Those were hit-and-miss. His mom's voice said today was a miss. "It was that man with the bagpipes. But other than the headache, it was good."

Ouch. "How many people turned off their hearing aids?"

She laughed. "You're terrible. I'm sure many of them enjoyed it." Then she paused. "There's no accounting for taste, I guess."

"I guess not," he agreed.

He listened to her ramble about her day for a few minutes as she related stories about the residents, who were prone to gossip outrageously, and then unexpectedly, she said, "Now why don't you tell me why you really called?"

Dante spoke to his parents multiple times a week. This suspicion seemed unfair, especially because she was right. "I can't just call and talk to my mom?"

"You can, honey, but usually I have to fight to get a word in edgewise." Ouch. Straight to the heart. He just always had so much to tell her. "Besides, I'm your mother. I raised you to adulthood. Neither of us would've lived this long if I didn't have a sixth sense about when you need to tell me things."

Reluctantly, Dante conceded that she had a point.

So it was overkill when she added, "Does this have anything to do with Gabriel Martin's news today?"

Forget sixth sense—his mother was some kind of witch. "Why would you say that?"

"I know my son." She made a *tsk*ing noise. "You're protective of your teammates. How many times did you get itchy mitts in juniors?"

Okay, so she wasn't clairvoyant, she was asking on account of his accrued penalty minutes. That made him feel better.

"Enough for you to see the pattern." He paused for a moment but couldn't just come out and say what he needed to—something that never happened to him. He'd have to build up to it. "The team was mostly okay. They were more surprised than anything. But I think it made sense to them. Gabe doesn't socialize much. Now they know why."

His mother paused tellingly. "*They*?" He could practically see her raising her eyebrows.

"I already knew." Dante bit his lip. "Um, I found out by accident." Did that make it sound like they matched on Grindr or something? "I opened the hotel door at the wrong time."

Or the right time, depending how you looked at it.

"Oh dear. That would've been a good time to engage the security chain."

"That's what I said!"

But she wasn't going to let him off the hook that easily. "So if your friend's not having problems with the team, and you're not in danger of jerseying your coworkers, then…."

Fuck it. He cleared his throat. "Mom, I'm bi."

"Ooooh," she said. Then, when she'd had a few seconds to process the ramifications, "Oh, honey. I love you. You never do anything the easy way, do you?"

The anticlimax washed him with relief. "It's not like I waited this long to reach enlightenment on purpose."

"Of course not." Another telling pause. "You know, this does explain a few things. All those half-naked hockey posters when you were younger—"

Dante had forgotten about those. "I promise I wasn't jerking it to those guys as a preteen, or it wouldn't have taken me this long to reach the bisexuality conclusion."

"Overshare, sweetie."

You'd think she'd be used to it by now. Dante's mouth was always ten steps ahead of his brain. At some point, he'd decided to lean into it. "I gotta be me." But his relief was short-lived. Now he had to ask the hard questions. "Listen, uh, is Dad home? I don't want to leave him in the dark, and I wanted to ask…."

"It's his games night with the boys." Her voice held fondness, amusement, and regret all in one. "But this is important. I can text him and tell him to come home." She knew Dante wouldn't want to talk to him while he was out.

"No, let him have his fun. But maybe ask him to call when he gets home?"

"It might be late," she warned.

"It's okay. I'm a good napper."

Once again his mother read between the lines. "You want to ask him about your abuela."

Damn it. "I wasn't worried about you and Dad." When he was younger, Dante thought his parents were trying to compensate for the fact that he was adopted by loving him so vocally. Eventually he realized they were just good emotional communicators who *did* love him that much.

Abuela, on the other hand….

"I'll make sure he calls you," she promised. "But Dante, whatever you think, whatever *anyone* thinks, you're not obligated to tell her. I know we raised you to be honest and straightforward about who you are, and your father and I are so proud of you. But you don't owe any part of yourself to her or anyone else."

"I know, Mom." He just wasn't sure how people were supposed to love him if they didn't even know who he was.

TRICIA GAVE Gabe a handful of options for handling the media feeding frenzy. None of them appealed— Gabe hated talking about himself—but as Tricia pointed out, the sooner they got the information out there the way they wanted, the sooner everyone would lose interest and Gabe could go back to his actual job.

He wasn't excited about doing an exclusive half-hour interview with a news anchor from SportsNet, but it sounded better than a series of videos for various online outlets. At least this way it would be over quickly.

They scheduled it for after their game against the To-ronto Shield.

At practice the day before the game, Coach looked him over head to toe, lingered on the dark circles under his eyes, and offered, "I could write you off as a healthy scratch."

Gabe had only ever wanted to play hockey. He hadn't given it up when he got moved up an age cat-egory and the older boys made fun of him, or when his mom left and he only had one parent to take him to games, or when the late timing of his growth spurt made him an even easier target for on-ice bullies. He wasn't about to give it up now. "No. I need to play." He felt adrift about a lot of things, but not about hockey.

Coach didn't look happy about it, and Gabe didn't blame her. He squirmed. "Unless you think it'll distract the team too much. I don't want—"

Coach waved him off. "They're going to have to deal with it sooner or later. We'll post extra security and move all media questions out of the locker room to offer you as much privacy as possible. Hopefully once your interview airs, that'll be the end of it."

"Thanks." If the state of the parking lot during practice was any indication, he was going to be grateful for that.

For the first time in ages, Gabe felt self-conscious walking into the locker room. But it seemed to be busi-ness as usual for everyone else—Bricks and Kitty had their heads bent together in the corner, Baller and Flash were diagramming plays on the whiteboard, and Olie was rolling bits of used sock tape into balls and flicking them at Yorkie. One of them had stuck in his hair. York-ie hadn't noticed.

Maybe there was a *slight* lull in conversation when he entered, but it only lasted long enough for someone to say, "So did you think about my cousin? Very nice boy!"

"Oh, so it's not genetic, then," Baller chirped, and things only got louder from there, until Coach came in and read them the riot act, telling them to get out on the ice already.

Gabe was practicing his stickhandling while he waited his turn for the shootout drill, one ear on Baller's rambling.

"Then we totally went to this nightclub, and like, it's shady shit, you know, because we're only eighteen, so nowhere where they check ID, right?" If Gabe was following, this was a story about underage drinking back in juniors, or possibly the AHL.

"—and the idiot totally starts hitting on this guy's girlfriend, even though—"

Leaning forward, Gabe flipped the puck onto the blade of his stick. Bounce. Catch. Bounce. Twist the blade, catch.

"Dude, are you even listening to me?"

Gabe dropped the puck. "What? Yeah, of course. You and your buddy got drunk in Vermont, which, honestly, is there anything else to do in Vermont?" Other than skiing, which was definitely not allowed during the season. Tapping maple trees, maybe?

"Wow, *rude*," Baller laughed. He made a play for Gabe's puck, but Gabe fended him off. "Just because you've got no imagination—"

That was as far as he got, because Kitty bumped them from the side and nearly sent them both sprawling. He skated off toward the net without another word or a single backward glance.

A hard pit formed in Gabe's stomach. Kitty was usually easygoing—possibly the least flappable player after Olie. But this, and the way he'd left the conference room yesterday… it spoke of a problem.

"Uh," Baller said awkwardly. "Speaking of rude." The corners of his mouth pinched a little, and his eyes went flat and hard. The look didn't suit him.

Gabe was grateful it was his turn next, because he didn't want to talk about it. He plucked a fresh puck from the pile on the ice and made for the net.

He scored high over Olie's shoulder and skated off to good-natured curses. But the satisfaction he usually got after a goal felt hollow.

THE GAME was a matinee, which Gabe didn't like. Middle-of-the-day weekend hockey never felt like a real game, and this one sucked from the get-go. The Shield—also known as the Ts, for the shape Toronto's city hall made on their logo—stifled them at every turn, barely letting them get a shot off, even on the power play. All the bounces seemed to go in Toronto's favor. Gabe managed to hit the crossbar and the post *twice*, but nothing went in.

Frankly it was impressive that the Dekes had had the puck long enough for Gabe to get that many shots. Careless and disorganized, they turned the puck over every shift, and now they were getting frustrated, which compounded the problem.

Frustration turned into sloppy plays. Gabe wished they could channel it into some goals instead, but he couldn't get himself together any better than the rest of the team. He went after the puck in the corner, his head down like a green rookie, when one of the Ts boarded him.

"Cocksucker!" the guy cursed as he skated away with the puck, an infuriating blur of white, blue, and yellow.

Gabe faltered for a second, smarting from the blow to his ego as much as the hit and the slur. But his legs held and nothing was broken. Like hell was he just going to stand there and take it, though. Still, Gabe couldn't assume anything was personal. It would fuck with his game.

Their game was fucked anyway.

It was only thanks to Olie's skill in net that the game ended in a 2–0 loss. Considering they got outshot 43–17, Gabe would take it... but he didn't like it.

The hall back to the locker room was crowded. The usual press scrum huddled around, but as Coach promised, none of them were allowed past the locker room doors.

A few of the reporters called Gabe's name, but he ignored them as he threaded past their mics and bodies. He wasn't the captain, he wasn't an alternate, and he hadn't made any plays unique enough to be worth talking about. He didn't have to talk to the press today.

In the locker room, Kitty avoided his gaze. But so did most of the other guys. Players tended to like their space after a frustrating loss. Gabe wasn't going to read anything into it. If he spent longer than normal under the punishing spray of the shower, no one commented, and no one seemed concerned about Gabe seeing them naked.

By the time he finished dressing, only Tips remained in one of the training rooms off the back of the locker room, icing his knee under the supervision of one of the trainers. Gabe stuck his head in. "You okay?"

Tips had taken a hit awkwardly and limped off halfway through the third.

Tips grimaced. "I'll miss a game or two, but it feels okay. Nothing permanent."

"Thank fuck." Gabe waved good night and braced himself for the trek down the hall.

He had to stop and think about an alternate route before he got to the end, because Baller was holding court with the press in a really inconvenient place. Fortunately the reporters were all watching him, so no one had seen Gabe.

"Dante, how has the controversy around Gabriel Martin impacted the Nordiques as a team?"

Anyone who didn't know Baller would have missed the irritated twitch of the corner of his mouth. "He's gay. What controversy?"

Gabe's sense of self-preservation sounded a warning, but he couldn't make himself move.

Some of the interviewers' voices didn't carry, which made eavesdropping a challenge, but Baller had taken at least *some* media training to heart, so Gabe heard his responses clearly. Someone must have asked about locker-room etiquette, because Baller rolled his eyes. He was lucky his smirk was so charming; if Gabe did that in front of the press, Trish would hand him his balls on a plate. "Gabe gives me exactly as much shit about my ass as everyone else. Now that I think about it, I'm kind of offended he doesn't pay more attention."

Gabe snorted.

An interviewer spoke again and, judging by the way Baller's easy body language closed off, they had crossed a line. The last of his patience evaporated. He clenched his jaw hard enough that Gabe could make out the flexing muscles from across the hall as Baller tried to refocus the conversation. "Does anyone have any questions about hockey?" he asked, a hint of desperation detectable under the annoyance. "You know, that game we get paid obscene amounts of money to play for you? Specifically the way we couldn't find the back of the net with both hands and a map, presumably because we never had the puck long enough to give it a try? Please. Anyone. Ask me about how bad we got outskated tonight. I hate losing, but I'd rather talk about that than my friend's love life."

Thankfully someone must have taken the hint, because Baller talked about the problems with their power play unit instead.

After double-checking to make sure he hadn't been spotted, Gabe went back down the hall and took the long way around to the players' exit. As Brigitte had promised, the players' parking area was secure. Anyone who wanted a shot of him getting in his car would need a telephoto lens. Gabe slid behind the wheel and gave himself a few moments to breathe deeply, leaning his forehead against the wheel.

That hadn't been that bad. He'd expected worse. Sure, the invasive questions were terrible, but tomorrow he'd do his interview with the SportsNet host, and then it would air, and things would go back to normal. Or not. But they'd settle down in time.

The way Baller had pushed back against those questions, though…. Gabe would be lying if he said that didn't mean something to him. It was one thing to support him in private and another to challenge the press on his behalf. He couldn't remember the last time someone had stood up for him like that off the ice. He never would've thought Baller to be the type—not because Gabe thought he was a bigot, but because he never seemed serious.

Gabe knew better now. Baller handled serious topics the same way he did everything else—head-on and flippant.

A sharp knock on his window had him jerking his head up to see Baller gazing at him in concern. Just how long had Gabe been sitting there?

He rolled down his window.

Baller tilted his head. "Everything okay?"

"Aside from the fact that I suddenly suck at hockey." Gabe tried to smile.

"Well, on the plus side, you're in amazing company." He took a step back and held his arms out, palms up, classic *look at me*.

Now Gabe smiled for real, in spite of himself. "It's amazing your head fits inside your helmet."

"What can I say, I'm a walking miracle." He put his hands in his pockets. "Listen, tell me to fuck off if you want, but you look like you could stand to blow off some steam. I understand if you want to be alone—"

"I don't," Gabe said. The words were out before he even thought about them. It was weird. He was an only child. He'd always kept himself apart from the team. He usually licked his wounds in private.

Now he had options.

If Baller thought Gabe's interruption was strange, he didn't show it. "Cool. So what do you usually do to unwind after a bad game? I know you don't usually come out drinking, and it's kinda early anyway...."

Gabe couldn't remember the last time he'd had someone from the team over, but what the hell. He had a cleaning service. The house was fine. Maybe he couldn't cook for shit, but he could order pizza.

And maybe it had been a hard week, and if he wanted to reward himself for getting through it by spending some extra time with Baller, who was nice to look at and actively doing his best to make Gabe feel less like shit, what was the harm?

"I'll text you an address," he said. "Wear something comfortable."

DANTE WENT back to his apartment to change, but he stopped short in front of his closet. What did *comfortable* mean? Like, lounging around on the couch comfortable? Playing basketball in the driveway comfortable? Beers on a patio comfortable?

It would be embarrassing if he showed up in sweats only to find Gabe wanted to go to some high-end bistro and drink vodka tonics. (Dante conceded at this point that Gabe and tequila was a love affair that was destined to be one-sided on tequila's part.) But if he showed up in nice jeans and a polo shirt and it turned out they were going to stuff themselves full of Chinese takeout and play videogames, he'd look like a tryhard *and* be uncomfortable.

Okay, this was ridiculous. Dante had spent less time considering what to wear before super hot dates. Just because Gabe was indirectly responsible for Dante realizing he was bi didn't mean Dante was into him. He was hot, that was all.

The point was, this was not a date. This was casual hangouts with a teammate, dress code comfortable.

Dante stripped out of his suit and grabbed a soft burgundy T-shirt and his fanciest gray sweatpants, the ones that were cloud-soft and looked like dress pants on casual inspection. There. Close enough.

The address Gabe sent was residential, in a nice area just outside the city. He'd sent a gate code too, which made Dante snort—68-96-53, the top line's jersey numbers, in order. Dante didn't know exactly who that kind of code was supposed to keep out. Maybe Gabe figured he was only in danger of being robbed by people who didn't watch hockey.

Dante parked in the circular driveway of a house that looked like it belonged in a magazine—stone, two stories, metal roof shingles, enormous detached garage. He whistled under his breath. Of course Gabe had money, but this was a lot of house for one person.

Maybe they didn't sell reclusive bachelor pads that came with their own entry gate.

He was wondering whether he should go up the front steps and ring the doorbell—Gabe's door was twelve feet tall and made of either very expensive wood or metal finished to look like it—when one of the garage doors opened.

Dante had expected fancy cars. This... was not that.

Gabe emerged from the garage wearing a sweat-wicking T-shirt that hugged his chest and arms, athletic pants, and sneakers. His hair was still damp from his postgame shower, and it was getting long now, curling above his ears and at his nape. Dante had gotten the dress code right—except on Gabe, it looked like *sweats, but make it sexy.*

Definitely hot. Damn.

"Hey." Gabe gestured around with a grin. "Welcome to my humble abode."

"We have different definitions of humble," Dante's mouth said, as usual several steps ahead of his brain.

Now that it was partially open, he could see that the interior of the garage had been divided into two. The cars must've been on the other half. This half was dominated by a bar, a high-top table with four stools, and a projector screen.

And... Astroturf?

Gabe ignored Dante's rudeness, which was probably for the best. "Pizza's ordered. It could be a while, though. They're always getting lost coming out here."

"That's cool," Dante said, gesturing to the front right corner of the garage, where an old-fashioned popcorn cart stood gathering dust. "If the situation gets dire, we can just make enough popcorn to bury ourselves alive. What *is* this?"

Gabe followed his gaze. "In my defense, the popcorn thing came with the house. I guess the previous owners didn't want to bother moving it."

Dante reminded himself that he had also entered the tax bracket of people who didn't have to sell their old stuff on Craigslist, but it still jarred him to hear that. "It's kind of badass. You should bring it next time Flash has a barbecue." He shook himself and pointed to the screen. "But I actually meant *that*."

"That's my baby." Unfortunately, Dante did not detect a single note of sarcasm. His despair only grew when Gabe walked over to a storage cupboard and withdrew a tall, narrow bag. "It's a video golf simulator."

Oh Lord. "Gabriel, I say this with love, but really. This is what you do in your spare time?"

Gabe's brow furrowed a little. Had Dante offended him? He didn't want to hurt the guy's feelings. "Yeah. My dad used to take me when I was younger." His cheeks went pink, like he was embarrassed.

"I've never tried it," Dante blurted.

The embarrassment disappeared under curiosity. Thank God. "What, really? *How*?"

It was a fair question. Pretty much everybody on the team golfed. The dads trip in Florida—golf. Various charity events in the off-season—golf. Somebody was getting married—golf.

Since they were bonding and everything…. "My parents spent all their money buying me equipment for the other rich white people sport."

"Oh." Now he looked sheepish. "Sorry, I guess I kind of assumed…."

Dante gave himself five adulting points for not saying something about assumptions making asses. "No, no, it's cool. I blow off steam by getting laid or blowing the heads off zombies in video games, and you…."

One corner of Gabe's mouth lifted. "I crush a tiny ball as hard as I can with a big metal stick and see how far I can make it go."

For a second Dante just blinked at him, reevaluating his opinion of golf.

Then he said, "Teach me."

The request turned out to be more complicated than he expected. Gabe had a couple spare sets of clubs—for which Dante side-eyed him suspiciously until he said they were his dad's old set and another set he'd picked up at a yard sale for fifty bucks. "They don't fit everyone, see?" He handed Dante his driver, which was too long to even attempt a swing with.

"You're not that much taller than me," Dante grumbled.

"We're just lucky you're not left-handed when you golf. The yard-sale clubs would be too short for you." Which was super weird. How could Dante shoot left in hockey and still be so right-handed at golf? "Here. Try this one."

The golf screen was actually kind of cool. It projected an image of a golf course, with a blue sky and trees and birds and the whole nine yards. A graphic in the bottom corner showed which way the wind was blowing and how fast. It tracked where the ball hit and how hard and projected where it would land on the virtual course.

Of course, Dante was terrible at it.

"Ugh!" he said in disgust when his third shot in a row landed in a virtual water trap.

Gabe, who'd just come back in from tipping the pizza delivery person, snorted and put the boxes down on the table. "Okay, here. Let me show you what you're doing wrong."

"*Please*," Dante begged. If he was going to play this dumb sport, he at least wanted to not suck at it.

"First, I know I said I like to crush the ball as hard as I can." Gabe grabbed one of the yard-sale clubs and dropped it on the floor between Dante's feet. He nudged it with his foot until it touched the back of his left heel and the toe of his right. He was close enough Dante could smell his bodywash. "But that's because I can hit the ball straight already."

"I feel obligated to make a joke here." Partly because that would keep him from being distracted. He almost felt light-headed.

Gabe rolled his eyes, but he was smiling. "Yeah, yeah, my golf shot is the straightest thing about me." Once the club was arranged to his liking, he took a few steps back. "Okay, see? When you pull back for your swing, you want to keep the club in your hands parallel to that line. Just for, like, a half-clapper."

That was far from a full swing, but Dante would like his ball to land on the grass at least once today, so he tried it.

"Better," Gabe said. Once Dante set another ball on the tee and reset his stance, Gabe returned and examined his hands. "You've got the grip right. Next time bring your arms back farther and get more of a swing, but remember to turn your shoulders. Keep that left arm straight."

Rinse, repeat. This shot went wildly to the left. Gabe was already laughing before he finished the swing.

"Okay, I see the problem now. You're not following through. In hockey you can't continue the swing because you'll take someone's head off. But no one should be that close to you in golf. It's making you kind of… choppy."

"Choppy," Dante repeated.

Gabe picked up a club and nudged him away from the Astroturf. "Just watch, okay?"

Dante watched. He watched as Gabe carefully adjusted his stance, legs apart. His shirt pulling tight over his shoulders and back. Muscled arms taut. Round hockey ass—not as great as Dante's, but whose was?—sticking out proudly. One smooth movement back, coiling like a spring, and then the release, all the way through, until the club practically wrapped around him like a hug.

Should Dante be jealous of a golf club?

Maybe he should've gone out and gotten laid instead. Then he could be having sex with a beautiful stranger, instead of realizing he wanted to have sex with his beautiful teammate.

He wouldn't, though. Hockey was too important to risk for sex.

"Too fast?" Gabe asked when Dante didn't say anything because his brain had disengaged.

"Maybe?" Dante hedged. He certainly didn't feel like he'd absorbed any useful technique.

"All right. Square up," Gabe told him as he put his club back in his bag. "And don't punch me."

Why would I—

The train of thought derailed when Gabe stepped up close behind him and put his hands on Dante's hips. "You're not rotating smoothly through here." Dante could feel the heat of him through their thin clothing. Suddenly the interior of Gabe's uninsulated garage in a Quebec October felt like a Louisiana a heat wave. "Swing again, slow motion. Try not to hit me with the club."

With the way Dante's nerves were firing with Gabe's hands on him, he'd be lucky to make contact with the ball. He decided not to try and concentrated on the advice Gabe had given him. Left arm straight. Wrists locked. Roll his shoulders into the backswing—

Gabe pushed on his left hip, moving it into the swing as he pulled the right side back toward him. "Good." Was his voice a little hoarse? Dante's brain was going to start leaking out his ears. "Now release and follow through—"

The problem with following through was that his ass, under Gabe's guidance, was brushing over Gabe's crotch, and it was hard to concentrate once he started wondering if Gabe was freeballing.

He must've done okay, because Gabe gave him a gentle slap of approval on the hip and stepped away.

"Not bad. But maybe we should eat before the pizza gets cold."

Dante took a deep breath and tried not to shiver now that he didn't have Gabe's warmth against his back. "Good idea. I'm starving."

Sitting at the pub table while Gabe grabbed a couple of beers from the mini fridge gave him a chance to get control of his reactions. Obviously his body had decided to do some catching up when it came to having sexual reactions to other men.

Nothing to worry about.

"I concede, I think." Dante wiped a smear of pizza grease from the corner of his mouth with his thumb. "There's definitely something therapeutic about whacking a tiny ball really hard. At least once you can get it to go where you want it to."

Gabe reached for another slice. "It's nicer when there's a real course involved." He flicked his gaze to Dante's, then shrugged a little. "My dad and I had all our important talks on golf courses."

For once, Dante managed to stay his tongue. That was the most adorable rich white-boy nonsense he ever heard, but Gabe didn't need to know that. "Yeah?"

"I came out to him on the green of the seventeenth hole at Richmond Centennial." He shook his head. "Two months later that's where he told me he and Mom were getting divorced."

Yeesh. And he still liked golf after that? Then again…. "We did all our important family discussions over food." At least until Dante realized he was bi when several thousand miles away from his parents. And those talks certainly hadn't put him off his feed.

His conversation with his dad had gone about like he expected. His dad said, "You will always be my son," as if that were in any doubt, and then admitted he had doubts about Abuela's reaction.

Dante didn't know what to do about that, so he hadn't called his grandmother in a while.

"What kinds of talks?"

Dante picked off a piece of pepperoni and popped it in his mouth. "Like why the other hockey moms gave my mom weird looks when they found out I was her kid, or why she had a shit fit when someone joked that I must look like my dad." Gabe tilted his head, and Dante realized Gabe didn't have all the facts. "My mom's white. Dad's Latino."

"Ah." He grimaced. "People are dumb."

"That's one word for it." Dante shook his head. "Or there were the times we moved. I always knew when we were moving again because Dad would make *mole*."

Gabe raised his eyebrows. "Army brat?"

Dante grinned. "No, just the regular kind. Dad works for a hotel chain. I didn't love all the moving around, but when I started getting older, he'd take the opportunities that put us closer to better hockey programs."

And it had been good practice for all the moving around in juniors, to the AHL, and finally to the NHL. He hoped he wouldn't get traded, at least not until he established himself a little better, but chances were it would happen eventually.

"Sounds like you're close."

Dante smiled. "Yeah. You?"

Gabe's shoulders hunched a little. "My dad and I are. Mom hasn't been in the picture for a while."

There was a story there, but it could wait. Dante picked up his beer bottle. "To good dads, then."

Gabe's glass clinked against his. "I'll drink to that."

"WHAT DO you think?"

Gabe stood in the green room with Flash, Tricia, and Erika, his agent, staring at his wardrobe options.

The first was a suit designed to make him look like every other hockey player—charcoal gray with a light blue shirt. No tie, at least, and a tiny You Can Play pin on the jacket.

Next to it, a pair of gray slacks and a sweater in lavender cashmere. Gabe thought that was a bold choice compared to the suit, but it was Hockey Fights Cancer month, and all the gear for that was the same lavender. There was a pin for this one too, this one with the hockey-stick caduceus logo on it.

The suit was comfortable, familiar armor, even if Gabe never would've picked this one to wear at any other time.

Gabe would look incredible in the sweater, no question, and unlike the suit, it emphasized the fact that he had an actual personality outside of hockey—and this interview was *about* his life outside of hockey.

"The suit's the safe choice," Trish said finally.

Hadn't Gabe made enough safe choices in his life? "The sweater, then."

Erika gave him a sidelong look. "Since when do you make risky choices?"

Since I dated a guy who decided to sell my sexuality to the tabloids. "I'm already out," he said. "Wearing purple doesn't make me any gayer. And at least I'll be comfortable."

Now Erika clapped him on the shoulder. "Proud of your personal growth," she said. "I'll let the crew know."

Flash furrowed his brow. "Why do they care?"

Trish and Erika exchanged glances. "Wardrobe will want to coordinate the anchor's tie."

Flash looked lost. "Why?"

"Optics," Trish replied as Erika left, presumably to speak to the camera crew. "It's a subtle way the network can indicate support for Gabe."

"Can't they just say they support him?"

Gabe had seen Trish's expression before, on the face of a *Game of Thrones* character. What was the line she'd said? *Oh my sweet summer child.*

"I'll leave you to get dressed," she told Gabe. "You're due in Makeup in ten minutes. And hey—don't forget to think about what we talked about, okay?"

She wanted him to consider doing something special for the team's Pride Night, which would happen in November, the day after they came back from a long road trip. Gabe wanted to dismiss the idea, but he admitted that it would look weird if he *didn't* do anything.

And part of him wanted to. But what would his teammates think? The rest of the league? Hockey fans in general? These days it seemed like people wanted to discourage athletes—especially hockey players—from having an opinion on anything more meaningful than whether a hot dog was a sandwich.

Even *that* could get you in trouble.

"I should've done this at home," Gabe grumbled as he put on the slacks.

"Because you really wanted strangers in your house for this invasive interview."

Flash knew him well. "We could've done it in the garage. Played the golf simulator. Very heteronormative."

"If you're like sixty years old, maybe."

"Hey, Baller liked it." Except now he was thinking about last night, and not just about how nice it had been not to sulk alone after a bad game. He was thinking about how easy the conversation had been, despite how different their lives were. After only a few minutes, he'd left the game and the associated media nightmare far behind him. Maybe Baller made some jokes at Gabe's expense, but he was just as willing to poke fun at himself… and if the past week had proven anything, it was that Gabe could use a few lessons in taking himself less seriously.

He'd even made a joke about Baller punching him when he helped him with his golf swing. Only that kind of backfired. Gabe was *sure* he was kidding when he said it—he certainly hadn't meant the touch to be sexual. Then he'd put his hands on Baller's hips and… well, mistakes were made. Baller was warm and he smelled good, and Gabe could feel the power in the muscular body under his fingertips.

He poked his head through the top of the sweater to find Flash eyeballing him. "You let Baller into the Fortress of Solitude?" Gabe wished Flash would stop calling his house that. "For *video golf*?"

Gabe didn't have anything to feel guilty about. He was allowed to make friends on the team. Flash had encouraged it, in fact.

So why did he feel like a teenager getting busted for breaking curfew?

"I caught the tail end of some of the questions the reporters were throwing at him after the game and I needed a minute." He shrugged defensively. "He found me sitting in my car and asked if I wanted company, so we ordered pizza."

Now Flash looked guilty. "He's a good friend. I should have been there."

"You *are* there. I could've called you. But you have a wife and four kids." Gabe couldn't take up all Flash's time. "Think of it as me saving the women of Quebec City from his terrible pickup lines, just for a day."

Flash snorted. "They should give you a medal." He reached out and straightened the fall of Gabe's sweater. It fit snugly, emphasizing his broad shoulders. "I suppose it'll do." He spun Gabe around and gently shoved him toward the door. "Come on. Let's not keep your adoring public waiting."

The anchor doing the interview was a former hockey scout named Rob McDonagh. He had graying hair and a slightly round, reddish face, and he had indeed donned a lavender tie for the occasion. He and Gabe had met a few times over the years—Gabe's draft day, during his time with Team Canada at the Olympics, and at one of the NHL media days in New York.

Rob held out his hand for Gabe to shake. "Hey, Gabe, good to see you again."

His handshake was firm, and his smile seemed genuine. "Thanks. You too."

For the interview, they were taking over one of the smaller conference rooms at the Amphitheatre, one usually used for filming social-media segments for the team. They sat kitty-corner at the table, with the film crew as unobtrusive as possible at the back of the room.

Rob gestured for Gabe to sit. "Erika said she went over my basic talking points with you. Do you have any questions or concerns before we start?"

Is there any way we can just fast-forward and get this over with? "Uh, no, I think I'm… *ready* doesn't seem like the right word." Erika had told him that the two of them had final say over what would make it into the televised version, so if he fucked up and said something stupid—his words, not hers—he had a get-out-of-jail-free card.

A sound tech pinned a mic to Gabe's sweater. "Just talk normally for me?" she asked.

"I can do that." Or he could fake it, at least.

"Volume's good. Okay, we're good to go here." She backed up toward the camera crew and gave them the thumbs-up.

While the techs adjusted the lighting, Rob went over what Gabe could expect one more time. Gabe listened with half an ear, trying to keep calm, until the producer said, "Okay, whenever you guys are ready."

Rob passed Gabe a water bottle. "Ready?"

Gabe cracked it, took a drink, and put it out of view of the camera. "Shoot."

"Tonight on this special edition of *Off the Ice*, join me as I talk to Nordiques forward Gabriel Martin about his recent media attention. Gabe, thank you for joining me today."

PR made me do it. "Thanks for having me" was the canned response that came out.

Oh well. Rome wasn't built in a day.

Rob eased him into the interview with a few softball questions about the team (Baller fit in nicely on first line, and Gabe was pleased with rookie Tom Yorkshire's progress), what it was like playing for a female coach (Gabe only had one other NHL coach to compare her to, but St. Louis worked them harder), what he'd done in the off-season (Pierre, mostly, but Gabe just said he golfed a lot).

Finally Rob gave Gabe the visual cue that they were getting into the serious questions. "Gabe, I'm sure fans watching at home have been waiting for me to ask this question. You recently released a statement to the media confirming that you are gay, after a former partner leaked intimate pictures of you to the press. What has the past week been like for you?"

Gabe wanted to reach for the water bottle, but at the last second, he remembered Trish's advice not to fidget because it made him look like he had something to hide. He was done hiding. "Uh, well, I've never spent so much time in the PR office. I think Tricia is sick of me." Not true—Tricia was great—but it gave him some time to come up with something more substantial. All his rehearsed answers had evaporated.

Rob gently prodded him back on track. "I imagine it hasn't been easy for you having your private life exposed like this."

Did he have to use the word *exposed*? That sounded so… explicit. The photograph was PG-rated.

Gabe cleared his throat. "It's been hard. All I ever wanted to do was play hockey, you know? That was the plan from, like, age five—just play hockey. At some point I guess I realized I would eventually get too old, but I sort of avoided thinking about what I might do afterward."

"Was that because you knew you were gay, and you felt pressure to keep that part of yourself hidden?"

This time Gabe did need to pause for a drink of water.

"It's fine," Rob said gently. "Just take your time. We'll cut it all together so you look confident in your answers."

Gabe hoped they had a good video-editing department. He chugged half the bottle, then set it aside again.

Rob repeated the question.

"It was never explicit pressure," Gabe said slowly. "Not external pressure, anyway. But growing up, there weren't any guys like me in the NHL. At least not that anyone knew about. And locker rooms then.... They're better now, and I do think teams are mostly willing to put in the effort, but back then locker-room talk included a lot of homophobic slurs. I figured if I was going to make it, no one could know the truth about me, so I made sure no one did."

"And how did that decision affect you?"

"To be honest, I'm still working that out. I think it made it hard for me to connect with my teammates, and that was lonely."

"But you've had a successful career. You were part of an Olympic-gold-winning team. You've won the Art Ross trophy. You've had tremendous impact on the ice. And yet...."

Gabe didn't know what he was going to say until he heard the words come out of his own mouth. "It was never enough that I felt like I could just come out and be me." *I lived alone in a huge house and played video golf by myself in my garage when I got upset.* "I never had it in my head to be anyone's role model for anything other than hockey. Like, I'll just be frank for a minute. Despite some progress, 'stay in the closet until you're well established' isn't bad career advice. But there's more to life than just a career. So...."

Be your own Phil Esposito.

Fucking Baller. Gabe would be hearing that in his head for the rest of his life. "A friend recently said to me that somebody has to be the first. Sometimes you have to be your own role model. And I guess if people are going to look at me as an example, I want them to know they shouldn't have to choose between their career and—" Love? Sex? Companionship? "—their personal life. They deserve both."

"Well, now that you mention it… are you seeing anyone?"

Gabe snorted. "My last relationship ended in blocked calls and pictures of me being sold to the media, so I am definitely single." He froze and backtracked. "Oh God, that's going to come across like I'm looking for a boyfriend, isn't it?"

"I'd be surprised if we don't get a few write-ins with guys' phone numbers after this airs."

Oh God. "And I thought my teammates trying to set me up with their gay cousins, college roommates, and brothers-in-law was bad."

That let them segue into less fraught territory, and Gabe relaxed. When the interview ended, he felt pretty good about it.

He shook Rob's hand, thanked the tech crew, and made his exit.

Flash was waiting for him at the door. "A friend, eh? I wonder who *that* was."

It was obviously a dig meant to get Gabe's back up, even if Flash was teasing. But Gabe wasn't going to rise to the bait. He felt too good, now that this was over with, to go on the defensive. He threw his arm around Flash's shoulders and steered him down the hallway. "Aw, Cap. You don't have to be jealous. You'll always be my favorite golfing buddy."

Flash shook his head and slung his arm around Gabe's waist. "The sad thing is, I believe you mean that."

FROM DANTE'S perspective, most of the guys who gave Gabe a wide berth after the photo leaked got their heads out of their asses once the interview came out. Dante wasn't about to give any of them awards for becoming enlightened members of society, but he got that some guys felt like they'd had the rug pulled out from under them. They thought they knew their teammate.

It probably would've been awkward for longer if Gabe wasn't the best player on the team, but he was… when he wasn't dealing with the enormous mindfuck of his personal life suddenly becoming very public.

And if Dante was harboring a tiny, teeny, insignificant flicker of *something*—call it pride—that Gabe had quoted him in his interview, however anonymously, for once in his life, Dante was keeping his mouth shut about it.

Dante was determined not to let his attraction to Gabe become a problem. There were lots of attractive people in the world, and Dante hadn't slept with most of them. But most of them weren't his boyhood idol, a man who had more in common with Dante than he knew about, who put in the extra time to help Dante, who was generous and humble and had a sneaky sense of humor.

Of course Dante *liked* someone like that. Not liking Gabe would be like not liking puppies or babies or junk food.

If they didn't work together, Dante would be all over that like cheese on pizza, but they did, so there was no point speculating. If that Pierre guy was Gabe's type, he probably wouldn't go for Dante anyway.

November arrived with the bite of winter in the air. The Dekes had gone on a few short road trips—some East Coast games, and the Prairies, which Dante was glad to get out of the way before that half of Canada froze for the winter. Not that it wouldn't be frigid in Quebec City too, but Quebec City couldn't compete with Winnipeg when it came to being an icy wasteland of despair. He spent a lot of nights in hotel rooms playing video games with Yorkie, or else taking turns exiling the other for phone calls and FaceTime. Dante mostly talked to his parents. Yorkie had to juggle parents, two sisters who didn't live at home, *and* his girlfriend.

Dante spent a lot of time playing games on his phone in the lobby to give him privacy.

The season hadn't started as smoothly as he hoped. While they notched a few decisive victories since the season opener against the Orcas, they suffered just as many humiliating defeats.

Then there were the losses that *really* stung, the 2–1 games where they played well—sometimes better than their opponents—but it wasn't good enough.

To make matters worse, their division was fiercely competitive, with four of the best teams in the league.

Sure it was early in the season, but if they didn't pull their shit together soon, they'd be out of playoff contention by February. And that sucked.

Dante couldn't help but feel like all the media bullshit had thrown Gabe off his game. And that was affecting the whole line—the whole *team*, since Gabe was their leading scorer. Coach had told them that if they couldn't start stringing together some wins soon, she'd have no choice but to break up their line and try something else. Whatever chemistry they'd had in the preseason had fizzled.

Dante hoped that this trip—a long haul to Arizona and Tennessee, with later stops in California—would provide a much-needed injection of enthusiasm, points, and confidence.

Then the puck dropped for the first game, and ninety seconds later it was in the back of the Nordiques' net, with Olie cursing in what Dante assumed was Swedish as the Scorpions' fans cheered their team.

But the game was still young. There was lots of hockey left to play.

"Okay, shake it off, guys," Flash said. He bumped his helmet against Olie's. "They got lucky. Anyone can get lucky, even us."

"I can definitely get lucky," Dante said, because he knew his cue when he heard it.

He didn't, though. The first period ticked away, and the Scorps potted another goal.

There was less than a minute left in the period when Dante's line came off the ice. He was resigning himself to starting the second down by two when one of the Scorps broke his stick attempting a shot.

Quick as anything, Bricks got on the puck and sent it knuckling out of the defensive zone just in time for Yorkie to pick it up as his line started their shift.

They'd caught the Scorps effectively short-handed. Yorkie hammered the puck over to Tips—it would've been a suicide pass if anyone had been close enough to check him. But Tips didn't have an angle. He snapped it back.

By the time the puck got to Yorkie, he had a practically impossible angle. Somehow he still got the puck on his blade and flicked it up just over the goalie's glove—his first NHL goal, a knuckler that squeaked in just before the buzzer.

The bench erupted in long-overdue cheers. Tips collected the puck from the crease and then joined the on-ice celebration.

In the tunnel on the way to the locker room, Dante got Yorkie in a headlock. "Nice one, roomie."

"Get off!" Yorkie laughed and shoved him away. "How am I supposed to score again if you throw my back out?"

"Dick," Dante said fondly. "Come on, we don't want to miss our pep talk."

First goals always energized the team, and this one was no different. For the first time in a week, the locker room felt unified, determined, hopeful. They went out for the second period and played the best hockey they'd managed all year—perfect defense, tight offense, not giving the Scorps anything to capitalize on. They peppered the goalie with fifteen shots. They didn't take a single penalty.

Nothing went in, but it felt inevitable now.

"I don't know what got into you guys, but keep doing it," Coach said before the third. "Great job out there. This is what I've been looking for from you all season. Now finish this."

Dante glanced to his left and caught Gabe's eye.

Dante held out his glove for a fist bump. "Wheel, snipe, celly."

It took them until halfway through the third period. The Scorps' goaltender was playing out of his mind, so the Dekes were still down 2–1.

Then Dante forced a turnover at the blue line and the race was on.

Gabe must have known he had the puck almost before Dante did. Flash stayed just behind them, between them and the opposing forwards who were racing back together.

Dante didn't have a shot. But he did have a tiny window to pass—right between his defender's legs, just like they'd done back in the preseason.

He didn't hesitate. A flick of his wrist and suddenly the puck was on Gabe's stick, with nothing between him and the net. Gabe held on, waiting for the goaltender to make a move—

And when he faked a shot low and near side, the goalie fell for it.

The goal horn went off and Dante slammed into Gabe, yelling. "Fucking *beautiful* goal!"

"Fucking incredible pass! Right through the legs!"

Dante grinned and slapped the back of his helmet as Flash crashed into them both. "Just like we practiced, baby."

Flash got an arm around each of their shoulders. "Let's do it again."

But just eight short minutes later, the horn sounded to signal the end of the period.

"Overtime," Olie said sourly.

"I tried," Dante protested. "Come on. That pass was amazing." The way they were playing tonight, it would be no problem to finish this off in overtime.

It wasn't long before they got their chance.

Overtime format meant three-on-three, and every second counted. Sometimes someone got stuck on the ice and ended up playing with another line. Dante was usually with Flash and Kitty, but Gabe couldn't come off without giving the Scorpions too good a chance.

One of the Scorps got Gabe up against the boards and came away with the puck, making for center ice, but Kitty caught him on the backcheck before he could take a shot.

Suddenly it was a mad rush back to the offensive zone. The Scorps did their best to wrestle the puck out of Kitty's clutches, but he deked around them.

Dante made a beeline for the net, hoping for a clear shot from the top of the circle, but the Scorps were too fast and blocked the passing lane.

But Gabe was completely open, only clear ice between him and Kitty—a clean shot to the net.

Dante tried to cycle around his defender to distract from the fact that Gabe was wide open with hot hands tonight. If Kitty got Gabe the puck—

Kitty passed to Dante, who cursed furiously when the Scorp guarding him intercepted it. What had Kitty been thinking? Gabe was wide open.

They rushed back down the ice, playing chase—except Gabe, who had to be exhausted from double-shifting. Flash replaced him, but by the time he made it to the defensive zone, the puck was in the back of the Dekes' net and the game was over.

What just happened?

Why would Kitty pass to him? Why hadn't he been able to hold on to the puck? Or even just tip it away. Gabe could've come in and grabbed it—

"Joder." Dante slammed his stick on the ice. It figured. Their best chance at a solid win in ages, a game they'd dominated for the last two periods, and it fell apart because….

Kitty and Flash were snarling at each other at center ice, looking like they were going to drop gloves and

go at it right there—air the team's dirty laundry in front
of twenty thousand Scorpions fans.

Perfect. Icing on the cake.

But his torment didn't end there. The ride back to
the hotel was tense. Everyone gave Kitty a wide berth,
which Dante figured was because it was that or someone was going to punch him.

He didn't have any intention of going out tonight—
he wasn't fit for human company.

"I'm gonna, uh…." Yorkie gestured over his shoulder, where Tips and Bricksy were waiting. "First goal
celebration drinks."

Dante wished he was into joining. "Don't let them
get you too drunk," he teased.

At least he'd have the room to himself for a bit.

He took off his shoes and suit and flopped on his
bed, debating. Part of him wanted to go talk to Gabe.
He'd seen Gabe's face when Kitty made that pass,
and… yeah.

Maybe Kitty had just made a mistake. It happened.
Not usually in so spectacular a fashion, but still.

But based on his pattern of behavior, Dante didn't
think Kitty made a mistake. He was pretty sure Kitty
purposely passed to Dante even though Gabe was wide
open and Dante wasn't. And the only reason he'd have
done that….

Was the same reason he'd left Gabe's impromptu
coming-out party without stopping by to talk to Gabe,
and the same reason he'd stayed at the other end of every gathering Gabe had attended since.

The reason being that Kitty was an asshole, and
now he hated Gabe because Gabe was gay.

Which meant he hated Dante too, or he would
when he found out the truth.

Given the circumstances and his state of mind, Dante had no idea what possessed him to answer the phone when his grandmother called.

"Dante! There you are, my sweet boy. It's been so long."

He smiled in spite of himself. "Hi, Abuela. I miss you too."

"Oh, you do not. You're far too busy to miss an old lady like me. But thank you for saying it."

"Thank you for calling." He turned onto his side so he could look out the hotel window, not that he could see much, just a vague orange-yellow glow from the businesses outside. "I forgot how tiring the first few weeks of the season are before I get used to the pace." Not to mention all the travel and the jet lag.

She *tsk*ed. "You need to take better care of yourself, mijo. Are you eating right?"

"As much as I can," he promised. "It's just an adjustment. I have a roommate this year on the road— Tom Yorkshire. If you saw the game tonight, he scored his first goal for us."

"I did see it! He seems like such a nice young man." Her tone darkened. "Not like that other one."

Fuck. Dante swallowed against a lump in his throat. "What do you mean?" he said. "All the guys on the team are pretty great." Except Kitty, but that can of worms could stay in the pantry.

"Oh, I know the bonds of brotherhood are strong, Dante, but you have to be careful. This man, Gabriel Martin, you don't want to associate with people like him. It's unnatural, what he is."

Dante swallowed around the lump in his throat. "Two months ago, when he was staying late after practice to help me, you liked him just fine."

Abuela huffed. "Well, of course, when I thought he had just seen your potential. But what if he was trying to take advantage of you?"

By running drills with me until neither of us could breathe? So sexy. How could I resist? "Gabe never tried anything, Abuela. He's a good man. He wouldn't do that." Even if Dante kind of wanted him to.

"Dante Baltierra, you listen to what I am telling you and heed my words. You be careful of this man and don't let him lead you into sin."

That was pretty rich. Dante did a lot more sleeping around than Gabe, and Abuela definitely knew about it. The only comment she'd ever made was to pat his cheek and tell him he'd meet the right girl someday, and mind he didn't do anything before then that he'd be ashamed to tell her about.

But he didn't have the fight in him today. He sighed, disgusted with himself and his lack of backbone. "I won't, Abuela."

They hung up a few minutes later, after a brief discussion of the church yard-sale fundraiser and the excitement of the neighbors three doors down finding an alligator in their ornamental pond.

Dante wondered what people were thinking, putting an ornamental pond in their yard in Louisiana, where gators were almost as common as humans. He tried to hold on to those thoughts instead of the darker, less happy ones.

He should've gone out drinking with Yorkie after all.

BY THE time Gabe returned to his hotel room, he was stewing. Had that really just happened? Had Kitty cost them their shot at the game because he wouldn't pass to Gabe? Because Gabe was gay?

Gabe didn't have any delusions. He knew it would take time for his teammates to adjust. He knew some of them were assholes. He'd just figured that their desire to win would outweigh their prejudices.

It sucked to be so wrong.

He felt like he should go out to celebrate Yorkie's goal, but he didn't want to bring the mood down. He didn't feel like celebrating. He felt like sulking, or breaking something, or whacking a tiny ball as hard as he could with a big stick.

But he wasn't going to find an all-night driving range at this hour, so he hit the hotel gym and ran five miles on the treadmill. They didn't have a game tomorrow. He could spend the flight to Tennessee recovering.

He almost jumped out of his skin when he turned the machine off, went to start his cooldown stretches, and found Olie watching him from the corner of the room.

"Jesus. Warn a guy."

Olie lifted his hands. One held a power bar, the other a bottle of Gatorade. "I come in peace."

Gabe snorted and bent his face toward his knee. "I was expecting the captain." Well, *most* of him was expecting Flash. A small part of him thought Dante might find him—he seemed to have some kind of sixth sense about when Gabe could use a friend.

"Think of me as his ambassador." He sat on the bench a few feet away, put the bribe down next to him, and let his hands hang between his knees.

Not that Gabe didn't appreciate being checked on, but... "What, he had something better to do tonight?"

"He's in a meeting with St. Louis."

Gabe winced. "Oh." Probably discussing what to do about Kitty's behavior. Not fun for Flash, and probably not a great time for Coach either. They'd have to figure out a plan, because they couldn't just have a defenseman who refused to pass to Gabe. But if that didn't work, they'd face going to management with *We need you to trade this excellent young defenseman because he won't play nice with the gay forward.*

"Fuck."

"Mm-hmm."

"Sorry," Gabe added after a beat. Defensemen and their goalies tended to form strong bonds.

When he glanced up, Olie was watching him closely. Gabe felt like a bug under glass. "It's not your fault he's a cave troll."

"Yeah." But if he'd been straight, or still in the closet, Kitty would've passed to him and they probably would've won.

He glanced toward the gym door.

Olie raised his eyebrows. "You expecting someone else?"

Not exactly. Gabe moved into his next stretch. "No. But I don't exactly want more company either."

A little white lie.

"Well, the look on your face says this power bar isn't gonna cut it." Olie tucked it back in the pocket of his hoodie. "So finish your stretches and we can order room service and talk about boys."

Gabe paused with his left foot tucked against the inside of his right thigh. "I'm not a teenage girl." He considered for a moment. "I pick the movie."

"Oh, goes without saying." Olie reached down to offer him a hand up.

Gabe took it and let Olie pull him to his feet. "And I'm ordering cheesecake."

"Good choice."

"And if you try to set me up with anyone's cousin, I'm kicking you out."

Olie threw an arm around his shoulders. "I would expect nothing less."

THE FLIGHT to Tennessee proved Gabe was wrong about the recovery thing. Even on the charter, he couldn't stretch out comfortably. Reclining barely helped.

Falling asleep sitting up in bed while watching movies probably hadn't helped either.

In the seat next to him, Baller looked like he'd gone three rounds with the sandman and lost.

"Did you go out with Yorkie last night?" Gabe asked, hoping for a distraction.

"What?" Baller blinked, his eyes bleary. "Uh, no. I was talking to my grandmother… lost track of time." He looked Gabe up and down, taking in the awkward splay of his legs and the way Gabe was sitting twisted in his seat. "What happened to you?"

"Self-flagellation."

Now he leaned back and did the once-over again from a greater distance. "Dude. What kind of kinky shit are you into by yourself?"

Gabe's cheeks went hot. "I was being literal. I spent some time in the hotel gym and didn't cool down well enough afterward."

Baller's lips quirked. "Getting old sucks, huh?"

He was lucky he was cute. "Don't be a dick. You got kept up late by your *grandmother*."

A weak smile. "Touché."

Something was off about that reaction, but Baller reclined his seat, stretched his legs out in front of him, and pointedly closed his eyes. "Wake me up when we land, okay?"

Definitely something going on. Was that why Baller hadn't come to see him yesterday? Had Gabe stepped in it?

"Sure," he said.

Damn it. Baller always managed to make Gabe feel better, and whatever Gabe had done made Baller feel worse. But how could he apologize for something he wasn't sure he'd done and that Baller wasn't acknowledging?

"Do you want to hang out after dinner?" he blurted. God, he sounded like a teenager asking his crush on a date. Worse, he *felt* like one.

Baller's eyes flickered open. He really did look exhausted. But he said, "Yeah, okay." And then, almost as awkward as Gabe felt, "Thanks."

A night off in Nashville meant steak and lots of it. Yorkie cornered Gabe at dinner to pick his brain about the Mustangs' goalie, clearly eager to turn his first goal into a streak. On his other side sat Symons, a rookie defenseman who'd been recalled from the AHL. Gabe suspected he was there to replace Kitty while management figured out what to do, but from the way he hung on Gabe's every word, he had every intention of making an impression. Gabe couldn't fault the kid's enthusiasm, even if it did mean his baked potato got cold.

The weather was mild, so they walked back from the restaurant. Gabe ambled along near the back of the group, not in any hurry to get anywhere. At least not until Baller dropped back next to him. "Kids talk your ear off at dinner?" he asked cheerfully. He must've had a good nap.

"It was you doing it not that long ago." Gabe preferred the relationship they had now, even if it sometimes felt dishonest on his part.

"Time flies." They fell into step. "Anyway, I learned something interesting." He paused for dramatic effect. "This hotel has a rooftop hot tub."

Gabe's muscles—still sore despite a nap, a shower, and a renewed attempt at stretching them back into their usual state—twinged in anticipation. "That *is* interesting."

"So I'm thinking... I'll bring beer. You bring snacks. And we both leave hockey out of it for one night."

"Sounds awesome." Weirdly, Gabe meant it, even though spending time with Baller wet and mostly naked should've been a nightmare. If all he felt was lust, it would have been. But it was like, now that Gabe was out, he couldn't keep that same stranglehold on his emotions, and he liked Baller more than he should like a teammate. He wouldn't act on his feelings—he'd hate himself if he ruined the bond they had—but letting himself *have* them for a person who knew the whole of him instead of only part was seductive in itself.

The dam had broken, but Gabe was swimming fine.

Later, after a quick conference call with Trish and Erika about the Pride Night plans, Gabe had to question his decisions. First, he arrived at the rooftop deck to find Yorkie and Symons already in the hot tub, giggling with the consumption of alcohol no doubt provided by Tips, who was their chaperone this evening.

There was plenty room in the hot tub, but he wasn't sure he wanted to subject himself to this… or whether he'd be welcome. Maybe his teammates would rather not hang out with him half-naked now. He could text Baller, figure out something else to do….

His indecision lasted until Yorkie noticed him standing there with two bags of chips and said, "*Gabe!* You brought snacks! You're my *favorite*."

That took care of some of his concerns, but it raised new ones. Gabe had just seen this child eat his entire body weight in beef. How could he already be drunk enough to have the munchies? Gabe looked at Tips. "If they puke in the hot tub, I'm selling you out to Flash."

"They used the puppy-dog eyes," Tips said defensively. If he was uncomfortable, he was a better actor than every other guy in the league. "What would you have done?"

Unfortunately Gabe didn't have an answer—he'd fallen prey to them enough times himself. So with a sigh, he dropped his towel on a deck chair and lowered himself into the water.

Bliss. He closed his eyes.

"Wow, am I late to the party?"

And opened them again to see Baller setting a six-pack at the edge of the tub. He was already shirtless, and his shorts, which might have been modest on someone else, clung to his ass and thighs, even dry. He hadn't gelled his hair today, so it was flopping over his eyes. It looked touchably soft.

Maybe it was a good thing Gabe had witnesses here to keep him from looking too much.

"Yes," said Symons, "but you brought beer, so you're forgiven."

Gabe flicked water at him. "Forget it, rookie. Get your own. Oh wait—you can't."

Baller sank into the tub with a near pornographic moan. "Sorry, Slimer. I only brought enough for two." He glanced over at Gabe, cheeks already pink from the heat. "Looks like I wasn't the only one with this idea." He handed Gabe a beer. "Cheers, I guess."

"Thanks."

Their knees bumped under the water, and a shiver went down Gabe's spine. He took a steadying breath. *You are twenty-eight years old,* he reminded himself. No excuse to behave like a teenager.

Then Symons said, "Tipsyyyy, come on. It's your turn," and Gabe realized that this wasn't just an underage hot tub party. It was also time for some kind of drinking game.

Tips sighed and tilted his face up to the sky. In a voice that implied he'd rather be watching paint dry, he intoned, "Yorkie. Would you rather... have to sing along or dance to every song you hear?"

Gabe said, "What?"

"Oh man, have you never played this game?" Yorkie turned wide, drunk eyes to him. "You're missing out! Gabe!" Then he frowned, evidently derailed from his train of thought. "How come you don't have a nickname?"

"Yeah! Everyone else has one." Symons winced. "Even if they don't deserve it."

"You threw up lime-green margarita all over Flash's patio at the barbecue," Baller said. "You earned that nickname, Slimer."

Was *that* how that came about? Gabe was glad he'd missed it. He glanced at Tips again. "You're limiting his consumption, right?"

Before Tips could answer, Yorkie continued. "I mean. There's Slimer. Flash. Olie. Tips." He enumerated these on his fingers. "How come I got stuck with Yorkie? I sound like a teacup dog."

"You are," Gabe and Tips chorused.

"And then there's *Baller*."

Baller preened. "Yes. I scored a nickname that means both 'awesome' and 'guy who fucks.' Both of which I have earned. Bonus, it's actually just a normal hockey nickname I came by honestly. Some of us were born lucky."

Gabe rolled his eyes.

"You should have a hockey nickname," Yorkie said earnestly.

Gabe didn't feel like he'd been left out—he'd have been mortified if his team saddled him with a nickname like *Baller*, though the teacup dog thing wasn't as awful. But… "Like what?" he asked. "It just doesn't work with my name."

"Take your last name's first syllable, then add *er*…." Baller wrinkled his nose. "Marter. Martyr? No. Too Catholic."

"See?" Gabe said.

"No no no," Slimer interrupted. "You gotta try with *sy*. So Martsy." He tilted his head in consideration. "I don't think that's better."

"Or Marty," Yorkie said, "but that's just a normal first name."

Exactly. "So you might as well just call me Gabe."

"We could try your first name! Gaber." It came out *Gay-ber*. Gabe cringed, waiting for the inevitable laughter… but Yorkie paled. "Oh. Yeah, I get why we don't do that. Gabe it is."

Gabe raised his beer in a toast. "Thank you. Now… who's explaining the rules of this game?"

"Yeah. I've always played the sex version. You know, who would you rather bang, your grandma or your high-school principal."

Gabe stared at Baller. "That's horrifying."

"Well, you can give two appealing options too!"

"Yorkie won't even *say* he'll fuck anyone except his girl, like, hypothetically," Slimer said. "So we adapted."

Would it be rude to laugh? Gabe pursed his lips to quell the urge. "I see. Who are we to doubt true love?"

Tips flicked Gabe's bottle cap at Yorkie. "Are you gonna answer or not, kid?"

He sighed. "Sing, I think. I *really* can't dance. And it would be distracting, you know, when they pipe music over the speakers between plays."

"You can't sing either, roomie. I have heard your shower serenades."

"Yeah, but most of the time I'm not mic'd up. Besides, what about driving? That could be dangerous!" Yorkie turned to Slimer. "Would you rather…?"

When Baller turned his face toward Gabe, Gabe tuned the rookies out. "We could chill somewhere else," Baller said quietly.

But Gabe didn't mind sitting there with them. For a lot of his career, he'd kept himself apart from gatherings like this. It felt like he was getting to experience some of the things he'd missed—although he sincerely hoped Slimer didn't give a repeat performance of the margarita incident.

"Hey! If you guys are gonna hang, you have to play. Fair's fair."

The twinkle in Baller's eyes and the twitch at the corner of his mouth said he was doing his best not to laugh. "What do you think?"

Obviously the rookies didn't care. Gabe looked over at Tips. "Aren't I too old for this?"

"Fuck no. If I've gotta do this, so do you. Kid's got a point." He shook his head ruefully. "Much as it pains me to admit it."

Gabe turned back to Baller. "What about you?"

"Oh, I'm definitely too old for this," he laughed. "But that's never stopped me from doing dumb shit before. Bring it on, rookies."

Gabe dragged over one of the bags of chips and opened it while Yorkie considered. "Baller. Would you rather… wear the same socks for a month or the same underwear for a week?"

Oh Lord. "I see what you mean by 'horrifying,'" Baller said to Gabe in an aside. "Underwear. Imagine the same socks in your skates for a month. If your feet didn't rot off it'd be a miracle. Who's next? Slimer? Would you rather meet the love of your life tomorrow, or be single forever and have a ton of hot one-night stands?"

Symons was, what, nineteen? Gabe expected him to vote for one-night stands, even if it was a lie. But he said, "True love, obviously. Duh."

And then Gabe's mild surprise turned to sheer shock when Baller shook his head and said, "Yeah, that was a dumb question."

Yorkie voiced Gabe's thoughts before he could even get his mouth to work. "*You*?" he asked, incredulous. "You're like Mr. Bar Pickups!"

"Yeah, 'cause I'm not opposed to having a lot of hot sex on the road to domestic bliss as well as afterward. And who's to say one of my bar hotties wouldn't be the one?" He shrugged. "Casual sex is fun for now, but it's not, like, the goal. My parents are super gross in love with each other. Who wouldn't want that?"

Baller would be good at love, Gabe thought. He worked hard for what he wanted. Sure, he could be obnoxious, but he was also kind and loyal and funny and honest. Those probably made good traits in a partner.

Too bad Gabe would never find out firsthand.

"Asexual people," Tips answered. Then, "Or aromantic people." He paused, brows knitted. "And probably some dedicated sluts."

And me? Gabe wondered. He hadn't given it any thought before he came out. Not that he didn't ever want to find "the one," but after hockey seemed like better timing.

Did he want it now?

Without meaning to, he glanced at Baller.

Baller caught him looking. "Oh, hey, just because someone said *sluts*. But fine." He waved vaguely. "Point made. Whose turn is it?"

Slimer turned his slightly lopsided gaze on Gabe. "Mine. Umm, Gabe. Would you rather have... a donut or a piece of pie?"

That seemed weak. Gabe glanced at Yorkie first—he seemed nonplused, but he was already pretty drunk—and then at Tips, who had his brow furrowed. Was he getting a dumb, uninteresting question out of respect? Because Slimer didn't want to make him uncomfortable? Because Gabe was gay and a sex question would make everyone *else* uncomfortable?

Or did Slimer just suck at this game?

"For clarity," Gabe asked, "am I eating the pastry or fucking it?"

Tips cackled.

"Can you fuck a single piece of pie?" Yorkie wondered out loud. "I mean, a piece of pie isn't that big." He gestured with his hands.

"If you're careful, you could fuck the donut and *then* eat it," Baller suggested.

"Boo, you could not!" Tips broke in. "What kind of two-pump chump are you that you could fuck a donut and have anything left after?"

"Hey, you don't always have to fuck hard—"

"So you're going to make sweet, tender love to a donut—"

"Where's the cream filling?"

Sighing, Gabe met Slimer's eyes over the heated debate from the other three. "Pie," he said, deadpan. "Cherry."

Yorkie laughed so hard they had to drag him to a potted plant so he could be sick in it. Gabe supported him under one arm while Baller got the other.

Baller's shorts were riding up his legs, and water droplets ran down his chest and arms, inviting Gabe to follow them with his eyes. He took a steadying breath and absently licked his lips as water pooled at the small of Baller's back where he'd bent over, his perfect ass on perfect display.

Fuck. Gabe needed to stop looking at him like that. Especially after Baller had been philosophizing about true love. Especially where their teammates might catch him. Especially—

Baller looked back over his shoulder, met Gabe's eyes, and…blushed?

Why was he blushing? Shouldn't he be upset Gabe couldn't control himself? Shouldn't he—

Yorkie groaned and heaved again, thankfully interrupting Gabe's train of thought. Wincing, he patted the kid gently on the back. "Hey, Yorkie. Would you rather hack up a hairball on a rooftop patio or all over your captain's backyard?"

KITTY WASN'T at morning skate in Nashville.

The official lineup, which Dante read not-so-stealthily over Coach's shoulder, said he'd be sitting out with a lower body injury.

"That's one way of saying he's got his head up his ass," Dante muttered, at which point Coach ordered him onto the ice with his squad.

Slimer slotted into the lineup with Bricksy. If anyone thought that was a lot of responsibility to give a kid who had never played an NHL game, no one brought it up to Coach in Dante's hearing. And maybe it didn't matter, because she obviously had other things on her mind. When they finished their light workout and regrouped in the locker room, Coach came in with her clipboard, wearing an expression like a thundercloud.

She exchanged a look with Flash, who nodded and moved from his stall to sit next to Gabe.

Dante could figure out where this was going. Judging from the muscles bunching at the corner of Gabe's jaw, he already knew about it too.

"I'm not going to beat around the bush," Coach said. "There's some kind of protest or picketing thing or some homophobic horseshit planned for tonight's game. The Mustangs are scheduling extra security and putting up barricades to keep them away from the arena, but it's going to be ugly. I don't want anyone unprepared. Do not engage them, don't look at them, don't read their signs, don't react. They won't be allowed inside the arena." She paused and then added, "*Fuckers*."

Dante felt sick. Gabe's skin had taken on a sallow tone, and his shoulders were hunched.

Flash said something quietly to Gabe in French, but Gabe shook his head, his face set in grim determination. So he planned to play.

Dante clapped his hands. "Let's show them what we can do, then."

"Fuck yeah!"

From the worried expressions on his teammates' faces, though, their confidence was not high. Dante couldn't blame them. They needed some decisive wins, or at least some solid goals so the ice would stop feeling like it was tilted away from them. With their superstar off his game and their best defenseman scratched for being an asshole, winning would be an uphill battle.

Falling asleep for his pregame nap took forever. Dante didn't usually have trouble sleeping. Even a baby could do it. Case in point, in the bed next to his, Yorkie was passed out on his stomach, drooling on the pillow, arms splayed like he was trying to hug the bed.

But Dante's mind kept spinning through what would happen tonight. A crowd of people would gather to protest… what? That a gay man existed? That he had the balls to play a professional sport?

That would've been bad enough. But tonight Gabe would walk into the arena convinced all those people were there only to yell at him. To hate him. To make him feel like shit. Regardless of how closely the rest of the team supported him—and Dante knew Flash and Olie were already planning bodyguard duty—he'd feel like he alone was the target of their hatred.

But he wasn't. Those assholes might not know it, but they hated Dante too. They should at least hate him to his face.

Only he couldn't come out now. It wouldn't take any pressure off Gabe, it would just shift the focus to whether they were sleeping together, which would definitely be worse for everyone. Dante would have to suck it up and deal for now. Maybe in the off-season....

With a quiet sigh, he rolled out of bed. He needed to drown out the noise of his brain without waking Yorkie. So he went into the bathroom, turned on the shower, and stood under the hot spray for a few minutes. He focused on the pressure on his skin, the steady beat of the water on the tile. He wouldn't have to hide forever. The situation sucked, but it was temporary.

Just like his inability to sleep.

Dante closed his eyes and leaned his hands against the wall. *Think about something else. Something relaxing.*

The sound of the water reminded him of the hot tub last night. That was a good memory; he concentrated on that. Laughing with his teammates. Teasing Yorkie for being so in love with his girl.

Catching Gabe looking at him when Dante's back was turned, literally. Seeing, just for a moment, that unmistakable flash of want in his eyes.

Feeling the answering heat in his own body.

Okay, that wasn't a relaxing thought. It worked as a distraction, though.

Dante had tried not to think about it. He knew what he looked like—knew people thought he was hot. He'd just never figured on Gabe being one of those people.

Of course, Gabe would never do anything about his attraction. Dante could tattoo *Kiss me, I'm bi* on his ass and do a striptease and Gabe would think it was some kind of performance art.

Gabe would never actually kiss him. He'd never put his hands on Dante's body with *intent*. He'd never

push so close Dante could feel his erection, and he definitely wouldn't reach down and wrap his hand around
Dante's cock—

Dante shuddered out a breath and blinked his eyes
open to see the shower wash the thick ropes of his come
down the drain. Well, that was one way to clear his head.
He shut the water off, grabbed his towel, and dried himself. Then he dressed and climbed back into bed.

Maybe he'd given himself a whole new set of things
to dwell on, but human biology put him to sleep anyway.

When Yorkie's alarm went off, they both got up to
get ready, but the atmosphere was strained.

"This is going to suck, isn't it?" Yorkie said. He
was retying his tie for the third time.

Dante slapped his hands away and took over. "Oh
yeah. But look on the bright side."

Yorkie waited. When Dante didn't continue, he
asked, "Which is?"

Finished with the tie, Dante sighed and nudged
him away again. "I was sort of hoping you'd come
up with something and fill in the blank. At least we're
handsome?"

Yorkie looked up at him, grimaced, then reached
out and touched the side of his head. "Actually your
hair's kind of doing a thing...."

Well, that happened when you went to sleep with
wet hair, but Dante didn't have time to shower again.
He combed and gelled it into place as best he could and
then they hustled out the door to meet the bus.

THE GROUP was big and loud, waving signs Gabe
didn't want to read but couldn't avoid. He forced himself to look away.

His hands were shaking.

"Calme-toi, mon vieux," Flash said quietly.

Gabe took a deep breath to try to shore himself up. "Tout sera bien?" he choked out.

Flash smiled in response. "Oui, exactement."

The bus stopped.

At the front, St. Louis stood. "All right. Just like we talked about, okay? Fuck these assholes."

A shout of agreement went up, and Flash pushed Gabe to his feet. He stood, numb.

"How are we going to do this?" Baller asked.

Gabe didn't follow his meaning until Flash said, "Surround him and get him in as fast as possible. You're shorter—take the back."

Bricks, who was six foot four inches of solid muscle, stood and rolled his shoulders. "No problem."

A few of the other guys got out of the bus first. They headed straight for the door, just like Coach told them to. "No lingering!"

With the bus a little clearer, it was easier to get organized.

"We don't have to—" Gabe started to protest, but Bricks cut him off.

"We do. They probably won't do anything, but I don't trust them."

Gabe was too relieved to argue.

They didn't talk much. Bricks, along with a few of the rougher players, got off first and waited by the bus door. Flash nudged Gabe out next and followed close behind.

Once they were all on the sidewalk, they moved fast. Flash kept tight to Gabe's side, as if to hide his face from sight. But he couldn't block out the jeers, and the noise and colorful signs seemed to jump around Flash to assault Gabe's senses.

Then they were at the door. Flash led Gabe down the hall, and his guard fanned out, leaving more space, but none of them wandered far.

Flash still had a hand wrapped around Gabe's arm when they reached the locker room, and he nudged Gabe onto the bench seat marked with his number. Gabe took a shaky breath.

Flash ruffled his hair. "Not so bad, *non?*"

Gabe gave a wan smile. "I made it."

"Yes, you did."

The door opened, and Gabe couldn't help but look over, his fight-or-flight still pumping. Baller stalked in and crashed onto the bench next to Gabe. "Fuckers," he muttered and bumped their shoulders together.

"Yeah." Gabe pressed back.

The locker room was subdued. No one seemed to be in the mood to joke. Guilt welled up in Gabe's stomach. They wouldn't be going through this if it weren't for him.

They made their way onto the ice for warm-up as a team. Some of the Mustangs skated to center ice to apologize, like it was their fault they lived in a city with a bunch of loud-mouthed assholes.

The fans seemed decent enough too. At least no one booed Gabe when he got on the ice at the start of the game.

But then everything went to shit. Like it always did lately.

Halfway through the first period, the ref called Slimer for tripping. As players skated around, changing up lines and getting situated, Gabe glanced toward the stands and froze. In the first tier, not too many rows up from the ice, a group of spectators had taken their shirts off. They'd each painted a letter on their pasty white bellies, spelling out DEATH 2 FAGS.

Gabe thought he might puke.

"Gabe," Flash called, but he couldn't look away.

Were they fans? Or had some of the nutters gotten inside?

"I thought there was supposed to be some fucking security," Baller snarled. He placed one gloved hand on Gabe's shoulder and pushed him around. "Stop. *Gabe.* Don't do that to yourself."

His hands were shaking again.

Flash skated up. "They're getting rid of them. Ref just called up to make sure Security knows and is taking care of it. He wants to know if you need a minute?"

That jostled Gabe out of his funk. "No. Hell no. I'm playing. Fuck 'em."

Baller smiled, sharklike. "Yeah, fuck 'em."

Flash nodded. "Good."

When Gabe got off the ice at the end of his shift, he glanced over to see the row half-empty.

Coach clapped him on the shoulder as he sat. "Good hustle." Then she leaned over the boards and shouted at Bricksy.

The rest of the first period passed unremarkably—still no score—and Gabe started to relax back in the room as he rehydrated, retaped, and listened with half an ear to Flash's rote go-get-'em speech. Across the room, behind Flash, Baller caught Gabe's eye and started mouthing along to the more well-worn passages. Gabe tried to shoot him a glare, but his mouth wouldn't cooperate. It wanted to smile.

Even Olie, who had grown dour as the losses wore on and tended to retreat from the rest of the team, seemed in decent spirits as they took to the ice for the second period.

Naturally it couldn't last.

Nineteen seconds into the second period, the Nags captain picked Baller's pocket and passed to their center, who tore off with Flash dogging his heels. Before the Dekcs' defense could make a play for the puck, he passed to the right winger, who blind-dropped it behind his back for his linemate. The puck went over Olie's shoulder almost before Gabe saw it move.

Fuck.

He breathed out heavily through his nose. Fine. One goal wasn't going to break them. They could come back from this. *Gabe* could pull them back from this.

Over the next several shifts, his teammates did an admirable job playing keep-away with the puck. Baller sat beside him for most of it, practically vibrating with energy. Olie only had to make a few saves, and the Dekes' shots on goal increased steadily, but the Nags' goalie was basically breakdancing on his helmet to shut them out. Watching it made Gabe's teeth hurt, he was gritting them so hard. Being on the ice for it was worse.

They tried everything. On paper, they did everything right. But despite two good chances for Baller and an incredible feed from Flash right onto Gabe's tape in front of the crease, they couldn't tie the game.

It ended 1–0.

Gabe sagged in defeat. In ten years in professional hockey, he'd experienced his share of slumps, both personally and as part of the team.

But it sucked that this one coincided with getting shoved out of the closet like a sixth grader with braces and bad breath.

The losses were wearing on his teammates too. Yorkie and Slimer were still too excited about being in the pros to let this get them down too much. But Baller was uncharacteristically deflated, which was just not right. He was supposed to be the loudest, brightest, happiest thing in the room.

Gabe had never been the go-to guy for off-ice problems, but he didn't have an excuse to keep to himself anymore. Baller had been there for him more than once over the past few weeks. It was past time Gabe returned the favor, even if he had no idea how.

He'd think of something. Baller deserved it.

THEY LOST the matinee game in Los Angeles 3–2.

At this point, Dante was starting to feel like they'd never win another game. This one was particularly tough because they'd been ahead 1–0 after the first period. He'd notched two points—a goal and an assist on Flash's third-period tally—and he still couldn't muster any enthusiasm.

He must've looked pathetic on the bus back to the team hotel, because Gabe skipped past his usual seat with Flash and dropped down next to him.

"You know," Gabe said, "if I'd scored tonight instead of you, I would at least pretend to be happy about it."

Gabe had two assists and looked only slightly less grumpy than Dante felt. Dante started to smile in spite of himself. "You would not."

"Yeah, you're probably right. But the point stands. This isn't like you." He paused. "You want to talk about it?"

God, did he, but what was he supposed to say? *I'm bi, my grandma thinks you're going to seduce me*

*and I'll go to hell, and I can't even tell anyone because
they'll assume the seduction is a done deal?* "That's....
Thank you, but no. It's just family stuff."

"Okay."

"But...." Dante bit his lip. "Maybe we can put
in some extra practice time? There's got to be a way
to fix—"

Gabe was already shaking his head. "I have a better idea. Come by my hotel room after team dinner?"

Dante firmly ignored the part of his brain—getting
louder with every day—that wanted to hear that as a romantic invitation. Gabe was just being a good mentor.

That didn't stop him from answering with, "It's a
date."

Predictably, Gabe only rolled his eyes.

Half an hour after team dinner, Dante knocked
on the hotel room door, as instructed. Gabe answered
in sweatpants and a T-shirt from his juniors days that
had probably fit him a lot differently back then. Now
it was threadbare and stretched across the chest. Dante
didn't have self-image issues, but the way Gabe's bi-
ceps strained at the shirtsleeves did make him feel some
kind of way.

"Well, I'm here," he announced. Then, "What *am*
I here for, exactly?"

"What, my company isn't enough?" Gabe gestured
him inside.

It was a standard hotel room—queen bed, dresser
and TV, tiny desk with an uncomfortable chair.

"Hey, you're the one who said you had a better
idea than extra practice." Dante sat on the mattress. As
usual, his mouth bulldozed ahead of his brain: "If that
meant hanging out together on your bed...."

Gabe's ears turned red, but he didn't take the bait. Which was probably for the best, because Dante didn't know what he'd do if he did.

"Take your shoes off if you're going to sit there. Show some respect, for fuck's sake."

Dante kicked his slides off while Gabe reached for the TV remote. "So, are we doing video review?" he asked. That might help. There had to be something he could work on to get them clicking better on the ice. "Do you think my wrist shot—"

He cut off when Gabe speared him with a look. "What did I say?"

Dante was having flashbacks to not knowing the answer in class because he'd been passing notes with Maisie Harris. "Uh... that you weren't going to practice with me?"

"Because you don't need practice." Gabe turned the TV on. "You had two points tonight. We hit a rough patch against a bunch of hot teams, and our best defenseman got scratched for being an asshole."

That was true, but it did not offer insight into how to start winning.

"The point is—losing streaks happen."

"Okay." Dante could accept that as the truth, even if he hated that it was happening to him. "So then what am I here for? If not to stop the losing streak."

"We're doing all we can for hockey." Gabe handed him a small white box, sat next to him on the bed, and fluffed a pillow to prop behind his back. "Now we're off the clock, so we do our other hobbies. I didn't pack my golf clubs, but...."

Finally Dante looked at the TV screen. "Wii Golf?" He laughed in surprise. "Where did you get this? This is, like, ancient technology."

Gabe gave him a wry smile. "In LA you can get anything delivered to your hotel room if you have enough money."

Dante shook his head, feeling a sudden rush of affection. "And you went for this instead of hookers and blow?"

Gabe offered him a flat look that hid none of his amusement. "I didn't think we had the same taste in hookers."

"Hey, I'll try anything once." Fuck, there went Dante's mouth again. "Except blow." Blow *jobs,* on the other hand—

Dante should've brought some snacks to keep his mouth occupied.

Fortunately Gabe didn't ask him to elaborate. "The *point* is…." For the first time tonight, he seemed unsure of himself. "I like golf. You like video games." He waved the Wii remote. "Seemed like a good compromise."

It was actually really sweet, more so because Dante knew Gabe didn't reach out like this often. "Hey, I came this far. And look, you already made a little Wii me." The on-screen bobblehead named Baller had medium brown skin and black hair, enormous eyes, and an orange shirt. It didn't much resemble him, but Gabe's curly-haired avatar looked like an anime character too. "Have you ever actually played this?"

"You're lucky I managed to get the thing hooked up." He shook his head. "I should've paid the guy extra for setup. Tech is not my thing. But I think there's a tutorial."

It was difficult to play sitting down, but there wasn't room to do it standing, so they improvised and ended up laughing when their constrained movements resulted in wild shots. Finally they quit for the night when Gabe accidentally flung his remote at the ceiling and they had to duck as it came back down.

Red-faced, still hunched to evade the flying remote, Gabe met Dante's eyes and they both burst into boyish laughter.

Then Dante glanced at the TV and cackled harder. "Gabe, oh my God. I think you figured out the secret." Somehow he got a hole in one on the shot.

When their giggles had subsided, they flopped back against the pillows. "What lesson was I supposed to be learning again?" Dante asked. "I think you were going for 'don't worry, be happy' but I came away with 'having money solves problems.'" He made a face. "Ugh. Which reminds me I need to get my truck serviced when we get back."

Gabe turned on his side to look at him. "Why 'ugh'?"

Now there was a loaded question. Dante sighed and considered his answer. "So like… this might sound weird."

"We're two professional athletes who just played Wii Golf sitting down. I think we passed 'weird' an hour back."

Dante released a slow breath. If anyone besides Olie on the team would get it, it would be Gabe. "So I still drive my grandpa's truck—Mom's dad's. He died when I was in high school." The truck was already six or seven years old then.

"Okay. I'm listening. Pickup trucks are built to last, right?"

Dante snorted. "Yeah, good thing, because I wasn't always gentle on it. Don't get me wrong, it's a good truck, and it has sentimental value—Gramps was the one who introduced me to hockey—but that's not why I drive it."

Gabe tucked a hand under his head. "Why do you?"

"Same reason I live in a one-bedroom apartment in an okay neighborhood." He gave a half smile. "You know how long it took me to get here?"

"Here, the NHL?"

Nodding, Dante elaborated. "I mean, I got drafted at eighteen, and at the time, that was everything, you know?" Especially getting drafted onto the same team as one of his personal heroes, which Gabe did not need to know. "But they said I wasn't ready for the NHL and stuck me in the A. And, like, they were right—I wasn't, not at eighteen. But the next two years, my coaches didn't do much to *get* me ready. I did everything I could, everything asked of me. I worked out, I stuck to the meal plan, I didn't complain when they moved me up and down the lineup or when less talented players got the call before me, because I figured my time would come."

Gabe pulled his pillow more fully under him. "Why do I feel like the next line of this story isn't 'and then it did'?"

"Probably because you know what hockey's really like." Dante shrugged. "I guess my agent has some kind of clout, because he called front office and said, basically, 'listen, call my guy up for a few games or trade him somewhere that'll let him play.'"

"And you found your feet right away." Gabe's vague, slightly confused smile gave way to a furrowed brow. "Didn't they fire the AHL coach a couple games after you got called up?"

Dante allowed himself a curl of satisfaction at that. "They did, yeah. 'Course, being a racist dick doesn't

exclude you from a lot of jobs in hockey, so he got another gig pretty fast."

To his credit, Gabe didn't argue or offer hollow
sympathies, he just nodded like he was absorbing what
Dante had told him.

Which brought Dante to the point. "Sorry for the
tangent, just—that's why I still drive the truck. I'm
here now, on an entry-level contract. No guarantee
of anything. My parents sacrificed a lot for me to be
here. I know they'd say that it's already worth it, but I
need to be able to take care of them, right? And if I get
traded—"

"Or if Coach gets fired for our losing streak and is
replaced with someone who sucks," Gabe filled in.

Good, so he got it. Dante nodded. "I could be right
back where I started. So until I hit that standard-con-
tract payday...." He lifted a shoulder and gave a wry
smile. "I will not be ordering hookers and blow."

"I understand. I mean, hockey players who live in
glass closets...."

Fuck, and that was an aspect of it Dante hadn't
considered. "Wow, this got maudlin." He grimaced. "I
don't think this was what I was supposed to take away
from tonight."

"Eh." Gabe waggled his hand. "The point was to
think about other things for a while. We did. Mission
accomplished."

Dante decided to push his luck a little. "So does that
mean you still won't practice with me tomorrow?"

"Oh God." Gabe laughed, rolling onto his back.
"Don't try it. Coach will bench you out of spite. Just
take the rest day. How often do we get one in California? It's gonna be a long winter."

True. Dante was glad they still had the Florida road trip to look forward to. "What's everybody doing? I was too busy moping to pay attention."

"Beach volleyball, I think."

Dante hummed the theme from *Top Gun*.

Gabe cracked up. "God, I'm glad you said it and not me. You're not into beach volleyball?"

"It's okay. I was just thinking...."

I was just thinking—I like you a lot. You care about what I think. You treat me like I'm smart, like I'm worth listening to.

I was just thinking—I could be traded at any minute. I could get another concussion.

I was just thinking—was Wii Golf really what I needed tonight? Or was it you?

I was just thinking—I want to go on a date with you.

He already knew Gabe was attracted to him, and that Gabe liked him enough to spend more time with him than anyone else. Yes, Dante had intended to err on the side of caution for once in his life. But the side of caution wasn't really his style. He didn't get where he was without putting himself out there.

He still had to work with Gabe, so he needed a plan. If he made a move, he wanted to be sure Gabe would welcome it or at least be able to turn him down in a way that let them keep their friendship intact.

Dante cleared his throat. "Did you know that I'm twenty-two years old and I've never been to Disneyland? That's practically un-American."

For emphasis, he put on his best puppy-dog eyes and hopeful expression.

"You want to go to Disneyland," Gabe said.

He was absolutely going to cave on this; Dante could tell by the smile hiding in the corners of his mouth. "It *is* the happiest place on earth," he said earnestly. "You want me to be happy, don't you?"

Gabe eyed him with evident horror. "That actually works on people, doesn't it?"

"All the time," Dante confirmed cheerfully. And it was going to work tonight too. "How 'bout it, Gabe? Are you in?"

With a sigh, Gabe reached for the tablet on his bedside table. "Fine," he said, long-suffering. He glanced back over his shoulder. "But only because I didn't bring my golf clubs."

Dante smiled, heart beating hard in anticipation. "I knew you'd see it my way."

SINCE THE whole thing was his idea, Baller tried to insist on paying for their tickets. But after last night's conversation, that didn't fly with Gabe.

"Not to hurt your feelings," he said dryly, "but I make ten times what you do." He handed his credit card to the ticket attendant. "You can buy lunch." Because of course he wasn't getting away with just a few hours in the afternoon. Oh no, they were there as the park opened, sunshine and happy families everywhere.

Gabe didn't want to admit it, but the enthusiasm was maybe a little bit contagious.

"Lunch *and* souvenirs," Baller bargained.

The ticket attendant gave Gabe a smile that said she thought they were the world's cutest couple and also that she had no idea who they were. Hooray for California.

"Deal," Gabe said as he let Baller usher him through the stiles and onto the railroad.

"You are really excited about this," he observed with mounting trepidation.

Baller threw his arm over Gabe's shoulders. "*Disneyland*, Gabe," he said, as if that explained everything. "We are going to have fun today if it kills us."

It actually might, if Baller insisted on being this enthusiastic about everything.

They got off the train at the first stop, and Baller stood there for a moment, beaming, like he couldn't imagine anywhere he'd rather be than Anaheim, California, in the middle of a losing streak. Gabe gave in to a rare sentimental impulse and snapped a picture with his phone.

"Pirates," Baller sighed happily. He grabbed Gabe's arm and herded him to the right. "Come on. Maybe they have some poor sucker dressed up as Will for you to ogle."

Gabe was reasonably sure the people dressed in costumes were for the *kids* to interact with, but he kept that to himself. Even if today did nothing more than deepen Gabe's pit of ill-advised feelings for his teammate, Baller still deserved to have a good time.

As it turned out, Gabe didn't have to worry about that. The line for the ride was short, and Baller spent the whole ten minutes bouncing on his toes, peering around at the scenery and humming "A Pirate's Life for Me" under his breath.

God, he was young, but for once, that seemed like an advantage. Having Baller around helped Gabe remember how to be young at heart.

That's a bit dramatic. You're only twenty-eight, he reminded himself. Maybe he needed more Disneyland in his life.

As they took their seats on the ride—Baller still vibrating with excitement—he shook his head. "Some days I forget you're only a baby. Today's not one of them."

"Stop being so old for five minutes and relax. I'm trying to cheer us up."

Gabe raised his hands in surrender. "Okay, okay. You're in charge. I'm just along for the ride. Rides."

Once he admitted that he was not in charge of the situation, it made for a pleasant day.

At the end of the ride, they emerged into the sunshine and Baller made a beeline for a cart that sold elaborate hats to match the theme. He tossed a tricorne at Gabe, then grabbed something in mauve with an ostrich-feather plume and shoved it on his own head. "What do you think?" He ran a finger along the brim, his eyes dancing.

Gabe had a sudden, powerful urge to kiss him, but he distracted himself by trying on his own silly hat. "Well, you're no Will Turner, but I suppose you'll do."

Baller stuck out his tongue and turned to the display of pins, but he did buy the hat.

Standing in the shade of a big tree by the Haunted Mansion, they ate Mickey Mouse–shaped ice cream for lunch.

"We going on this one too?" Gabe asked.

"Everyone knows you have to work up to Splash Mountain." Baller threw his stick away and licked a drip of ice cream off his thumb.

It probably wasn't purposely pornographic.

Probably.

After the Indiana Jones Adventure, Baller tried to buy Gabe a fedora that looked even worse on him than the tricorne.

"How many ridiculous hats can one man need? Only douchebags wear fedoras," Gabe protested.

Baller smirked and took a picture with his phone. "So, no problem, then."

Gabe made a face.

"You said I was in charge," Baller reminded him.

"I didn't think that meant control of my wardrobe."

Baller rolled his eyes. "Spoilsport." He tossed a headband with Mickey Mouse ears at Gabe instead. "Compromise?"

At least the team wasn't here to witness Gabe's humiliation. He would never have heard the end of it. Flash would chirp him forever. But today was a happy day, so he sucked it up and put on the headband.

It probably said something about him that this outing with a teammate was the closest thing he'd had to a normal date in his adult life. He didn't go to restaurants with romantic partners. He went to clubs—discreet ones.

That was a bit pathetic, actually. Worse now because he'd somehow developed feelings for Baller, who was so far removed from the type of man Gabe usually dated that he might as well be an alien. Baller was friendly and warm and tactile and in touch with himself in a way that was fascinating to Gabe, who preferred not to examine his own psyche too closely.

Somehow, talking to his teammates about his sexuality must have eroded that barrier in his mind that kept him from ever thinking of them in romantic terms. It was the only explanation. And it was very inconvenient.

But that was Gabe's problem, not Baller's, and he wasn't enough of a jerk to let it ruin their fun. Just because he was setting himself up for heartache, that didn't mean he couldn't enjoy sunshine and theme park rides and Baller's very stupid hat.

At least the hat was keeping him from getting burned, Gabe thought, which prompted him to duck into one of the shops for extortionately priced sunscreen before his own situation got any worse.

In midafternoon, they hit a different kind of challenge.

"On this ride, you get to shoot things with lasers. It keeps score." Baller's body language was all competition.

Gabe looked at the sign—Buzz Lightyear Astro Blasters. "Loser buys drinks the next two nights out."

"Oh my God, what's happening? Are you committing to multiple nights of debauchery?"

Fortunately Gabe's already reddened skin would hide his blush. "I only committed to the drinking."

Baller laughed in delight. "All right. You're on."

The cars of the ride swung side to side to allow riders to aim, and Gabe could've sworn he needed shoulder pads, because Baller kept shoving him over to throw off Gabe's shots. Not to be outdone, Gabe pushed right back and laughed in triumph when he hit a higher-scoring target.

He was pretty sure he was bruised when they stumbled out of the ride for the fourth time, but he was smirking. "Another rematch?" He'd bought a souvenir photo after the first go around—they were jostling each other, shoulder to shoulder, laughing as they tried to disrupt the other's game. It showed the score.

"Screw you, no, you smug bastard." Baller pouted, but he couldn't hold it—his grin won out a second later. "Seriously, I thought I was supposed to be the one who's good at video games. Did you stay up all night practicing with the Wii or something?"

"Maybe I just have better hand-eye coordination than you." Gabe adjusted his ears as he preened. They hurt his head, but Baller had to wear his stupid hat as long as Gabe kept the ears on. Gabe wasn't going to give in first.

"That's not what the statistics say, buddy." Over their past four games, Baller beat him in points. "In fact, I—" He stopped midsentence and cocked his head at Gabe, an odd smile twisting his lips. He took a step closer and raised a hand to Gabe's headband. "Duck your head a little? You've got something on your...."

Gabe froze when Baller grabbed his right wrist for balance as he reached up. His hat tipped back precariously, but Gabe couldn't have made a grab for it if his life depended on it. He was stuck, not breathing, while Baller shuffled closer until Gabe could see his pores. He brushed his fingers over Gabe's mouse ears.

"I think you walked into a cobweb. You've got a leaf.... There." Baller pulled his right hand away but left the other clasped around Gabe's wrist. There was a papery sound as whatever he'd pulled from Gabe's head hit the asphalt.

Their eyes caught.

For one eternally stupid second, Gabe was waiting for Baller to kiss him.

Then the moment passed, and Baller let go and took a step back. He slapped Gabe on the arm. "Much better. Good thing you have me to look after you."

Gabe forced himself to unfreeze and shake his head in mock disbelief. "Right," he said as they started walking again, toward Space Mountain this time. "I'm such a handful."

Baller snorted. "You know better than to feed me a line like that."

"I'll feed you *something*."

Baller tripped over nothing on the pavement. Gabe grabbed him by the back of his shirt before he could take a dive. Crap. He'd gone too far and just about injured his teammate.

Huffing at himself, Baller righted his hat and then poked Gabe with his elbow. "Sausage?" he suggested.

Gabe's mouth dropped open. Then he realized Baller was gesturing with his other hand toward an actual honest-to-God sausage cart. "What the hell. We already killed the diet plan."

Baller grinned. "That's the spirit."

By the time they returned to the hotel for team dinner, Gabe had forgotten all about their headgear. When they walked into the lobby, Flash looked over from the concierge desk, a gym towel slung over one of his shoulders, and barked out a laugh. "I guess I don't have to ask what you two got up to today."

"We went to Disneyland," Baller said unnecessarily. The feather on his hat flopped from one side to the other in time with his enthusiasm.

"So I see." Flash rolled his eyes and reached up to flick Gabe's ears.

Gabe took them off.

"You'd better have enough energy for the game tomorrow."

Gabe bristled. "What? I got him home in time for curfew."

Affecting wide-eyed, earnest innocence, Baller nodded. "Yeah, Dad. He was a total gentleman. Didn't even try to steal second."

Gabe braced himself for a knowing look from Flash, but he just smacked the brim of Baller's hat down over his eyes. "Hurry up and get ready for dinner or we're eating without you."

Their nearly late arrival left only enough time for a quick shower and a change of clothes. Gabe ran into Baller again waiting for the elevator. It was easy to fall back into step and into conversation, chirping each other about Buzz Lightyear and stupid hats.

They sat next to each other at dinner, but Gabe quickly got drawn into a conversation with Flash, Olie, and Tips on his left, while Baller entertained Yorkie and Slimer's questions on his other side.

"Disneyland?" Tips asked, eyebrows raised.

"Baller wanted to go." What was Gabe supposed to do?

Flash rolled his eyes. "He's, like, twelve years old. Of course he wanted to go to Disneyland."

That hit him right in the guilt complex. "It sounded better than beach volleyball," he grumbled.

Olie snorted. "That is either the most or least gay thing you've ever said."

Gabe didn't have any defense for that, so he didn't try to mount one. Instead he finished his dinner and socialized for a few more minutes and then excused himself for the night. A whole day in the California sunshine had taken it out of him, even though it had been an excellent distraction.

At least from hockey. When it came to his feelings for Baller, it had been the opposite.

DANTE CLOSED the hotel room door behind him, leaned against it, and bit down against an impossible smile. Who knew what kind of noise might come out if he didn't?

Their date at Disney couldn't have gone better if he'd scripted it. They'd had fun, and if he flirted outrageously, Gabe didn't seem to mind.

Exhaling slowly, he took stock of the situation. Point the first—Gabe wanted his bod. The whole hot tub staring incident had convinced Dante of that. Point the second—Gabe liked him enough to voluntarily spend time with him and enjoyed himself doing it (even if he totally undersold what a good time he'd had at Disneyland). Point the third, the game-winner, the golden goal—when Dante stopped Gabe to pull the cobweb out of his headband, he'd looked at Dante with wide, expectant eyes, his lips slightly parted. As if he wanted Dante to kiss him.

Which was *awesome*, but Dante wasn't going to do that on a road trip the day before a game. Especially since they were flying back to Quebec City right afterward. If Dante knew Gabe, he was going to need time to think—or, more realistically, to panic, regroup, and then think, which he wouldn't get. The schedule had them landing in the wee hours of the morning. Then they would get the day off to recover from jet lag before playing again the next day.

And Dante really did need to get his truck serviced. He wasn't fucking with their dynamic until that game was over, so any servicing on his dick would have to wait.

Besides, they had a game tomorrow—a game Dante wanted to win.

He fell into bed and dropped off to sleep, still smiling, before Yorkie returned from dinner.

His good mood was still in place the next morning. Disneyland must have worked up an appetite, because he awoke starving. By the time Dante decided he needed to get breakfast ASAP, Yorkie was still lazing in bed, making noises that said he was only awake out of necessity.

"Yo, hey, where are you going?" Yorkie asked.

Dante turned around. "To get food?"

Yorkie coughed. "I know you're, like, a total exhibitionist. But put some pants on first, maybe?"

Okay, fine, so Dante was a little distracted. Who among them had never had a daydream?

"I can't believe they let little smartasses like you in the NHL," Dante grumbled as he went back to his suitcase for clothes.

Yorkie sat up and picked up last night's jeans from the floor. "So who's the girl?"

"What makes you think there's a girl?" Yorkie knew he'd gone to Disneyland with Gabe, right? So what was up with this question? Or had he not put two and two together?

Yorkie hopped into his jeans. Dante would never be able to pull off that move; he had too much junk in the trunk. "I don't know, the fact that you haven't tried to pick anyone up in like three weeks?"

Yeah, that was probably going to give him away to more than one person. "Haven't been feeling it," he lied. He'd definitely been feeling *something* lately. It was just himself, more often than not. "Losing streaks. Not great for the libido."

"Can't relate," Yorkie said lightly.

Asshole.

Dante stuffed his feet into his shoes. "Are you ready to go or what? I'm dying of starvation over here."

Maybe the rest of the guys had also had a good day yesterday, because for the first time on this trip, the chatter in the locker room before the game felt light. Olie was smiling again, Yorkie and Slimer brought youthful enthusiasm, and without the elephant—well, Kitty—in the room, Gabe was joking with Tips and Bricksy, giving them a hard time about their respective rookies.

"Like you can talk." Tips rolled his eyes. "I don't think you're supposed to have to babysit them once they turn twenty-two. At least Yorkie didn't make me take him to Disneyland."

Dante flicked a Gatorade cap at him. "Don't be jealous, Tips."

"Yeah," Yorkie piped up, turning earnest puppy-dog eyes on him. "I would've gone to Disneyland with you if you asked."

Coach broke up the party with a sharp whistle. "All right. Cut the chit-chat. Let's go. Warm-ups!"

Dante bumped his shoulder against Gabe's as they walked down the tunnel to the ice. "I just want to warn you, I want revenge for Buzz Lightyear. I'm scoring so many more goals than you tonight."

Gabe checked him lightly, but he was still grinning. "Dream on."

During warm-ups, the cheerful mood continued. Slimer scored on his shootout drill and earned a squirt from Olie's water bottle and high-fives from everyone except Bricks, who shoved Slimer's face into his armpit in a gesture of brotherly love.

Gabe faked a release by bringing his stick *over* the puck but not touching it, then doubled back and scored high over Olie's shoulder while Olie was still trying to find the puck between his pads.

Dante whistled under his breath. "All right. Jeez, save some for the game."

With a smirk, Gabe lifted the blade of his stick to his face and blew on it as though putting out a match.

Back in the locker room, though, things got serious. For the first time, Dante noticed the dark circles under Coach's eyes. "Since you're all in such a good mood, I'll keep this short and sweet." She cleared her throat. "Get out there and beat the Piranhas so I don't have to come up with new line combinations to keep my job." Then she sighed and smiled. "And I can't lose my job when I'm about to have another mouth to feed."

There was a short but complete silence, and then Yorkie said, "Oh my God, Coach, you knocked up Henri?"

The flurry of congratulations carried them until they had to get back to the ice for the anthem.

And then it was game on.

The whole game, the Dekes seemed like they were flying. In the first period, Gabe bailed the puck out of the corner backhanded, and it landed on Dante's stick like Gabe had eyes in the back of his head. Dante hammered it home with a whoop of triumph and let his momentum carry him into the boards for a bone-crushing celly.

Then, with thirty seconds to go in the second, Slimer poke-checked a Fish at center ice and Yorkie sped after the wobbling puck. The goalie blocked the shot, but Slimer picked up his first NHL goal on the rebound.

The Fish came back with a vengeance in the third. Dante felt bruised from hip to shoulder. But Olie shut the doors on them.

Gabe sealed the win with a filthy lacrosse-style goal as he sped around the net halfway through the period. Forty seconds later, just for insurance, Flash backhanded in a dirty goal right from the paint.

When the horn went at the end of the period, it felt like they'd won a playoff series.

"I can't believe we have to get on a plane!" Slimer said mournfully. "What about my first-goal night out?"

He got a first-goal pie-in-the-face while doing his media interview instead, but Dante made a note to pick up a bottle of something at the airport if he could. The kid deserved a celebratory drink, at least.

Dante would've liked to have said he was too keyed up to sleep on the plane. But it turned out that being a professional athlete was exhausting even if you did take three-hour naps in the middle of the day. The cabin lights went out after takeoff and he reclined his seat… and didn't wake up until the plane touched down in Quebec City.

Slimer never did get his drink, but Bricks promised to take him out after their next game, as a makeup.

A handful of flurries fell as Dante drove back to his apartment, mindful of the weather. Part of his service appointment was getting the winter tires put on, which he should've done weeks ago. But the old truck handled perfectly. He parked in his designated spot and went inside, where he fell right back asleep.

Fucking road trips.

He woke up to insistent pounding and surprising brightness.

The pounding was audible, at least, and not in his head. The brightness was due to the fact that according to his phone, it was just past noon.

He was going to be late for his service appointment if he didn't hurry.

With a curse, Dante jumped out of bed. For once he'd put his laundry away before he left for the trip, so his jeans were easy to find. He shoved his toothbrush into the corner of his mouth as the pounding at the front door continued. "Okay, okay," he grumbled as he un-locked the deadbolt and opened the door. "Are you that eager for me to find Jesus—"

Kitty stood on his doorstep, hulking shoulders hunched, face miserable.

"Uh," said Dante. A dribble of toothpaste threat-ened to escape his mouth. Dante sucked it in and took a step back. "Yust uh fec."

He retreated to the bathroom to spit.

What was Kitty doing here? What possible reason could he have to think that Dante wanted to see him? Dan-te had made it pretty obvious where his loyalties lay.

He guessed he was about to find out.

When he returned to the living room, he found Kit-ty had barely moved. He was standing just far enough inside to have closed the door behind himself to keep the heat in.

Confrontation time.

Dante put on his least friendly smile. "Look, I don't know what you're here about, Kipriyanov, but I have plans today and I need to get going."

At first Kitty seemed to shrink a little farther, but then his whole face sort of puckered and he straight-ened his spine and shoulders. "I'm—I can drive you? I need… help."

You sure do, bud, Dante thought. He'd been a lit-tle surprised how much Kitty's betrayal had hurt, giv-en they didn't know each other that well. Then again, considering Dante hadn't told anyone aside from his parents that he was bi, not many people had had the chance to hurt him like that. "I have to take my truck in for service," he said, "so driving me is out."

"I can follow?" He must be desperate. "Please. I know I'm not deserve—but I fuck up, with Gabe. I think, I'm apologize—except how?" His thick eyebrows drew down and together like a moody thundercloud. "How I say sorry for something so big?"

Dante let out a slow breath. Maybe Kitty didn't deserve a second chance. Plenty of people wouldn't give him one.

But Gabe probably would, and Dante was invested in the team's success.

And if Kitty could apologize well enough that *Dante* forgave him, then Dante wouldn't have to go around feeling hollow whenever he spotted Slimer on their blue line.

"All right," he said finally. "Meet me at the garage by the Tim Hortons with the good Timbits—you know the one?"

Everyone knew the one. "Da," Kitty said right away. "Thank you."

Despite the cold weather and his enormous frame, Kitty had driven a compact two-seater sports car, as though determined to get as many days' enjoyment out of it as possible. Dante had him run through the drive-through for a forty pack of Timbits and demolished a third of them sitting in the parking lot before he felt generous enough to say, "Okay, talk."

Kitty only paused a moment. "In Nashville, people bring horrible signs."

Dante shivered. Kitty glanced at him and then stabbed the button for the passenger seat heater.

He cleared his throat. "Thanks. Uh, yeah, they were pretty bad."

Kitty glanced toward the box of Timbits as though to gauge whether Dante would shank him if he reached for one. Sighing, Dante offered the box. He'd already eaten all the birthday cake ones anyway.

Kitty selected sour cream. Weirdo. "In Russia, we have problem," he said. "Problem is everything… what's word, means 'big government lie'?"

Dante blinked. "Conspiracy?"

"Nyet. Like… like stories that say politician can lift horse, or saves babies?"

Ooooh. "Propaganda?"

"Yes. Sometimes, is hard to know what's real, what's make up, until you see…." His brow furrowed and he swallowed. "In Russia is very bad for gay people. Is not like here. Is more normal to say—say things those people say."

Dante's stomach twisted as a shiver went through him.

"Here, I forget, little bit, things I hear growing up, things maybe I think and not know I think. When I find out Gabe is gay… I am angry. I feel like my friend lies about who he is. But Gabe doesn't lie, he doesn't change. He is the same. Only I am reacting with part of me that doesn't think."

Kitty paused for another Timbit. Dante shoveled in another one too, if only to keep himself from jumping in. This seemed like something Kitty needed to get out, and if Dante had to hear it, he was going to eat his feelings about it.

"Then Nashville happens, I see these angry people saying things I hear in Russia—things maybe I have in head. They hate so much, so loud. Is like mirror, you know?" He paused, looking at his hands, picking off flakes of sugar. "Now I see clear. Only I don't like who I see. I'm think, 'Misha, Gabe thinks you are like these people. He thinks you wish—'" He couldn't finish the sentence.

Dante offered him the Timbits again. Kitty took two and shoved them in his mouth one after the other.

Dante opted for chocolate.

Eventually Kitty croaked, with one hand over his eyes, "Can't both be right. And usually when someone thinks someone else should die, they wrong. Now, because I'm stupid, because I'm not think, my friend Gabe thinks I wish he is dead."

Dante's stomach felt like it was weighted with rocks. "Not just Gabe," he blurted.

Kitty jerked his head to look at him.

Shit. He hadn't meant to come out to Kitty first, of all the guys on the team, but there was no going back now. "Me too," he said.

Kitty's eyes went wide. "*You're*—you and Gabe…?"

"We're not together!" Dante said. *Yet*, he added mentally, but if he told Kitty he wanted to bone Gabe, the guy's head would probably explode. "Gabe doesn't even know I'm bi." When Kitty only blinked, Dante clarified. "I like guys and girls."

Now Kitty tilted his head, assessing. "You tell other guys yet?"

So they could ask the same embarrassing question? "No."

"But you tell me first? Even after I'm…?" The corners of his mouth turned down, and his eyes drooped in defeat. "Whole team hates me, and I deserve. But can I fix?" He fished out another three Timbits. "*How?*"

Dante leaned back against the warmth of the seat. They were done talking about his sexuality, apparently, which suited him fine. But he didn't have any ideas... until he dug out the last birthday cake Timbit, which had been hiding.

That... might actually work. "I have an idea," he said.

He explained the concept.

Kitty looked at him, then looked at the box. "We gonna need a lot more Timbits."

Damn, Kitty could really put them away. "You're still hungry?"

"Not for me. For *bribe*."

GABE STAYED after morning skate to film his video clip for the night. Then Tricia put him to work signing pucks, photos, and a jersey for the raffle. When he stopped to make sure he didn't smear Sharpie all over the back of the rainbow-colored 53, he noticed the little crocheted Gabe doll on her desk had acquired a rainbow scarf.

"Bet I could make a bundle auctioning a couple of those off," she said when she saw him looking. "Too bad I haven't had time to make more."

"It's cute," he said with a smile.

She grinned back. "Thanks. So, listen. I know this is kind of last minute, but we need you on hand for a photo op with some local LGBT charity leader before the game. Literally just a photo. I guess this person is a big fan. Can you get here half an hour early?"

Gabe hid a grimace as he signed the last card. "You promised if I did the video, you wouldn't make me socialize."

"It's not like I pimped you out for a whole dinner! That's why we're doing it before the game—there's literally only time for a handshake and photograph."

Gabe didn't understand why they weren't doing it after the game, when they'd have the proceeds from the raffle and a big check to hand over for that photo op, but it wasn't his job to understand. "Fine," he agreed, a hint of humor in his tone, "but only because you make such cute crafty things."

Three months ago he couldn't have even imagined today's events. Now, Gabe was barely anxious enough to worry that they might impact his afternoon nap.

He managed a respectable three hours asleep and called his dad on speaker as he got ready to leave the house.

"How are you feeling?"

Mother hens had nothing on his dad. Gabe shrugged into his jacket. "Better than draft day?" he offered. "I don't know. It's weird."

"You know, this could be good for you."

For fuck's sake. "Not you too."

His dad chuckled softly. "A father can't worry about his son? You've been alone a long time—"

"It was a guy who got me into this situation," Gabe grumbled.

So of course his dad pointed out, "And he couldn't do it now."

Gabe was wading into dangerous territory—his dad could always tell when Gabe was keeping something from him. But Gabe didn't have it in him to snap. His dad hadn't dated since Gabe's mom left. Maybe that was why he was suddenly interested in Gabe's love life.

He took a brief moment to be thankful his dad had never met Baller. If he saw the two of them together, he'd know how Gabe felt about Baller right away. Talk about embarrassing.

"Just because I'm out now doesn't mean I'm going to start, I don't know, dating publicly." Like his life was a season of *The Bachelor* or something. Gabe shuddered.

"Oh, God forbid." Then, more gently, his dad added, "I just want you to be happy. I don't want you to be my age sitting around the house playing Spider Solitaire by yourself like your old man."

Ouch. His dad wasn't pulling punches tonight. With a soft sigh, Gabe admitted, "I know that. I'm just…." *Dealing with unexpected feelings for a straight teammate.* "It's already a big change. I need time to get used to it." And it wasn't even a lie.

"Well, knock 'em dead tonight, yeah? A repeat of the game in Anaheim would be ideal."

Now he snorted. "Did you make another bet with Nelson down at the pub?"

"That would hardly be ethical."

Riiiight. Gabe shook his head "No promises."

He pulled into the players' lot five minutes ahead of schedule and made his way into the arena, but before he got more than a few feet in the door, Tricia pulled him aside. "Good, you're here."

Gabe furrowed his brow. "I said I would be."

"Yes, and very begrudgingly too." She directed him to stand in the perpendicular hallway, with the camera crew just in front of him, facing the main doors.

Why *was* the camera crew all the way down here? Sometimes they took photos of the guys coming in like it was some kind of fashion show, but no one else would be arriving for a while yet.

Gabe felt suspicious. "What did you do?"

"Actually, I'm innocent." Trish gave him a smile. "And while these shots are going out on our socials, none of them will be of you, all right?"

Why didn't that put him at ease? "So you lied to me about the handshake thing."

"*Lie* is such an ugly word...."

A few minutes later, a rental truck pulled up at the players' entrance and two men got out. They conferred with the security guards, who nodded them in, and then unrolled....

"Wow," Trish said. "It is even sparklier in person."

Gabe didn't even know what to call it. He didn't think it could be termed *carpet*, since carpet didn't reflect so much light. It looked like someone flattened a disco ball and turned it into a floor runner.

God, he hoped this wasn't for *him*. Sparkles and disco were not his vibe.

"Ten minutes!" Trish's PA chirped.

The delivery guys secured the floor runner to the concrete using adhesive strips and checked that it would stay in place. "Win us one tonight!" the taller one said as they were leaving. "My dad's a Voyageurs fan and I like to rub it in."

Gabe laughed. "I'll do my best." Then, when there was no one from outside the organization to hear anymore, he finally had to ask. "Trish... why does the players' entrance look like a seventies nightclub?"

"It's cute that you still think this was my idea."

True, the disco vibe was significantly more... more....

"Where is that music coming from?"

Was that "Don't Stop Me Now"?

"Oh my God." There were plenty of guys on the team who'd get on board with a scheme like this… and only one of them who'd plan it himself. Gabe covered his eyes. "Trish. Please tell me he didn't."

Trish put her hand on his shoulder. "He did." She patted him a few times, mock soothing. "But your re-action's not for public consumption, so just enjoy it, okay?"

The door to the street opened just as Freddie Mer-cury sang about being a shooting star, and Flash came in wearing a deep red suit Gabe had never seen before. At least he wasn't dancing, just walking down the hall, sunglasses still on like he belonged in a Corey Hart song. He'd only gotten halfway to Gabe when the doors opened again and Tips entered, dressed head to toe in the most eye-popping tangerine Gabe had ever seen.

He did a horrible finger-gun dance down the run-ner—it was genuinely hard to watch, so Gabe was glad when Flash got close enough to hug.

"I can't believe you're doing this to me," he said into Flash's shoulder. His eyes were burning.

Flash squeezed him once and then let him go with a pat on the back. "Not my idea."

Gabe surreptitiously wiped the corner of his eye. "Yeah, I guessed."

He and Tips bro-hugged, and then the door admit-ted Olie, Slimer, and Yorkie in yellow, green, and pow-der blue.

"That color's a bold choice," Gabe told Slimer, who was in a lime that matched his margarita mishap.

Slimer just grinned and fist-bumped him. "YOLO, man. We can't all pull off color like this guy." He gestured to Olie, whose ensemble included a mustard fedora that looked unfairly good on him.

Gabe didn't get away with a bro hug this time; Olie practically lifted him off his feet. "Oof! Uh. Thanks." His throat was closing up again. He wanted to say *it means a lot*, but the words wouldn't come out.

"Should've done it weeks ago." Olie released him and stepped back with a wink. "Adele loves this fit, you know." He did a little twirl.

Gabe managed a laugh. "She's got taste."

By now the music had reached its wildest, fastest, loudest moment—so of course that was Baller's cue to saunter in wearing a tailored plum suit. His crisp white dress shirt had one too few buttons fastened for Gabe's heart rate, and he was wearing the pirate hat from Disneyland.

He was also grinning like this was the most fun he'd ever had in his life.

Fuck, Gabe knew it had all been his idea, but now he felt—he could hardly put it into words. He felt seen, accepted, and loved.

And deeply, unexpectedly sad, because it hit him how much he liked Baller, beyond what a friend should, and nothing could ever come of it.

He expected another fist bump from Baller, or even a bro hug like he'd shared with Tips. They weren't exactly the hugging kind of friends.

So it surprised him when Baller wrapped his arms around his waist and squeezed... and didn't let go.

Swallowing, Gabe hugged back, grateful for Trish's promise about the cameras. "Always gotta be a grand gesture with you, eh?" He hoped keeping his voice quiet would disguise some of the emotion.

That made Baller squeeze extra hard and finally release him. When he pulled back, the grin Gabe had expected was more of a warm smile, almost private. "I am who I am," he agreed.

Then he gestured to the camera crew, and they started packing up.

"But actually," Dante continued, "this isn't all me."

The last of the song died out, but the door opened again. This time it admitted Kitty—in Pepto Bismol pink—carrying a coordinating gift bag.

"No more cameras," Baller said quietly. "Plausible deniability."

"Well," Gabe said, choking up again, "he absolutely is going to wear that suit on a regular basis, isn't he?"

"Kinda surprised he didn't already have one that color," Baller agreed. He murmured something to the rest of the group, and they all moved away. "We're gonna give you guys some privacy."

So that was why this had started so long before the game.

Gabe was alone by the time Kitty got to him, but he didn't feel it.

Kitty thrust the gift bag toward him. "I... this is for you."

Bemused, Gabe took it—only to immediately sag under the weight. "Holy—what's in here?"

"Apology vodka." Oh, well, of course. Kitty put his hands in his pockets, but he managed to meet Gabe's eyes. "Gabe.... Sorry. I'm sorry." His eyes were shadowed, and the words felt heavy. "I know now, is not okay, to do what I do. To make you feel how I do. It's... I'm little bit lost, sometimes. Things different here. Sometimes bad different. Food terrible. Vodka *most* terrible." He said this with a scowl, like he was personally affronted by the lack of quality alcohol.

Then Kitty softened again and raised his eyes to meet Gabe's. He looked miserable and sounded worse. "Other things… good. Better. This, definitely better."

Gabe swallowed a sudden terrible lump in his throat. "Okay."

Kitty shrugged in obvious discomfort but held Gabe's gaze. "Just… need time. You tell me when I fuck up. We play together again, score lots goals. Beat Montreal. Yes?"

"Hell yes," Gabe agreed.

"And then we drink vodka!"

"How did I know you were going to say that?"

Kitty must have apologized to Coach too, because he dressed for the game and she scratched Slimer. In the locker room, Gabe shook his head and told Baller, "I can't believe that kid bought a suit that ugly for a game he's not even getting paid for."

Dante gave him a sideways look. "He didn't."

Gabe blinked. "You're saying he just *had* a suit that color?"

"Uh-uh." Baller stood and rolled his neck, then shook out his shoulders. "I'm saying Kitty paid for all of them. And supplied like every tailor in the city with enough coffee and Timbits to make sure they got done on time."

It was a hell of an expensive apology, but Gabe didn't have time to think about it—he couldn't afford to get emotional again. Now was the time for hockey.

For the first time in his life, Gabe didn't feel like a hypocrite in his rainbow-themed jersey. Most teams had Pride Nights once a season and they'd raffle off the sweaters worn during the pregame warm-ups.

The Dekes had decided to actually play in rainbow gear tonight. But some of their opponents, the Voyageurs, had rainbows on their jerseys too—a colorful band around the right sleeve.

In the stands, the first three rows had coordinated their outfits. A group at the end wore red shirts, sitting next to a half-dozen people in orange, followed by yellow, green, blue, and purple. They'd created a rainbow behind the home bench.

A kid in yellow stood on her seat, waving a heart-shaped sign with #53 written in the center.

Fuck. Gabe was not going to cry.

Baller hip-checked him. "Wake up, Phil Esposito. It's hockey time."

Gabe turned to him and smiled wide. "Yeah it is." But he took a detour to his spot on the ice, grabbed a spare stick, and tossed it over the glass to the girl with the sign.

Then they lit the ice on fire.

Flash won the faceoff and passed to Baller, who took it left down the ice. They kept it in the zone, in front of the net, for two shots on goal before one of the Voyageurs stole it. He skated back down the ice, Flash in hot pursuit. Then Kitty snaked in and slipped the puck off the Voyageur's stick.

Kitty passed to Gabe—another rush of pure joy went through him. He took the puck into the offensive zone, skating hard, untouchable. And when he got to the net, it was so fucking easy to just tap it in.

Baller and Flash collided with him so hard he hit the boards. He couldn't stop grinning—a grin that only got wider when Kitty launched himself on top of their group hug.

They scored again before the end of the first period. Baller flicked Gabe's pass in with a cool no-look backhand that made Gabe's mouth water.

Baller was laughing and dancing, singing along to his goal song loud enough for the other players on the ice to hear.

"Come on, Jagger, let's get back to the bench." He got one gloved hand on Baller's shoulder and pushed.

The Dekes scored again in the second—Yorkie off an assist from Bricks, Tips off one of Kitty's rebounds. By the time they skated on for the third period, things were looking pretty one-sided at 4–1. Montreal scored again, but Tips corralled a loose puck into the empty net.

Baller slapped him on the ass as they skated back toward the tunnel. "We're going out tonight, yeah?"

"Oh my God, *yes*," Yorkie said fervently.

"Da."

"Oui."

Gabe blinked as the rest of the team weighed in, all in the affirmative. "Maybe we should make reservations."

But first, Gabe had a job to do. After a night like this, there'd be no avoiding the press.

"GABE, HOW does it feel to have a game like this tonight, on Pride Night, of all nights?"

Gabe couldn't believe the question didn't make him want to run screaming. Instead he only kept smiling. "It's amazing." He cleared his throat. "Just... knowing the team has my back, the fans have my back... uh, that would've been great on its own. But then to give the fans a decisive win like this at home.... It feels pretty great. Definitely a weight lifted."

The first reporter squished over to make room for another one, but she kept her phone pointed at his face.

"You got a special welcome home from a section of season ticket holders tonight. Can you comment on that and its impact on your performance, coming off a road trip where you had sort of the opposite experience?"

"Yeah, it was definitely… we had a few really unlucky games, and we weren't playing our best before that, and after the sh—mess in Nashville, coming home to that meant a lot." He tried for a smile and had a feeling it came off watery, which sucked, but whatever. It wasn't like he'd be the first professional hockey player to cry on camera. "We really have the best fans. I know everyone says that, but when you come home to that kind of reception after the record we've had lately— yeah, we won our last game, but it was a nine-game losing streak before that. I don't know that a lot of fans would show up for their teams in that way."

Trish must have given the reporters some kind of signal after that, because they thanked him and swarmed away to bother Olie and Flash, leaving Gabe to hit the showers in peace.

DANTE WAS having a good night. Lots of goals, his suit looked amazing, and they'd all started drinking Kitty's vodka in the locker room, so they were loud and feeling good by the time they hit the club. That would've been enough for him, but Gabe actually came with them—to an *actual club*. There was a dance floor and everything.

If this was the end of days, at least Dante was going out on a high note. Maybe he could get the DJ to play "Don't Stop Me Now" before the asteroid hit.

Yorkie tapped out early to call Jenna before bed—
she was up late studying, apparently—so Dante slid his
untouched beer toward himself. Shame to waste it.

Slimer pouted. "I was gonna drink that."

Dante tilted the bottle at him. "You snooze, you
lose. Besides, I thought you were going to dance?"

"Dude. That's why I need the beer. Liquid
courage."

Now Dante pointed with his bottle hand toward
the middle of the room. "Bar's that way, my friend."
Honestly. Dante had only just moved up this far in the
pecking order. This was his beer now. He'd earned it
through years of being the guy getting pecked. Slimer
would get his turn in a couple years.

"Yeah, but—" Slimer followed his finger. "Dude,"
he exclaimed, delighted. "Gabe's totally picking up."

Dante inhaled so sharply the beer stung his nose.
Oh, no *way*. He opened his mouth to tell Slimer so in no
uncertain terms—in no universe would Gabriel Martin,
superstar Nordiques winger and noted recluse, pick up
a man in a bar with the rest of his team watching.

Except before he could inform Slimer just how
wrong he was, he saw exactly what Slimer did. Gabe
was leaning one elbow on the bar, relaxed and smiling.
His body language said *I'm interested.*

That asteroid could've struck and Dante wouldn't
have noticed.

Of course guys were openly hitting on Gabe now.
Might as well shoot their shot, right? Dante couldn't
blame them… in principle.

In practice, he was plenty ready to blame everyone.
Didn't this guy know Gabe was here with his team?
That they were all here celebrating him and his impact
on their game tonight? Didn't he realize how mortified

Gabe would be if, in the morning, someone blogged about hockey superstar Gabe Martin going home with a random Quebec City townie? Not that Quebec City had a lot of blind-item gossip sites or whatever. Still—

Slimer raised his phone and pointed the camera toward the bar.

Dante put a hand on his arm and jerked it down. "No."

"What? C'mon, I was just gonna chirp him a little—"

For fuck's sake. "And what happened the last time a picture was taken without his knowledge? It ended up in the press, remember?"

Slimer's mouth worked for a moment. Then he said, "Oh."

Dante released his arm.

At the bar, the man flirting with Gabe upped his game, leaning forward and resting his hand on Gabe's wrist. He had a nice smile, Dante thought, but he was kind of scrawny. Objectively speaking, Dante was better-looking. He probably made more money too.

Dante's mood soured. Why was Gabe wasting time on this guy? Sure he was friendly… and available. But so was Dante! *And* he had a better ass. Why would Gabe waste his time with this guy when he could be with Dante?

Oh yeah. Because Gabe had no idea he *could* be with Dante.

The bar flirt said something, and Gabe laughed politely. But he didn't pull his hand away.

Dante should be the one making Gabe laugh like that. He should be the one with his hand on Gabe's wrist.

"I gotta take a piss," Dante told Slimer, nudging him out of the booth.

He washed his hands for longer than necessary as he considered. He knew what he wanted. Not acting on it might be the smart, mature thing to do, but Dante didn't get where he was by not taking calculated risks.

It was time to take the shot.

But when he got out of the bathroom, he didn't see Gabe or his friend. The spot at the bar was empty. Gabe didn't seem to have rejoined their teammates either.

What if Dante was too late and Gabe had gone home with this guy and they fell in love and got married and adopted kids together? What if—?

No. There was Gabe, walking away from the other side of the bar, where the cash register was. Dante still had time.

He caught up and grabbed Gabe's arm to get his attention. "Hey. Can I talk to you for a second?"

Without waiting for an answer, he dragged Gabe toward the door.

"Uh," Gabe said. He followed along behind Dante but didn't protest out loud. "What's going on?"

Dante waved at the bouncer on their way out, but he kept going to the narrow smoker's alley between the bar and the next building. At least they'd be out of the wind.

"Did you run into an ex-girlfriend or something? Or hit on somebody else's?" Gabe stumbled when Dante abruptly let him go. "Do you owe somebody money? If you're in some kind of trouble—"

An incredulous laugh bubbled up out of Dante's mouth. "Not that kind of trouble," he promised. "I saw you with that guy in there."

Oof. Not smooth.

Gabe's brow furrowed. "What? Jean-Claude?" Then he paused. "Wait, you were watching? Was everyone…?"

Leave it to him to focus on the wrong thing. "Slimer pointed it out. He thought it was cute." This conversation needed to get back on track. "That's not the point, okay? I know that guy is… is smooth and available and convenient and decent-looking, and he made you laugh, and you were probably thinking about having sex with him"—oh God, mouth, was this really the time?—"but don't go home with him."

And then Dante's mouth did the first smart thing it had done since the game ended—it kissed Gabe.

He was still holding Gabe around the forearm, and the heat from his skin radiated through the cloth of his shirt. Gabe's lips were soft and smooth and just a little slick, and the slide of them against Dantes's made every hair on his body stand up.

For the longest, achingest, most heart-stopping moment, Gabe didn't react.

Then put his hand on Dante's neck to tilt his head back and stepped closer, until he had Dante almost pinned against the brick wall of the building next door. Dante opened his mouth with a small, surprised sound and Gabe licked into him, one deep exploratory thrust and then retreat, a teasing slide across Dante's tongue and lower lip that flooded Dante's whole body with heat. His pulse beat wildly under Gabe's palm. The space between their bodies crackled with electricity, sparks looking for something to ignite.

God, yes.

And then, just as quickly, Gabe pulled away. In the light of the streetlamp, he looked blindsided, like he'd just gone headfirst into the boards. "Uh," he said. "What…?"

"Don't go home with him," Dante repeated. "Go home with me."

Gabe sucked in a sharp breath. "You want to—"

Dante grabbed his hand and put it over the fly of his pants, where it was pretty obvious what Dante wanted.

That might've been a mistake, because Gabe moved the heel of his palm over the base of Dante's cock and pressed just right, curling his fingers around Dante's length as much as he could through the fabric.

Dante's breath caught in his throat.

When Gabe spoke next, his voice came out in a rasp. "Go settle your tab."

Gabe must've been planning to pick up tonight, because by the time Dante had paid, he was idling out front, and he never drove if he'd had more than a few beers.

Lucky for both of them.

Dante slid into the passenger seat and closed the door behind him. Gabe had turned the seat-warmer on like a polite Canadian.

Gabe didn't look over at him. "Are you sure about this?" he asked.

"No," Dante said sarcastically, "I dragged my gay teammate out of a bar and kissed him on a whim." Wait, that sounded exactly like something he'd do. "It's not a whim, Gabe. I've been thinking about it for months. Which I could tell you about *in detail*"—oops, that sounded like a threat—"but maybe not until you're done driving."

Without further comment, Gabe put the car in gear.

SECOND PERIOD

TRAFFIC THIS time of night was dead—and thank God, because if the drive had taken longer than ten minutes, Gabe might've lost his nerve.

What was he doing, taking home a teammate for sex? A teammate he had feelings for?

Then Baller put his hand on Gabe's thigh, and any remaining good judgment went out the window. Gabe hadn't gotten laid in months, and he'd lost track of how long he'd been lusting after Baller. A better man might be able to resist.

He didn't bother parking in the garage, just left the car in the driveway and made a beeline for the front door, Baller hot on his heels.

"Shoes off," Gabe said automatically when they stepped inside. He would've been embarrassed about it—talk about an awkward impression—but Baller just snorted and bent to unlace.

"Are you always this demanding?"

Gabe's mouth went slightly dry as he admired the view, but Baller might as well know. "Usually I'm worse." He toed his own shoes off and nudged them onto the mat. "At least now they're not in the—mmf."

Baller cut him off with a kiss. Well, if he was going to be like *that*.

Baller's mouth was soft, his lips wet from being licked. The touch of them zinged down Gabe's spine, leaving goose bumps in their wake, and he opened his mouth instinctively, desperate for more.

Any thought of the consequences fled. Baller opened up for him and let Gabe sweep his tongue in, then gasped when Gabe scored his teeth along his bottom lip.

They devoured each other for a frozen moment. Baller threaded his fingers into Gabe's hair. Gabe moved his hand from Baller's hip to his ass.

Even through the fabric of his jeans, Gabe could feel the warmth of his skin, the firmness of the muscle. He dug his fingers in and brought their groins together as Baller's mouth went slack on a moan.

Fuck. The heat of Baller's cock against his sent a thrill up Gabe's spine. Baller was *really* into this.

"You have a bedroom here somewhere, right?" Baller said breathlessly into the humid space between their mouths. "And not just, like, a charging station?"

"Up the stairs, double doors at the end of the hall."

Somehow they made it without tripping, even though they couldn't keep their hands to themselves. Gabe was grateful his cleaning service had been in today when he pushed Baller backward onto the neatly made bed and settled over him.

When he let himself think about it, he'd figured Baller would be hesitant in bed, at least the first time. Gabe was sure he'd never had sex with a guy. But he'd been stupid to think so. Baller never let anything come between him and what he wanted. He wasn't afraid to touch Gabe—not his hair or his chest or his ass or his thighs—and he definitely wasn't shy about thrusting his erection against Gabe's.

His *still-clothed* erection. They could do better than that.

Gabe stopped grinding their hips together and sat up to breathe. Baller was panting, wrecked, his lips swollen. Begging to be abused further. "Fuck, I wanna get you naked. You good with that?"

Baller made a hot noise and arched his hips up. That was more than just a yes. "You...." He fumbled for his belt and fly, but his hands were shaking. Gabe batted them away and took over. "*You* are into dirty talk?" Baller said. "*You*?"

Gabe's stomach tightened, because that was definitely approval. "I'm into getting active consent." He raised his eyebrows and waited for Dante's nod before working the belt open and dragging down his zipper. "And yes. I'm a complex guy."

"I don't *believe this*." At Gabe's hip pat, Baller lifted his ass. Gabe worked his fingers under his waistband and pulled down until Baller could kick his pants and boxers off. He had a nice cock, thick and hard and perfect. "Say something else."

God, he was going to be trouble. "You like hearing me talk? You want me to tell you what I'm going to do?"

"Will it make you touch my dick any faster?"

Not usually, but he wanted to reward Baller's enthusiasm, so he wrapped his hand around him. "If you ask nicely."

Baller bucked into his grip. The buttons on his shirt strained with the movement. "Oh my God. Uh. Please?"

Not *quite* good enough, but Gabe hadn't exactly been clear. "Tell me what you want." He smeared fluid down the length of Baller's cock. It twitched in his grip, eager and responsive. Gabe licked his lips. "I could jerk you off. I'd rather suck your dick, though."

Baller mewled, and his cock leaked precome all over Gabe's fingers. "Yes, God, yes, I want—stop *teasing* me and put your money where your mouth is." Then he laughed—lust-filled and borderline manic—and said, "Or maybe put your mouth where *my* money is."

But the desperation in his tone belied his sass.

"Cute." Gabe climbed between his legs and ran his hands up Baller's thick thighs.

"Gabe," Baller whined when Gabe tickled the crease of his groin with his thumbs. "Seriously, man, don't tease me, I'm so close to—"

Yeah, he was, and Gabe wanted to push him over the edge. He mouthed at the moisture leaking from the tip, and Baller bit his lip and keened. His cheeks had flushed a dark pink, and his hands were clenched into fists. The salty, bitter taste made Gabe's mouth water. He laid his left arm heavily across Baller's abs and held him down as he sucked.

"Fuck! Oh, fuck. The stubble, that's—" Gabe hadn't shaved since that morning. Too much? "—so fucking hot."

Apparently not. Gabe pulled off and rubbed the side of his face against the smooth, sensitive skin on the inside of Baller's thigh.

"Fuck, you're good at this. You should—you should teach me."

Gabe had been doing a decent job ignoring his own cock, but he wasn't a saint—that mental image made him groan. "You're a menace."

"You—" Gabe put his mouth back on Baller's dick. "Hnng. You like it."

He loved it, but he wouldn't give Baller the satisfaction of hearing him say so. Instead, he pushed Baller's thigh out to give himself more room to work and slid his mouth down as far as it would go, pushing past his gag reflex. He wanted to make sure Baller jerked off to this for the rest of his life.

Gabe probably would.

When he slid his hand down to palm Baller's balls, his thighs quivered and the muscles under Gabe's forearm tensed. Was he sensitive there? Or was he anticipating Gabe might touch him somewhere else?

"That feels…." Baller writhed. "Can you…?"

He *was*.

Gabe slid his fingers farther back, until they reached the hot cleft between Baller's legs.

Baller curled his hands in the bedsheets and begged, "Fuck, fuck, Gabe, *please*."

Then Gabe let the pad of his index finger ghost over the sweat-damp skin of Baller's hole. Baller made a wet choking noise and flooded Gabe's mouth with come, his thighs tensing hard under Gabe's body. Gabe swallowed the first mouthful and then pulled off to jerk him through it, drinking him in with his eyes—the flush on his cheeks, the wet sheen on his mouth, the spatter of come on the shirt he still wore making it translucent. Baller's heart beat so hard and so fast, Gabe could see his pulse pound in his neck.

Gabe's dick was leaking in his pants.

"Oh my God," Baller panted. "Fuck, gimme five seconds to catch my breath and we can start on that lesson."

He seemed determined to give Gabe a heart attack. Gabe took his clothes off while, beneath him, Baller scrambled to get out of his own shirt, heedless of the come smearing over his belly.

Baller had seen him naked before, so Gabe shouldn't feel nervous. But there was a difference between being naked in the locker room and being naked in bed, just like there was a difference between being into having your dick sucked and being the one doing the sucking.

Before Gabe's dick could get any kind of performance anxiety, Baller looked over from pulling his socks off and said, "Oh wow, I am *super bi*."

As far as endorsements went, Gabe thought that one was pretty good. He stepped out of his dress pants, toed off his socks, and didn't even make it half a step closer before Baller was up on the side of the bed, reaching for his cock. "Can I...?"

This had to be a fever dream. Gabe nodded, half dazed, as Baller—Dante—wrapped a hand around him and smeared precome around the head and down the shaft. They weren't in the locker room anymore, and Gabe would never think of him as just a teammate again.

Dante's grip was firm and callused, the pressure just right. Gabe bit down on a groan and pushed into the touch.

Dante's breath caught, and he flicked dark eyes up from Gabe's crotch to meet his gaze.

Then he slid to the floor, and all the blood in Gabe's brain flooded south along with him.

"So, uh." Dante exhaled shakily, but his grip stayed sure as he stroked Gabe's cock. "You probably don't actually have to walk me through this." A corner of his mouth teased up. "But I bet we'll both enjoy it if you do."

Fuck. "A menace," Gabe repeated with a slight shake of his head. He took half a step back and gripped the base of his cock. "This is gonna be a short lesson."

Dante lowered his eyelashes. "Looks long enough to me."

Groaning, Gabe slid his hand into Dante's hair. It was very fine, and the strands were soft, the ends prickly. He'd had it cut recently. Gabe liked the way it felt in his fingers. "A *quick* lesson, then." He coaxed Dante's head back. "Open your mouth."

Gabe expected another smartass comment. Instead, Dante opened his mouth, lips red and wet and waiting. His eyes were dark and hot and full of promise... and challenge.

Gabe was so fucked.

He traced the head of his cock over Dante's mouth, smearing fluid over his lips. Dante tried to take him in, but Gabe's grip on his hair kept him from getting what he wanted. He hissed in pleasure at the pull on his hair.

Gabe must be having an out-of-body experience. It was the only way he hadn't come already. But soon he wouldn't be able to hold back. The hunger in Dante's eyes was eating him alive.

Finally he pushed the head of his cock inside and rasped, "Suck."

Dante sucked.

A shudder ran through him as Dante's lips closed around him. His cock was thick, and spit and precome leaked out the corners of Dante's mouth as Gabe thrust gently in and out, controlling the pace with his hand in Dante's hair.

When Gabe stopped thrusting and let his dick rest on Dante's tongue, Dante let out a low, deep moan.

He was already so good at this, and he *loved* it. Of course he did—he loved using his mouth in every other context. "Fuck, that's good. I love how much you like this." He pushed his thumb into Dante's cheek until he could feel his own cock. Dante shuddered around him. "You want more?"

Dante offered a look of lust-filled challenge, and then he tried to move down on Gabe's erection.

Gabe's cock pulsed precome in his mouth. Well, if that was what he wanted—he pulled Dante forward slowly, watching his face and body for his reaction.

Dante closed his eyes and made a needy sound Gabe felt more than heard. He brought his left hand up to clutch Gabe's ass, as if he needed something to hold on to, but his right hand was in his lap, moving over his own cock.

How was Gabe supposed to deal with that? "You getting off on this?" Another groan—deeper, more desperate. Some part of him thought he shouldn't push his luck, but maybe Dante was a bad influence, and now Gabe was the one who couldn't control his mouth. "On sucking a cock for the first time?"

His balls tightened. He wouldn't last much longer.

Dante's breaths came fast and hard through his nose.

When Gabe couldn't take it anymore, he pulled out to jerk off into his own fist. Dante made a bereft sound and never took his eyes off Gabe's dick, even as he spilled over his own fingers.

Gabe saw the heat and speculation in Dante's eyes when Gabe wiped his hands on a fistful of Kleenex and thought, *I've created a monster*. But he was pretty sure he hadn't had anything to do with it.

"I could've handled it," Dante said huskily.

Yeah, if Dante'd had the opportunity to talk, he'd have been goading Gabe into coming in his mouth. Just one more reason for Gabe to keep said mouth occupied. "Sorry," he said dryly as he offered Dante the Kleenex box. "Swallowing is not part of the Rookie Cocksucking course."

"Oh, so there's a graduate-level class?" Dante tossed his tissues into the waste basket—a perfect three-pointer. He looked up from his knees and grinned. "Advanced Oral Seminar? Is that before or after Intro to Facials?"

Okay, fine. So he probably didn't need to worry about Dante having a sexuality crisis. Gabe rolled his eyes and dragged him to his feet, then gestured him toward the master bathroom. Kleenex could only do so much. "Forgive me for trying to be polite."

"Forgiven," Dante said magnanimously as he turned on the sink. "Though you should know better. I like giving head."

"I noticed."

"On women, I mean. So I figured I'd like this too." He washed and dried his hands while Gabe did the same at the other sink. Then he rubbed his fingers along his chin. "Might have to see about growing some stubble, though. Hey, it's Movember, so the timing's good."

Yeah, right. "You're too vain to stop shaving for a month." This conversation was surreal. Where was the panic? Dante didn't seem like he was in a hurry to leave. Here he was, casually joking about facial hair improving his blow-job performance.

Gabe concentrated on drying his hands and hoped that hid his confusion.

"I do end up looking like I forgot to wash my face." Dante leaned against the bathroom doorframe, looking as completely at home as he did in the locker room. "You're expecting me to freak out, huh?"

Damn it. "The thought crossed my mind."

"Sorry to disappoint." He smiled—not the shit-eating grin, not the manic look that said *I dare you*, but a soft, private thing. "So… think we can talk now?"

Gabe swallowed, his heart suddenly in his throat. "I guess we better."

FIRST THEY detoured to the kitchen, because Dante had gone more than three hours without eating and was on the brink of starvation. Gabe shoved a couple of pre-packaged dinners from a meal service into the microwave and leaned against the counter, like he thought he needed to keep his distance from Dante and the kitchen wasn't quite big enough.

Dante could've told him he didn't bite, but he wasn't going to make promises he couldn't keep. "So," he said instead, "I like you. Sexually."

Gabe flushed an adorable shade of pink, but he nodded. "I… gathered."

Now for the harder sell—for Gabe to buy it, and for Dante to say out loud. "Also, uh, romantically. Like, I'm pretty into you. So…."

Gabe squirmed like a worm on a hook, but Dante was pretty sure that wasn't a *how do I let him down gently* squirm. This was the guy being uncomfortable with feelings, which probably happened when you'd been professionally in the closet your whole life. "You… want to date."

He said it like he was verifying a fact. Dante decided to treat it like a question. "What a great idea!" He smiled broadly. "Now that that's settled…."

Finally Gabe laughed and ran a hand over his face. "*Why*?"

Some people just couldn't take the easy out when someone offered it. "Fishing for compliments?" He didn't wait for an answer. "I could say it's because you're hot and good at hockey, but that's not why, even if it's true." This time he did pause. "You listen. You take me seriously, even though you have way more experience than I do. You helped me when I asked for it." And the last thing, the hardest to admit, but also the most important. "You make me feel like I belong here. Like I don't have anything to prove."

The microwave beeped, but Gabe made no move to open it. He swallowed visibly. "You've been thinking about this."

"Since September. Yeah." Dante was a pretty chill guy most of the time, but his stomach was in knots. He'd laid it all out there and Gabe was still hedging. How much more could he push without being an asshole?

Gabe turned and pulled a couple plates from the cupboard. He put one meal on each, grabbed a handful of cutlery from a drawer, and brought everything to the table. At least he wasn't fleeing in terror. "You're not out," he said as he slid Dante's plate across the table. It wasn't a criticism.

"It's a work in progress." Dante grabbed a fork and dug into his chicken pasta. "My parents are cool with it, though." His lips quirked as he remembered his slipup from the day before. "And Kitty." The meal was pretty good, considering its origins.

Gabe blinked at him. "You came out to *Kitty* before me?"

Dante swallowed his pasta. "In fairness, it was mostly an accident. And given my mouth, I think it's impressive I haven't told the whole world."

"Why haven't you?" Gabe paused. "Uh, definitely no judgment from me, right? I know the obvious reasons. Just… you know. You did mention a skywriter."

"Ha. So I did." Suddenly Dante wasn't quite so hungry. He poked at a noodle. "First reason—my grandma's a homophobe."

There was a silence as Gabe digested that. Then he said, "The conversation that kept you up at night…."

Dante winced. "Yeah."

"Fuck." Gabe rubbed a hand over his face. "Sorry. That was… I shouldn't have teased you about that."

With some difficulty, Dante shoved his complicated feelings about Abuela back into their box. Tonight was about him and Gabe. "You didn't know. That's… whatever. The other reason is more important." He squared his shoulders. "I knew you'd hate it. Everyone would think we were together even if we weren't. You had enough to deal with answering personal questions about yourself. It didn't seem fair to add questions about me to the mix."

"Doesn't seem fair to tie you up in the closet either."

Dante speared a piece of chicken and then speared Gabe with a look. "The only thing you want to do less than answer questions about the relationship you aren't in with me is answer questions about the one you are."

"Yeah," he admitted moodily.

It was a problem they could deal with another day. Dante was focusing on the positive. He pointed his fork at Gabe. "So you admit there's a relationship."

That startled Gabe into a small smile. "You're very persistent."

"One of my finer qualities," Dante agreed.

"I'm kind of a disaster."

Dante waved this off and forked up another bite of pasta. "I got drunk and mooned a cop last year." It had been all over those hockey message boards too. "Next."

Gabe's lips twitched. "I can't cook."

"Good thing you're rich."

Now he put his fork down and his crossed his arms on the table. A little color came into his cheeks, but his jaw was set—he wasn't joking. "I prefer to top."

Was Dante supposed to pretend to be surprised? "Sweet. Do you know how many girls these days have strap-ons? I love the twenty-first century."

Gabe gave him a pissy look. "I'm being serious."

For fuck's sake. "*So am I.*"

Oh, the shoe was on the other foot now. "Uh," Gabe said. His ears were turning red. "Really?"

He was totally getting turned on imagining Dante getting railed by a girl with a strap-on. Aww. "You're not the first to notice how great my ass is, but if it makes you feel any better, you can be the first to explore it with a flesh-and-blood cock."

Finally Gabe gave up and raised his hands. "Okay. You win." But he was smiling—a shy, hopeful thing that made Dante's heart go pitter-patter. He nudged Dante's foot under the kitchen table. "State your terms."

Dante fist-pumped. "Okay. Uh, I want exclusivity." He was nonnegotiable on that. If he was going to do something as dumb as getting into a relationship with his teammate, he was going all-in.

"Done."

Yeah, he didn't expect Gabe to fight him, but it still felt nice to hear. But now that the easy one was out of the way, he had to get on with the hard stuff. He bit his lip. "I want you to meet my parents if we're still together next time they're in town. As my boyfriend."

Gabe looked a little green, but eventually he nodded and exhaled the breath he'd been holding. "Okay. Okay, I can do that. I think."

He must've thought the worst was over, because he picked up his fork again to resume eating.

Unfortunately, Dante had one more bombshell to drop. "I'm coming out eventually, though. Details to be determined." His shoulders wanted to hunch, because he knew Gabe would hate it. "There's, like, timing to consider. If we break up, I'll probably wait longer. But I'm not good at keeping my mouth shut." He coughed. "As you know."

"All right." Gabe exhaled slowly. "That's fair."

"All right," Dante repeated. Then he grinned. "So hey, which side of the bed do you sleep on?"

GABE WOKE up warm, content, and unwilling to move, which made it a challenge to discern why he'd woken. His alarm wasn't going off. The curtains were still closed.

Then Dante's voice, rough with sleep but laced with amusement, broke through his clouded mind. "So when you said you slept on the left side, you actually meant… *my* left side?"

The warm, comfortable thing under Gabe moved unpleasantly. "Mmmrf," he grumbled.

Something poked him between his ribs. "Not that this isn't charming, but maybe you could get off me so I can pee?"

"Ugh." Gabe rolled over to go back to sleep.

When he woke up the second time, Dante was back in bed with him, passed out on his stomach with the sheets barely covering his ass. The view was… well, *all* of him was awake and inspired.

So. Last night… happened. And now he was in a relationship with his teammate, who was immune to sexuality crises and into pegging.

Now that he thought about it, none of this surprised Gabe except for the part where Dante had kept it a secret.

Agreeing to this relationship was probably stupid. One misstep could implode the team as well as their careers… but Gabe trusted Dante not to let it. They had both made too many sacrifices for hockey to let a failed relationship take it away from them. Dante might be brash and impulsive, but he wasn't reckless. And as for Gabe's heart, it was at least halfway too late for that. He might as well try to make this work.

He was trying to resist the alluring swell of Dante's backside when it shifted obscenely as Dante stretched, pushed his knees and shoulders deeper into the mattress, and lifted his ass toward the ceiling. Dante made a contented noise and then relaxed his shoulders and shoved his pelvis into the mattress instead.

Gabe licked dry lips. "Good morning."

"Mmm." Dante turned his head toward him. Even with bedhead and pillow creases lining his face, he was gorgeous, his dark, sleepy eyes framed with heavy lashes and his full lips turned up in a lazy smile. "Looks promising so far." He stretched again, and this time he rotated his body until the sheet was only covering his dick out of sheer bad luck on Gabe's part.

Gabe was about to agree when the floor started to buzz. A few seconds later, the alarm on his phone went off.

"Spoke too soon," Dante groaned. He flopped over the side of the bed and rooted around on the floor for his phone, which must have fallen out of his pocket yesterday.

Sighing, Gabe rolled toward his nightstand and picked up his own. After their intense road trip and yesterday's home game, they didn't have practice today. So why had he set an alarm?

Reminder—Habit de lapereau fundraising fair

"Ah… fuck." He'd volunteered for that back in the preseason, before his whole life got upended. Habit de lapereau was a Quebec City charity that raised money to make sure kids had warm outerwear for the winter. Gabe had volunteered for it a few times; it usually involved things like face-painting and ball hockey for the kids, while the adult hockey fans got to rub elbows with the stars of their team.

He'd forgotten about it, which wasn't like him. He wondered if it was too late to call Trish and have her cancel. Maybe they wouldn't want him anyway, now that he was out.

Dante heaved himself back onto the bed, phone in hand. He had completely escaped from any modesty the sheet might have provided, and Gabe had to drag his gaze away from the enticing trail of sparse dark hair that led down from his navel. "So apparently Flash's kid is sick and Trish wants to know if I can step in for him at something called… I actually have no idea, but it appears to involve rabbits."

Close. "It's a thing so lower-income families can make sure their kids have snowsuits this winter."

Dante blinked at him. "How did you get that from 'rabbits'?"

The name was a mix of *habit de neige*, snow suit, and the word for a baby bunny. Gabe dropped his phone on the bed and rubbed the sleep out of his eyes. "I got conscripted too. Except I forgot about it or I'd have asked Trish to cancel for me." Though if Flash had already canceled, he probably couldn't get away with it. Charities advertised their celebrity appearances and counted on their supporters paying for the privilege. A player not showing up due to a family illness was one thing, but Gabe and Flash were the two most popular players on the team. They couldn't both not show.

So he was going to have to sack up and deal.

"Ah." Dante eyed him carefully. "Presumably not so you could spend all day in bed with me."

Gabe huffed a laugh. "No, although that would've been a nice side benefit if you weren't going to this thing too. Just... I haven't done a lot of one-on-one fan interaction since the whole, you know." He gestured with his hands.

"Are spirit fingers inherently gay?" Dante wondered with a fond, teasing smile.

"That wasn't spirit fingers, that was just—" Gabe exhaled sharply through his nose. Dante was winding Gabe up on purpose.

Well... at least if things went terribly, he'd have someone to commiserate with. With a great mustering of willpower, he sat up. "I guess I should drive you to get your car."

"I could get an Uber. Save you the time." Dante had gone half over the side of the bed again, presumably looking for his underwear.

"Not a great idea," Gabe said. He hoped he sounded calmer about it than he felt. The idea of some stranger coming to his gate to pick up his boyfriend—still wearing last night's suit….

His stomach churned.

"Why not?" Dante yelped and fell the rest of the way out of the bed. His boxers must've been just out of reach. Then he stuck his head up so Gabe could see it over the mattress. His hair was wild and his face was red from being upside down. "Oh. Right."

"Maybe if you hadn't been wearing the world's most conspicuous suit last night," Gabe teased.

"Excuse you, did you get a load of Kitty?"

"Kitty didn't have a purple hat with a feather in it."

"Yeah. Shit, I think I left that in the locker room. Hope no one stole it."

It was *adorable* he thought that was a possibility. Gabe tamped down on a smile. "Come on. Get dressed and I'll give you a ride. I'll even spring for breakfast at a McDonald's drive-through."

"Gabriel Martin, I may swoon."

Gabe snorted. "You'd swoon from hunger if you tried to eat my actual cooking. McDonald's seems like the least I can do."

Besides, nobody looked too closely at people in a drive-through.

Once he'd dropped Dante off, Gabe called Tricia and let her know his concerns.

"I was expecting this before now, really," she said. "You surprised me."

Gabe sighed. "I forgot."

"That explains it." He could hear her smiling. "Look, I got a call from the director of the program the day after your announcement in support of you. I told them not to make a big deal out of it, but anyone who's a homophobe can just put their tickets in some-one else's raffle box."

Hopefully not Dante's.

That didn't exactly address all Gabe's concerns, but considering how late he'd left his freakout, he prob-ably couldn't complain. "Okay. Thanks."

"And obviously I'll be there for a few hours in case of emergency."

Gabe should get her a really nice Christmas pres-ent this year.

He pulled up to the community center just before noon. Though he was early, the parking lot was already half full. As he closed the car door, Olie pulled in a few spots over in his shiny silver Mercedes.

Gabe waited for him outside the doors. "Trish roped you into this too?"

Olie gave him a flat-eyed look. "Like a good pillar of the community, I volunteered." They fell into step as they entered the building and he added with a shrug, "Adele works for one of their partner organizations."

Of course she did. Beautiful, quirky, worked for a nonprofit—she was a perfect match for Olie.

Trish met them just inside the doors. "Hey, guys. I don't suppose you've seen Tom and Dante?"

Gabe fought down a blush. He'd seen a lot more of Dante than Trish needed to know about. "No, not yet."

"Well, come on in and wait in the ready room. You'll get enough public exposure when things kick off." She smiled teasingly at Olie. "Don't worry about your French. We have plenty of bilingual volunteers who can translate."

Good thing for Dante and Yorkie.

Miraculously, the two of them showed up just a few minutes late, and Trish gave them a brief outline of how the fundraiser worked. Guests who made cash or clothing donations received access to the room and a number of tickets they could use for activities or raffles. "We're going to set you up in the main room. There are plenty of other attractions, not just you."

Apparently this year they'd managed to get Bon-homme, the city's famous anthropomorphized snow-man, as well as a handful of amateur actors dressed up as cartoon favorites.

"You mean I could've come dressed as Elsa from *Frozen*?"

Yorkie looked Dante up and down. "You're really more of a Sven."

When no one else laughed, Trish said, "Sven is the reindeer."

Olie coughed and fist-bumped Yorkie behind Dan-te's back.

After a short orientation session, Gabe found him-self in an armchair, reading kids' books to a bunch of three-year-olds. As the only decent French speaker among the four of them, he was the obvious choice, and as a bonus, it didn't offer a lot of opportunities for awkward questions.

Besides, the books the group had chosen were hockey-themed, so this wasn't totally out of his wheel-house. He'd spent enough time with Flash's kids to be comfortable. All he had to do was read, show the pic-tures, and pause at the appropriate moments so the kids could have a giggle, which was very cute. It was like scoring on an open net.

On the other side of the gymnasium, things were going at a different pace. Yorkie had gotten the rookie assignment—ball hockey. Though a divider separated the two sections, occasionally a shout of PG-rated English chirping ("you shoot like my grandma!") or clumsy French encouragement ("Good… stick!") broke into story time.

Gabe's first time volunteering for this charity, he'd gotten stuck with ball hockey. For weeks, his shins looked like a Dalmatian's.

Olie had the other half of Yorkie's side of the gym for basketball by process of elimination—he was too smart to get stuck with ball hockey, but his French wasn't good enough for story time, and apparently he wasn't much of an artist.

Meanwhile, Dante had the spot opposite Gabe's for arts and crafts. Gabe was too busy to pay much attention, but he caught the occasional snippet of bad French as Dante complimented Marie-Philip's sunflowers or remarked on how much Simon liked the color purple.

Finally Gabe had read through every book twice— the kids and their minders rotated through the various stations—and was released from his duties. He retreated to their designated break room as quickly as he could without being accused of running away and chugged two bottles of water to soothe his dry mouth.

"Almost done," Trish said with an encouraging shoulder pat. "I know you hate this stuff."

Gabe sighed. "I don't hate it." Okay, that sounded like a lie. "I'm glad I can help. I always help with this— you know that. This is just my first year doing it without something to hide behind." That veneer of presumed heterosexuality had been so comfortable. This felt like he was standing in the net without any pads on.

"Uh-huh." Trish wasn't buying it. "You're an introvert. It's okay. Weird career choice, maybe," she teased.

Gabe didn't think it was all that weird—he played hockey, which meant spending time with the same group of people in concentrated doses and then having a lot of naps. But he played along anyway. "Hey, we can't all be—"

"I love kids." Dante swanned into the room with a stack of drawings thicker than a hotel Bible. "Look at this art! Little geniuses."

Trish grinned. "Case in point?" She turned to Dante. "I should've known you'd be a hit with the munchkins."

"I feel like you mean that to be insulting, but I'm not insulted because kids are awesome." He slid a piece of construction paper over toward Gabe. "Here's a drawing of me getting beheaded by a Voyageurs player. I'm not sure, but I think it's supposed to be Van Houten."

Gabe snorted. "Well, that's something he would do." The blob in the Dekes jersey did have Dante's black hair… and also a huge red geyser spewing out of its neck. Possibly Van Houten wore a manic grin. More red dripped from the blade of his stick. "Wow. I take it the artist is a Montreal fan."

"Ehhh." Dante waggled his hand back and forth. "I think I talked her around. Good kid. Talented, obviously." He grinned. "How were the rug rats?"

"Fine. *Normal*," Gabe stressed. "No one mentioned any homicidal tendencies."

Trish interjected, "Gabe does story time every year."

When Dante raised his eyebrows in question, Gabe said defensively, "Gabe doesn't like having his shins hacked to pieces by ten-year-olds." Plus the toddlers were adorable.

"I do kinda feel like we should've given Yorkie some Kevlar or something." Dante dropped into the chair across from Gabe. "What's next? It's gotta be almost time for the lunch thingy, right?"

After a quick glance at the clock, Trish finished her water and put the bottle in the recycling. "Yeah. I should go rescue Olie and Yorkie—I mean, Isak and Tom. The sports ones always run over."

Gabe was sure Yorkie would be happy for the reprieve.

When she'd gone, Dante leaned back in his chair with a happy sigh.

Gabe couldn't resist a dig. "You enjoy spending time with kids your own age that much?"

Dante made grabby hands for one of the bottles of water on the counter behind Gabe, and Gabe passed him one. "Come on, kids are awesome. Adaptable, hilarious… no filter. After your story time, one of the Anglo ones asked if I know why his teacher dresses like Frog and Toad."

"Did he not see your suit from yesterday?"

Dante finished cracking open the bottle and shot him the finger. "No, but I drew him a picture. Used the whole purple crayon." Well, he'd have needed it.

And then he proceeded to break Gabe's brain. "Whatever. So I like kids. Always figured I'd be a model hockey player and have, like, four."

Gabe's train of thought took an abrupt turn toward an out-of-service bridge, *Looney Tunes* style. "Uh."

"What? Flash has four. I think Bricks has three already. Tips has two with a third on the way." Gabe must have missed that announcement. Dante paused, head tilted to the side, eyes suddenly serious. "You don't want kids?"

Somehow Gabe found his voice, even though his fight-or-flight response was clamoring for attention. "Never thought about it," he answered truthfully.

Dante stared. "Never?"

"I mean...." Gabe gestured. "Never thought I'd be out and still play, and obviously I wasn't going to, like, go adopt kids and single-parent them while playing professional hockey. I just figured it was something to think about when I retired."

"Okay, but, like, every guy on the team has kids, just about. You never thought, 'Oh, one day...'?"

The first time Gabe had held Flash's youngest, what had he felt? She was warm and cute and tiny and terrifying.

The first time he'd seen Dante holding her, he'd thought, *Dante would make a good dad.* And he'd felt... wistful.

And those were thoughts he was absolutely not going to reexamine on the first official day of their relationship. Yikes. He wasn't going to start beating himself up because he'd caused the tiniest sliver of possibility that Dante might not be a dad.

"Nope," Gabe said.

Fortunately, before the conversation could get any more awkward, Olie and Yorkie stumbled back in. Yorkie collapsed in the chair next to Dante and nearly faceplanted on the table. "Ow."

Dante patted him on the back. "You look as ready for a nap as the kid who burst into tears when she found out the orange crayon was broken. Poor sleepy rookie. The kids wore you right out, huh? Did you get any good pointers, at least?"

"Birth control is very important," Yorkie said to the cradle of his arms. He sounded one yawn away from unconsciousness.

Dante nodded seriously and poked him in the stomach. Yorkie wheezed. "You gotta wrap it up." He winked at Gabe.

Gabe felt his face heating, so he turned the conversation to Olie. "How did you enjoy basketball?"

Olie gave him a wry look. "About as much as any tall Black athlete who doesn't play it."

Everyone in the room winced in sympathy.

Then Olie grinned. "Nah, just kidding. I killed it. Obviously."

The Dekes didn't sit together at the lunch. While the kids were occupied with their activities, the parents had been bidding on silent auction items, including which table the celebrity guests would sit at. Adele seemed to have won the bid to have Olie at her table— probably with his own money, but it would go to the charity, and the rest of her table would enjoy it. Nobody would complain.

As for Gabe, the pleasure of his company had been won by a lesbian couple who ran a local textile shop and had started a knitting drive for matching hats, scarves, and mittens, all of which had been donated. They didn't ask a single question about his love life, but Vero was *very* interested to learn about his golf simulator.

By the time the raffle winners were announced, Gabe was ready to go home. The four of them signed their jerseys and posed for photos, and then it was time to leave.

Gabe let out a long, slow breath as he left the community center and breathed in the fresh, crisp November air. He'd done it. He'd made it through the day without being confronted with anyone's overt homophobia and without letting on that he'd started sleeping with Dante. It had been just like any other fundraiser.

Except, no—because Vero had mentioned that she and her wife were brand-new hockey fans, and they might not have bid on him at all if it hadn't been for all the publicity. People liked to talk about "growing the game" and what that meant, but it usually was just talk, or at least it felt like it.

This was different—special.

Trish came out of the building behind him. "Oh geez, you scared me. I thought you'd be long gone by now."

No, he just needed a little space. "Actually, I wanted to talk to you. Uh… do you think you can get the names of the couple who bid on me?"

She blinked at him. "The foundation will have it, but I don't know if they'll give it to me. Depends on why, probably."

"They're new hockey fans." And they'd just dropped a lot of money to have Gabe as their guest. Sure, the donation was a tax write-off, but still. "I'd like to make them my guests at a home game sometime soon. Can you coordinate that?"

Now she smiled. "Yeah, I'm pretty sure the foundation will at least pass on that message for us. I'll set everything up."

"Thank you."

The door behind them opened again. "Hey, Gabe, do you want to—oh, hi, Trish." Dante's cheeks went slightly red. "I didn't see you there."

So much for being completely beyond suspicion.

"Wow," Trish said. "I feel so appreciated." She rolled her eyes. "I'm out, guys. Gabe, I'll email you details for that game, okay?"

"All right. Thanks again."

Once she'd gotten into her car, Dante turned to Gabe. "Sorry, uh—anyway, I guess Yorkie's having some kind of relationship drama, so me and Olie are going to take him out for dinner. You in?"

"We just ate," Gabe said.

Dante scoffed. "So? Like you couldn't eat another three plates." He leaned in and lowered his voice. "And then later…."

The words set Gabe's blood to a low simmer with their implicit promise.

But this was already a lot, really fast. Gabe needed to decompress. He'd spent the past forty-eight hours with people. He wanted to lie on his couch alone for a couple hours.

Even if he did also want Dante naked and writhing in his bed, it seemed… responsible… to take things slow.

Slow-*ish*.

"You three go," he said. "I'm pretty beat."

"Oh." Dante glanced around. "I guess it's been kind of a busy few days for you, huh?"

Gabe snorted. "You could say that."

Dante cleared his throat. "I could come over after…?"

Fuck. Yes. No. Was there a tactful way to say *I really want to fuck you, but I need to watch TV by myself*? Without hurting someone's feelings?

This was why Gabe mostly stuck to booty calls.

When he took too long to respond, Dante shook his head. "You can tell me no, Gabe."

It was nice that he thought so. But at least he was letting Gabe off the hook. "I've got a lot to process, that's all. Don't think I don't want to…." He wasn't going to say it out loud in public, even if they were apparently alone. "But I'm going to go home and decompress. You should be with Yorkie anyway. If Jenna breaks up with him, he's going to be a train wreck."

"Oh, he is." He shook his head. "Poor kid. I hope things work out for them. I guess she was being 'weird' when he called her before lunch. I don't know why that warrants this level of mope, but whatever. He's a kid; he gets a pass."

He's a kid. He was closer to Dante's age than Dante was to Gabe's, but Gabe was trying not to dwell on that. He didn't need to do any more second-guessing. "Just do him a favor and don't take him to a strip joint, all right? His head will explode."

Dante barked a laugh. "God, he'd never forgive us." He grinned. "I'll talk to you later, yeah?"

"Yeah," Gabe agreed. Okay. This wasn't so bad. "Later."

IF DANTE thought Yorkie was a train wreck after the fundraiser, it was nothing to how discombobulated he was the next day at practice.

They didn't have an early morning, just a midday skate with another home game the next day. Usually the practices that started later had a more relaxed, fun vibe. Today's was spoiled because Yorkie couldn't pay attention to save his life.

"Dude," Dante growled, butt-ending Yorkie with his stick because he was staring off into the stands instead of focusing on Coach's instruction. "You're going to get scratched."

Dante did not give up a potential night of filthy, spine-meltingly hot sex with Gabe to cheer Yorkie up only for him to pull this the next day. Not cool.

"Yorkshire! Baltierra! This isn't third grade."

"Yes, Coach!" Dante said quickly. Great, now *he* was in trouble.

"Sorry, Coach," Yorkie mumbled.

Fortunately for Dante, he wasn't on a line with Yorkie, so he kept his nose clean for the most part… until they were scrimmaging against each other and Yorkie caught him with a high stick to the jaw.

"Ow. Motherfucker." Dante shoved his glove under his armpit and raised his hand to his face. Yep— blood. Well, he was bound to lose his good looks in this game eventually. He just hadn't thought it would happen during practice.

"Oh shit," Yorkie said. His eyes went huge. "I'm so sorry—"

Tips pulled him off to the side as Flash and Gabe skated up to Dante.

"How's it look?"

With one gloved hand, Gabe tilted Dante's head up and to the side. Despite the sting of the cut, Dante couldn't help but flash back to the night before last.

What do you know—he could get hard in hockey gear after all.

"It's bleeding like a motherfucker," Gabe said. "Looks clean, though."

It probably wouldn't scar, then.

"Just need some glue," Flash suggested. He nodded over to the trainers' bench. "And disinfect." But he glanced over at Yorkie, and Dante didn't skate off right away. "He's acting weird to you?"

"I don't think he did it on purpose," Dante said, and then his brain ran that through the French-speaking English to native English decoder and he amended, "But he hasn't been sleeping well. And yesterday he maybe had a fight with his girlfriend? I don't know, the two of them are super weird about each other."

Flash muttered something under his breath and skated off after Yorkie, and Dante went to the bench and let the trainers subject him to a disinfectant wash and glue stitches.

"What do you think?" Dante asked Gabe later as they peeled out of their gear after practice.

"I think he's going home with Flash to be subjected to family time, a home-cooked meal, and probably a massive guilt trip to figure out what's going on with him. With an option for diaper duty." When Dante raised his eyebrows knowingly, Gabe shrugged. "Not that I'd know from experience or anything."

Right. Sure. That probably wasn't exactly how Gabe ended up coming out to Flash. "What about you?" Dante asked, deliberately casual. "Dinner plans?"

And that was how Dante ended up following Gabe home and getting an introduction to the dual rain showerheads in the master bathroom. Of course, that was only fun until the water hit the glue on his face, and then he had to move off to the side because it turned out neither of them was into blood.

"Hey, you know what we should do?" Dante gasped when Gabe had him pushed chest-first against the shower wall with a hand around his cock and his erection pressed tantalizingly between Dante's cheeks.

Gabe slowly stroked his thumb over the head of Dante's dick and licked a line up the side of his neck. "I'm not fucking you today either."

God, why was it so hot that Gabe was telling him no? "Kinda… kinda feels like you wanna." Dante tilted his hips back to get Gabe closer.

Gabe scored his teeth up the side of his neck. Dante's legs shook with it. "Didn't say I didn't want to." He thrust his hips just enough for Dante to feel it. "We have a game tomorrow."

"Oh God, are you serio—ooooooh my God." Gabe had his other hand around his own dick now and he was rubbing the head against Dante's clenching hole. "For the last time. I can take it."

That was a lie, though—they both knew it wouldn't be the last time he said it.

"And you can prove it tomorrow night." Gabe was relentless—rubbing, stroking… talking. "When I will fuck you as hard as you want."

Shuddering, Dante braced himself against the shower wall and thrust into Gabe's hand, then back against the tease of his cockhead. His mouth dropped open. He was so close—

"If you're fine the next practice, no more kid gloves. Promise."

Dante could live with that. Except…. "And what if, what if I can't?"

Gabe chuckled against the side of his neck. "Then I'll fuck you as slow as *I* want until you can," he said, and Dante's cock sprayed all over the shower wall.

He was still catching his breath when Gabe pinned his shoulders with one hand and jerked off all over his ass.

"*Fuck.* Is it tomorrow yet?"

Gabe gave his hip a wet smack and nibbled at his ear lobe. "Patience." Then he pulled away and, in the same tone, said "Dinner?"

On cue, Dante's stomach rumbled. "Yes, please."

That night, when he was on his way home, Dante's phone rang. He answered on the hands-free. "Hello?"

"So you are still alive!"

And there went his good mood. But if he let it show in his voice, he'd be in for an epic guilt trip. "Sorry, Abuela. You know the schedule gets crazy this time of year."

"Oh, I'm just giving you a hard time, mijo. I know you're a busy boy." Uh-huh. He smiled wryly. "I saw your game the other night. That was a nice goal you had."

She was talking about the Pride Night game. Dante braced himself. "Thanks. It was a good game."

"You were due for some good luck."

"Past due, I think." He flicked on his signal to change lanes.

Abuela must have heard the ticking of the signal, because she said, "Oh, did I catch you at a bad time? You know you don't have to answer when you're driving."

He ignored the impulse to question her sincerity. Abuela might be a world champion guilt-tripper, but she'd lost her husband to distracted driving way back before there were even laws against answering a cell phone while in control of a car. "It's okay, Abuela, I'm using the hands-free, I promise. I was just on my way back from G—a friend's house."

"Just a friend?" Abuela asked shrewdly, and Dante almost caused an accident after all. "Mijo, you're allowed to have a girlfriend, you know. You don't have to hide it from me."

"I'm not," Dante said, hoping he didn't sound as panicked and strangled as he felt. Out of an abundance of caution, he took the next right and pulled into a strip mall parking lot. "Why would you think that?"

She *tsk*ed at him. "It's seven o'clock and you're coming back from a friend's house? That's early to be coming home from dinner, isn't it? Hm?" Shit, it was, especially in Quebec. "You couldn't have been there very long—I know young people these days have their *arrangements*, but you could at least stay for coffee afterward—"

"Oh my God," Dante yelped.

"Or buy her dinner, Dante. You don't have to go out all the time, you can get delivery—"

"Abuela!" Dante protested. "I wasn't with a girl. I was at a teammate's house. That's why I'm going home so early. We had lunch together after practice. It's not like I went over to someone's house when they got home from work at five just to…." Yeah, he wasn't finishing that sentence out loud to his grandmother. Especially since he *had* gone over to Gabe's house after work to dot-dot-dot. Apparently he did have a functioning brain-mouth filter.

He didn't know if he felt worse about his grandmother's assumption that he was on his way home from a booty call or that he couldn't correct her with the truth because she'd disown him.

"You don't have to sound so scandalized, mijo. I know what sex is."

Dante's organs liquified with mortification. He slouched in the driver's seat, one hand over his face.

"Was it your roommate you were spending time with?" Oh good, a subject change. "He seems like a good boy."

"Yorkie? Yeah, he's a good kid, but no. I went out to dinner with him last night, though. He's having girl problems."

"At his age? Bless him."

Finally some firmer ground. Dante pounced on the chance to steer the conversation away from what he'd been up to tonight. "He's really devoted to his girlfriend, but they're fighting right now and he doesn't know why."

Another *tsk*. "Young love. Everything is so intense at that age. I remember when your grandfather and I—"

This was Dante's punishment for his chronic oversharing. He just knew it.

Or maybe it was his punishment for not sharing at all.

YORKIE'S FOCUS didn't improve during the game the next day. He took three penalties, turned the puck over just as often as he managed to complete a pass, and got in a fight in the dying minutes of the second, when they were up 3–2.

Fuming, Coach benched him for the entire third period. Dante didn't blame her and didn't know what to say to Yorkie, who was the picture of misery, sitting on the end of the bench with his head down. Dante was just glad this wasn't happening on the road, because he didn't know what he'd do or say. Sure, sometimes his emotions got the better of him and he lost control of himself on the ice. And everyone had bad days sometimes.

But they were *professionals*. They couldn't expect to have days like this without consequences. You couldn't take your personal life on the ice with you.

Of course, that was easier said than done. Dante knew that.

He was still annoyed, though, on top of his concern.

Most of the annoyance fled in the last few minutes of the third, when Dante dug a knuckling puck out of the corner to Flash at the top of the circle. He feigned a shot and passed to Gabe, streaking around behind the net, who put it in with a filthy backhand the goalie never saw coming.

The goal was pretty good. But what saved Dante's mood was when the arena speakers started playing Warrant's "Cherry Pie" to celebrate the goal.

Who had told? It wasn't him, and Slimer was back down in the minors, so it had to be Tips or Yorkie.

"Was this you?" Gabe accused into their celly. He looked half amused, three-quarters embarrassed.

"I wish. This is hilarious." Dante fluttered his eyelashes. "I mean, I can't promise *cherry*—"

Gabe face-washed him, which was disgusting and worth it.

It was a Sunday night game, which meant nobody was going out afterward. Flash had collared Yorkie and it looked like he was going to drag him home for some tough love, so Dante could officially let go of any feeling of responsibility there. Adele was waiting for Olie in the hallway. With Flash occupied, Gabe, Dante, and Kitty handled media. Dante didn't need Trish's training to know to acknowledge Yorkie had made mistakes without throwing him under the bus, but her pointers on *how* to do it definitely came in handy.

And then they were free.

"So," Dante said as he fell into step next to Gabe on the way to the parking garage, "your place?"

Gabe's shoulder bumped against his. The heat from the shower was still radiating off him, and his damp curls lent him a boyish look—though the promise in his voice was anything but innocent. "My place," he agreed. "I'll stop for takeout on the way. Any requests?"

Dante blinked. "Not too much garlic?" Seriously? He could eat as much as any hockey player, but they were going to have dinner first? *Why?*

With a minute shake of his head, Gabe clarified, "The food's for after."

Well, that was nice. Dante would probably need to refuel. "Protein. Carbs."

"Got it."

If Gabe was getting dinner, though…. Dante probably had time to make a stop on the way too.

He pulled into Gabe's driveway twenty-seven minutes later. The lights were on inside.

Fuck it. He forgot all about the box on the front seat. He only barely remembered to take the keys out of the ignition.

By the time Dante got up the front steps, the door was swinging open to reveal Gabe in only his obscenely clinging boxers. Dante had a second to appreciate the view before Gabe dragged him inside by the tie and took his mouth in a kiss.

Getting to the bedroom without taking his hands or mouth off Gabe's body was a lot easier now that Dante knew where it was. And this time, Gabe had helpfully already done most of Dante's work for him, so he got to appreciate how hot it was to have someone strip his suit off him, one article at a time.

The jacket went first. Gabe slid his hands up Dante's chest and over his shoulders, under the lapels, in a bold, smooth, confident movement that made Dante's nipples pebble beneath his shirt. He let go of Gabe to allow the fabric to slide down his arms.

Gabe caught the jacket without looking and draped it over a chair even as he reached for Dante's belt with the other hand. His lips never left Dante's mouth, and he never stopped guiding Dante backward toward the bed.

Dante hoped his brain was up to the task of remembering all the ways Gabe was going to blow his mind tonight.

The belt buckle slid open, but Gabe didn't move to take off Dante's pants. Instead, he brought his hands up to Dante's neck.

Dante was a professional hockey player. He put on a tie several times a week. He was also lazy and usually just loosened the damn thing and pulled it over his head.

So he wasn't prepared for how sexy it was to hear and feel the rasp of the silk around his neck coming slowly undone as Gabe untied the knot and pulled the material so it caressed Dante's chest before he dropped it next to the jacket.

If Gabe didn't take Dante's pants off soon, his dick was going to grow thumbs and deal with the problem itself. Because Dante's actual hands couldn't help—he couldn't stop touching Gabe's skin. His sparse chest hair prickled under Dante's palms, but his skin was hot and smooth. Gabe felt broader than he looked. Dante's fingers skipped into the valley between his pecs, then lower, until he could count Gabe's abdominal muscles by feel.

Not that he had the concentration to count.

With one last, thorough sweep of his tongue, Gabe withdrew from Dante's mouth only to move his attention to the side of his neck while he painstakingly unbuttoned every. Last. Button. On Dante's shirt.

Dante could afford another shirt. Gabe could just rip this one off him. It would be worth it.

He must've voiced this out loud, because Gabe muffled a laugh against the side of his neck. It tickled in a way that gave Dante goose bumps. "Patience."

Dante made an outraged sound. "Says the guy who answered his door practically naked."

Gabe nipped the skin below his ear. "Strategic advantage." But he finished with the buttons.

Then he gently tugged Dante's shirttails out of his trousers.

Fuck it. Gabe could undress Dante as slowly as he liked, but Dante was done pussyfooting around—or whatever you called it when there wasn't any in sight. He slid his palm down Gabe's sternum and over the waistband of his boxers until he had Gabe's hard cock pressed along his wrist and palm.

"Gabe." He wouldn't have called it a whine. That didn't make it untrue. "At this rate I am going to die of old age before you get your dick in me."

Snorting, Gabe gave him a gentle shove. Dante's knees hit the mattress and he tumbled onto it. "What's the hurry?"

Dante would show him what the hurry was. He tugged Gabe down to straddle him and grabbed his hand. "*This*, Gabriel. This is the hurry." He pressed Gabe's palm against his cock. Pants, underwear, whatever—the pressure felt good, and he bucked into the touch.

"What?" Gabe sat back and looked Dante over. He worked his hand over his length. "Your dick have an expiry date?"

Groaning, Dante arched into the touch. "I'd prefer not to come in my pants."

"I dunno. Could be hot." Gabe stroked him with a little more pressure, and Dante's mouth fell open as the hot, damp material shifted against his erection.

God damn it. That did sound like a filthy kind of fun. But… "Rain check?" he gasped. "Come on. You promised to fuck me."

Finally Gabe released him. "I did." He closed his hand around Dante's wrist and unbuttoned one cuff, then the other. Then he sat back on Dante's thighs until Dante had space to sit up and shrug out of his shirt.

Dante thought Gabe would go back to teasing him. Instead, he slipped his fingers under Dante's waistband and slid backward, taking the trousers and underwear with him, until he was kneeling between Dante's feet. He peeled his socks off too. The gentle caress on the inside of his ankle made Dante shiver.

Or maybe that was just the cool air on his bare dick.

Hell, maybe it was anticipation.

Gabe must have finally felt some of his urgency, because now that Dante was naked, he didn't waste time climbing back onto the bed. They explored each other's bodies with greedy hands. Dante dug his fingers into Gabe's thick thighs, then slid them under the hem of his boxers, edging closer to his goal. If Gabe wouldn't rush himself, Dante would coax him along manually. So to speak.

"You really...." A thrill went through Dante when Gabe actually jerked his hips into his touch. "You want it that bad?"

Dante almost groaned in frustration. "Have you not been paying attention? There's, like, one thing on my mind tonight. I've been pretty up-front about it." He paused. "Is this slow seduction thing because you're trying to give me time to change my mind?" Gabe didn't just want an engraved invitation, he wanted it *notarized*.

"No," Gabe said, slightly too late for Dante to believe him.

Fine. Gabe seemed determined to drive Dante out of his mind... but two could play at that game. Dante was up for the challenge.

But before he could act on the decision he'd made, Gabe said, "When you showered after the game—"

"I was *very thorough*," Dante said, perhaps just as too quickly as Gabe had been too slow. In fairness, "Way more thorough than you should be in a public shower, but I regret nothing."

"Jesus." Gabe shook his head. "They're gonna write that on your tombstone."

"Yeah, when I die of sexual frustration."

Finally Gabe teased the crease of his thigh with the tips of his fingers, and Dante decided he didn't need his dignity but he did need to move this past second base. He licked his lips and lowered his eyelashes. "If you need me to beg for it, I will."

Gabe looked gut-punched. His long, fat cock— yeah, maybe Dante was a little apprehensive, but nothing fucking ventured, right?—twitched between his legs.

"You're not the only one who can talk," Dante promised.

Gabe's hand slid a little farther, until his fingers brushed the sensitive skin of Dante's balls. Gabe swallowed. "Get up on all fours."

Yes. Dante scrambled to move, his cock swinging heavy between his legs. The position felt ridiculous, but he didn't care.

Especially when Gabe moved behind him and pressed a kiss to the base of his spine. Then lower, on the curve of his ass.

It was possible that Dante had overstated his ability to form words.

Gabe's warm, soft breath ghosted over his skin. "You want—"

"*Yes,*" Dante managed to hiss between clenched teeth. "I want you to—"

But the rest of the sentence died on his tongue when Gabe parted the globes of his ass with his thumbs and rubbed his stubble on the insides of his cheeks. Dante's arms trembled. Sweat prickled on the backs of his knees and the insides of his elbows. His pulse thundered in his ears.

All Gabe's hesitation disappeared at once. He buried his face in Dante's ass and flicked his tongue over his hole. Just once, at first. Then again, wetter, lighter. A tease. Then again.

Dante collapsed onto his arms under the onslaught, and he rested his forehead on his wrists as a thick, choked sound escaped his throat. Heat suffused his body. He flushed everywhere, up to his hairline, every nerve ending on fire with want.

He forgot about getting fucked. All that mattered now was making sure Gabe never stopped.

Gabe made a hungry noise against skin alive with lust. He spread Dante wider and changed from teasing flicks to firm stabs of his tongue, and Dante's mouth fell open against the comforter. "Oh fuck," he said. He sounded faraway to his own ears. "Oh fuck, Gabe, oh my God. That feels—that's so—"

It felt like the fabric of the universe was unraveling around him. His dick was leaking steadily, his balls throbbed, and his ass had beard burn. He was more turned on than he'd ever been in his life and Gabe *still wasn't fucking him*.

And suddenly this was completely unacceptable. "Gabe, come on. Fuck, I want it so bad. You know that, yeah? Your mouth is so good, but give me—"

Gabe pulled his mouth away and pushed his thumb into Dante's hole.

"Yes!" Dante half shouted, half sobbed. That was what he wanted—to be filled. Gabe obliged and pushed his thumb in farther, short and thick, tugging at Dante's rim. Then the click of lube and two fingertips instead, thrusting shallowly, a hint of what would come. Dante was out of his mind with it. He forced himself up on his hands and pushed back into the invasion until he'd taken Gabe's fingers as deep as they'd go. "Fuck—Gabe, *fuck me*."

"Yeah," Gabe said. *Finally.* His voice sounded raw. "The way you take my fingers, you're gonna take my dick like that?"

Dante hoped to fuck that was a rhetorical question.

For one strange, gut-clenching moment, Dante was empty. Then there was a telltale crinkle of foil and latex and finally a hot, blunt pressure at his entrance.

Like hell he was waiting for Gabe to decide he was ready now. Dante bore down and pushed back and somehow, miraculously, Gabe didn't make him wait anymore.

Gabe's cock had more give than Alice's strap-on, but it was longer too, and thicker. The pressure of it made Dante's eyes cross as he adjusted to the sensation.

A distant murmur of praise fell from Gabe's lips. The crescents of his nails dug into the flesh at Dante's waist.

Something sparked in the back of Dante's brain, something primal and hungry.

"Wait," Gabe said hoarsely. He shifted his grip to Dante's hips and tilted.

Dante's nervous system lit up like a slot machine hitting the jackpot. "Hnnng." A wordless, desire-filled sound escaped him. "Yeah, that's—there, like that—"

Gabe drew back and then fucked forward again, pulling Dante back to meet his thrusts.

Dante's mouth fell open. "Oh fuck. Oh fuck. God." His eyes lost focus, so he squeezed them shut.

Gabe didn't speed up. The bed thudded rhythmically against the wall. And Gabe kept rolling his hips as Dante clenched around him.

"I knew you'd look good like this," he said.

Dante moaned. "I knew you had a thing for my ass."

When Gabe scratched at it lightly with his fingernails, Dante rewarded him with a hiss and arched his back—only to nearly fall forward on his face again as the shift had Gabe hitting his prostate just right. A sharp, shocked sound escaped him.

"There?" Gabe asked. "Like that?"

Dante didn't dare move. "Like that, keep—keep going." He held himself still, braced at the perfect angle for Gabe to keep fucking him just right.

His balls throbbed. His cock was so wet it was dripping everywhere, but Dante couldn't think about touching it. He'd lose his balance, and he didn't want Gabe to stop.

Apparently Gabe had other ideas. "Fuck, I need to see you." And suddenly Dante was flat on his back on the bed with Gabe pressing forward between his knees.

Dante had no time to appreciate the manhandling. Gabe was already pushing his knees up. Dante gripped one around the back of his thigh and let the other fall over the small of Gabe's back as Gabe pushed back in.

"Oh God—fuck—Gabe, Gabe, I'm gonna come. Harder, come on, just a little more—"

He curled his free hand into the pillow, as if letting go might mean flying off the bed. He was so close, he could taste his orgasm, just out of reach.

Gabe leaned down for a shallow, sloppy kiss. The briefest brush of his stomach against Dante's cock was almost enough.

Then he pulled back and batted Dante's hand away from his leg. Gabe pushed his knee farther out, exposing Dante further. "I wanna see."

God, yes, and Dante wanted Gabe to see him. He wrapped his hand around his rock-hard shaft and managed two strokes before he accidentally met Gabe's eyes.

That was it. Dante came apart, clenching hard around Gabe's cock in his ass, his balls emptying. He worked himself through it, thumbing at the sensitive head as it pulsed come all over him.

Gabe kept nailing his prostate until finally he closed his eyes and opened his mouth and shoved in deep and hard, twitching against Dante's ass, heaving for breath.

Holy fuck.

Gabe carefully withdrew from Dante's body—not Dante's favorite part of the experience—and collapsed next to him.

Dante watched him through hazy, half-lidded eyes, feeling orgasm stupid and content. When he'd inflated his lungs enough to speak again, Dante said, "Hi."

"Hi," Gabe said back, sweet and attentive.

Dante turned his head on the pillow and kissed him, unable to keep his self-satisfaction from his smile. Gabe could probably taste it. But of course he was smug. He knew he'd been right about the sex. Gabe should've listened to him.

Oh well. Dante had a feeling there weren't any more kid gloves in his future.

Finally Gabe broke the kiss. His cheeks were pink, but he didn't look much less smug than Dante felt. "So...."

Yeah, Dante could give him this one. "Okay."

Gabe blinked. His face was as blank as Dante's brain felt. "Okay?"

"Uh-huh." Dante nodded. He had to close his eyes for a second to remind himself he still had control of parts of his body. "Okay. As in, okay, I concede that fucking your way is awesome."

Gabe rolled onto his back and laughed at the ceiling. "I said I'd fuck you as hard as you wanted. I said nothing about how fast."

"You sneaky little bastard," Dante said admiringly.

Gabe turned his face toward him and grinned. He was just so *handsome*—it seemed wild that it had taken Dante years to notice that Gabe wasn't just attractive, *Dante* was attracted *to him*. And he was funny, and he treated Dante like he was important, and looking at him now made Dante feel like...

... like he wanted to stay curled up in this bed with Gabe forever.

Which was certainly a lot to be feeling on a Sunday night not a week after you started dating someone.

Then a loud, rumbling sound disturbed the peace of the moment, and Dante snickered and hid his face in the pillow. "Sorry."

"I think that's my cue to offer you the shower while I use the microwave," Gabe said wryly.

"Perfect romance," Dante said sincerely. "Think I can borrow some sweats too, or are we dining al fresco?"

"I'm pretty sure that doesn't mean 'naked,'" Gabe said, wry. "Second dresser drawer. Help yourself."

Sweet. Dante had never dated someone whose clothes he could borrow, though many a girlfriend had borrowed his shirts. It would be interesting to be on the other side of the equation for once.

The microwave was still going when he got out of the shower, so he dried off and grabbed a pair of Dekes sweatpants and, smirking to himself, a worn-out golf-branded T-shirt from the dresser.

It was freezing outside, but fuck if he was putting shoes back on now. He sneaked out and grabbed the box from the front seat of his truck.

"I brought dessert," he announced as he walked back into the kitchen. Gabe looked over from manning the microwave, lips quirked in amusement.

With a flourish, Dante opened the box. "It's pie. Cherry."

GABE COULDN'T have said if regular sex or finally being out to his teammates had an effect on his hockey, but since the media had run out of new things to say about his sexuality, he'd been on a tear. The last week of November, he scored five goals in three games and was made the league's first star of the week.

Off the ice and out of the bedroom, he spent more time with his teammates in November and December than he had all of the previous season. One memorable off day, when Dante was trying to distract Yorkie from whatever was going on with Jenna, Gabe—suddenly unused to spending time alone—ended up playing on the golf simulator with Flash and Kitty, who lived a few streets over.

"What's with the sudden urge to socialize?" Flash asked over the hum from the electric heater. "Are you feeling okay?"

Kitty looked around in feigned confusion. "Why you buy a house so big if you never have a party?" He narrowed his eyes and adopted a teasing tone. "Or maybe I'm just never invited?"

"Neither of you is funny." Gabe ignored them and took his shot—a perfect drive to the green. Eat that, Flash. "Or good at golf."

"Gabe was afraid that one look at his interior decorating would give away his sexuality," Flash deadpanned. "Now his secret is out, so it's safe to have people over."

Gabe waited until Flash was squaring up to hit the ball to say, "Just avoid the basement. It's been a while since I hosed down the sex dungeon."

Flash shanked the shot horribly. Kitty laughed and touched his beer bottle to Gabe's.

But something about the shot wasn't quite right. Gabe tilted his head at the way Flash was holding himself. There was tightness around his eyes—more than the little lightning-shaped scar could account for. "Hey, Cap—you okay?" His form was *awful*. Sure, Flash didn't get out on the golf course as much as Gabe did— the guy had four kids and a wife to spend time with— but still.

Huffing, Flash dropped his club back in the bag. "We play hockey together every day, but you notice something in my *golf swing*?"

"I'm usually a little busy to watch you play hockey," Gabe said. "It's your hip, right?" Gabe could tell by the hitch in his swing—that hadn't all been Gabe's interference.

Flash heaved himself up onto one of the barstools. "Yes, you busybody. The trainers are keeping an eye on it."

So it was serious. "Surgery?"

"Probably in the off-season." Flash glared at him. "Don't be a nag. I don't need everybody knowing." He glanced at Kitty. "You too, Kipriyanov."

Kitty raised his hands in a gesture of innocence. "Don't look at me! I don't say nothing!"

Fine. Apparently they weren't talking about it. "It's your shot," Gabe reminded him. "Don't forget about the wind shear."

Flash waited until Kitty lumbered over to hit the ball—he seemed to find golf hilarious—to lean forward across the bar and ask Gabe in French, "Seriously, though. You're not dying or something, are you? You seem too happy to be dying…."

Only the little death, Gabe thought, but he tried to keep his expression neutral. "I'm not dying."

"Mm-hm," said Flash, obviously suspicious, but then Kitty made a triumphant sound and distracted them both.

"Ha! Hole in one!"

At last—some competition.

"I DON'T know," Yorkie said doubtfully as Dante un-locked the truck. "It was kind of anticlimactic."

"What, because there wasn't a lineup wrapped around the building to get in?" Dante popped open the back door and heaved his bags onto the rear floor-boards. Black Friday shopping in Quebec didn't have anything on the US, but Yorkie had been missing his family, and he was still worried about Jenna, so Dante figured they could give it a try.

Yorkie took to retail therapy like a gator to a swamp. Mission accomplished. Dante was the best roommate ever.

"It just feels like it doesn't count if you don't have a turkey hangover."

Dante snorted. "Can't argue with that, I guess." He shut the door and missed whatever Yorkie said in reply. "What's that?" he asked as he slid into the cab.

Yorkie gave him an odd look. "I didn't say anything."

Dante frowned. "I swore I heard—"

There it was again. Dante paused with the key half-way in the ignition. "Did you hear that?"

Yorkie met his eyes and shook his head. "I don't—"

Then he stopped, and Dante could *see* that he heard it this time.

They both reached for their seat belts at the same time.

"Where do you think it is?" Yorkie asked, peer-ing under the running boards. "Like, shouldn't it not be able to hide somewhere dangerous?"

"What, do I look like I design trucks now?" Dante shone his phone's flashlight up into the wheel well. Nothing.

But then he heard it again—a faint, pitiful, heart-rending sound.

Meow.

He stood up so fast, he whacked his head on the side mirror. "I think it's under the hood!"

It took them twenty minutes and a trip into the grocery store for a can of tuna to coax the thing out from Dante's engine block.

The kitten was black, or at least covered in grime, tiny and ragged-looking and *loud*. It clung furiously to the front of Dante's shirt, its nails digging in like hooks.

"What are you going to do with it?" Yorkie asked, sitting in the passenger seat once again. Dante had started the truck in the hopes that some warmth might get the kitten to relax enough to let go of him. So far, no dice.

"I don't know, man. He's pretty cute." And purring up a storm despite the clawing. "But my apartment building doesn't allow pets." He glanced at Yorkie. "Think Jenna'd want him? You know… keep her warm at night and stuff?"

"Jenna is a dog person."

Dante worked very hard not to laugh out loud.

Yorkie rolled his eyes. "Yeah, yeah, I know. But she lives in the dorms anyway. They're not even allowed to have, like, goldfish. There's no way she can have a cat."

"I'll have to take him to a shelter, then, I guess." Which was too bad, because Dante was already getting attached. "You think you can hold him while I drive? I'll take you home and then take him to the vet or whatever."

But the kitten would not be dislodged, and Dante was worried about hurting him if he pulled too hard to try to make him let go. "Guess I'll just drive really carefully."

He dropped Yorkie and his obscene pile of gifts off at his apartment, then did a quick Google search on his phone for the nearest veterinarian.

Shit. He hoped they spoke English.

Three hours and a couple hundred dollars later, Dante had made no progress delivering the cat to a shelter. But he did look much cuter now. Under the grime, the kitten was a tuxedo cat with a little dab of white on his nose. The vet tech gave him a quick bath and inspection, of which Dante understood mostly that the cat didn't have fleas and was very young—barely old enough to be away from its mother.

He also understood that the tech wanted his phone number for personal reasons, but for once, Dante played the oblivious card. He paid for the checkup and all the shots and even a cat carrier, because he wasn't going to ruin his career getting into a car accident because a kitten tried to claw his nipple off while he was driving.

And then he went into the parking lot, put the cat carrier on the front seat, and looked at the kitten.

The kitten meowed.

"This isn't a good idea," Dante told him. Everybody knew you weren't supposed to get people pets as presents. Even really cute pets. Even—especially—for significant others.

The thing was, Dante didn't want to give Gabe a cat. He wanted Gabe to give the cat a place to live temporarily until Dante had a home that allowed pets.

"You're going to need a really cute name and a lot of stuff. And I'm going to need, like, a bribe. Think we can pull this off?"

Meow.

"I'll take that as a yes."

One expensive trip to PetSmart later, Dante pulled into Gabe's driveway. He'd texted from the store—just *You home? Ok if I stop by?*—which, in retrospect, definitely read like Dante wanted to come over for sex.

Which wasn't inaccurate. Dante was down for it, and also up for it, pretty much all the time. It just wasn't the primary motivator this time.

Either way, Gabe said yes, and now here they were. "Be cool," Dante told the cat, and then he juggled the bags into one hand so he could ring the doorbell.

WHATEVER GABE had been expecting after Dante's text, it wasn't this. He opened the door to find Dante and a lot of *stuff*—bags and bags of it in one hand, and a weird-looking black-and-white thing tucked under the opposite arm.

This didn't *look* like a booty call, but it was Dante, so anything was possible. "Uh. Hi?"

Dante said, "Here, could you hold this?" and shoved the black-and-white thing at Gabe before pushing past him into the house.

Then he bent down to take off his boots, so at least some of Gabe's etiquette lessons had stuck.

"What—?" he said, and then the thing *mewled* at him.

And that was when Gabe noticed he was holding a tiny, warm, fluffy, wriggling, adorable creature.

Oh no. Why had Dante brought him a cat? Gabe shifted his grip, praying he wouldn't get clawed, and hip-checked the door closed.

The kitten mewled again.

"Mario says hi too."

That was when Gabe noticed the logo on the bags. PetSmart. Oh God.

"Did you…?" He took a moment to collect himself. The kitten took the opportunity to squirm out of his arms and hide in his front closet. "Did you never watch those PSAs about not getting other people pets as presents?"

Even if this was easily the cutest cat he'd ever seen in his life. The little rings on its tail! Its tiny white feet!

"Hey, no, this is my kitten. I paid his vet bills and everything. I'm just loaning him to you until I find a place that allows pets." The boyish hope on his face wasn't going to sway Gabe. Damn it. He had to be strong about this. He was gone too often to have a pet.

"Where did you even get him? *Why* did you get him?" It felt mean to point out that their relationship was too new for them to be co–pet owners when Dante had just said this was his kitten… even if that smelled like BS.

Dante looked guilty. "I found him under the hood of my truck when I was leaving the mall. Yorkie and I just got in, and I thought he said something, but he said no, he hadn't, and then we both heard it again, so we looked. Poor little guy almost got barbecued."

There was a rustling from the closet, proving that while the kitten had escaped death by engine block, its survival instincts hadn't improved. One more rustle and then a *thunk* as the broom Gabe kept in there for sweeping up ice melt fell over.

Dante continued, "It's so cold, you know? I didn't want him to freeze to death either."

Gabe was being played. He *knew* he was being played. "You could have taken him to a shelter—"

Another, louder crash echoed from inside the closet—probably a bag of hockey paraphernalia tipping over—and then a lone puck rolled out across the floor. After a second the kitten scrambled out in hot pursuit, skidded on the tile of the entryway before somersaulting over the puck, and sank its rear claws into the rubber, its black-and-white-ringed tail twitching like crazy.

Obviously spending so much time with Dante had weakened Gabe's defenses. He wanted to coo.

"I already got him checked out, and the vet gave him his shots. She says he's perfectly healthy. Doesn't even have fleas."

The cat let go of the puck and stretched out on its back, showing off a white bib, paws, and belly, and bright yellow eyes.

"Please can he stay? I swear it's just temporary. I can start looking into other options when I get back from visiting my parents after Christmas."

Gabe didn't know what was worse—Dante's puppy eyes or the cat's fluffy tuxedo belly. Not that it mattered. He'd been doomed the second he opened the door. *I don't even like cats*, he told himself firmly. But what he said was "You're paying for the pet sitters when we're gone. And any vet bills. *And* anything he destroys."

Dante broke out into an enormous smile, and Gabe's heart fluttered. Oh no. Gabe didn't even want to think about the things he'd do to get that expression aimed at him again.

Dante grabbed him by the shirt front and pulled him into a brief, hard kiss. "*Thank* you. Seriously, you're a lifesaver. I promise this is just until my lease is up and I get a place that allows pets."

Somehow Dante's blinding grin roped Gabe into setting up cat things—a scratching post, a litter box that went in the corner of the laundry room, a bed Dante insisted on putting in the prime patch of sunlight coming in through the front window. He'd even bought an automatic food and water dispenser for when they were away on short trips, apparently having foreseen Gabe's arguments about no one being there to look after it.

While Gabe fiddled with the screwdriver, trying to get the stupid battery cover back on the water dispenser, Dante rolled the puck for the kitten.

That reminded Gabe—"What did you call him?" Dante had used a name when he first came in, but Gabe had been so distracted by a kitten being in his house that he missed it. But if they were going to be roommates, he should at least know the cat's name.

Dante scooped the cat up and cradled it like a baby, stroking its bib. Gabe couldn't believe the thing didn't claw his face off. "Mario."

"Mario," Gabe repeated. Okay, whatever. It wasn't the worst cat name he'd ever heard.

"Mario Lemew."

Oh my God. "Seriously? Not Phil Es-paw-sito?"

Dante gaped at him. "Where were you when I was filling out the paperwork? It's too late now. Mario Lemew it is." He set the kitten down, and it wobbled over to its bed and faceplanted in the weak sunbeam of the day's last light. Dante stood and brushed his hands off on his jeans, his body language going from playful to predatory in an instant. "Now are you finished with that thing? Because I was thinking today might be a good day for that advanced seminar."

THE TEAM only got three days off for Christmas, but Dante hadn't seen his parents or his grandmother for months, so he wasn't passing up the opportunity for a visit. Gabe dropped him off at the airport on his way out of town, since he was spending the holiday with his dad in Ottawa.

Dante was only a little sad they'd be spending their first Christmas together, well, apart. But on the other hand, they definitely weren't ready for family integration yet.

His parents met him in Arrivals with a big sign that had his jersey number inside a big heart, because they were big supportive dorks. Dante spent the first twenty-four hours basking in their attention and love, stuffing himself with his dad's cooking, and playing dominos with Abuela.

Then, when she left, he spent an hour sitting on the couch while his parents watched *It's a Wonderful Life* and he texted with Gabe.

He didn't realize he'd been caught with a goofy smile on his face until suddenly the TV stopped making noise and he looked up to find the movie over, his dad nowhere to be found, and his mom watching him with a fond expression.

Busted.

She cleared her throat. "New girlfriend?"

"Mom!"

"I'm sorry," she said wickedly. "I should say 'partner,' shouldn't I? I don't mean to pry—"

"Yes, you do." She couldn't help it. She loved him, and he'd never kept secrets from her before—not important ones, at least. And now, well, he was pretty obviously seeing someone, so it was probably driving her nuts.

He hated not being able to talk about it too. It was harder to hide that from himself now, when he didn't have the distraction of Gabe around. And with the exception of the *secret* part of their relationship, Dante *was* happy—the kind of happy people gloated about. Dante was a champion gloater. Having to sit on his happiness was killing him.

And this was his mother, who loved him and who would never betray his trust.

Who would hopefully understand why he'd agreed to something so against his own nature as keeping his mouth shut.

"Gabe and I are together," he said before he could change his mind.

His mother's face went carefully, completely blank. Then she said, "Gabe your teammate and mentor."

He closed his eyes. "Yes."

"Gabe the guy whose poster used to hang on the wall in your bedroom."

God damn it. "Yes."

A hint of laughing incredulity crept into her voice. "Gabe the man you went to Disneyland with last month."

"Mom," Dante complained, opening his eyes.

"*Dante*," she said in the same tone. Then she snickered. "I'm sorry. It's just—I'm very conflicted! Because on the one hand, that's sweet and adorable and hilarious. And on the other hand, is it also kind of sketchy and predatory?" Her brow furrowed and her tone went philosophical. "Would I react the same way if you were a woman, or if Gabe was?"

The only time Gabe was even remotely predatory was in the bedroom, but Dante was not telling his mom that. Especially because he'd have to explain that he liked it. "It's not like that." How much was he going to have to tell her? "I made the first move, okay?"

Now she laughed outright and patted him on the knee. "I'm sure you did, honey. I don't know why I was worried. At least not about that. But it is a mine-field, you know, getting romantically involved with a coworker."

He sighed and put his phone down. "I know. And Gabe's—I mean, I get it, he's been around the league longer than me, he's got hang-ups I haven't had time to develop because I've been bi for like five minutes. He also doesn't want to tell anyone about us. I understand the way he feels, but also I hate it."

His mother hummed thoughtfully. "It isn't like you to hide, definitely. But it's hard not to empathize with him too. And—how long did you say you've been together?"

"A couple weeks."

"So it's a bit early to be sending out save-the-date cards."

Jesus. "Mom!"

"Sweetheart." She echoed his tone again, but this time she was gentler. She patted him again. "How many times in your life have you told me you're dating someone?"

That brought him up short. He thought about it as a tiny, dim lightbulb went on somewhere in the back of his brain, where he could hopefully ignore it a little longer. "Uh...."

"Never, baby. Not one time in almost twenty-three years."

That couldn't be right. "I had girlfriends," he protested.

"Girlfriends you mentioned in passing, sure," his mother agreed. "You even had girlfriends you introduced me to, because you were still living at home and had no choice. But you've never said, 'by the way, Mom, Maisie is my girlfriend now.'"

Technically he hadn't done that this time either. At least not on purpose. "I haven't exactly done a lot of traditional dating in the past couple years."

"Yes, I have a vague idea of what the sex life of the average single male athlete looks like, thank you, and I'd prefer to *keep* it vague," his mom answered dryly. Dante hoped she didn't read any hockey message boards, but he wasn't going to ask about her sources. "I'm sure you had plenty of casual friends. That's my point."

That this was not casual. Dante couldn't deny that. "I'm listening," he hedged.

"Just… oh, I don't know. I don't want you to compromise who you are, and I'll always be on your side. But I don't think your boyfriend had a very nice time with his coming out experience. It's not unreasonable that he doesn't want to feel responsible for putting you through that as well, especially when you've only been together a few weeks."

"It wouldn't be him 'putting me through it,'" Dante grumbled, but he saw her point. That would put a lot of pressure on Gabe, even if Dante's perspective was that he'd prefer to be out either way. "I get it, though."

"Mm-hmm." The way she said that made it clear he'd missed the point she was really making. "And you

can keep that in your back pocket when Dad gets bent
out of shape on your behalf."

Ooooh. He smiled. "Wow. You're a genius." That
actually would be helpful. Between that and the impending shitstorm when his grandmother found out, he
should be able to get his dad to cut Gabe some slack.

"When it comes to your father, yes, I'm the leading expert," she teased. "Now, it's time for good little
boys to go to bed. Santa doesn't come when you're not
sleeping, you know."

Dante got up and kissed her cheek. "I know. Good
night, Mom. I love you."

Really, he thought the conversation with his mom,
and later, his dad, went well. Maybe they had concerns
because he'd never dated another man, never mind one
he worked with, but they were just happy he was happy.

He held on to that the next day, when he opened his
last gift from Abuela—a small, carefully wrapped box
that contained a simple gold band on a platinum chain.

The ring looked uncomfortably familiar. He swallowed. "Abuela… is this—?"

With weathered hands, she took the ring and the
necklace from the jewelry box, placed them in his hand,
and curled his fingers around them. "I know young people these days want something flashy," she said. "But
there's still value in old-fashioned things."

Dante uncurled his fingers and stared at the wedding ring that had been his grandmother's. "Don't you
want to keep it?" He knew how deeply she'd loved his
grandfather.

"Oh, I can't wear it anymore these days anyway."
She rubbed her hands together. "My arthritis is too bad.
That's what happens when you get old, mijo."

That was the thing about moving away, he'd noticed. He was gone for such long stretches of time that she seemed to age in fast-forward. "You're not old," he protested.

Abuela laughed. "Lying is a sin, you know," she teased. Then she grew serious again. "It would do me good to see you settled down before I die. I just want you to be happy, mijo. A nice boy your age shouldn't be alone."

I'm not. But the words died before they could reach his lips. "I'm glad you look out for me," he said through a tight throat. "Even if it doesn't seem like it."

"Oh, Dante. I love you."

Fuck. He closed his eyes. "I love you too, Abuela."

He let her hang the chain around his neck. Then she cupped his face and beamed at him, pride evident in every beautiful brown wrinkle. "There." She patted the ring where it rested against his chest. "Maybe it will bring you luck."

DANTE WASN'T sure if Yorkie had patched things up with Jenna, if he'd needed the holiday break, or if he just finally learned to compartmentalize, but whatever had happened over the break, the rookie had improved. No more turnovers, and he tallied three assists in Detroit. In the locker room, at least, his smile was back.

But he still had hockey-bag-size dark circles under his eyes, so the sleeping thing probably wasn't going much better.

"Didn't hear you come in last night," he said around a yawn the morning after the game.

That's because I didn't sneak back in until four this morning. He'd passed out in Gabe's room after their victory celebration. "Yeah, you were pretty dead to the world."

"I took some ZzzQuil," Yorkie admitted. He sat up and rubbed his eyes. "I can't, like, get my brain to shut up at night."

Dante hoped he hadn't been up *too* late before he self-medicated. He would be completely fine letting Yorkie know what was going on, but Gabe would shit a brick. "Have you tried talking to someone? Like, I'm pretty sure there are trainers for this stuff."

"For *sleeping*?" Yorkie said incredulously.

Probably they were actually therapists at that point, but Dante wasn't going to use that word and potentially put Yorkie off talking to them. "Yeah, man. You're a professional athlete now. Every physical need catered to."

He shook his head. "I guess."

"Anyway." Dante got up and stretched. "I'll take first shower since it seems like you're still fighting to keep your eyes open. But don't be too long—we've got to be at the bus in an hour." They didn't often play back-to-back road games, but Chicago and Detroit were at least reasonably close together.

Dante got out of the shower to find Yorkie had fallen back asleep half sitting up. He looked wiped out.

Think my roomie is Going Thru It, he texted Gabe, along with a picture. Then he went to wake him up. "Come on, dude. Go get in the shower. I'll throw your shit in your bag, okay?"

"'Kay," Yorkie mumbled, and he tottered off toward the bathroom.

Gabe hadn't replied yet, so Dante added, *What do I do?*

Idk, let him sleep when he can I guess. The three dots blinked at him for a moment before the next message came through. *He still hasn't told you what's up w Jenna?*

It's like he's suddenly locked up tighter than Fort Knox. Which was super weird because Yorkie wouldn't shut up about her normally.

Considering it wasn't exactly an early start, the bus was quiet. Dante figured Yorkie needed an opportunity to talk to someone who wasn't him—maybe Tips, or maybe Flash or Gabe, someone who might have actual advice to give—so he sat in the row behind him instead of next to him. Yorkie didn't even notice; he just collapsed into the seat and leaned his head against the window.

Gabe came in after them, met Dante's pleading gaze, and then swung himself into the empty seat beside Yorkie.

Dante was *so good* at giving hints.

"Morning, rookie."

Yorkie barely turned his head. "Hey. Baller crash with you again last night?"

Oh *shit*. Had Yorkie figured out what was going on? Why hadn't he called Dante on it?

Dante felt dumb.

On the other hand, Yorkie had said it casually, without any innuendo. Maybe he just thought they played Wii Golf until the wee hours of the morning.

"Uh, yeah. He's a glutton for punishment, I guess. Likes getting his ass beat at video games."

Dante bit back on a snort. He liked getting his ass something, all right. It might even rhyme with *beat*.

He shouldn't be listening to this. He was going to give them away.

Gabe cleared his throat and went on. "You okay?"

Yorkie rubbed his face. "Just haven't been sleeping well."

Leaning back in his seat, Dante tuned them out. Gabe could handle Yorkie.

He didn't have time to second-guess his decision, because Flash took the seat next to him. "Well if it isn't my second-favorite winger."

Honestly, was Dante supposed to take offense at being second to one of the best players in the league? "Flattery will get you everywhere."

"Why am I not surprised?"

Rude. "Did you come to show me baby pictures?" Dante asked hopefully. Sure, he was enjoying being a grown-up with his own place and a boyfriend, but that didn't mean he didn't occasionally miss hanging out with Flash's rug rats. "I can trade you."

Flash raised an eyebrow. "For?"

"Kitten pics."

Now the other eyebrow went up too. "There's no way your kitten is as cute as my kids."

Dante held up his phone. "Wanna bet?"

So they spent the quick trip to the airport going back and forth with their phones, Flash showing off Baz's first skate, Dante playing video of Mario going so wild for his toy he flopped off the couch and then ran away with his back arched. Dante figured he was safe—Flash had never been to his apartment, so he had no reason to suspect the pictures weren't taken there.

Until Flash said, "Isn't that Gabe's house? I recognize the ugly tile."

And, shit, the floor in Gabe's kitchen was a particularly horrible and distinctive marble tile Dante had given him shit for on more than one occasion. Gabe said it came with the house and he didn't cook anyway, so who cared?

"Um," Dante said. "Yeah."

Flash had a very calculating expression. He wasn't going to ask. He was just going to wait until Dante incriminated himself further.

Jerk.

"My apartment doesn't allow pets," Dante said feebly. "So Gabe said the kitten could live with him until I get a new place."

"That was nice of him," Flash said. It sounded like *I know exactly why he said that.* Which wasn't fair. Gabe thought Mario was cute too.

Dante was about to tell Flash that he was the one cleaning the litter box when they were home, but at the last second he realized that made it sound worse. "Well, you know Gabe. He is a nice guy."

Yikes.

Flash's expression made it clear that he wasn't fooled, but fortunately they were pulling up to the airport, so Dante was able to make his escape.

He caught up with Gabe on the flight. At first he intended to warn him that Flash was onto them, but something made him stop. Flash wasn't going to make a big deal out of it or he'd have said something to Dante. Letting Gabe know would only upset him. So instead he asked, "Any idea what's eating our rookie?"

Gabe shrugged and shook his head. "Homesick, maybe."

Maybe. They'd just come back from Christmas—sometimes that triggered a wave of it. "The first year can be tough. Whatever's going on, we'll get it out of him later." They'd given Yorkie long enough to work it out. Flash had tried. Tips had tried. Now it was time for a tag-team.

"Take him out for dinner or something," Gabe agreed.

Dante wrinkled his nose. They always went out for dinner, and public restaurants weren't the best setting for hard talks when you were mildly famous and hormonal. "If he's homesick, we should cook for him instead."

Gabe's dry look said it all. "If I cook for him, he'll be dead."

"And you think *I'm* a disgrace to adulthood." When Gabe's raised his middle finger, Dante just laughed and said, "Fine. *I'll* cook, but we're doing this at your place. You have a better kitchen." Aside from his ugly tile.

Gabe rolled his eyes, long-suffering. "Fine."

THEY PUT up a good fight in Chicago until the second, when Flash took a hit that sent him tumbling. It was a clean hit, but he went down weird and landed hard on his right side. He didn't get back up.

Fuck. His hip.

There was a whistle as Chicago flipped the puck over the boards and out of play, and Gabe made a bee-line for Flash and crouched on the ice. "Flash, ça va?"

Flash rolled onto his stomach and groaned. "Non. C'est—"

Glancing up, Gabe looked toward the bench to see one of the trainers rushing out. The trainer settled on the ice and spoke to Flash in rapid-fire French.

The trainer met eyes with Gabe. "Help me get him up?"

"You're sure we won't make it worse?"

Flash said something in French laced with enough religious curses to make it very clear that he would be leaving the ice on a stretcher over his dead body.

"Machismo is actually going to kill one of us one day," Gabe grumbled.

The trainer shook his head. "It should be okay. Just to the tunnel and we'll get him in a chair."

Gabe moved in close on his right side and pulled Flash's arm over his shoulder for extra support.

They shifted forward and Flash gasped. "Maybe," he continued in French, "no weight on the right side."

The trainer nodded. "Okay, Flash, we're going to get you off the ice. Right foot up and lean to the left. Put your weight on me. I'm going to guide you across the ice and we're going to get you in the back so we can figure out what's going on."

They exited the ice to stick taps from both teams, which left Gabe to deal with his teammates.

Dante met him first. "What's going on? What happened?"

"His hip. I don't know…." He shook his head.

They regrouped. Coach set out a new lineup, cursing under her breath. She moved their fourth-line center to take Flash's place and rotated the other players through to take the strain off the extra minutes everyone else would play.

Gabe tried to focus on the game, but things fell apart. Flash was hurt badly and would be out for some time. All the progress Yorkie had been making over the past few games evaporated under the stress.

Missed passes, dropped pucks—they were practically giving the scoring opportunities away on a silver platter. Gabe was disgusted with himself at how poorly he played.

By the time they reached second intermission, they were down 3–0.

Olie, who was the sole reason they were still in the game, was frowning angrily in the locker room. Gabe suspected he was more upset about Flash than the score.

Coach gave them a rousing speech, reminding them to earn their keep and quit fucking around, then left to get an update on their captain.

Back on the ice, Chicago scored goal number four one minute into the period.

Before the next faceoff, Olie waved to Gabe, Dante, and Tips.

"If I hear their goal song one more time tonight, I'm going to skate out of the crease and lodge my stick up your asses. Try to keep the puck in the offensive zone for more than thirty seconds this period. I can't do all the work."

As far as inspirational speeches went, it wasn't bad, but it wasn't enough.

Chicago scored twice more, and Gabe wanted a drink. Getting shut out sucked. 6–0 shutouts sucked more.

But none of that really compared to his level of concern about Flash.

Off the ice, Gabe found Coach for an update.

"They're sending him for imaging."

That meant X-rays as well as an MRI—bone and tissue.

Flash was thirty-four. An injury this severe almost definitely meant surgery. Hip surgery now meant long-term injured reserve—he'd be out the rest of the regular season.

It also meant cap relief, so theoretically the team could bring someone in to bolster their lineup while

Flash recovered. Sometimes teams got "rental" players whose contracts would be up at the end of the regular season, in exchange for draft picks. But usually trades meant someone had to go the other way.

In other words, if this injury was as bad as Gabe thought it was, roster changes were inevitable.

He cleared his throat. "I'm gonna go say hello."

"Be warned. He's pretty high."

Gabe would imagine so.

He walked in on the tail end of a phone conversation between Flash and his wife. "'Vette, 'Vette, 'Vette," he crooned. Gabe could hear the tinny sound of her response but couldn't make out the words. Whatever she said, though, made Flash screw up his face. "Non, non," he mumbled. "Je t'aime. Je t'aime."

He raised his head a little when Gabe entered, then said, "The Anglo Angel is here to save me."

Yvette must've said something in his ear, because Flash raised the phone. "She want to talk to you."

Gabe had no idea why Flash was speaking English when Gabe's French was fine, but he put it down to the drugs. "Hi, Yvette."

"Gabriel. Thank you for talking to me. My husband is a bit unhelpful at the moment."

Flash was still crooning Yvette's name at the ceiling.

"He was in a lot of pain, but he's not anymore." The situation wasn't exactly funny, but sometimes you had to make lemonade. "He mentioned there was an issue a while ago? This seems related."

Yvette swore. "I told him he should have had that treated in the off-season." She sighed. "Do they know anything yet?"

"No. They're sending him for diagnostics. Then they'll probably send him home."

"He's going to be so mopey."

Only when he's not high. "Yeah." He breathed out. "At least it's the end of the road trip." Flash would have an easier time knowing they weren't on the road without him.

"Small mercies," Yvette agreed. "Thanks for talking to me, Gabriel. Can I say good night to my husband?"

Gabe handed over the phone and pretended to be very interested in a spot of chipped paint on the door frame while Yvette and Flash said their goodbyes.

It was weird. He'd never envied their relationship before. He'd made a decision about his love life and intended to see it through, and there was no point regretting it because he was living his dream otherwise.

But now....

Gabe had had his share of minor injuries, but only one truly nasty one, when he'd been laid up with a knee injury and couldn't bend his leg. His options had been pain or nausea from the meds, getting off the couch had taken every ounce of his willpower, and he'd been so bored and sick of his own company, he teared up when Flash stopped by to play cards.

Flash wouldn't be alone for his recovery—though with four kids at home, there'd probably be times when he *wished* he were. He'd have Yvette to lean on, to cheer him up and help him shower and tell him to stop feeling sorry for himself. To remind him he wasn't alone, that people loved him for more than what he could do on the ice.

And now Gabe wanted that—the general concept he'd never let himself want before. But he wanted it with someone in particular. He wanted it with Dante. And he wanted to be the one there when Dante needed him.

His stomach twisted. Gabe didn't know how to want these things, much less make them happen. He didn't know how he'd held Dante's interest this long to begin with.

Just one more thing to worry about.

THIRD PERIOD

"THEY'RE FLYING him to Boston for the surgery," Yvette told Gabe when she answered the door. No greeting—she obviously wasn't herself today. "Day after tomorrow."

Gabe had been summoned to Flash's house not even ten hours after their flight landed back home in Quebec City. He was barely conscious, but he didn't want to put it off.

Apparently the doctors felt the same way about Flash's surgery. At least he wouldn't have to wait. "Are you going?"

"Yes. His mother's coming to watch the kids." She sighed and gestured for him to come in. Her normally immaculate hair was frazzled, and she hadn't put on makeup. Gabe wasn't sure he'd ever seen her without it; she was usually as put-together at home as she was in the courtroom. "I hate leaving Dominique when she's so young, but it's just for a few days."

Gabe nodded and set his shoes on the rack. "How's he holding up?"

"Hah. You know how he is." She shook her head. "He won't snap at the children, but he's miserable. I'm surprised he wanted you to come by."

"Maybe he wanted to be miserable to someone he's not married to. Get it out of his system."

Yvette laughed and hugged him, seemingly on impulse. "Oh, Gabriel. You really are an angel if you're signing up for that. Go on in. He's in the study."

Truthfully, Gabe had no idea what Flash wanted with him. He was probably doped to the gills and still uncomfortable. But showing up when requested seemed like the least Gabe could do.

"It's open," Flash said in French when Gabe knocked. His voice had that same slow, not-quite-slurred quality it had had in Chicago once the doctors gave him something for the pain.

Gabe pushed the door open to find Flash draped over his couch in sweats and a T-shirt. His face was sallow, making the lightning bolt scar stick out that much more, and he looked vaguely green. Gabe knew that feeling; the good pain meds hit him the same way.

"Hey."

"Hey," Flash echoed in English, with an intentionally obnoxious accent. "Close the door, would you?"

"Are we discussing mafia business?" Gabe raised his eyebrows, but he closed the door anyway. Leaving it open would be the same as inviting the kids in. Obviously he was here for a serious talk.

Flash affected a surprisingly good Don Corleone. "Gabriel, my son, someday, I will call upon you to do a service for me." He waved at the armchair kitty-corner from him. "Sit."

Gabe did, and then Flash swore. "Damn, I should have told you to get yourself a drink first."

If the remark had come from anyone else, Gabe might've started to freak out, but he had experience with Flash when he was drugged up. "I'm fine." He settled deeper into the chair. "Are you going to tell me what's up?"

Flash sighed deeply and sagged into the pillows. "You can never just make small talk, you know that? Always has to be right to the point. All business." He lifted his head. "You should work on that."

"Your criticism is noted." And probably valid. But Gabe could practice his conversation skills after Flash had told him what was on his mind. "Don't change the subject."

Flash let out a disgusted noise and made a face at him. Then he heaved himself half upright, with his right leg out straight on the couch and his back braced against the armrest. Some of the color drained from his face, but he didn't flinch. "I'm going to miss the rest of the regular season."

Despite the fact that he'd seen this coming, Gabe felt a cold knot of dread form in his stomach. "Yeah, I figured." Hip surgery was a big deal.

"It'll be playoffs by the time I'm back. And I'm not getting any younger." That *did* make him grimace, and Gabe's heart twinged in sympathy. "It might be an if, not a when."

"Don't talk like that." Jeez, was he trying to jinx himself?

"Gabe." Another long sigh, and then he switched languages. "I am doing this all wrong. Maybe we try it in English."

That usually meant he thought Gabe's French wasn't up to the task. Maybe Gabe had been missing some nuance. But he didn't think Flash had been particularly subtle—*I'm having surgery and won't be back until April* was pretty straightforward.

Then Flash said, "Baller is good to you, yes?" and suddenly Gabe was glad he hadn't stopped in the kitchen for a drink.

"Uh," he stuttered. That couldn't be what it sounded like. "I think you mean 'good for me'? Like, the way he makes all his friends loosen up and have a good time?"

Flash snorted. "Oh, I am sure you have a good time. And he is good for you. But I meant what I said." He paused. "I said what I meant? Both. He's good to you, Gabe. He dotes on you. It's very sweet."

Suddenly Gabe was on the edge of panic. He cleared his throat, wondering if he should try to convince Flash there was nothing going on. His heart beat too fast in his throat. "What makes you think…?"

"Gabe. Baller thinks you hung the moon. He looks at you with his heart on his face."

Gabe didn't have time to correct the idiom—or die of embarrassment—because Flash went on.

"You took him to Disneyland for your first date. You are together all the time. You have a cat together."

Fuck. "It's Dante's cat," Gabe protested weakly.

Flash shot him an unimpressed look. "Oh, *Dante's* cat. Who lives at your house. *It's your cat*, Gabe!" He paused and frowned. "*Votre* chat." Emphasizing *you*, *plural*. "You're good together. Anyone can see it. I'm happy for you."

Okay, he wasn't upset about Gabe dating a teammate, but—"*Anyone*?" Gabe croaked.

"This is what you focus on?" Flash rolled his eyes. "Anyone who knows you, yes. All of a sudden you are smiling and sociable. You are much less grumpy when you are getting laid. We are happy for you. You are letting people know you. This is a good thing!"

Finally Gabe's heart stopped trying to claw its way out of his mouth. So they hadn't been as under-the-radar as he thought. Flash knew. That was fine. He was probably overestimating how many other guys on the team had figured it out, and he wasn't the type to gossip—at least not about Gabe.

Gabe took a deep breath and let it out slowly. "All right. Uh. Thanks."

Flash waved him off. It seemed that Gabe's relationship status was not the point of this meeting. "It's important, this growth you are doing. You are spending more time with the team. Yorkie says you invited him for dinner."

Which Dante was going to cook. Yes, Gabe could see how they'd been less subtle than he thought. "Um. Yeah."

"Good. I haven't been able to help him as much as I should. I'm grateful you were able to step up." Flash switched back to French now. "I've had extra physio for my hip. And I have four kids now"—despite his obvious discomfort, his face lit up at this, because the man adored his children—"and we are on the road a lot as it is. I don't want to miss seeing them grow up."

Had Gabe let his guard down at the wrong moment? This conversation seemed headed down a dark road. He swallowed. "What are you saying?"

"I'm stepping down as captain."

No. "What?" It could be worse. With an injury like this one, he could be looking at retirement, voluntary or not. But Flash had been a constant on the team since Gabe arrived. He'd gotten used to Flash being their leader. Knowing that he had an ally in the captain had made him feel as safe as a closeted gay man could feel in a professional sport.

"It's time," Flash said. "Everything changes. That's life. But this will be a good change."

Gabe had never met a change he liked. He crossed his arms, realized that made him look angry, which wasn't fair, uncrossed them again, and squirmed back in the chair. "Who's even going to replace you?" As if anyone could.

Flash gave him a grown-up version of that proud father look. "You are."

Gabe's mouth dropped open. "What?" he said again. "No. I'm not—I couldn't—"

"You can," Flash interrupted. "You're already doing the work. You put in time with Baller earlier this year getting him ready. You spend time with the rookies, making them feel included, helping them with the transition to the pros. You even made up with Kitty, and no one would have blamed you if you'd never spoken to him again."

"But...." Gabe floundered for another excuse. He never imagined being made captain. If he set modesty aside, he could admit he was one of the best players in the game right now. He'd always been good at hockey.

But he hadn't always been good at people. He'd been too afraid to let his teammates get close. But now... he *did* enjoy spending time with his team outside the arena. He'd gotten to know the guys as individuals and not coworkers. He liked them. Too much socialization still wore him out, but he'd started to get bored if left to his own devices too long.

Flash waited patiently for Gabe to work through all this in his head, and then said, "You are ready, Gabe."

He swallowed, his stomach still in knots. What if Flash was wrong or—worse—what if he was right? "They're not gonna make me the first openly gay captain in the league. That just... that screams publicity stunt."

"Oh, yes, no team has ever made their top scorer captain before."

Gabe felt that level of sarcasm was uncalled for. "What about Dante?" That, at least, felt like a more valid objection. He didn't want to tell front office they were dating. "I would be...." How did he say it in French? He switched to English. "Dating someone while in a position of authority."

Another eye roll. "Don't ask me to validate your kinks."

Gabe let out a sound of pure frustration and buried his face in his hands. "Did the meds they gave you make you extra sassy?"

Flash gave a groaning sigh. "No, but the painkillers are wearing off." He leveraged himself into a more upright position. "As someone who has lived and worked with the man, I can tell you Dante Baltierra is going to continue to do exactly what he wants. Which, currently, is you."

Gabe wasn't touching that.

"And you care too much about winning to let your feelings influence how you run the team."

Gabe couldn't object to that either.

"So it'll be fine," Flash concluded. "Congratulations. Stop making this harder for me and say yes. Coach already picked you. It's a done deal."

Finally, through uncooperative lips, Gabe managed to say, "Okay."

Flash beamed. "Okay. I'd hug you, but I can't get up. So you can just, you know. Have Baller do it for me. No groping, though."

Just what had Gabe gotten himself into? He managed a weak smile. "No promises."

DANTE DIDN'T sleep well the night after the game. Who would, after a game like that? On top of replaying every mistake he'd made, he was worried about Flash and what his injury might mean for the team. He woke up late, still groggy, and poured himself an enormous cup of coffee, hoping it would wake him up.

A lot was riding on how they performed the next couple of weeks. A poor performance and they'd miss playoffs. A middling performance that barely got them in would mean they could expect a first-round exit— sort of the worst-case scenario, since it meant a lower-round draft pick as well as disappointment.

But the way to prevent that first-round exit was to trade for replacement players. Flash was injured and couldn't be traded. A handful of other players had no-movement clauses that meant they'd have to approve any new team they went to. Everyone else was fair game… including Dante.

The Dekes probably wouldn't trade him. He was worth more to them than he cost. But there weren't any guarantees.

By the time he finished his coffee, he seriously needed breakfast and he had a text from Gabe. *Come over? It's important.*

He could get breakfast on the way. Or, well, more like lunch.

At this point they were beyond the stage of Dante ringing the doorbell, so he let himself in, took a few steps, remembered his shoes, and backtracked to put them on the mat.

"Gabe?"

He didn't get an answer, but he could hear a television, so he followed the sound into the den. Mario was body-slamming his scratching post while Gabe watched game tape.

The man needed to learn how to unplug. "Knock, knock." Dante threw himself onto the couch next to Gabe and paused the replay. "Reporting for duty as requested." Oh God, he was watching the video from the Chicago game. "Why are we punishing ourselves with this when we know we're going to have to watch it at practice tomorrow?"

Gabe took the remote and turned the TV off. Then he scrubbed his hands over his face, shoulders hunched. "Maybe I shouldn't tell you this." He sighed. "But you're going to find out tomorrow anyway."

Dante's stomach did a flip. That didn't sound good.

"Flash is out for the season. Maybe longer." He ran a hand back through already riotous curls and finally met Dante's eyes. "He's stepping down as captain. There's going to be a press conference tomorrow after practice."

"Oh shit." No wonder Gabe had been reviewing this game—he was probably trying to figure out how they were going to manage without their captain on a regular basis. "That sucks."

But from the expression on Gabe's face, that wasn't the whole story.

"You know who the next captain's going to be," Dante guessed.

Gabe lifted his head, gave a mockery of a smile, and halfheartedly spread his arms. "Ta-da."

Oh *wow*. "Seriously?" Did that sound too incredulous? "Gabe, that's—that's amazing. Uh." Now that was too enthusiastic. "I mean. It sucks for Flash, obviously." He'd said that already.

Gabe's smile twitched a little farther toward genuine. "He says he wants to spend more time with his kids anyway."

"They *are* adorable." Dante pulled his feet up on the couch and sat cross-legged—basically an invitation for Mario to climb up in his lap, which he did, purring like mad. Dante scratched him between the ears. "They're practically a vacation after managing a whole hockey team."

Gabe snorted and bumped Dante's elbow as he reached out to pet Mario too. "I don't think I'll tell him you said that."

"Yeah, I don't mind babysitting, but I wouldn't call it a relaxing pastime." Mario purred manically, batted at Gabe's hand, and flopped over on his side.

"It's a trap," Gabe warned.

"I know." Dante petted the cat's belly anyway. He got in four strokes of the ultrasoft fur before Mario tried to murder his fingers. "We should go on vacation."

Gabe lifted his head and looked at him, bemused. "We can't."

"In the off-season," Dante said with a roll of his eyes. "Somewhere with a swim-up bar where they put the pink umbrellas in the drinks. You can wear a tiny little Speedo and slather me with sunscreen. It'll be hot." Literally and figuratively. Nice weather, cold drinks, and no pressure—they could just relax together.

"Why am I the cabana boy in this scenario?"

Dante patted his knee. "Don't worry. We can take turns." He used his index finger to pet under Mario's chin. "Seriously, though. It's been a stressful season and it's not even over yet. We should go away together. It'll be fun." Now he was getting really into the idea. What better way to cement their relationship? He'd never been on a vacation like that with a partner. It sounded awesome.

"Kind of hard to plan a trip when you don't know when you're going to be done work," Gabe argued. "I don't want to jinx it."

"Dude, unless something goes very wrong, we're not gonna have playoffs in July. I think we're safe." Unless Gabe meant he didn't think they'd still be together in July? Which Dante guessed was possible, but like, he wasn't talking about renting a superyacht. They could afford to take the L on a resort vacation. Especially once he got his first big-boy contract.

"I guess." Gabe didn't sound too enthused by the idea, but he was probably preoccupied. Dante decided to let it go for now. They could talk about it when Gabe wasn't using up all his brain cells trying to figure out how to be the best hockey captain ever.

After one last chuck under Mario's chin, Dante extricated the cat from his lap and stood. "Put a pin in that thought for now."

Blinking, Gabe looked up at him. He raised his eyebrows.

"You're just going to sit here stewing about the press conference tomorrow and what people are going to say about a gay man being captain of a hockey team." Dante held out his hand. Gabe took it, and Dante pulled him to his feet.

"Maybe," Gabe said, rueful. "What are you going to do about it?"

Dante leaned in slowly until their mouths almost touched and the sides of their noses brushed. "Come upstairs and find out."

Fillion Out Indefinitely; Martin Named Captain
By Kevin McIntyre

GM Brigitte Ballard and Head Coach Hayley St. Louis announced at a press conference today that with Jacques Fillion expected to miss the remainder of the season after hip surgery, the team has named right wing Gabriel Martin captain.

Despite a rocky start to the season, Martin has rebounded and averaged better than a point per game over the past two months.

With this announcement, Martin becomes the NHL's first openly gay team captain.

The Nordiques play tomorrow night in Ottawa.

GABE'S FIRST match as captain was an away game in Ottawa. If he couldn't have a home crowd, having his dad in the audience was the next best thing.

Even if it did mean Trish had a camera crew film it for their social media.

"I am so proud of you," his dad whispered fiercely as he pulled him into a tight hug.

Gabe just swallowed hard and hugged him back.

Then he took a deep breath, turned around, and took the jersey Trish was holding out. It was only fitting that his dad get to be the first person to see him wearing the letter.

His dad patted the brand-new C on Gabe's chest and looked up at him. "It's a good day."

Fuck it. He better not start crying.

Gabe cleared his throat. "I wouldn't be here without you."

There was some manly back-patting, and for the next few seconds, nobody looked at a camera.

If it was fitting for his dad to be the first person to see him in the captain's jersey, it was probably equally right that Dante was next, after the camera crew. Gabe was on his way back to the locker room when Dante intercepted him and directed him into a trainer's room.

"Dante." Gabe appreciated the heat in his eyes, but this wasn't really the place.

"Shhh," Dante said. "I know. I just wanted to...." Unlike Gabe's father, he ran *both* hands over Gabe's chest. The sensation it evoked was decidedly different. Gabe couldn't actually feel the heat from Dante's palms through all his gear, but you wouldn't know it from his body's reaction.

He let Dante give him one brief, hard kiss—maybe even reeled him in by the waist, a little bit—and then broke away. "Okay. You leave first."

Dante mock-shivered. "Ooh. Maybe I'll develop an authority kink."

God help them both. Gabe groaned and gestured to the door. "Out!"

With Flash out, Gabe and Dante needed a center. At first Gabe worried Coach might move him off the wing and make him do it—he *could*, it just didn't come naturally—but she said he had enough change to be dealing with at the moment. They would rotate in centers from other lines and see if any of them fit first.

Tonight that meant Yorkie was their starting center.

Since defensive responsibility was Yorkie's main weakness, Coach had changed up the way the defense rotated so Kitty and Bricks, their strongest D pairing, would usually be on the ice with them.

That's more change to deal with, Gabe had thought when she told him, but it seemed like a reasonable plan. He was even looking forward to the experiment, in a way.

Right up until they set up for the puck drop and the Tartans player opposite him, number 27, leaned forward and said, "Whose dick did you have to suck to convince them to make you captain?"

Gabe froze for a second in complete shock, but recovered just in time to collect Yorkie's pass and take off down the ice.

Gabe believed the best way to deal with homophobes was to play better hockey than them. Naively, he hoped that would be it. The guy'd gotten it out, it hadn't affected Gabe's play, now hopefully he'd move on to another tactic and they could be done with this one.

They weren't done.

"You letting them all fuck you?" the guy asked after pushing Gabe up against the boards to try to get the puck Gabe was sheltering between his skates.

Gabe butt-ended him, got away with it, and got a clean pass off to Yorkie to boot.

"Or are you screwing Baltierra?" he asked while they waited for another faceoff.

Maybe Gabe should just drop the gloves and fight the guy. It was his first game as captain, and it would really set the tone. But his team would pay for it when he ended up in the box. That wasn't how a captain should behave. He needed to lead by example.

Then 27 skated up close during a stoppage to whisper low while everyone was distracted trying to retrieve the puck that had gotten stuck in Olie's pants. "It's disgusting they let you in the locker room. You watching your teammates naked?"

Gabe kept ignoring him, but the idiot was obviously looking for a weak point.

He found it in the second period. The game was still scoreless. Despite himself, Gabe was starting to feel hunted. He just wanted to play hockey, but no matter what he tried, he couldn't shake this asshat. He and Gabe were scrambling for the puck in the corner when he said, "I hope all the parents are complaining about your management letting you sign autographs for kids. Disgusting kiddy—"

Gabe punched him in the face, still wearing his gloves.

His new enemy sneered in triumph. "You punch like a girl."

Gabe punched him again, this time with his gloves off.

The ref and a linesman pulled Gabe off him, Gabe still trembling with anger.

"Five for fighting." The ref pointed him toward the box. They had less than that left on the clock, so Gabe headed straight for the locker room.

Once there, he tore off his helmet and tossed it aside as he sat heavily on the bench. His shoulders slumped, and he pressed the heels of his palms to his eyes. He was not going to fucking cry just because some dickbag thought it was okay to accuse him of being—

He swallowed hard, then took several deep breaths.

Worst of all was the burn of shame and disappointment. He never should have risen to the bait. Letting the guy know Gabe was rattled was just plain dumb.

And on his first game as captain, no less.

He sat on the bench and silently berated himself for taking such a stupid penalty while the PK ran down on the ice. They'd be starting the third period with a penalty too. Gabe hoped he hadn't done too much damage to the score of an already close game.

When his team filed into the room, they were *loud*.

"Fucking asshole!" Kitty yelled. For one startled second Gabe thought Kitty was talking to him. Then he continued, looking murderous, "I'm punch him myself next."

Gabe's stomach twisted. "You heard him?"

Kitty gave a sour smile. "Good hearing. Too bad for him, he not know what hit him next period. To say you hurt *kids*—?"

"He *what*?" Dante snarled, red-faced.

The locker room erupted in cursing.

Fuck. Gabe needed to get them under control. What would Flash do here?

Probably his dumb whistle. God, was Gabe going to need to learn to make that noise? "Hey!" he shouted. "Hey! Everybody shut up!"

At least they were all fired up now. Maybe he could direct that.

Miraculously, the room quieted… and in that moment, Gabe realized the team really did have his back. Even when he lost his cool and gotten slapped with a five-minute major.

"I'm touched that you're all ready to defend my honor," he said. Several of the guys nodded. "I'll have a word with the linesmen and see if they can keep an ear out, because he *will* get suspended if one of them overhears. Actually—" He glanced over his shoulder to see Coach standing in the doorway. "Can we get me mic'd up?"

She nodded to one of the trainers, who went off to find the equipment.

Gabe turned back to the team. "In the meantime, I'd rather win the game than a fight, so aim your anger at their net."

Coach took over from there to talk strategy, but Dante leaned in close to Gabe's elbow. "Good speech."

Gabe glanced over his shoulder at him. "Yeah?"

Dante nudged him, smiling proudly. "Yeah."

But apparently Dante didn't take the message to heart, because the first chance he got to lay body on the guy, he lowered his shoulder, leaned into the hit, and dropped 27 like a sack of potatoes.

The refs called Dante for boarding. He went to the box with a satisfied smirk.

Gabe sighed. They were supposed to be trying to win the game, not giving their opponents power play chances.

Ottawa capitalized on the penalty with a goal in the first thirty seconds, which left Gabe steaming. "This is exactly what I didn't want to happen," he said when Dante was released from the penalty box.

Dante's mouth set in an unhappy line. "What, so it's 'do as I say, not as I do'?"

That wasn't fair, Gabe thought—the guy had been talking about Gabe, not him. But before he could say so out loud, a voice in the back of his head piped up that yeah, the guy would've said the same thing about Dante—he just didn't know Dante fucked men too.

For Gabe, that would've made it easier to ignore. For Dante, it would've been the opposite.

"Fuck it," Gabe said. "Let's just get one back, okay?"

And they did, on their next shift. Dante shouldered a Tartan off the puck in the neutral zone and passed it to Yorkie, who got the puck into Ottawa's end. Gabe could see how it would play out, and he skated for the far side of the net while the defenders set up to protect their goal.

Yorkie drop-passed for Dante, who came in hot behind him, with Yorkie screening him from the goaltender. Somehow the goalie made the save—but Gabe was whipping around the back of the net, and he poked the rebound just over the tip of the goalie's skate.

Damn.

"Nice play!" Gabe shouted to Yorkie, who went pink at the praise. But it was deserved—Gabe didn't know a lot of rookies who could have pulled that off.

"Nice garbage goal," Dante said, a little coolly, like he was mad Gabe had yelled at him for taking a completely unnecessary penalty.

Gabe was still annoyed, but he didn't have a leg to stand on since he'd punched the guy in his ugly face, so he just said, "I'm used to picking up your trash," and grinned when Dante laughed.

Number 27 kept his mouth shut for the remainder of the period. Gabe was pretty sure his own captain had had a word with him. And the Dekes played a tight game after that, not giving up a penalty and keeping good control of the puck. But for all their work, it looked like the game would go to overtime.

With under two minutes on the clock, Dante robbed one of the Tartans of the puck and saucered it past two defensemen to land right on Gabe's tape. He didn't have a lane clear to the net, so he took the puck around behind, looking for an opening.

When he spotted the Dekes' colors in front of the net, he passed without thinking. Yorkie put a wrister through the goalie's legs and the goal light went off.

Gabe crashed into Yorkie in celebration. This could work—*they* could work. Maybe Yorkie wasn't Flash, but he was young and fast and a quick learner. Gabe could adapt.

Dante joined the huddle a split second later and clapped Yorkie on the bucket like he was ruffling his hair. Kitty and Bricks brought up the rear.

"Best team," Kitty said, knocking his visor against Yorkie's.

The three of them watched the last seconds of the game tick by from the bench. Even after Ottawa pulled their goalie, the Dekes' defense held firm. When the buzzer sounded, the whole bench let out a collective sigh of relief, and Gabe whooped and jammed his shoulder pads into Yorkie's. "Think they'll give you first star?"

"I...." And then Yorkie burst into tears.

Hoo boy. So maybe this couldn't wait until their dinner.

GABE GOT through the media interviews by repeating praise of his teammates and the standard boilerplate about his captaincy that Trish had drilled into him—it was an honor, he'd do what he could to live up to it, he wanted Flash back as much as the next guy. Then he had to add that no, he didn't know anything about number 27 getting a disciplinary hearing, and he had no comment on anything that might have been said on the ice.

It wasn't like he could say, *That asshole should be thrown out of the league.*

By the time he got to the locker room, Dante was out of the shower and Yorkie had composed himself. Nobody was talking to him, so Gabe had to wonder if anyone else had even noticed his breakdown in their excitement over the win.

But maybe it was better if nobody *had* noticed. It gave Gabe an opportunity to sneak in without Yorkie getting suspicious. He detoured past Dante on his way to the showers. "Get him back to the hotel and convince him to order room service, yeah?"

Dante flicked his gaze up to meet Gabe's, then over at Yorkie, who was smiling as Kitty and Bricks reenacted Dante's hit on 27. "Yeah."

Relieved that the press hadn't held him back too much, Gabe followed the rest of the team back to the hotel and headed for Dante and Yorkie's room.

When Dante opened the door, Gabe walked in to find Yorkie sitting cross-legged on his bed, wearing sweats and worrying at the sleeve of his hoodie.

"You guys order food?"

Dante nodded. "Yeah, should be here any minute. I ordered you fish and a bulgur salad."

"Awesome, thanks." Gabe plopped down into the armchair the hotel had placed between the double beds. "So, what's up?"

Dante shrugged. "Yorkie and I were just talking about how awesome we are."

Gabe rolled his eyes at the statement, but he smiled at Yorkie. "Well, we were pretty great tonight. Good recovery from the last game. And I appreciate getting a regulation win on my first game as captain, so thanks for that."

Yorkie gave a halfway decent smile. "Thanks. Playing with you is fun."

"You too, kid."

"Geez," Dante grumbled. "What, no love for me?"

So needy, Gabe thought with an internal smile. Of course Gabe—

Oh.

For a second his brain froze up in total panic. Then muscle memory kicked in and the instinctive retort came out. "Screw you, like your ego needs it."

Gabe could deal with his personal shit later. Tonight was for Yorkie.

Someone knocked at the door, and Dante answered for room service. "Come and get it, boys."

For several minutes, eating monopolized their attention. Figuring Yorkie needed the calorie boost, Gabe refrained from asking any questions until after their plates were clean.

And then, steeling himself, he finally put the words together in no uncertain terms. "So, look. We've tried the subtle approach. We've tried just being there for you. But you're not taking the hint to talk about it. It's affecting you on and off the ice. What's going on?"

Gabe had gone through his mental checklist of possibilities. There was homesickness, or a sickness or death in the family. Then he considered anxiety, depression, or some kind of physical ailment. He didn't think it was a substance abuse issue—Yorkie wasn't showing any of the signs of that—but you never knew.

Whatever it was, they could deal with it. Someone on the team would have experience, or know someone who did, and they could get the rookie through it—with Gabe's support, obviously.

Yorkie pushed the remnants of his spaghetti Bolognese around with his fork. "I don't know—"

"Don't even front," Dante said. "This has been going on since before Christmas."

Yorkie made a face and put his fork down.

"We don't want to push," Gabe said. A total lie. If Yorkie had a breakdown on the ice, they were fucked. Gabe would push as hard as he needed to. "But maybe if you get it off your chest—"

"Jenna's pregnant."

Gabe stared at his rookie, feeling decidedly off-balance.

Impending fatherhood had not been on his list. He had no idea what to say. His first impulse was to ask *Are you sure it's yours?* but he was pretty sure that was an asshole move for multiple reasons.

Fortunately Dante had never met a silence he couldn't fill. "Shit, man. That—fuck, that blows? I mean, not because babies aren't a good thing, but who the fuck knows what to do with one at nineteen."

Thank you, Gabe mouthed at him.

Yorkie nodded. "I know. Not that…. Jenna doesn't know what she wants to do. She's still got time to, you know. End it." He looked down. "I know it's her choice and all, but I don't think I want her to. I don't think *she* wants to. And that makes me even more scared, because what do we know about babies? And my mom"—his voice broke—"is going to be so mad." He smeared a hand over his face.

For the second time that day, Gabe participated in the manly ritual of pretending no one in the room was crying. They ought to give him honorary membership into the heterosexuality club.

"Okay." He rallied his scattered thoughts. "Okay, let's think about this." He grabbed the hotel notepad and pen from the bedside table. "What are the main problems, if Jenna decides to have the baby?"

Yorkie blinked red-rimmed eyes at him. Dante cleared his throat and passed him the box of Kleenex, pointedly not looking at his face.

God, they were all disasters. Poor Yorkie. At least Flash had experience with what to do with a kid.

Yorkie took a Kleenex and wiped his eyes, then blew his nose loudly. "Uh. Well, she lives in the dorm. So she'll have to move, because you can't have a baby in the dorm. And nobody our age is going to want to live with a kid."

Gabe wrote *housing*.

"And she's still in school. She's not going to be able to play hockey when she's, you know." He held his hands out in front of his stomach. "So, so, is she going to lose her scholarship?"

School, Gabe wrote. *Tuition*.

"And then! Neither of us knows what to do with a kid, and who'll take care of the baby while she's at class? I don't want her to drop out because of this, but I can't take care of it either when we're gone all the time and I don't even live in the same city."

Child care. And, after a moment, *guilt*.

"And there's my parents. My mom's going to kill me. She'll think I didn't pay attention in sex ed. But I did! We use condoms *and* she's on the pill."

For a second Gabe was sure Dante was going to make a joke about slipping one past the goalie, but he restrained himself.

Gabe wrote *parents' expectations*. "Is that it?" he asked. Then he realized that sounded like he didn't think that was a lot, which wasn't the case. It would've been a lot for a full adult to handle. Yorkie was barely done shopping for his *own* clothes in the juniors department. "I mean, those are the big ones, right?"

Yorkie nodded… and looked at him as if he was waiting for Gabe to hand him the answers.

Gabe did not have any answers, but he did have a lot of experience bullshitting to the media. "Look, Yorkie—Tom—I know it's her choice, but the best thing to do would be to stay honest about what you want. Wasn't Jenna supposed to come to the game tonight?"

Another nod. "Yeah, but she, uh, she was getting some morning sickness. I guess it's not, like, strictly a morning thing. So she stayed home."

"Okay," he said for what felt like the hundredth time. But a plan was starting to come together. "I know it's kind of late, but do you think she's still awake? Would she come talk with us if we sent a car?"

"Uh," Dante interjected. "Just to clarify—we don't want her to feel, like, ganged up on. This would be a support-only talk."

Good thing Gabe had him around to interpret Gabe to English. "Yeah—solely offering resources and options. I can see if Bricks is still awake. He's our union rep. He'll know if Jenna's entitled to anything as your life partner, even though you're not living together."

Now Yorkie was looking at him like Gabe had actually *given* him answers, or at least the hope that he might get some.

"My dad lives here in Ottawa. He probably knows someone who can recommend a nanny," he continued.

Anything to prolong that relief he could feel pouring off the rookie.

Yorkie sagged, nodding. "Yeah. Yeah, a nanny, that's... we probably need one of those, huh?" He shook his head and picked his phone up from the bed, presumably to text Jenna. "Like, live-in help would be awesome. Except first, Jenna needs to find a place to live."

Actually.... "I can help with that. I—" Gabe stood, dug his hand into the pocket of his jeans, and pulled out his keys.

Yorkie said, "What?"

"I have a condo in Ottawa," Gabe said. "I stay there in the summers sometimes when, uh...."

When he was visiting his dad and he wanted to entertain company.

Dante put a hand over his face, obviously having put two and two together.

Gabe coughed. "Anyway." He separated the key from the others. "It's two bedroom, two bath. Maybe not ideal for a live-in nanny situation, but...." *I'm probably not going to be using it this summer anyway.*

He needed to stop having these revelations during a crisis conversation with his rookie.

"Wow," Dante said. "Giving him the keys to your bang pad."

"Oh my God," Yorkie said in mortification.

Gabe was right there with him, but he pushed through it. "There's a covered parking spot, and it's walking distance to the university."

Yorkie looked like he was going to cry again.

Shit. "Just—you've got friends who'll support you. You've got a team of guys who will help however they can, and a lot of WAG mothers who will be there with advice. You won't be alone. No matter *what* you and your girlfriend decide." Gabe tapped his foot against Yorkie's.

Yorkie gave him a watery smile.

Great. So that was Yorkie's concerns dealt with, or at least as much as they could do in one night when Jenna hadn't arrived yet.

Now for the other side of the problem. "Have you talked to Trish? From PR? Because I didn't, okay, and that was a mistake."

Yorkie looked like he might throw up. "Oh God. I have to tell front office, don't I?"

Gabe waved his hand, hoping he could play this off like it was no big deal. "They call it controlling the narrative or something. Basically, she'll help you work out a plan of what you want to say if the media gets ahold of the story before you're ready to go public, give you advice on when to break the story if it doesn't happen on its own. I didn't tell her I was gay, and I ended up looking like a closeted asshole instead of, I don't know, a guy who likes privacy."

"Yeah, but you are a closeted asshole. Well, you were. Now you're an out asshole." Yorkie wiped his face with his sleeve—the Kleenex box was *right there*—proving that he really was an actual baby. Oh God, he was going to be a dad. This was a train wreck.

"And you're a nineteen-year-old professional athlete who knocked up his girlfriend. But with Trish's help, maybe you're just a couple who's stupidly in love and about to welcome a baby." Gabe paused as something horrible occurred to him. "You do love her, right?"

Off a shaky sigh, Yorkie nodded. "It'd be easier if I didn't."

Gabe wouldn't know about that.

Dante piped up with more good advice. "You should call your agent too. He and Trish can, like, figure out a strategy together."

Yorkie looked like he'd rather take a slapshot to the nuts, which Gabe could relate to. "In the meantime, I think this merits a night off from the nutrition plan."

Dante met his eyes and quirked half a smile. "Ice cream?" he asked hopefully.

"Maybe a little variety," Gabe said, remembering they were going to have company. "I'll call room service back." After all, it would only be polite to have food for Jenna.

And maybe he could introduce them both to his dad. At least then they'd have some support in the area.

Later that night, when Yorkie and Jenna obviously couldn't take any more helpful advice, Gabe said, "Uh… why don't we leave you two alone?" He glanced at Dante, hoping he was coming across as casual in front of their audience. "You could crash with me."

If Yorkie or Jenna thought this was an odd offer, they didn't so much as look at him. They were sitting on Yorkie's bed, bodies angled toward each other, deep in quiet conversation.

Dante quirked a wry smile. "I'll get my stuff."

It was late enough that they were just going to brush their teeth and sleep. That in itself was new and strange and a little bit wonderful for Gabe, who'd never been in a relationship with anyone long enough to make a habit of sleeping in the same bed without having sex first.

Now he understood what he'd missed out on. Jenna and Yorkie were basically kids, and they knew more about supporting each other as a couple than Gabe did.

Sure, they were in for some rocky times, but they *wanted* to be together long-term. At their age, Gabe couldn't even have imagined having that.

He could barely imagine having it at twenty-eight.

"What're you thinking about?" Dante asked, turning his head toward Gabe's on the pillow.

Gabe shook his head, and that hazy, indistinct vision of a possible future vanished. "Nothing," he said quietly. "Just too tired to think."

Then he reached up and turned off the light.

FOR ALL his hesitation about the job, Gabe took to being captain like a pro video gamer doing a speed run.

No surprise there, at least not for Dante—Gabe liked being in charge. Part of him wondered if all these years he'd been chafing under someone else's leadership, half convinced Flash was doing it wrong. But that felt mean; Gabe and Flash had always been close, and Flash was a good captain.

Flash being a good captain didn't make Dante feel all warm and fuzzy inside, though.

They had a few days before their next home game, so Gabe, Yorkie, and Trish skipped the chartered flight back to Quebec City. Nobody asked Dante, but Dante had never been the wait-for-an-invitation kind. He'd make it back in time one way or another. Right now being there for his roommate—and his boyfriend—was more important.

His decision had nothing at all to do with the fact that they'd decided to hold their meeting at Gabe's dad's house instead of the hotel, for privacy and comfort's sake.

Or at least that was what he was telling people if anyone asked.

Dante had met Chris Martin a handful of times over the years. He came to a lot of games and had come on last year's fathers' trip. He was a kind man with a kind face and the same bright blue eyes as Gabe, except with laugh lines. His blond hair was shot through with gray, and he had kind of a dad-bod thing going on. Dante wasn't going to tell Gabe his dad was hot, like, to his face—he was saving that revelation for a special occasion—but that didn't make it untrue.

"Wow," Chris said when he opened the door to the Dekes contingent on his porch. "The gang's all here, eh?" He stepped back and let everyone inside. "Come on in. Tom, is it? I'm Chris."

There were handshakes and introductions all around, with Dante hanging back. When it was his turn, Chris looked at him, tilted his head, and smiled slightly. "Dante. Good to see you again."

They shook hands.

"You too." Despite his Southern upbringing, Dante managed to avoid tacking on a *sir*. That would look suspicious.

"I didn't realize you were involved in this situation."

Dante panicked. Oh God, with his reputation, Chris probably thought he'd had a threesome with Yorkie and Jenna and was potentially the father or something. "Uh, I'm not. Just… moral support, you know?"

Maybe he'd protested too much—now Chris looked like he was going to laugh. "Well, they're lucky to have you. Come on in."

Miraculously, Dante remembered to take off his shoes without prompting.

As he'd expected, he was pretty much useless in terms of input, but it wasn't really that kind of meeting. First Jenna and Yorkie went upstairs into a bedroom to make the call and let their parents in on what was happening. Now that they had a plan, including somewhere to live, he guessed the idea of telling their families was less daunting.

Speaking of a place to live, Dante was carefully not examining his feelings about Gabe having a secret apartment to fuck men in, because it seemed sordid. Gabe didn't treat casual sex the way Dante did—something to be celebrated and enjoyed. He didn't have any hang-ups in the bedroom—not as far as Dante could tell—but he still felt like he had to hide that he had sex at all. Sure, no one wanted to bring home company for the night and risk being observed by their parent, but this didn't feel like that.

Dante hated that Gabe owned real estate because he felt like he had to hide who he was. It would've been different if he lived there in the summers, but he'd as good as said he didn't.

"Dante?"

Shit. He'd spaced out sitting on the couch with Trish. Gabe and his dad were in the kitchen, getting drinks. "Sorry, just… thinking."

She raised an eyebrow. "You're not going to tell me you've got the same problem as Yorkie, are you?"

Double shit. He cleared his throat. "Well, not the *same* problem." Unfortunately, Gabe's advice to Yorkie—that not talking to Trish was a mistake—kept ringing in Dante's head. He knew that advice should apply to him too. Even if Dante put off his coming out, he should have a contingency plan in place. That was only smart.

Now her eyes went wide and she looked toward the kitchen.

Fuuuuuuck. Dante needed to divert her before she jumped to the correct conclusion. Gabe wouldn't be happy if he outed them to her. "Uh, maybe we can talk sometime this week?" He didn't have to tell her what was going on with Gabe, but at the very least he wanted a sounding board to make a plan for his own coming out.

"I'll check my schedule," she said faintly.

Fantastic.

Before the situation could deteriorate, Yorkie and Jenna returned, Gabe and Chris came in with the drinks, and the focus shifted to the other crisis. Dante sat back and watched Trish do her thing, with Gabe providing the veteran-hockey-support angle.

Maybe he should've just gone back to Quebec City. He was not needed here.

He hated warming the bench.

Then, while Yorkie and Trish were going over the third draft of the statement, Chris turned to him and said, "You want to help me make some lunch?"

Dante could've kissed him. "Yeah, sure."

Chris's kitchen was half the size of Gabe's and three times as functional, and featured not one single ugly tile. Dante set to work putting together sandwiches on fresh rolls that must've been bought that morning, while Chris diced vegetables and slid them into an enormous pot.

"What're we making?" Dante reached for the butter.

"I figured you can't go wrong with chicken soup." He smiled ruefully. "Seemed like a good day for it."

Dante couldn't disagree. The wind outside was howling. He hoped they made it home before the snowstorm hit. "So how come you can cook but Gabe burns water?"

He laughed. "That's a two-part answer. One, I worked as a sous chef when I was an undergrad." He added the carrots and celery to the pot. "Two, I think when Gabe's mom left.... Ah, I don't know. I spoiled him. Making food is my love language, I guess. I was focused on that and not making sure he could fend for himself in the kitchen."

Dante smiled. That was sweet. "My parents are the same way. My grandmother taught me to cook."

Fuck. Time to steer away from that topic. He grabbed the mayonnaise.

"Oh—don't put any—"

"No mayo on Gabe's sandwich," Dante finished. "I know." He had some kind of weird thing about the texture.

Chris cleared his throat. "Seems like you and my son know each other pretty well."

Had making lunch been a carefully laid trap? Or had Dante's mouth just gotten him in trouble again, as usual? "Um, yeah. I mean, we eat dinner as a team a lot, so...."

Which was true, but not what Chris was really asking. And now Dante was squirming like a worm on a hook because he hated lying.

Before he could panic further, Chris snorted. "You can relax. I'm not going to pry. I know what my son's like."

It was official—Dante was going to die of embarrassment. He hadn't even known he could still *get* embarrassed.

"He just seems a lot happier lately, more sure of himself. I guess some of it could be explained by not

being in the closet anymore, but I think he's met someone. I *hope* he's met someone."

Dante wished he could confirm it out loud. Since
he couldn't, he concentrated on the sandwiches. But he
couldn't help a small smile. If Gabe's dad had noticed
that his son was happier... if Dante was responsible for
that, even in some small way.... "He's pretty special,
even if he can't cook."

Chris touched his shoulder, and Dante had to look
up and meet his eyes. His face was soft and warm and
open and welcoming, and his eyes held an uncomfortable depth of emotion. Dante realized Gabe had probably never introduced him to a partner before. And, well,
he still hadn't, but that was sort of a technicality. "Glad
we agree."

DANTE FOLLOWED Gabe home later that day under
the guise of missing his cat, but Gabe wasn't fooled.
While he did spend a few minutes consoling Mario—
he was being well taken care of by Gabe's neighbor,
who sent him daily emails about the kitten's antics—it
was a pretty transparent ploy.

Not that Gabe was going to complain.

"So." Dante stood and draped his arms around
Gabe's neck. "We never got a chance to celebrate your
first game as captain."

The man was insatiable, which Gabe also wasn't
going to complain about. He tucked his hands into Dante's waistband. "No?"

"No." Dante shook his head. "*And* I never got to
express how hot I got watching you fight that asshole."

Gabe's lips tried to twitch into a smile, but he clamped down on it. *He* wasn't proud of himself for it. "I should've held my temper."

"Hmm." Dante walked his fingers down Gabe's chest to his belt buckle. "That guy had it coming."

"What about me?"

Dante laughed, a low, throaty, sexy sound. "You've got it coming too."

Usually Gabe was the one who wanted to slow down and take his time. Tonight Dante seemed determined to squeeze every moment of pleasure out of both of them. He laid Gabe out on his back on the bed and rode him so slowly Gabe could feel the muscles in his thighs trembling with the strain of control.

When that control snapped, Gabe rolled them over, wild with lust and whatever thick emotion filled the air between their bodies. Dante pulled him down for a kiss that was more shared breathlessness than anything, and when Gabe thrust in one more time, Dante clenched around him, shuddered into orgasm with a cry against Gabe's lips, and dragged Gabe over the edge with him.

Afterward Dante stretched in the bed, lazy and sated and smug. In comparison, Gabe felt soft around the edges, as if he didn't quite know where all his limbs were. He was used to being hyperaware of his body—he needed to be, in order to play his best game, but also because he'd always so strictly controlled his mannerisms, sure the wrong set of his hips would give him away.

Now he pillowed his head on his arms and watched Dante sprawl out in his bed like Mario in a sunbeam.

"I don't know if I learned my lesson," Gabe admitted, feeling come-dumb.

Dante grinned and turned toward him, tucking his hand under his face. "That's okay. We can go over it again until you get it."

"I'll let you catch your breath first."

Again, that warm, low laugh. Then Dante reached between them and took Gabe's hand. "I have a confession to make." His accent slipped a little, the way it did sometimes when he was tired or worked up. Gabe had come to love the slurred consonants and drawn-out vowels.

"Oh?" Curious, Gabe let Dante curl their fingers together.

Dante squeezed gently. "I think your dad sussed us out."

Gabe's mouth went a little dry. "What makes you say that?"

"Ah, well, he definitely thought it was weird that I knew you didn't like mayo. He went on a fishing expedition." He shrugged. "I didn't confirm anything, but I wasn't exactly going to deny it. He seemed happy, though."

Gabe took a deep breath and let it out slowly. He could deal with his dad knowing. He probably should've told him by now; his dad had been hinting for a while that he knew something was up. Of course his dad would be fine. "He's been pushing me to start dating 'for real.'"

Dante's brow creased. "Why didn't you tell him? Before now, I mean."

Why hadn't he? "I... don't know. Force of habit, I guess. And maybe I didn't want to admit that he was right."

Dante's forehead smoothed out again; obviously he accepted that answer. "Well, the cat's out of the bag now."

"I guess so." Gabe smiled, hoping to show he wasn't upset. He rubbed his thumb over Dante's knuckles. "I can put up with a couple I-told-you-sos."

"See, that's what I love about you," Dante said, teasing. "You're so easygoing."

Gabe froze, and that fuzzy-edged feeling sharpened. Was that—was Dante—? Did he mean…?

Dante had frozen too, his eyes locked with Gabe's. His cheeks were red, as if his mouth had run away with him, as if he hadn't intended to say those words at all.

But not as if he hadn't meant them.

Gabe's heart thundered. Dante did mean them, and Gabe knew it. If he could be honest with himself, he'd admit that he'd known for a while.

It was his own feelings he hadn't been sure of until this moment.

Love.

But the words wouldn't come out. Gabe was too much of a coward to take Dante's words at more than face value. "That's me," he said with forced lightness. "Captain Casual."

Dante's smile went a little crooked. Gabe was sure Dante knew he'd copped out, but he didn't know how to apologize, so he pulled Dante's hand to his mouth and kissed his knuckles. *Please understand.*

He didn't know why he couldn't answer, but it filled him with shame.

Maybe Dante got it, because the crookedness softened. "All right, Captain. Well, I'm going to go rinse off before I glue my asscheeks together. And then, what do you think? You want to go out for a late dinner? I could eat."

"When can't you?" Come to think of it, Gabe was hungry too. "I've got a couple catered meals in the freezer. We could do dinner and a movie and hang out with Mario." It didn't seem fair to leave the kitten alone again already.

"Perfect romance." Dante crossed the space between them and planted a soft kiss at the corner of Gabe's mouth. "Meet you downstairs."

They fell asleep on the couch in the middle of a Marvel marathon, only for Gabe to wake up to Samuel L. Jackson staring at him judgmentally in the credits, with Mario attacking the arm of the couch next to him.

Ugh. He was stiff. "Hey." He nudged Dante. "C'mon, wake up so we can go to bed." Also so Gabe could regain some sensation in his thigh, since Dante had fallen asleep with his head on Gabe's leg.

They were doing it again, he realized as they crawled under the covers—getting into bed together just to sleep. Because that was what couples did, and they were a couple. Partners. Boyfriends. Whatever you wanted to call it.

Dante loved him.

Dante was already asleep again, breathing those deep, heavy breaths that always made Gabe fall asleep too. But before he did, he found himself back in that soft-edged state, where nothing quite felt real and the borders between *me* and *him* blended together.

"I love you too," Gabe whispered into the darkness.

One day he would be able to say it when Dante could hear him.

THE SNOW fell steadily throughout the night and into the next morning. Word came down early from Coach that practice was canceled; front office didn't want anyone driving in this much snow. That suited Gabe.

He could make do with what was in the freezer. And somehow, he even had a handful of moderately fresh ingredients Dante must've put on the list for his grocery service at some point, and—conveniently—a boyfriend who knew what to do with them.

So he was pretty happy to be spending a lazy day around the house with the cat, even if it started with Gabe cleaning the litterbox while Dante made pancakes.

"I could do it after breakfast," Dante said. He had flour on his nose and he was wearing black boxers and a workout shirt that could have belonged to either of them. Gabe was a little concerned that he wasn't sure who.

"It's fine. I got it." Gabe kissed his cheek and then, smirking, dusted his hand in the flour Dante had spilled on the counter and left a big white palm print on his ass.

"Joke's on you!" Dante laughed after him as Gabe retreated to the laundry room and the cat box. "These are your underwear!"

Gabe had thought they looked familiar. No wonder they were so tight. "Try not to rip these ones!"

"Fuck you!"

Yeah, Gabe definitely wasn't complaining about getting homemade pancakes for breakfast.

He was just washing his hands when the doorbell rang.

Figuring his neighbor probably left something behind when she was looking after Mario—though why she'd want to come out in a storm like this rather than wait for the snow to subside, he couldn't guess—Gabe dried his hands and went to answer the door.

The last person he expected to see was Kitty.

"Uh," he said. "Hi?"

Kitty was wearing a winter jacket along with a scarf and toque, all liberally coated in snow, including on his eyebrows. He didn't look cold, just miserable, and Gabe automatically stepped back to let him in.

Kitty brushed the worst of the snow off before he did, then stood on Gabe's mat, looking baleful. "Hi. Sorry for not call, but I leave my phone in car. Car is in garage. And"—and here he cursed, or so Gabe assumed, because whatever Russian word that was, it didn't sound polite—"builders, they install stupid door wrong so it only opens out. Already too much snow to open door."

Kitty was renting his place from a former player who'd retired and moved back to Sweden. Gabe remembered him complaining about bizarre design choices, but not being able to open the door to the garage due to snow was pretty bad. Gabe probably would've sold the place. "What about the big door?"

Kitty cursed again. "Stupid opener broke again! Have to open manually from inside garage."

Which he couldn't get to because of the snow.

"Right," Gabe said. "Uh, I guess you want to borrow my snowblower?" To get it over there he'd have to clean out his own driveway.

"Da," Kitty said, sagging in relief. "Please."

"Sure," Gabe said. "Let me just—"

And then Dante, whose presence Gabe had completely forgotten about in his surprise at seeing Kitty, yelled from the kitchen, "Hey, Gabe, where do you keep the maple syrup?"

Kitty met Gabe's eyes.

Gabe panicked. "Um."

On cue, Dante emerged from the back of the house. "Breakfast is just about—uh. Hi, Kitty." He flushed.

Kitty looked at Gabe. "I'm hope maple syrup is for breakfast."

Oh my God.

Gabe panicked some more. "We were just, um—"

Kitty took pity on him. "Gabe. I don't care what you um."

"I guess you wouldn't believe me if I said this isn't what it looks like?" Dante said sheepishly.

"*Looks* like maybe you lie to me," Kitty said. "You say, 'Hey Kitty, I am bisexual.' I say 'Hey Dante, is okay, you and Gabe are together?' You tell me no." He gestured. "This doesn't look like no!"

Dante flushed deeper. "What was I supposed to say? 'Not yet'? That's cocky, even for me."

This conversation was getting out of hand. "Can we focus!" Gabe said.

Both of them looked at Gabe. Now *he* was the one blushing. He sighed. There was no use denying anything now. The best he could hope for was that Kitty would keep his mouth shut. "Kitty. Would you like to stay for breakfast? Dante made pancakes. Then we can go dig out your garage."

"You have maple syrup?" Kitty poked his tongue out in a tease.

Gabe sighed again. "Yes. It's on the fridge door, Dante. Bottom left."

"Roger that." He turned to go back to the kitchen, revealing the floury handprint Gabe had left on his ass.

Kitty looked at Gabe, obviously holding back a laugh. "Maybe you get him some pants before breakfast too."

That was probably a good idea.

PART OF Dante expected Gabe to have a meltdown once they'd freed Kitty from the four-foot snowdrift in front of the side door to his detached garage. He didn't, though, at least not an outward one. Dante was taking that as a good sign, even if Gabe had kind of let him down last night.

Dante told himself it wasn't like he'd actually said *I love you* and Gabe had left him hanging. His mouth just got ahead of his brain again and he'd said *That's what I love about you*. He was teasing when he said it. Just because he actually meant it didn't mean Gabe was obligated to say it back.

Of course Gabe hadn't said it back. He was more skittish than a long-tailed cat in a room full of rocking chairs, as Dante's maternal grandmother would have said. That didn't mean he didn't feel it, though, right?

At this point Dante caught himself toying with the ring on his necklace and dropped it in self-disgust. It was time to quit agonizing over what he wanted and do something about it.

So, after Kitty had been liberated and reunited with his phone, and after they'd spent an hour in Gabe's home gym to keep up their conditioning, and after they'd had another meal from Gabe's seemingly bottomless frozen-catered-dinner drawer, he said, "I'm going to take your advice and talk to Trish about me being bi."

Gabe, who was washing the morning's frying pan, stuttered just perceptibly. "My advice?"

Dante swallowed. He knew Gabe was going to hate this, but he was going to have to deal. "Yeah. You told Yorkie not preparing her was a mistake, so…. What's good for the goose is also good for the goose."

"Technically, I think you're both ganders." Gabe picked up the sponge again and finished with the pan.

While he rinsed it, Dante reached for the dish towel. "She's going to ask if we're together," Gabe said.

"Probably." Dante kept his voice even. "But this isn't about that. I will make that clear."

"She'll still know."

"Probably," he said again. Dante's stomach clenched and his chest felt tight. "Look, I know we said we'd wait to tell people, to make sure. And we did. It's been months. I'm not changing my mind about us." He paused, his heart pounding too fast. "Are you?"

"No," Gabe said quickly. "No, of course not, I'm just…." He huffed. "I am not great at letting people in."

Dante snorted. "Yeah, I noticed." He bumped their hips together and put the dried frying pan back in the drawer. "But look… I'm just putting this out there. Your dad knows. Kitty knows. More people are going to find out. The world isn't going to end."

"I know that." He didn't look happy about it, though. "You're just going to make a plan? Not actually do anything?"

Frankly, Dante would rather have the whole thing over with. He was proud of who he was and hiding it made him feel like he had something to be ashamed of. But he understood why Gabe wasn't ready. "Just a plan for now." Then he added, because he felt like he had to, "But I can't wait forever. I hate this."

"I know."

"Okay." Dante had pushed hard enough for now. "I'll see when Trish is available. Thanks for understanding."

Gabe nodded, and Dante considered the subject closed.

On to happier thoughts. "So—dream vacation. Don't think about it, just answer. Where are you going?"

"Scotland," Gabe said right away.

Dante boggled at him. "Seriously? That is the most white-boy—*Scotland*?" Not that there was objectively anything wrong with Scotland, beyond the existence of haggis. It was just so... pedestrian? A place that spoke the same language Gabe did, with a somewhat similar climate. Wouldn't he want to go somewhere for a change of scenery?

Then he realized the truth. "Oh my God. You just want to go golfing!"

"Not *just*," Gabe protested. "There are other things to do."

"Like what? Walk through castles?" Dante rolled his eyes. Gabe was not the castle type. "Are you going to traverse the misty moors in a long coat and a kilt, searching for your ain true love?" He paused. "Actually that would be hot."

"Shut up," Gabe muttered. "I guess you probably want to go to Cancun or something."

"Cancun? What are we, college students?" Dante scoffed. "Fuck no. I'm going to, like, Fiji. Somewhere far away and exclusive with beautiful beaches, where they have those little cabins that sit on the water. I will do nothing but swim, drink, and eat poke."

"That's it, eh?" Gabe quirked a smile.

"Well," Dante amended, "and fuck. Provided I have the right company." He batted his eyelashes.

"I guess that doesn't sound *terrible*."

"That was an invitation," Dante said. He backed himself up against the kitchen counter and pulled Gabe after him by the belt loops. "You know I'm going to go. I'd rather go with you than without you."

Gabe took the bait and bracketed Dante's body with his arms. "I got that from the sex part."

But he wasn't going to accept the invitation today, apparently.

One battle at a time.

DANTE GOT in to see Trish the next day, after a strained conversation with his agent in which he promised multiple times he had no intention of coming out before signing his next contract, and his agent muttered about how much scotch he deserved.

"Hey, Dante. Come on in and have a seat."

Dante closed the door behind him and dropped into the chair across from her and smiled at the little crocheted Gabe doll with the rainbow scarf. He smiled and picked it up. "Thanks for making time on such short notice."

"That's why they pay me the big bucks," she said wryly. "What's on your mind?"

"I'm bi."

Tricia looked at him. She looked at the little Gabe doll he was holding and its rainbow scarf. She put two and two together and got four.

She opened her mouth.

Dante blurted, "I am not, uh, taking questions at this time." Because if she asked, even if he lied his ass off, she'd know the truth and have no plausible deniability.

She closed her mouth again. He couldn't tell if she wanted to laugh or scream. Maybe both. "Okay. Can I ask why you're here, though?"

Oh. Right. Some questions were maybe needed. "I don't want you to be blindsided like you were with Gabe. I want a plan in place in case I get outed. Preapproved statements. That kind of thing."

"But you're not planning on coming out." She was still looking at the doll.

Dante carefully placed it back on her desk and fought the urge to sit on his hands. "No." It was half a lie. He did plan to come out. Just not until he'd made sure he was getting paid, and that meant lawyers and an offer sheet and an outside PR firm, probably. Which all sounded horrible, but Dante wasn't fucking up his career. Some people didn't have ten-million-dollar contracts already.

Trish exhaled loudly and picked up her pen. "Okay. Let's get the wording down. And can I just say up front…."

Dante lifted his gaze in expectation.

Trish leveled him with a mock stern look. "No Grindr profiles."

Dante cracked up.

THE THING was, Gabe knew he was being an asshole. It wasn't fair of him to ask Dante to stay in the closet. But it seemed inevitable that everyone would know the truth about their relationship the second Dante came out as bi, and how would that look? Gabe was the captain now. He was supposed to be in a position of authority. Wouldn't their relationship make him look like a creep?

And what was he opening Dante up to? Gabe's stomach still turned when he thought about Ottawa Tartans number 27 and his disgusting remarks. If someone like that made a comment about what Dante was like in bed, Gabe would get suspended for the rest of the season, if not his life.

What Dante was like in bed was for Gabe to know and that asshole to dream about. Maybe not even that.

Meanwhile, the team won six straight games and jumped to third place in their division. Gabe had been working with Yorkie to improve his defensive game, and the extra practice was paying off—probably just as much because Yorkie had less on his mind now.

Gabe could hardly believe his rookie was going to be a dad.

But his main concern at the moment, beyond hockey, was—

"Hey, we don't have a game next Thursday, do we?"

Dante had the same access to the game schedule Gabe did, but Gabe had it memorized farther. "No. Why?"

Dante looked over. He was lying on his back on the couch with Mario on his chest, purring like mad, so his face was sort of upside down. "It's my birthday. I was thinking we could check out that new steakhouse downtown."

Some of the guys on the team had mentioned it; Tips said it was worth the price tag. "You want me to see if I can get a reservation for like twenty?" Gabe asked. Considering the place was brand-new, that could be kind of a big request. "I can throw my name around." He didn't like doing that, but he could suck it up for Dante.

But Dante shook his head. "Uh, no." He sat up, displacing Mario, who flopped onto the floor and went after the toy shaped like the hockey puck. "I was thinking maybe just the two of us could go. Like a date."

Gabe's palms went damp at the idea.

It was stupid. Before they started sleeping together, he'd been fine with taking Dante to Disneyland—objectively a lot more suspicious than going out for dinner on his birthday. Teammates went out to eat together all the time, in big and small groups, and no one batted an eye—not even when it was just one of them with Gabe.

"Oh," he said, feeling dumb. It was such a small thing. Gabe could do that, couldn't he? "Okay."

"Cool." Dante smiled, his eyes crinkling in the corners.

So that just left figuring out a gift and playing hockey. Gabe could do those things too.

This could be their year. He never said it out loud, and he avoided reading articles about it when he could, but the beat reporters kept asking, kept hinting, kept pushing.

And wouldn't that be something to shove down the throat of every Number 27 who'd ever thought they could get away with spewing hateful garbage? To say that Gabe, the first out gay captain in the NHL, led his team to the Cup just a few months after being outed?

He wanted that so badly he could taste it. And in three months, he'd have a chance to make the dream come true.

DANTE WAS on the treadmill when his phone rang.

He glanced at the call display—his grandmother, probably calling to ask what he wanted for his birthday, as though she still needed to buy him things. He dialed the speed down to a walk and answered the call on his earbuds. "Hola, Abuela."

"Dante Baltierra!" she shouted, so loudly he cringed and reached for the volume. "Please tell me that my ears are deceiving me in my old age!"

He turned the treadmill off as a cold suspicion settled on him. "That—" His voice cracked. "That depends on what you heard."

She couldn't know he was bi. How would she find out? His parents wouldn't have told her.

"Tell me you're not—tell me you don't think you're in an abomination of a relationship with that disgusting pervert!"

Dante's heart turned to lead in his chest. He sat down, his legs suddenly heavy. Through a dry mouth, he asked, "What pervert, Abuela?"

"Don't play games with me, Dante. You know the one I mean. The faggot. Your *teammate*," she spat. "They should have kicked him out the second those pictures surfaced."

"He's the best player on this team." That was easier to respond to than the rest.

"So you admit it!" she accused. "You are a—a sodomite!"

If his eyes hadn't been filling with tears, he would have laughed. *Sodomite.* Fuck's sake. "Yeah, I am," he said. "I'm a sodomite, Abuela. And a cocksucker. And a lot of other things too."

"How could you do this to me? To our family? Do you know the shame—"

"I *don't* know any shame," Dante interrupted. "I won't be ashamed. I haven't done anything wrong."

"Haven't done anything wrong!" she shrieked. "Only broken your grandmother's heart. Only committed a sin that will see you burn in hell! Dante, I beg you to leave this man. It isn't too late. God will forgive you."

Dante would never forgive her, though. He'd never forget the hatred and disgust in her voice. But it was freeing too. He didn't have to care what she thought about him anymore. "No. I'm not going to do that."

"If you love your family—"

"I do love my family," he said. He tried to be firm even though his whole body was shaking in grief and anger. "I love my family, and my teammates, and they love me. And I love Gabe, and I'm not going to leave him."

He tuned out the next half a dozen sentences she spewed, but even though he wasn't listening, the words ate at him like acid.

When he caught something about begging for forgiveness, he cut her off. "I'm not going to ask your forgiveness, just like I didn't need your permission. I don't need it and I don't want it."

Her scream of rage froze the pieces of his broken heart, and he couldn't take any more.

He hung up the phone before she could say anything else.

Dante's hands continued to shake until he dropped the phone on the floor. He buried his face in his palms and dug his fingers into his hair, hoping that the physical pain would distract him from the gaping hole in his chest.

On the floor, his phone buzzed again. The screen showed his mother's face.

How had Abuela found out? His parents wouldn't have told her. She must have been eavesdropping, and his parents hadn't been careful. And now his mother was calling because she knew—

He couldn't face his mother's guilt on top of everything else. With one last swipe across his damp face, he stood and returned to the treadmill.

The miles pounded away beneath his feet. He lost track of how far he'd run, or for how long. But no matter how hard he pushed himself, he couldn't escape it. His vision blurred with sweat or tears. One more mile. Five more minutes.

His lungs were already burning when his shoelace caught in the side of the treadmill. Jerked off-balance, Dante flailed to catch himself, but he hadn't attached the stupid safety clip. The treadmill threw him off and he landed on the floor, jarring his right arm. Searing pain jolted up through his shoulder, and he cried out and reached for his elbow.

But his elbow wasn't where it should have been. Or it was, but it was also someplace else, because his humerus and his ulna weren't meeting anymore.

He'd dislocated his elbow.

Dante closed his eyes and let his head fall back against the floor. "Fuck."

By the time Gabe arrived at the hospital, his heart had slowed to only half frantic. He tried not to let that show on his face as he walked through the lobby doors, looking around for a familiar face.

He found Coach standing with Dr. Zahn, one of the team's doctors, and made a beeline for them. "How bad is it?"

Coach gave him the side-eye. "Nice to see you too."

Gabe tried not to bristle. He didn't need to pick a fight with a pregnant woman, and he *had* been rude. "Sorry. I'm just worried. Hi, Coach. Dr. Z. How are you?"

"I'll be better when this kid stops standing on my bladder," Coach groused.

Dr. Z inclined his head. "I'm fine, Gabriel, thank you for asking. As for Dante…."

Now Coach took over. "Dislocated elbow," she said shortly.

Fuck. Gabe winced. That sounded painful. No wonder they'd called Gabe to come pick him up and drive him home.

At least he didn't have to worry about why they'd called him. Dante didn't have family in Quebec City. As captain, Gabe was the de facto backup.

But how had Dante managed to dislocate his elbow on an off day by himself? "Timeline?"

"Well, he was smart and lucky. He didn't try to set it himself, he got to the hospital quickly, and it doesn't look like anything tore too badly. But it's a soft tissue injury, so it's tough to predict. Could be three weeks. Could be three months."

That meant injured reserve. Gabe's heart sank. He could be out until playoffs or later. And just when the team had started to get some momentum. Gabe didn't know who he felt worse for, Dante or the rest of the team.

He'd been so sure this could be their year. They could've done it without Flash. But without him *and* Dante?

But this wasn't the time to get upset about it. "All right. Take me to him?"

Dante was in a curtained-off bed in the ER, shoulders slumped. His right arm was in a sling. He looked like the picture of dejection.

Gabe cleared his throat. "Hey."

At the sound of his voice, Dante looked up. His eyes were red and hazy, unfocused. "Gabe... I fucked up." He lifted his injured arm, then immediately winced and brought it back tight to his chest.

"Accidents happen," Gabe said gently. "It'll be okay. Are you ready to go? Dr. Z gave me your discharge instructions." It was pretty obvious Dante would need to stay with someone for a while. He'd be in the sling for at least a week.

"Yeah, I…." He frowned at his legs, which were hanging off the end of the bed. With only one arm and a head full of drugs, he seemed to struggle with how to push himself closer to the edge so he could stand up.

Carefully, Gabe wrapped an arm around his waist and gave him a gentle tug until he could slide off. Dante didn't release him right away, though. He leaned his head against Gabe's shoulder for a few alarming seconds before righting himself.

Gabe couldn't help but wonder if there was more going on here than just the injury. "Come on. I'll take you home."

An afternoon cuddling Mario would do him good.

The drive was uncharacteristically quiet. Dante leaned his head against the car window and didn't say anything. He didn't even fidget.

Gabe realized before they got more than five minutes that he didn't have much food suitable for people trying to keep down industrial-strength painkillers. He didn't think frozen dinners would appeal. So he stopped at the grocery store.

"I'm going to run in for some staples." God help him; he didn't remember the last time he'd gone grocery shopping for himself. "You want anything special?"

Dante didn't move his head from the window. It looked like he was trying to meld with it. "Abuela used to let me have ice cream when I was sick."

Gabe didn't think that sounded good for his stomach, but he could worry about that later. "Okay, ice cream. Flavor?"

"Chocolate."

At least that would be easy to find. Gabe loaded a basket with ice cream, bread, bananas, apple sauce, eggs, yogurt, and rice. When he returned to the car, Dante had his eyes closed, his breath fogging the glass of the window.

He drove home slower than he might have otherwise because he didn't want to wake his passenger.

Dante woke up when Gabe pulled up in front of the house. He wiped at gummy eyes with his left hand and mumbled, "You're not in the garage."

"I'll get you and the groceries inside first."

By the time Gabe got back inside and put the food away, Dante hadn't moved from the couch where Gabe had left him. Gabe wrapped the designated injury bag of frozen peas in a tea towel and brought it out. "Here. Ice for twenty minutes."

Dante took it with a grimace. Gabe helped him prop his elbow on a pillow.

Then he sucked it up and said, "Uh. Do you want to talk about it?"

Something had to *be* wrong, beyond the injury. There was no way Dante was this subdued just because he was stoned and in pain.

Dante's face crumpled like a deflating balloon, and he raised his left hand to the chain around his neck— the one with the plain gold band on it that he'd been wearing since he came back from Christmas. "My grandmother called."

Oh God. "Is everything okay?"

"She found out," Dante said hollowly without looking at him. "About—I guess she must've heard my parents talking. She always did like to eavesdrop. Mom called me after to apologize, but I was kind of—I'd already fallen and hurt myself so I'm not too clear on the details."

Gabe filled in the blanks. Dante's grandmother had eavesdropped on his parents and learned that her son was in a relationship with a man. She'd called him to spew something vile.

And then Dante had hurt himself.

"What happened to your arm?"

"Fell off the treadmill." He tilted his head back toward the ceiling. If he was worried about Gabe seeing him cry… it wasn't like he hadn't seen Gabe at his worst. "Thought I could outrun my problems. Jury's out on that, but I couldn't outrun my fucking shoelace."

So on top of being heartbroken and angry, he felt stupid for injuring himself and guilty that he'd put the team in a bad situation.

Gabe didn't know how to make any of that better, so he said, "How many bowls of ice cream do you want?"

Dante gave a tiny, short laugh, but it hitched at the end and his face crumpled again. This time it didn't smooth out.

"Shit," Gabe muttered. But instinct made him slide over on the couch until he could pull Dante awkwardly into his arms. "I'm sorry. I'm so sorry. I know it—it sucks." The words couldn't contain the feeling. He knew that.

For a few minutes Dante just breathed wetly into the front of Gabe's shirt while Gabe carded his fingers through his hair.

Before Gabe could think of anything else to say, Dante fell asleep.

Well. Thank God for cell phones. Gabe worked his out of his pocket and navigated to the website he'd bookmarked a few days ago. He couldn't fix Dante's arm and he couldn't fix his grandmother, but he could still do something extravagant for his birthday.

A little research showed that Fiji might be okay for a gay couple, but Bora Bora would be better. Gabe figured that was close enough and booked an overwater bungalow suite with a pool. Would a week be long enough? No, that was too far to go for just a week. Better make it two.

When the total came up on the screen, Gabe didn't blink. What else was he going to do with his money? He put it on his credit card, then logged in to his banking app and paid the card off.

Dante was still sleeping.

The discharge instructions said Dante should leave the sling on for a week before being reevaluated. That meant he still wouldn't be able to use his arm on his birthday.

Gabe felt a stirring of misgivings. He'd decided going out to dinner with Dante was probably harmless, but that was before. The reservations were at a steakhouse. How was Dante supposed to eat steak with only one hand?

The idea of having to cut it for him in public made Gabe's skin crawl. He could imagine people watching him, judging him. Judging *them*. Wondering what they did together. He would be too paranoid to enjoy himself, he'd behave like an asshole, and it would ruin Dante's night.

Better to reschedule. They could go when Dante had use of his right hand again.

Cancel reservation.

Gabe clicked the link, then set his phone down. He might as well catch a few z's himself.

DANTE STRUGGLED with being on IR.

As Gabe had expected, the painkillers zapped Dante's appetite, and he only picked at the dinners Gabe

reheated or brought home. He ate a lot of toast and bananas, and the protein shakes Gabe had put in the fridge
steadily disappeared over the next week, but it wasn't
really enough for a healthy young athlete to maintain
his muscle mass.

Not that Dante was allowed to do anything more
strenuous than ride the stationary bike in Gabe's
home gym.

Meanwhile, Gabe still had to go to practice and
play games. He suspected Dante spent most of his time
snoozing in front of bad daytime television, because
when Gabe got home, he usually found him on the
couch, remote in his left hand, Mario next to him or
on his lap.

Truth be told, Gabe wasn't much better company.
They scraped out a win their first game without Dante,
but dropped the two after to teams they should've beat-
en. Without Dante's skill to compensate for Yorkie's
inexperience, they had to break up the lines, so Yorkie
got moved down and Gabe shifted to center. He hated
it—he was never satisfied with his faceoffs—but it was
only temporary. He could deal with it for now.

He knew what the sudden slip meant for their
roster. No one in front office wanted to miss a shot at
playoffs. But Gabe had no idea who'd go on the block.
Their backup goaltender? Tips? A couple of the guys
from the minors?

Or Gabe himself?

Gabe didn't like to consider it, but he was having
an amazing season. A couple of would-be contender
teams could afford him. And the return for the Nordiques could make it worthwhile. Either they'd take
a bunch of high draft picks and solid prospects and
bide their time for a serious playoff run, or they'd take

two good but slightly less talented players. The media seemed to have lost interest in sensationalizing Gabe's sexuality—probably because he hadn't given them anything to talk about—so he was a more acceptable risk now than he had been.

Of course, he had a modified no-trade clause. If front office decided they wanted to deal him, he'd have twenty-four hours to give them a list of acceptable teams.

So when he got called into Brigitte's office an hour after morning skate the day before Dante's birthday, it filled him with dread.

The office door was still closed when he got there, three empty chairs sitting outside it. He could hear murmuring from the office, but nothing distinct enough to guess who was in there or what they were saying.

He was too fidgety to focus on a phone game, and it would probably be unprofessional to have his cell on for this anyway. He took it out and turned it off, then slipped it back into his pocket.

Shit, or maybe he should have left it on? What if his agent was trying to get hold of him?

Gabe stared down at his feet as he paced, not wanting to meet anyone's eyes by accident if someone came around the corner unexpectedly.

The sound of the door opening made Gabe raise his head, and the bottom dropped out of his stomach. Oh God.

"No," he said, and it sounded broken even to him.

Kitty stared back at him, his eyes glistening suspiciously, his body language defeated. His mouth turned down when he spoke, a thick rasp on top of his usual accent. "Sorry, Gabe. Sorry. I—"

Gabe cut him off with a hug.

Kitty put his long arms around Gabe's back and crushed him to his chest until all the breath rushed from his body. Gabe turned his face into Kitty's shoulder, pressing tight.

Then he rallied himself enough to speak past the emotion and pulled back to look his friend in the face. "Where?"

"Pittsburgh." Kitty made an obvious attempt at a smile he just as obviously didn't feel. "Is okay. With me there, we win Cup easy."

"God, you probably will, you asshole." Gabe took a deep breath and let it out slowly. Pittsburgh was in their conference, so they'd play each other often.

It didn't really cheer him up, but it was worth a try. "I'll miss you."

Kitty put a huge paw on either side of Gabe's face and tilted it down to kiss the top of Gabe's head. It felt like a benediction, like goodbye. "Gabe. Me too."

DANTE KNEW he was a shitty patient. His arm was useless, and it hurt, and *he* hurt, and he was angry—angry at himself for falling off a fucking treadmill because he was upset and didn't notice his shoe was untied, angry at his grandmother for being a homophobic asshole, and angry with his parents for outing him.

He felt bad about that last part. They hadn't done it on purpose; they were talking about whether they might get to meet Gabe properly if they came up to watch a game. It wasn't their fault. His family never knocked when entering each other's houses.

But maybe now Abuela wouldn't be going to his parents' house at all.

He tried to keep his mind off of that and on productive things, but he wasn't allowed to go to practices
or even work out beyond some time on the stationary
bike, in case he managed to fall or otherwise injure his
arm. Gabe wouldn't fuck him for the same reason, and
he couldn't jerk off, so his only sexual release came
from Gabe's tormentingly slow blow jobs or hand jobs
in the shower—both of which were amazing but felt
like adding insult to injury when it wasn't what Dante
really wanted.

The day before his birthday—two days before he
was supposed to be able to take the sling off, pending
Dr. Z's evaluation—he couldn't take it anymore. He
was bored and lonely and if he had to eat another meal
from Gabe's freezer, he would die. Now that he'd eased
back on the painkillers, his appetite had returned, and
he was at the point where he'd shank a man for some
fresh vegetables. So he ordered groceries to be delivered and carefully took the sling off. It wasn't like he
was going to lift weights.

Cooking buoyed his spirits. Sure, his arm hurt, but
once he'd done all the chopping, he could stir with his
left hand. The smell of the rich mole sauce filled the
kitchen and permeated his brain. For the first time in a
week, he started to relax. He set his phone on the counter and pulled up a Top 40 playlist on Spotify and let
himself enjoy it.

When he'd finished cooking and he'd eaten his
portion of fork-tender chicken mole with brown rice
and a salad of spinach, strawberries, and almonds,
he took an anti-inflammatory and called his dad. His
grandmother might have ruined their relationship, but
he was damned if he was going to let her ruin chicken
mole—or his relationship with his parents.

He hadn't spoken to his parents since his accident, so it was no surprise his dad picked up on the second ring. "Dante! I was hoping you'd call, mijo."

That was when Dante realized it was the middle of the day on a Wednesday and his dad was probably at work.

He took a deep breath. "Hi, Dad."

"How's your arm? Do the doctors have an estimate on when you might be back on the ice?"

"Not yet. I'm supposed to see the doctor the day after tomorrow." Speaking of the arm, he should put the sling back on. He reached for it and pulled the strap over his head. "For the record, dislocating your elbow is a zero out of ten experience. Do not recommend."

"I'll make a note." But before Dante could be glad his dad was taking his cue to keep things lighthearted, he said, "Son, I want—" His voice broke. "Please let me apologize—"

Fuck. "Dad." Dante was having a hell of a week. He didn't have it in him. The anger had fled the second he heard his dad's voice. "Don't—"

"I didn't hear her come in. I never would have said—"

"*Dad*," Dante said more desperately. He could not handle his dad's guilt on top of his own. "It's not your fault Abuela's a homophobe, okay? Let's just—I can't talk about her right now."

For a week he'd been hearing the echo of her hateful words to him. He'd never forget them as long as he lived. She was as good as dead to him.

"Okay," his dad said after a moment. "Okay. Tell me about—something. Anything. How's your cat?"

Dante could *always* talk about the cat.

After the initial part of the conversation, he felt better. He lost track of time catching up on things in his parents' lives, until his dad checked the clock and realized he'd talked through his lunch break.

That made Dante check the time too. He'd been expecting Gabe home just after noon, but it was quarter to two—which at least gave him time to clean up the evidence of his illegal cooking adventure.

He made up a plate for Gabe and put away the leftovers. Gabe probably went out for lunch and forgot to text.

The door opened a few minutes later, and Dante went to meet Gabe in the entryway. "Hey," he said. "How was…?"

But he stopped.

Gabe's face was tight and drawn, and he was biting his lip.

Dante's mood fell back into blackness. He knew what that face meant. His heart jumped into this throat. "Who did they trade?" *Not Gabe. Please not Gabe.* "Yorkie? Bricks?"

"Kitty."

No. That didn't make any sense. Why would they trade one of their core defensemen? They couldn't have. Dante shook his head. "Why would they?"

Gabe flattened his lips. "Pittsburgh needed defensemen, we needed forwards."

"But…."

Who would he beat at darts? Who would make fun of him about maple syrup and *um*? Who would buy him an amazing purple suit as an apology for being a jerk?

"Who's gonna play D?" he asked pathetically.

Gabe cleared his throat. "I guess—they think Slimer might be ready."

Fuck. Dante ducked his head and let Gabe just hug him. "Fuck, fuck, fuck. I'm such a fuckup. Why didn't they just get rid of me? Why did it have to be *Kitty*?" Why did it have to be this week? Couldn't Dante have had a little longer to lick his wounds before the universe rubbed salt in them?

Gabe leaned back far enough so he could cup Dante's face in his hands and look him in the eye. "You can't blame yourself for this. You start taking the blame for accidents and trades, it's never going to stop. It's how the game works, okay? People get injured and players get traded." His voice rasped over the last word. "And it fucking sucks to lose a teammate, but he's still our friend. It's not like we'll never see him." He stroked a thumb along Dante's cheekbone. "He's even still in the same conference."

Dante sighed and leaned into the touch. "I just… it's Kitty, you know? He looked out for me right from the start. And he knows about us," he said in a rush. "About me." No one else did. He knew it was petty and petulant and unimportant in the grand scheme of things, but—"And tomorrow's my birthday."

"I know." Gabe kissed his cheekbone. "It sucks." Then he paused. "It smells amazing in here…." His voice was laced with equal measures hope and suspicion.

"Don't lecture me about the arm right now, okay?" Dante asked. "Just… you want some lunch?"

Dante had no delusions that he'd escaped the mother-henning, but Gabe nodded and smiled. "All right. Lunch sounds great. Thanks."

DESPITE THE absolute shit show of the rest of the week, Dante's birthday started pleasantly. Aside from normal morning concerns, there was no pressing reason to get out of bed—no practice and no game today, and Gabe had moved his workout with the trainers to mid-afternoon to give them more time together.

One thing Dante had learned—Gabe *really liked* to take his time. He teased Dante with his mouth on his dick and three fingers in his ass and backed off every time Dante got too close to the edge, until Dante's chest was heaving and his shoulders were tight with the strain.

"Fuck, Gabe, you gotta let me come or I'm gonna hurt my arm—"

Finally Gabe took pity on him, and Dante came until he felt like he'd been wrung dry.

After that he got to put his new deep-throating skills to the test. All in all, a very satisfying start to the day.

They showered together, which wasn't energy efficient no matter what anyone said, but Dante couldn't feel bad about it today.

Then, while he went downstairs to feed Mario, Gabe went out and picked up Cinnabon for breakfast.

"It should be my birthday every day," Dante said in bliss. Carbs and sugar made a perfect breakfast—at least if you didn't have to play hockey later.

"You'd get sick of these." Gabe licked a glob of frosting off his thumb.

Dante scoffed. "Never."

But he didn't have any decent clothes at Gabe's place, just the sweats he'd been living in for the past week, so when Gabe went into town for his workout, Dante asked to be dropped off at home.

On the drive over, Dante decided to test his luck. After all, if a guy couldn't be a brat on his birthday, when could he? "What do you think about the Seychelles?"

he asked, looking out the window. Wet, dirty, cold
snow everywhere. A little escape fantasy to some white
sandy beach was just what the doctor ordered.

"… I think they're some islands in the Pacific, but
I'm not totally sure."

Fine. Dante could spell it out for him. "I mean for
our summer vacation. I bet they have at least one golf
course."

Another too-long pause. Then Gabe said, "I don't
know. Can we talk about it later?"

Which meant he hadn't wrapped his head around
the idea of a vacation where someone might spot them
together and learn the truth. Not a big surprise, but
Dante would be lying to himself if he tried to pretend
he wasn't disappointed.

Still. It was an argument for another day.

Dante's apartment smelled stale, so he cracked
open a few windows, figuring the chill would be an im-
provement. But before he could make any wardrobe decisions, Kitty swung by to say goodbye and drop off his
keys, since Dante had agreed to supervise some work
being done to the house in his absence.

"Will miss you and best cat," Kitty said gruffly.
"Even though you cheat at darts."

Dante squawked. It was better than feeling sorry
for himself or apologizing for being the reason Kitty
got traded. "How can someone cheat at darts? That
doesn't even make sense."

Once Kitty left, Dante wandered into his bedroom
to check out his closet for something to wear to dinner.

Things deteriorated during the afternoon. He'd cut
back on the painkillers, so he was sore and irritable by
one o'clock. He accidentally bumped his arm against

the door frame in the laundry room and dropped his clean shirts on the floor.

At two, his mom called to wish him happy birthday, which was fine… until she also tried to apologize for accidentally outing him.

"Your father refuses to speak to her until she apologizes to you, so they're at a standoff."

Dante knew she meant it as a show of support for him, but it only made him feel worse. A few minutes later, he changed the subject and made an excuse about needing to get ready for his date that night.

By three he was starving, but when he opened his fridge, he realized that at some point while he was at Gabe's, the thing had given up the ghost. The air was barely cool and smelled like the inside of Dante's hockey bag. He left a voicemail for his landlord and then spent half an hour cleaning it out with one hand.

So it was a crappy afternoon. But tonight he and Gabe would get out of the house that had started to feel like a prison and go out in the world as a couple—even if they were the only ones who knew it. Dante would order the best steak on the menu and drink whatever overpriced wine the server recommended. Then Gabe would take him back to his place and they could have a repeat of this morning.

That thought kept him going. Steak. In public. With his boyfriend, who had many hang-ups but was being pretty great when it came to looking after Dante while he was injured.

Even if he still couldn't commit to a hypothetical vacation.

The new guys from Pittsburgh had arrived, and Gabe had met them that afternoon, so he filled Dante in on what they were like as he drove them back to his place. They were experienced players with statistics to match, which was great for the team, but maybe not so great for Dante. He could be fighting to get his spot on first line back when he'd healed.

But he couldn't think of it like that. If the team didn't get some help, the season could be over before Dante was ready to rejoin them. He'd just have to make sure he worked hard to rehab and come back strong.

They pulled into the driveway, and Gabe parked in the garage. Dante vowed to leave the bad mood there with it.

God, he couldn't wait for steak. Skipping lunch had made him ravenous.

Dante let himself into the house and kicked off his shoes. "So listen, don't judge me, but I'm starving." He picked up Mario, who'd come running to say hello, and kissed the top of his head. Mario purred and bumped his face into Dante's chin. "Should I have a snack before dinner?"

Gabe came in behind him and straightened both sets of boots on the mat. "I'm not the boss of you," he joked.

Laughing, Dante raised his eyebrows. "What, unless we're in bed or on the ice?" He set the cat back down again. "What time's dinner?"

"It should be here at six thirty."

Dante's heart sank. "Be here?"

Gabe nodded and gestured Dante toward the kitchen. "Yeah. I mean, it didn't seem like there was a lot of point going out."

No. It was only Dante's birthday, after the worst week of his life. "No point?"

"It's not like you'd be able to enjoy it." Gabe shrugged and got a bottle of wine out of the fridge.

Apparently he'd missed the edge in Dante's voice. "Everyone staring at you, wondering when you're going to be back on the ice, and you can't even hold a knife…."

Everyone staring at you. "Wow. Projecting much?"

Gabe paused his decorking. "Uh…?"

"People staring is a you problem, Gabe. I own a purple suit. I'm not exactly a shrinking violet."

Finally Gabe seemed to realize he'd fucked up. "Okay, but do you really think a steakhouse would be enjoyable right now? I'd be cutting up your porterhouse."

Dante stared at him. "I could've ordered fish. Or pasta." A kind of mania overtook him, as if to compensate for the anger simmering beneath it. "And yeah, Gabe. I do think a steakhouse would be enjoyable. I would enjoy the *fuck* out of going out to a nice restaurant with my boyfriend. Because it's my birthday and I've been bored out of my mind all week. My grandmother disowned me. I dislocated my elbow and got a good friend traded. And my boyfriend won't even commit to a hypothetical vacation."

"Hey, whoa." Gabe held his hands up. "You're right, it's been a shitty week. But do you think that maybe you're overreacting a little?"

"Do I think I'm overreacting?" Dante repeated. "Well, Gabriel, let's see. I've been in a relationship with a man who has asked me to make myself small for his comfort, and I did it because I understand where he's coming from and I thought he just needed time. But I'm coming to realize that no matter how much time I give him, his comfort is always going to come before my happiness. It's never going to be the right time for me to come out. There's always going to be an excuse. And we can't even go out to dinner as friends because someone might see us together and come up with a wild story that's actually true. That we are in a relationship.

"But no one will ever come to that conclusion again, don't worry," he went on. "Because God forbid you should lower yourself so far as to cut up a steak for your boyfriend in public." All the resentment he'd let fester over the past two months combined with the hurt and disappointment he felt tonight, and it all spewed out of him. "I am proud of who I am. Every part of me. I'm sorry that your mom didn't love you or whatever, but I can't be with someone who's ashamed to be seen with me because he's ashamed of himself."

He watched those words land like a blow. Gabe flinched, but his expression was as much bewildered as hurt. He was still holding the wine bottle. It would have been comical if it didn't hurt so fucking much. "Are you breaking up with me?"

Oh fuck.

"Yeah," Dante said. Fuck, he was breaking up with his boyfriend at his boyfriend's house and he couldn't even drive away.

"Okay," Gabe said. He let go of the wine. His hands curled and uncurled on the countertop. "Um, do you want a ride?"

"I'll get a cab," Dante said. Shit, fuck, what a disaster. He just wanted to be alone and he'd have to endure a twenty-minute drive first. And then—"I'll be back for my cat."

He didn't wait around to see what else Gabe had to say. He turned toward the door, put his shoes and coat back on, and let himself outside.

The winter air stung his skin, and he realized he'd dressed for a night out, not the outdoors. He'd be cold if he was going to wait for a taxi.

But he had his house keys in his pocket… which meant he had the keys and code to Kitty's place. That was only a ten-minute walk. Dante's arm might still be in a sling, but there was nothing wrong with his legs.

Hunching his shoulders against the cold, he let himself out the gate and walked out into the night.

OVERTIME

GABE DIDN'T know what to think when Dante left. He stood rooted to the spot in the kitchen, staring at a bottle of wine that should've been the precursor to a nice night in. He'd ordered a special meal prepared by a private chef; it was supposed to be delivered at six thirty. He'd even bought some candles and set the table in the dining room for once.

But it hadn't been good enough. Of course it wasn't. Gabe should've known. Dante was... exciting, dynamic. He needed to be seen by people, he thrived on attention. Gabe never had a prayer of holding his interest long-term.

At least he hadn't put himself through the public spectacle of coming out as a couple for a relationship that had no chance of lasting. And there was a silver lining to Dante being injured now; at least Gabe wouldn't have to see him for a few weeks. They'd have time to make sure they could go back to their jobs as professionals and not let their personal lives interfere.

It was probably for the best.

But it sucked. Gabe really thought he could have something with Dante. He knew it wasn't perfect, but he also knew Dante made him better. He was a better hockey player, a better teammate, and a better captain because he'd learned from Dante.

And maybe it was stupid, but he'd been sure Dante loved him. The way he looked at Gabe, the things he said, the way he paid attention to Gabe's little quirks. He knew what Gabe was going to order from room service before he did it. He knew when to leave him alone and when to bring out the Wii and when to distract him with sex. You didn't invest that much time and effort in someone's happiness if you didn't care about them.

Right?

Gabe had just poured the bottle of wine down the sink when the doorbell rang with dinner.

He ate his portion at the kitchen island and tossed the leftovers in the garbage.

Then he went into the living room to watch TV. It was too early to go to bed and too cold to whack golf balls in the garage, but he needed some kind of distraction. Mario meowed plaintively from the floor next to the couch when Gabe turned the TV on, and Gabe scooped him up and set him down next to him.

Mario meowed again.

Gabe sighed and petted him between the ears. "I'm going to miss you too."

WITH NO Gabe to occupy him, Dante threw himself into rehabbing his arm. The day after his birthday, he got cleared to take off the sling. Two days of physio and he had reasonable range of motion without pain and was able to start doing basic resistance exercises.

Once they cleared him to drive, he waited until the Dekes had a game and picked up his cat.

Kitty's landlord, a former player named Lars who lived in Sweden, had asked if Dante would move in so the place wouldn't be empty, since Kitty's rent was paid up until the end of the season anyway, so Dante didn't have to worry about bribing his landlord to make a pet exception. Lars took additional payment in cat videos, which Dante happily provided. It wasn't like he had much else going on. One video of Mario "helping" Dante with his rehab exercises made him an overnight Catstagram celebrity.

At least he didn't have to see Gabe right now. He would have to be mature and collected and prove to himself that their relationship hadn't been a mistake from the get-go, and while he was sure he could do it, it was nice to have some time to lick his wounds. He'd been so sure Gabe loved him. He'd convinced himself that Gabe just needed time, that he'd get used to the idea that it was okay that people knew he was in a relationship with someone—another player even—and then everything would be smooth sailing. He thought Gabe had grown.

But he hadn't. He was okay with being out publicly because he had no choice, but the idea of the world knowing he loved another man was too much. When Dante wasn't too busy being pissed off about it, it made him sad.

He focused on the anger. It was more productive. But sometimes the sadness intruded and there wasn't anything he could do about it.

Like when his mother called and asked how he and Gabe had celebrated Dante's birthday.

Dante inhaled sharply.

"Oh," his mother laughed, "I don't need *details*, sweetheart, that's not—"

"We broke up."

After everything—after his grandmother disowning him, after the discomfort of hiding their relationship, after making a plan with Tricia for what to do if he happened to get outed as bi, after consults with his own agent and a PR firm about how to handle coming out intentionally.

Dante hadn't changed his mind. He still wanted to come out. He was still going to wait until he had a qualifying offer from the team. Nothing had changed… except that when everything happened, he would no longer have Gabe's support, and his grandmother and his parents weren't speaking to each other.

"What?" His mother sounded alarmed. "Honey. Oh, no. I'm sorry. What happened? I thought things were going well."

"So did I." This was also hard to admit because she'd told him, hadn't she? *I don't think your boyfriend had a very nice time with his coming out experience. It's not unreasonable that he doesn't want to feel responsible for putting you through that.* But this hadn't even been about coming out. Dante just wanted to go to dinner. "I thought he was more okay with us being together than he was, I guess. It was fine for a while, but when he wouldn't even go out for dinner with me on my birthday…."

"That would be very disappointing."

Disappointing. No. It was heartbreaking. "It sucks." And it sucked worse because—"Please don't tell Dad yet."

"Dante—"

"No, look, Mom." His breath shuddered when he released it. "He's not talking to Abuela because of me right now. I don't want him to think that's—that it's for nothing."

His mother's tone went steely. "Dante, if you never even looked at another man, the things she said to you would be unforgivable."

Dante put a hand over his stinging eyes. "I didn't mean to cause all this trouble."

"Honey. This is on her, not you. And that's the end of it."

He inhaled shakily. "Okay."

But it turned out not to be the end of it, because the next day his father called to let him know Abuela had had a stroke.

"I know I said I wouldn't speak to her," he said, and the guilt and grief in his voice twisted Dante's insides.

"Dad. Of course you have to go." She'd hurt him badly, and he knew her actions had hurt his dad too. But she was still his mother, and she didn't have anyone else. His parents hadn't told Dante much, but they'd said enough for him to know that Abuela wasn't going to come out of the hospital again.

His father let out a long breath of relief. "You're a good man," he said through emotion so thick Dante could feel it. "I'm proud that you're my son."

The general down trend of Dante's mood continued as the Dekes went on a winning streak. Dante couldn't help but watch every game. He longed to be on the ice, even if it meant being in close quarters with Gabe. Having to watch the two new guys score goals and celebrate with Gabe was just pouring salt in the wound—both of his actual injury and the breakup.

But while the doctors said he was making good progress, it wasn't good enough to let him go back to practice.

"Let's talk about it next week," Dr. Z said after he'd had Dante run through his range of motion. "You're coming along. We don't want to set you back by okaying you for something you aren't ready for. The team's doing well. There's no rush."

Dante didn't know how to explain that the team doing well *was* the reason for his rush. He didn't want to lose his spot. What if he got healthy before the trade deadline and they decided to deal him? What if he got healthy but they decided to scratch him because the new guys were working out so well?

At least healing and physio left him so exhausted that he wasn't having any trouble sleeping.

His appetite was another scenario.

Lars's kitchen was much nicer than the one in his apartment, and he threw himself into cooking. He even had Yorkie over for dinner one night, like he and Gabe had planned to do.

"Dude," Yorkie said. "This is way nicer than your apartment."

"The food's better than room service too." With a flourish, Dante set a plate in front of him. "Buen provecho."

"Thanks."

But even though Dante knew he needed to eat, and even though he'd done everything right, and even though it smelled amazing, the food didn't taste as good as it did in Gabe's ugly kitchen. While Yorkie plowed through his plate and a second helping, then half of a third, Dante struggled to finish one.

Finally Yorkie pushed away his plate and wiped his mouth with a napkin. "Is something bugging you?" he asked. "I mean, like, beyond the obvious?"

Dante was not going to lay his problems on a guy who was about to become a dad. "No, nothing, just the painkillers fucking with my appetite." He hadn't been on anything stronger than Advil in weeks.

Yorkie stuck his thumb in his mouth to suck off a glob of pasta sauce and gave him a skeptical look. "So you and Gabe didn't break up?"

Dante's mouth fell open. "Uh... you knew about that?"

Yorkie rolled his eyes. "Duh. Like suddenly you were never in the room anymore when I went to bed and sometimes I'd catch you sneaking in? Also, one time Gabe's room was right next to mine. Hotel room walls, you know?"

Dante winced. "No wonder you weren't sleeping well."

"Oh, don't flatter yourself. You weren't what was keeping me awake." He took a sip of his milk, because he might be legal drinking age, but he was taking no chances driving under even a little influence with a baby on the way. "But seriously, do you want to tell me what happened?"

Dante was desperate to tell someone on the team, and he couldn't go to the captain for obvious reasons. But... "Won't that be awkward for you?"

"More awkward than hearing you two fuck?" He pushed the plate away a little farther so he could lean his elbows on the table. "Come on. You know how we gossip."

"Yeah, but...." He shrugged. "I don't know, Gabe's the captain, right? So it feels like shit-talking him behind his back."

"So you were the one who broke up with him."

Even not telling Yorkie things was telling Yorkie things, apparently.

When Dante didn't say anything, Yorkie snorted. "It doesn't take a genius, dude. The guy's kind of a control freak. You… are not."

"I mean… that sums it up." Without getting into details Yorkie didn't need to know, anyway. Dante didn't need him angry on Dante's behalf. He needed the team to make the playoffs so he could come back this year. That meant no unnecessary beefs with the captain, including his own.

Ugh. *Maturity.*

"Okay," Yorkie said doubtfully. "But if you're not going to vent about your relationship problems, can I?"

"Oh sure." Dante could use some perspective. He was mopey and heartbroken and that sucked. "Lay it on me."

"So you know how me and Jenna are getting married? Since we can't live together while she's in school or whatever, Bricks said the best way to make sure she and the baby are eligible for our health care stuff is to get married."

As if Yorkie had needed an excuse to marry this girl.

As if Dante had somehow forgotten, when Yorkie hadn't talked about anything else for more than five minutes in the past two weeks.

He propped his chin on his hand and leaned on the bartop. "Uh-huh."

"Well, I thought, you know, maybe she'd want to go shopping for something nice to wear? Since we're just doing the city hall thing. So I asked if I could take her shopping next weekend to pick something out and she got mad at me!"

This sounded like a pregnant person problem, but Dante wasn't going to say that out loud. "Like… how mad?"

"Hard to say." Yorkie huffed. "It was easier to know how bad I fucked up when we were in the same place. Over the phone, it's hard to know when you're getting the silent treatment. But when she started texting back one-word answers, I figured I better call her."

Dante smiled. "A novel concept. And?"

"And I guess she was mad because she thought I meant, like, a wedding dress? And that we wouldn't have a 'real' wedding—with, like, the dancing and the cake and the dinner and stuff? And she didn't want to be pregnant in her wedding dress, and she thought I wanted her to buy something nice because none of her clothes fit and she's fat." He was wide-eyed and bewildered.

"Dude."

"Right?" Yorkie said. "First of all, *I haven't even seen her in weeks*. How would I know if she's getting fat?"

Dante hoped he hadn't said that to Jenna.

"But like, just because we're getting shotgun married for benefits doesn't mean we can't have a real wedding. I will give her a real wedding. I will wedding the *shit* out of her. All she had to do was say that's what she wanted."

"So when you said you wanted to vent about your relationship problems," Dante said slowly, "you really just meant you wanted to brag about how in love you are and how you don't *have* problems."

Yorkie made a face at him. "I *do* have problems. Pregnancy hormones are ninety-nine of them. Poor Jenna." Then he shook his head. "I'm just annoyed because, like, how was I supposed to know what she wanted?

Or that she was getting sensitive about clothes? She didn't tell me!"

"Yeah," Dante agreed. "Were you supposed to read her mind?"

And then he felt uneasy. Because wasn't Dante guilty of expecting Gabe to read his mind? Sure, he'd made it clear he wouldn't stay in the closet forever… but he'd never made it a point to push for a timeline. He'd said he wanted to go out to dinner for his birthday, but he hadn't given any indication that failure to make a reservation would result in the death of the relationship. Instead, he'd bottled up his frustrations about feeling like a shameful secret and then vented them all at once, explosively, right in Gabe's face.

Which said as much about Dante as it did about Gabe, and none of it was flattering.

"What?" Yorkie prodded after a moment, and Dante realized he'd been silent for too long.

He mustered another smile. "Just, like—tell me you didn't say you didn't know she was getting fat."

Yorkie laughed. "Oh, fuck you. I'm not an idiot."

No, he wasn't… but Dante might be.

By the beginning of February, Gabe had found a good rhythm with his new linemates. But after their first few games together, they faced a slew of difficult opponents and started sliding just as Toronto and New York hit hot streaks.

It figured that despite the painful trade, they still might not make the playoffs.

Gabe did what he could to keep the team focused and motivated. But lifting others' spirits when his own were low didn't come naturally, and he found himself on the phone with Flash every other day to pick his brain.

"For God's sake," Flash finally said, when Gabe called on a day they didn't even have practice. "You're doing fine. It's just growing pains. You're trying to integrate new guys on your line. That doesn't happen overnight."

Gabe groaned in frustration. "Yeah, but it seemed like we clicked right away the first game, and now we're—"

"Now your new teammates don't have anything to prove," Flash interrupted. "They're not going to play like it's their first game with a new team and they have to impress the fans and coaches every night. That's not sustainable. Find the level that is and learn to work with that."

Somehow Gabe felt betrayed. "Are you telling me I can't expect 110 percent every night?" he said, mock-outraged.

Which set Flash off on a rant about dumb English idioms and the state of the Ontario public school curriculum, but at least Gabe laughed. He hadn't been doing a lot of that lately.

He hadn't realized how much space Dante took up in his life until suddenly he wasn't in it anymore—no video games, no movie nights, no sex, no surprisingly tasty dinners cooked in the comfort of his own kitchen. He missed having Mario around underfoot to throw toys for and give treats to and nap on the couch with. Gabe's house, which he'd always lived alone in, felt empty and cold.

Road trips weren't much better. By this point in the season, most of the guys had established seat partners for flights and bus rides. Gabe still had more friends than he had before the season, so it wasn't like he was the odd man out. But with Flash and Dante out, Kitty traded, and Yorkie now rooming with Slimer, it was a change to his routine, and he hated that on principle. At least Olie didn't mind putting up with him—although Olie's usual pregame routine involved listening to angry Swedish death metal on his headphones and ignoring everything else, so Gabe's bus rides weren't very chatty.

The time he felt most alive—most like himself—was on the ice, with the puck on his stick and an opposing player chasing him. But their new guys didn't read him the way Dante did, didn't make him laugh the way Dante did. He never caught either of them yowling the lyrics to "Moves Like Jagger" at the top of their lungs. Even celebrating a goal with them was bittersweet. Neither of them fit against his side the way Dante did.

They came back from squeaking out an overtime win in Detroit to a fresh dusting of snow and an almost-unheard-of weekend off.

Gabe went to sleep in his cold, too-large bed and woke up to his phone ringing. He fumbled to answer it without raising his head from his pillow. "Hello."

"Good, you're awake," Flash said cheerfully.

Gabe groaned. "What time is it?"

"Time to wake up. Yvette's throwing a dinner party. You're invited."

Gabe wiped the crud from the corners of his eyes. "What time?" *Why* was a moot point; when Yvette got it in her head to host a dinner, you didn't miss it.

Besides, it would do him good to get out of his empty house and spend some time with people. Maybe the activity would keep his mind off Dante for an hour.

He showed up with his customary bottle of whiskey to find himself the fifth wheel. Yvette's sister and the nanny had taken the kids, and Olie and Adele were in the living room, already equipped with glasses of wine.

"How's the hip?" he asked as Flash handed him a glass. He was walking normally, but that didn't mean much.

"No hockey talk!" Yvette interrupted. She waggled her finger at Gabe. "You know the rules."

He held up his hands in surrender. "I'm sorry. I'm out of practice."

"Yes." Now she gave him a speculative look. "It's been some time since you had time in your schedule to visit us."

She had just said they weren't allowed to talk about hockey, so Gabe could only assume she was talking about his social schedule. He glanced at Flash in alarm, but Flash had turned away to talk to Olie and Adele.

Shit. "You know," he said, waving his hand vaguely. "Being captain…."

The skeptical lift of Yvette's eyebrows said she wasn't buying it, but she didn't call him on it. "Mm-hmm." She gestured him into the sitting room. "Come on and sit down, I think the lovebirds have an announcement."

Lovebirds.

Gabe sighed and sat in the armchair kitty-corner to the love seat—aptly named—where Olie and Adele sat with their hands twined together.

Oh.

That's a big rock, Gabe thought wildly. He'd only ever thought of fancy rings like that in hockey terms— one day he wanted a huge, gaudy Cup ring. But not because he actually wanted to wear it—he wanted what it represented.

Kind of like the way an engagement ring represented a relationship, really. So in that respect, having a wedding band made sense. But still, he'd rather have something solid and plain and subdued. Like the one Dante wore around his neck—

Fuck.

Olie and Adele did actually make their announcement just after dinner, and when Gabe congratulated them, he was there in the moment, sharing in their joy, and he meant it.

But when that moment passed, his own thoughts sucked him back in. Why was he so lonely now? Had he felt this way before but been unable to recognize it because he didn't know what he was missing?

He'd always told himself there was time for love after hockey. He'd never let himself think about it beyond that. And maybe this was why. He'd known, deep down, that if he ever looked closely at his life, he'd see how empty it was—not because there was anything wrong with being single, but because he'd closed himself off to the possibility of love.

Good grief, he was getting maudlin. How strong was this wine? He pushed his glass away and tried to refocus on the conversation.

"… make sure we tell all our loved ones before one of the hockey boards gets ahold of the story," Adele was saying.

Gabe frowned. "Hockey boards?"

Adele and Yvette both rolled their eyes expressively, while Olie and Flash groaned. Apparently this was a fertile conversational ground.

"Did I say something wrong?"

"How do you not know about the hockey boards?" Yvette shook her head. "I was nine months pregnant with Baz, standing in line at the grocery store, no make-up, wearing my pajamas because I couldn't stand the feel of anything else on my skin, and someone snapped a photo and put it online. Opposing counsel tried to show it in court! Thank God the judge was a woman. She tore him a new one."

"Wait, *what*?" Gabe said, aghast.

"Have you been living under a rock?" Flash asked. "Really? Or just because you don't date"—he winced like he knew that was a sore subject—"you never had to deal with it?"

"I mean, I think I had my share of bad media attention on people I date." Maybe it was just one incident, but it was a really *big* incident.

"But, what?" Adele asked, tilting her head. "You didn't think you were the only one, did you?"

"Uh." He *had*. "I guess I never really thought about it."

"Oh, lucky you." Yvette passed him a plate of dessert—baklava. But Gabe had lost his appetite. "Did you hear what happened with poor Jenna? One of her teammates decided to go and start an internet rumor that the baby isn't Tom's. He had me threaten legal action. Very satisfying."

Gabe had heard about that, but only tangentially. At least Yorkie knew better than to go to Gabe for legal advice. "This is a thing people spend time on?" he asked. "Why?"

"Who knows why people do anything?" Yvette gave him a wry look. "You hockey players are not all that. It isn't all bad, though. For every disgusting misogynist, there's someone sending positive messages of support and calling people on their bullshit."

"I had to start including the brands of my sneakers in my Instagram posts," Adele said. "Everyone wants a pair."

"Well, they are fabulous."

"Yeah, and now companies are sending me free shoes!"

Gabe zoned out again and picked at his dessert. It looked like he'd had his head up his ass on more than one issue. His coworkers and their partners were also under the public microscope. Maybe the attention was a different flavor, but it was still there. All this time he'd felt singled out because he was gay, when his teammates were dealing with the same thing. Even if he were straight, people would gossip about his personal life. He could either not have one, or deal with the attention.

And truthfully, how much would that attention impact his life? Trish was good at keeping the media in line and focused on hockey questions. Erika never put him in contact with people who wanted to talk about anything that would make him uncomfortable. So what was the big deal? What was he afraid of?

He'd been so proud of himself for finally opening up to the team, making friends, getting to know people. He'd thought it was a big step forward. But that was just a mask he'd hidden behind, because in the end, he'd still acted like a closeted asshole.

It was one thing to be a private person. But he'd been so busy falling into old habits that he hadn't seen that what worked for him was suffocating Dante. He knew damn well they wouldn't be able to keep their relationship secret forever, but he'd happily kept kicking that can down the road rather than face the problem like a good partner.

Now he knew what he wanted. He knew it was worth putting the effort in to get it.

The question was, how did he atone?

And would it matter if he did?

DANTE'S GRANDMOTHER died on a Friday.

He didn't know what to do with himself, but he wasn't allowed to practice yet anyway, so he got on a plane and flew to Louisiana to be with his parents.

They met him at the airport, eyes red-rimmed with dark circles underneath. They engulfed him in their arms and just held on. Dante sank into it, soaked it up.

The night before the funeral, his dad knocked at the door of Dante's room. "Can I come in?"

Dante turned off the hockey game—Edmonton at Calgary. "What's up?"

His dad sat on the edge of the bed. "It didn't seem right to tell you about this on the phone. But I think… your grandmother wanted me to give you this."

It was a note, folded and refolded like Dante's father had been worrying it in his hands. He must have read it—he wouldn't have agreed to give it to Dante otherwise.

With no small amount of trepidation, Dante opened it.

The words were only barely legible, no trace of his grandmother's usually steady and precise handwriting.

Mijo,

I am afraid for you. I can't understand why you do this. But I don't have to understand to love you.

Dante swallowed as he put the letter down on the bed and covered his eyes with one hand. His dad put an arm around his shoulders and pulled him close.

He'd thought she was dead to him forever—the woman who'd disowned him, the woman who'd taught him to cook and doted on him and watched telenovelas with him after school.

And no matter how stubborn he was, or how he tried to harden his heart, part of him had hoped she'd change her mind. That she'd apologize, beg for his forgiveness, prove that she could accept Dante and embrace the man he loved.

It stung to have that chance ripped away now, like antiseptic on a cut. But at least this way it wouldn't fester, wouldn't scar.

He didn't remember packing the ring on its chain, but he found it in his toiletries when he was gathering his things after the funeral.

It was too late to fix anything with Abuela.

But looking at the ring and the chain it hung on made Dante think it wasn't too late for everything. Maybe it could still bring him some luck. He'd have to see.

PERHAPS THE hockey gods were granting miracles, because Dante got the all-clear to start practicing with the team again two days after he got back from Louisiana.

He was too relieved to be back on the ice to worry about Gabe, at least until he returned to the full locker room and remembered their stalls were next to each other.

But he was determined to be an adult and deal with his problems head-on. Even if that problem was "I see my hot ex naked all the time at work and I'm still in love with him even though he broke my heart."

Considering that they hadn't been as discreet as he thought—or at least, not as discreet as *Gabe* thought— he wondered if he wouldn't feel the tension in the room when he returned. But he never had a chance.

"Oh shit, look who it is!" Bricks stood and clapped him on the back with a meaty hand. "Nice of you to grace us with your presence."

"You're right—it is." Dante went in for the bro hug, then high-fived Olie and Slimer on his way to his stall.

Gabe was there waiting for him. Dante didn't think he was imagining the determination in his jaw, but he held out a hand. "Welcome back." Then, softer, cautiously, "I'm sorry about your grandmother."

It wasn't what Dante wanted, but he'd take what he could get—and a little more. He let their hands linger a little too long and pushed the words out past the roughness in his throat. "Thanks, man."

Gabe looked away first.

It was a start.

He wasn't allowed any contact for a week, so he wore a different-colored jersey as a visual reminder for everyone to back off.

It sucked the first time he managed to put a puck past Olie, because he wanted nothing more than to be in the middle of a celebratory hug with Gabe, but he wasn't allowed that either. And it was awkward to turn around expecting it and see Gabe skating toward him, only to remember—both the injury and their breakup—and then wince, stop short, and pat him on the helmet instead.

Horrible.

But it was all worth it when he got the all-clear for regular practice.

"Well, I wouldn't go so far as to call it a medical miracle," Dr. Z said, "but I can't see any reason to keep you out any longer."

Thank God.

So that was one less thing to worry about.

It was another three games before Coach put in him, and he had to suffer through playing ten minutes on the fourth line the first night. He made up for it by sniping in a goal from the top of the circle.

He got hugs from his lineys and fist bumps from the bench, but it wasn't what he really wanted.

Until he returned to his regular spot in the lineup, he wasn't going to get what he really wanted. Maybe not even then. But he'd made up his mind—he needed to work his way back onto Gabe's line. He had to prove they could still play together even if their relationship didn't work out. *Then* he could try to fix his heart as well as his arm. So he just had to suck it up, play his best, and keep his fingers crossed.

And make sad, beseeching eyes at Coach when she was putting the lineup together at pregame skate.

His third game back was in Raleigh. They'd dropped the last two, and they were neck-and-neck for the last wildcard slot.

Coach didn't finalize the lineup until the last minute, which meant Dante was already at the rink when he heard.

"You're in, Baltierra." Moser, their new left winger, high-fived him. "Maybe you can keep up with this guy." He gestured at Gabe. "I'm so busy chasing after the puck to get it to him so *he* can score, I never have time to hit anybody anymore."

Dante laughed. Moser was six and a half feet tall and liked to make sandwiches… out of himself, the boards, and their opponents. "See, there's your problem—you don't skate to where the puck is—"

"—you skate to where it's going to be," Gabe finished. There was an awkward second when he and Dante met eyes, and they both seemed to acknowledge what had passed between them. Then the moment broke and Gabe thumped Moser on the back. "It's okay, Moser. We'll always have the penalty kill."

Apparently they'd developed a bond while Dante was out, because Moser mock swooned. "Aww, Cap. You say the sweetest things."

They didn't have more than a few minutes before the game, but Dante suddenly couldn't wait any longer. "Gabe."

Gabe snapped his gaze back to Dante.

Dante cleared his throat. "Can we…?"

Gabe looked at the clock. Then he glanced around the locker room, which was emptying rapidly. He liked to be the first on the ice for warm-ups, but he must've decided this was more important, because he nodded with something like relief in the corners of his eyes and said, "Just—meet me in the trainer's room?"

Did Gabe wanting privacy bode well for Dante's chances, or the opposite? Probably a stupid question. It was just Gabe being Gabe, hating the thought that anyone might know his business.

But he didn't leave Dante waiting long. He'd only been in the room for thirty seconds when Gabe closed the door behind him.

Dante opened his mouth not totally sure what was going to come out of it and was surprised when Gabe beat him to the punch.

"Here." He thrust out a dark blue envelope bearing Dante's name in Gabe's obsessively neat block printing. "I just… before anything else. I wanted to, well." He huffed. "Happy belated birthday."

For a second all Dante could do was stare at the envelope like it might bite him. The edges were worn, like Gabe had been carrying it around in his bag for a while. He must've been. Otherwise why would he have brought it all the way here, instead of giving it to Dante at home?

"Thanks," he finally said, the reflex of manners kicking in at last. Without consciously deciding to, he slid his thumb along the flap and broke the seal.

A kid's birthday card sparkled up at him, complete with a glittery rainbow unicorn. In front of the giant 3, Gabe had drawn a 2 in Sharpie. Not very Gabe—but pretty Dante, really. He smiled in spite of himself and opened the card.

Sorry it's not Fiji, Gabe had written. *Maybe we can go there next, if this place sucks.*

Happy birthday.

Then there was a little, poorly drawn heart that nonetheless made Dante's squeeze in sympathy, followed by Gabe's name.

Tucked into the card were a printout of a flight reservation confirmation for two and a brochure for a resort in Bora Bora—a two-week stay in both their names. The email was dated the day Dante dislocated his elbow.

Dante was going to faint.

"I can still change the names, I think," Gabe said hastily. "If you don't want to go with me, but I thought—"

You fucking idiot, Dante thought, biting down on what he was sure was a truly deranged smile. "You got me my dream trip for my birthday."

Gabe shifted from foot to foot, which Dante only knew because he could hear it. He was still staring at the brochure. God, that water was so blue. It would feel so good. "If you don't like it—"

"You got me my dream trip for my birthday and then you *let me leave you* because you *didn't make restaurant reservations*." Dante didn't know whether he was going to laugh or cry. "What the fuck, Gabriel!"

"… Do you not like it?"

Dante gave up any pretense at getting his emotions in check and pushed Gabe against the door. Then he poured everything he hadn't said over the past few months into a brief, desperate kiss. Gabe made a noise of surprise into Dante's mouth and fisted his hands in the sides of Dante's jersey, holding on.

God. They'd been so stupid.

A buzzer sounded distantly, reminding Dante that they were, in fact, still being stupid. Reluctantly, he pulled away. Gabe looked pleasantly dazed, his curls in disarray. Dante had a vague sense memory of getting his fingers all up in it.

"We still need to talk," he warned.

Gabe nodded mutely, but he was starting to smile.

It was contagious. Dante tried to keep a stern face. He pointed a finger. "And don't think that you can just buy me a vacation to Fiji every time you fuck up!"

Gabe's smile widened. "It's Bora Bora."

"*Whatever*," Dante said. "We're talking after the game!"

"Okay," Gabe agreed easily, looking no less thoroughly kissed. He made no move toward the door.

Dante wanted to keep that look there forever, but also, he needed Hockey Gabe back so they could make the playoffs. "Okay," he repeated. "So let's get on the ice already!"

Finally the dazed look slipped off Gabe's features, to be replaced by a slight flush. "Right."

As ready as Dante felt, it didn't stop the game from being brutal. Carolina was on the bubble too, and every game counted. After skating only ten or twelve minutes in the past two games, Dante felt the burn in his quads after the second period. The game was tied at nothing going into the third. Dante wanted something to celebrate.

Well. Something *more* to celebrate.

Coach's intermission pep talk was to the point. "I know you guys can do this. You're playing a solid defensive game. Look to exploit the weaknesses we talked about in practice. The refs slapped us with that penalty late in the second, so they'll be looking for a makeup call. Draw that penalty and let the power play do their job. My back hurts. My feet are swollen. Let's put this away in regulation and get some barbecue."

Gabe didn't try to outdo her. "You heard the lady. Let's go!"

They were all filing past to get to the ice when Dante had a wild idea. He stopped next to Coach with Gabe just behind him. "So this is probably inappropriate on a lot of levels, but uh…." He held up his gloved hand and wiggled his fingers. "Can I touch your belly for luck?"

Coach looked at him for a long moment. Then she shook her head. "That's not even close to the weirdest thing I've done for hockey. Couldn't hurt."

Dante couldn't feel much through his gloves, so he just gave the bump a gentle pat. "Thanks, kid!"

Maybe it worked or maybe it was a coincidence, but Dante drew a holding penalty on his first shift, just like Coach wanted.

They set up for the faceoff, and the puck found Dante's stick. He sent it up the ice to Gabe.

Gabe shot and missed—but at just the right angle for Dante to redirect it over the goaltender's stick and into the net.

"Fuck yeah!" Dante whooped. He raised his stick in victory and then *oof*ed out a breath as four guys collided with him one after the other. Gabe was the closest. Dante let himself lean into it.

"Like you never left," Gabe chirped.

Then their eyes met, and for a minute their teammates didn't exist.

The moment didn't last, but their good fortune did. With four minutes left, Carolina pulled the goalie and turned up the heat in the Dekes' defensive zone. Dante blocked a shot ten feet from the blue line, but the sting hardly registered—the shot had deflected into the neutral zone and there was no one between him and the empty net. One shot and it was in—2–0.

This time, when he skated by the bench for fist bumps, he leaned over the boards and wiggled his fingers at Coach's belly.

She laughed.

Carolina's goaltender went back in, but the Dekes had momentum now, and Dante wasn't going to

let his foot off the gas. Even if said foot was, technically, gassed.

With a little less than two minutes to go, his line
got stuck on the ice, cycling the puck in the offensive
zone, looking for that third goal. Dante's legs and lungs
were burning, so he was mostly standing in front of the
net as a screen—so when the puck ended up in the net
again, he didn't care how it got there, he was just glad
he could get off the ice.

The linesman credited Gabe with the goal, and
they dutifully did the celebrating, and thirty seconds
later the horn went off to signal the end of the game.

Obviously Dante wanted to celebrate the win, but
his preferred method of celebration involved having
that talk with Gabe first. But when Gabe came back
from an interview, shaking his head, the chances of getting to do that went up in smoke.

"What's so funny?" Dante asked, rubbing a towel
over his wet hair.

Gabe tossed him a puck, which Dante caught
left-handed. "Looks like that last goal was a deflection
off your skate." He paused. "Congratulations on your
hat trick."

It must be Dante's lucky day. Now he *definitely*
couldn't get out of going for barbecue.

DANTE DIDN'T bother trying to talk to Gabe at the
restaurant. In fact, they didn't even sit close to each other. He didn't think the tension between them could've
held. He'd probably have ended up with his hand on
Gabe's dick under the table.

Which, like, maybe someday, but preferably not in
Raleigh.

The team wandered back to the hotel in groups. Dante was on his way up when Gabe's text came through with his room number.

Yeah, he wasn't going to bother stopping by his own room. He let Yorkie know not to expect him, ignored his "get it, Baller!" and turned his phone off.

He barely remembered the trip up in the elevator, or walking down the hall, or knocking on the door. But then it opened and there was Gabe, and all at once the outside world rushed back in, and now he was firmly rooted in the present, with Gabe looking at him like he was the Stanley Cup and the Art Ross and an Olympic gold all wrapped up in one.

Gabe did terrible, wonderful things to Dante's ego.

But once Dante came inside and sat down—at the desk, because they really did need to talk, and if he sat on the bed, Dante's mouth would talk plenty but it wouldn't say anything useful—Gabe started pacing like the hero in a period drama.

Oh Jesus. Gabe was wringing his hands.

He must've noticed himself doing it, because all at once he grimaced, flexed his fingers, and pointedly moved his arms to his sides. Then he took a deep breath and said, "I owe you a huge apology."

Somehow, Dante's racing heart rate kicked up a notch. "Okay."

"But it's hard to know where to start." Gabe made that face again and sat on the edge of the bed. He shoved his hands between his knees as though that would keep him from fidgeting. "I treated you like you mattered less to me than privacy I don't have—and I've *never* had it, however much I thought I did. I thought I changed. I thought I was dealing with the reality of being out, but I wasn't. I might have been shoved out of the closet, but I never got over that instinct to hide. I made you feel like I was ashamed of you, and that couldn't be less true."

And that was when Dante knew for sure. They could fix this. It might take work and compromise and patience and understanding—and maybe only one of those things was his strong suit—but they could do it.

It would mean owning up to his own shortcomings, though. Dante knew he had kind of a complex about not just being the best at things but being *seen* as the best. And when Gabe wouldn't let anyone else see him being a good boyfriend, Dante had stopped being one.

"It wasn't all your fault. I wasn't exactly Mr. Clear Communication about things that were bothering me."

Gabe gave him the ghost of a smile. "Yeah… usually you're not shy about saying what you want. Why not this time?"

Time to bring back that honesty, even if it hurt. "I thought if I told you I wanted to stop hiding our relationship, you'd say no." Dante gave a small shrug. "I knew that when that happened, I'd probably break up with you, and I didn't want to, so…."

Gabe huffed out a breath. "That's… fair."

"Yeah." Dante rubbed his damp palms over his quads. Now for the important stuff. "So… I miss you." That one was easy.

But the naked relief on Gabe's face made him think maybe it wasn't so easy for Gabe. "I miss you too."

Even with the encouragement, the next one was harder. "I still—" *love you. I love you. I love you.*

He couldn't be the first this time. "I still have feelings for you."

Gabe exhaled shakily. "I… yes. I do too." He swallowed and then asked, voice laced with hope, "Do you want to start over?"

A quick, unprompted laugh escaped Dante's mouth. "No." But before Gabe's expression could register more than hurt and surprise, he said, "I don't want to go backward. I want to pick up where we left off. I want to sleep in your bed and make you breakfast and get matching Stanley Cup tattoos that get sunburnt in Bora Bora." He allowed himself a rueful half smile. "That's probably not, like, the best idea, though."

Now Gabe echoed his hesitant laughter. He ran a hand through his hair and rubbed at the back of his neck. "Yeah, I don't think anyone's going to be holding us up as an example of rational decision-making."

"Nope," Dante agreed. But it had more or less worked out for them, hadn't it? It seemed that way now. "Look, if we're doing this, there has to be some middle ground. You can't ask me to hide indefinitely, and I… I mean, I'm kind of—" He gestured around himself. "Loud? A lot? Extra?" Part of it was a defense mechanism, and he was grateful that he didn't feel like he had to be that way when it was just him and Gabe. "But I can try to tone it down—"

"No," Gabe said right away.

Dante blinked at him. "No?"

Gabe's cheeks were red. "No. Don't be anyone but who you are. You're uncensored. You say what you think." He paused. "I love that about you."

"Okay," Dante said weakly, over the pounding of his heart and the tingling rush of emotion. "I am absolutely going to jump you for that, but I want a plan first. Hiring the skywriter and hiding forever are both off the table. What's left?"

"Hear me out, because this is going to sound bad at first." He bit his lip. "But what about nothing?"

That did sound kind of bad, but Dante was willing to hear more. "Go on."

"I'm not talking about hiding. We do all the stuff we always did"—he winced—"and all the stuff you wanted to do and I was an ass about. We don't try to fool anyone. If you want to post pictures of us together or talk about our cat on social media, go for it. We can be open with the guys on the team. If someone asks, we answer." Gabe shrugged. "That's the short-term plan."

Dante had to admit that made sense, especially for a high-profile couple that had recently split up. A big announcement seemed premature. "And longer term?"

"I'm not sure. But I have a lot of money and the number of a good PR agency." He took another deep breath. "I'm never going to be the kind of guy who's excited to talk about his personal life to the media. But if you want to, then you should, and if it's important to you, then I'll be a part of it. Maybe once you have your offer sheet, or maybe after playoffs. We can decide on a timeline."

It sounded suspiciously like everything Dante wanted. How was he supposed to say no?

Good thing he didn't plan to. "Deal." He smiled. "And I promise not to hold my tongue until I explode ever again."

Gabe laughed. "Good. I missed you running off at the mouth. There's just one more thing."

Right now he could ask Dante for the moon. "Name it."

"Can I come visit Mario? I miss him a lot for a cat I never wanted in the first place."

Oh God—Dante hadn't told him. He grinned. "Yeah, you can visit, but uh, surprise—turns out Mario's a girl."

Gabe's mouth dropped open. "How did you miss that?"

"Apparently it's hard to tell when they're kittens!" Dante said defensively. Then he admitted, "Okay, also I may have misunderstood something the vet tech said. But only because French has unnecessarily gendered words! Why is 'cat' male, anyway?"

"Spanish *also* has gendered nouns."

"And *you* also missed that Mario's a girl."

Gabe laughed. "Touché."

"Anyway," Dante said, standing up at last, "who cares about the cat? We have more important things to talk about."

Talking was the last thing on his mind, and he could tell by the way Gabe was watching him that Gabe knew it. "Oh?"

"Yeah." Dante toed his shoes off and put one knee, then the other, on the bed, until he was straddling Gabe's lap. "What do you think? Scoring three goals and having sex with the captain in the team hotel—a Dante Baltierra hat trick."

IT TURNED out they didn't need to worry too much about coming out to the team after that night. When they arrived at breakfast together, Bricksy took one look at them, dug out his wallet, and handed Yorkie a wad of cash.

Yorkie turned bright red.

"You couldn't have waited another week?" Bricks grumbled, but he didn't seem particularly upset.

Gabe was mortified, but at least it saved him the trouble of figuring out how to bring it up.

Dante salvaged the situation further when he plucked the money out of Yorkie's hand. "Unsportsmanlike conduct, rookie. That's insider trading." Then he fanned the bills out at Gabe. "What do you think? You Can Play donation?"

That sounded like a fair deal to him.

The Dekes still hadn't cinched a playoff spot by the last game of the season. They were tied with Toronto and one point behind New York, with Carolina having dropped out of the race. People had been laying bets for weeks. Since New York's final game was against last-place Buffalo, most analysts assumed they would be going, and the remaining spot would go to Toronto or Quebec City.

Gabe hated that they were so close to the playoffs with everything hinging on chance. If the Dekes lost and Toronto won, or if they both lost or won, the Shield would go to the playoffs, since they had more wins overall. It was frustrating that another team's upcoming game influenced their chances so heavily.

The Dekes lined up against the Voyageurs.

"At least it's a home game," Flash offered. He wasn't back to playing yet, but Coach had made an exception and let him into the locker room.

Well, sure. But Quebec City had gone without a professional hockey team for long enough that the audience held just as many Voyageurs fans as Dekes. Still, Gabe nodded breathlessly and squared his shoulders. They could do this.

The first period passed scoreless, and the crowd's expectations weighed heavily on Gabe. Coach had made them hand in their cell phones before the game so they couldn't get distracted checking other scores. Now she stood leaning against the locker-room wall, rubbing her stomach and grimacing. "Don't you dare disgrace this baby by losing now. We've worked hard for this all year. You've bled and sweated ice. Don't let this season beat you."

Gabe locked eyes with Dante, then Yorkie, then Bricks. They could do this.

The Voyageurs opened scoring in the second period, a back-and-forth combo almost too fast for Gabe to follow. Screened by his own defensemen, Olie never had a chance to get his stick on it.

Gabe came off shift just after, buzzing with the need to get their momentum back. He slapped Yorkie on the shoulder. "Go get 'em, kid."

Thirty seconds later Tips slipped a wrister past Montreal's goalie off Yorkie's rebound.

The rest of the second period passed in a flurry of checking and slick stickhandling, but no more goals.

Now, in the third, it was time for Gabe to remind people why the Dekes made him their captain. He knocked shoulders with their new center and then bumped his helmet against Dante's. "Now we prove we've earned our places."

They went scoreless for three shifts, hanging on to the puck by the skin of their teeth. Then Bricks went to the boards with an opposing forward and came out with the puck. He saucered a pass to Gabe over chewed-up ice, and he took it down past the Voyageurs' defense.

He didn't have a good shot, but he did have a teammate. After faking a shot on net, Gabe dropped a no-look pass to Dante. He was rounding the back of the net when the goal light went off and "Moves Like Jagger" blared from the overhead speakers.

Dante slammed him into the boards, whooping.

Gabe and Tips each scored again after that. The Voyageurs couldn't keep up.

They won, but it wasn't time to celebrate yet.

Everything in the amphitheater stopped as the announcer came on the PA. "The buzzer just sounded in New York. The final score is Buffalo 5, New York 1."

"Holy shit," Yorkie said in the brief moment of dead silence before the theater erupted in cheers. "Holy shit!" New York's loss coupled with their win put the Dekes ahead in points. It didn't matter what Toronto did now. They were in.

Tips was still doing his victory lap, and the rest of the team boiled off the bench to join him. Gabe made a beeline for Olie, got there just after Bricks, and crashed into the two of them as they leaned their helmets together, screaming in each other's face. "Fucking right!"

It was another few shouted expletives before Gabe saw the familiar 68 on a sleeve next to him, and he made a split decision. One hard yank on the back of that jersey, and Dante spun 180 degrees, red-cheeked and beaming, helmet discarded somewhere in the celebration, sweaty hair stuck up all over.

Gabe fisted an ungloved hand just above Dante's Dekes logo, yanked him forward, and planted a smacking kiss on his cheek—nothing other guys hadn't done in the heat of playoff excitement, but Dante and Gabe knew it was for them.

Fuck what anyone else thought. Fuck the media and society's expectations and everyone who said a gay man couldn't be good at hockey, and fuck every homophobic coach and teammate Gabe had ever had growing up who'd made him believe it.

Gabe *could* have it all. Love, sex, hockey. And he was going to do everything in his power to hold on to all three for as long as he could.

IT WAS late when they returned to Gabe's house. Dante was still buzzing with adrenaline, the thrill of victory humming under his skin. He took it easy on the booze, because honestly, he'd lost a little too much weight lately. He didn't need to go getting dehydrated or lose his balance and fall and reinjure himself.

The victory, and Gabe at his side, were reason enough for his energy.

But even with the win coursing through them, something kept their movements slow and deliberate. The space between them disappeared. Dante should have felt desperate with it, but the touch of Gabe's skin settled something inside him. The energy became intensity, focus.

That feeling of being seen and known and held pushed him over the edge and into bliss.

Afterward they lay facing each other in bed, exhausted and grinning as the triumph of the night reasserted itself, and suddenly Dante couldn't wait any longer. "I want to tell you something, okay?"

Gabe squeezed his hand and his expression became serious. "Okay."

Swallowing, Dante drew away and pulled the chain over his head. Then he pressed the body-warm piece of metal into Gabe's hand and curled his fingers around it.

Suddenly Gabe's eyes were wide-awake.

Dante took a deep breath. "When my grandmother gave me this at Christmas, she was not-so-subtly telling me to stop fucking around. She wanted me to settle down. She wanted me to 'be happy.'"

Gabe's throat worked as he swallowed.

Now Dante exhaled shakily and let the ache of sadness flow out with it. "She left me a note, you know? Said she didn't understand, but she loved me." He cleared his throat. "Anyway. I want you to have this. To wear it for me. It's—the team's done so well since I started wearing it, but… ever since she gave it to me, I've known it wasn't for me."

There was only one person he could imagine giving it to.

Gabe opened his hand, and Dante heard his breath catch. But he didn't make a move to put the chain around his neck. His voice was hushed. "You want me to…."

Dante felt himself go pink, but he quirked his lips and made himself meet Gabe's eyes. "I love you, okay?" he said, with no small amount of exasperation. "You complete idiot. Now would you put the ring on, please?"

Gabe's eyes were soft and bright when he opened his hand again and lifted the necklace over his head. The ring settled against his chest like it belonged there.

Dante breathed out a sigh. "Thank you."

"You have it backwards," Gabe told him. He brushed his thumb over the curve of Dante's cheek and kissed him, soft and sweet. "I love you too."

THEIR FIRST playoff game was two nights later in Philadelphia, and everyone's nerves were frayed. The Firebirds had eked out the top spot in the division.

Even though Gabe loved and believed in his team, he was still surprised when they snagged the first game of the series 3–2 in regulation. Like most of his team-mates, he wasn't too proud to start celebrating and laughing on the ice when the buzzer went.

No matter what else happened, they had this moment.

But then they had it again two nights later, once more on Philadelphia's ice.

Game two was a bloodier battle, with the Birds playing furious and rough, obviously ashamed of having dropped the ball on home ice. And who could blame them?

But the Dekes held out and battled hard to keep the puck in the offensive zone and push a couple of goals in the net. Neither of them was pretty, but looks didn't count. When the buzzer rang at the end of the third and the score was tied 2–2, Gabe didn't care about pretty.

It went to second OT. Everyone was exhausted, but both goalies held their ground, denying everyone—until Dante picked up the puck in the neutral zone, tore down the ice, spun to avoid the Firebirds's defensem-an, and backhanded the puck into the net. But they lost game three 1–0.

The locker room was quiet after, everyone dis-heartened to lose the first game at home. But Coach was having none of it.

"We're still up two games to one, and they might have outscored you tonight, but they didn't outplay you. Tomorrow night you'll do better." She winced and put a hand on her stomach. Gabe guessed she'd been kicked somewhere sensitive. "Or else."

They did do better. Winning their third game of the series at home was a high unlike any other. They screamed at each other, whooped and hugged on the ice. Yorkie got buried beneath a pile of exhilarated teammates appreciating his game-winning goal.

Up 3–1, they headed to Philly for game five. Gabe and Dante weren't the only ones vibrating in their seats, filled with anticipation. They were on the brink of advancing to the next round, but no one said it out loud. No one wanted to jinx it.

The Firebirds were desperate. They fought hard and mean in the hope of staving off a Dekes win for one more game. Midway through the first period, one of the Birds hit a slapshot. Bricks took it in the face.

It knocked him to his knees. He spat blood onto the ice, and Gabe thought he could see teeth.

The trainers ran out, quickly got him on his feet, and pressed a white towel to his face.

Both teams gathered around their benches, waiting to see how things played out. Coach paced back and forth, muttering. When the trainers guided Bricks away, the Dekes clattered their sticks on the ice.

Filled with indignation over the injury, they rallied. But their 2–0 lead didn't last, and they left the ice with a 2–2 score.

At intermission they learned Bricks lost two teeth and needed forty-nine stitches, but the shot hadn't broken any bones. He looked disgusting, but the doctors predicted he'd be back for the next game.

Before they could feel relieved, Coach tore them a new one for throwing away the lead.

The second period was just as brutal. Coach scowled and paced behind the bench. The refs called no penalties, content to let the players half murder each other on ice. The Firebirds led 4–3.

During second intermission Coach yelled at them some more, rubbed her belly angrily, and reiterated how hard they'd worked to get this far.

In the third, the Dekes scored twice in a row to make it 5–4… and they kept the lead.

And that was it. The Dekes won their first series.

The on-ice celebration culminated in a big, sweaty group hug, and Gabe kissed Olie's glove and blocker. For five minutes, Coach watched them all with an odd half grimace, half smile, rubbing her stomach. Then she shouted them into the handshake line.

They bubbled into the locker room, still ebullient. Gabe had a text waiting from Kitty—*thanks for eliminate Philly for us, sad we have to beat you next*. He snorted and saved it so he could think of a good return chirp later.

Before the media came in, Coach clapped for their attention. "Okay! Thanks for getting that done. I appreciate it." They all laughed, but Coach shook her head. "No, seriously. I'm proud of the way you played tonight. You showed the league we deserve our spot."

Gabe flushed with pleasure, and Dante nudged his shoulder and squeezed his hand.

Then Coach said, "Now I have to go talk to the media, and then one of you idiots needs to get me to the hospital. I can't believe I'm having this kid in Philadelphia." Her gaze lit on Yorkie. "Rookie, you're gonna need the practice. Get in the shower."

Yorkie went white, then started pulling at his clothes. "Yes, Coach."

Trish poked her head in then and looked around. "Are you guys ready for this? Because there is an actual media frenzy going on out here and there's gonna be a riot soon."

Coach put her game face back on and squared her shoulders. "Let's do this."

THEY LOST to Pittsburgh in six.

The handshake line seemed endless. Dante tried to keep up a brave face. He didn't want his mug showing up on any hockey blogs with a caption about how he shouldn't play hockey if he couldn't lose without crying. It wasn't like the loss was a surprise, but he didn't have to be happy about it.

At least the loss meant Dante could shave his travesty of a playoff beard. It itched and it was doing terrible things to his skin. Maybe next year he'd just buck tradition and skip it entirely. His face didn't deserve this treatment.

Halfway through the line, he found himself touching gloves with Kitty, who made a noise of dissatisfaction and leaned down to engulf him in a hug instead. "You play good," he said in Dante's ear. "Maybe get us next year. Rematch?"

Dante squeezed back—even in hockey gear Kitty gave the best hugs—and then pulled away and slugged in him the shoulder. "We'll definitely get you next year."

Kitty smacked him on the ass when he moved on to Gabe.

"Well, he called it," Gabe told Dante as they continued the handshakes.

"What, Kitty?"

Gabe nodded. "Yeah. He said they'd win the Cup easy."

Now that was just *rude*. Dante gave him an affronted look. "We didn't make it *easy*." And Pittsburgh hadn't won anything yet.

Back in Quebec City, Gabe planned a backyard barbecue to cap off the season. Dante took one look at the scale of it—he'd put up an actual whiteboard in the kitchen to diagram the "plays"—and called a caterer. There was no reason to subject a team full of hungry guys and their families to the barbecue equivalent of burnt toast and crunchy scrambled eggs, and Dante wasn't cooking for fifty.

He still hadn't made peace with the season being over, but he knew the team had given it everything in the tank. He'd led the team in playoff scoring and edged out Gabe by two points, though Gabe had more goals. Pittsburgh's goaltender had personally told him Dante gave him nightmares.

But it wasn't enough to keep Dante from being disappointed.

Then, the day before the party, Dekes front office called him and his agent in to give him his offer sheet and talk about his official contract. Brigitte, the general manager, had a real way with words, because she managed to imply that the intention to sign him wouldn't change if Dante did something wild like out himself as being in a relationship with the team's captain, without implying that Dante was in fact in said relationship.

He came away from the meeting with the feeling that Brigitte should've been a diplomat and found that his disappointment over the season ending had pretty much disappeared.

The party itself was low-key as far as these things went. Gabe didn't have a pool, and it was still too cool to enjoy one without a heater anyway, but he'd borrowed Flash's volleyball net, and Dante had gone to the local toy store and bought them out of goggles and water guns, which he preloaded and arranged just inside the back gate.

By the time the party was over, Dante had a sunburn and a smile and a whole camera roll full of pictures for his Instagram, a handful of which had already been approved by their PR firm to use as the soft launch of their relationship to the world at large. He and Gabe went over them in bed, propped up against the headboard with pillows.

"What do you think?" Dante asked. "These ones?"

The first was the shot of Gabe kissing his cheek after the last regular season game. In the second, Dante had a tie knotted around his head Rambo-style while Gabe, slung over his shoulder, laughed and aimed his water gun at Baz.

The third was Gabe asleep on the couch the day after their playoff exit, Mario curled up on his chest.

"Kind of subtle for you," Gabe commented.

"I don't know," Dante said after a moment's thought. "I think I disagree. I'm not posting them to tell the whole world we're boning." Instead they showed two professional hockey players being happy and in love and domestic and a little silly.

"Well, I like them." Gabe kissed the side of his head. "Go for it."

Dante thumbed down to caption the photos. *This season didn't end the way we hoped, but it's not all bad I guess. See you in October! #catdad*

After some consideration, he amended that to *#catdads*.

His phone made a little chirping beep to confirm the upload. Then Dante set it on the nightstand, curled up on the bed facing Gabe, and let out a dramatic sigh. "I really wanted that trophy."

Gabe mirrored his pose and tucked one hand under his cheek. "I'm shocked." The ring on the chain around his neck settled against his bare chest, and he hummed thoughtfully as Dante touched the warm metal. "I'll make you a deal to keep you motivated."

Dante met his eyes. That sounded promising. "I'm listening."

"When we do win the Cup together, I'll kiss you at center ice. On the mouth."

Dante mock gasped. "Scandalous." Then he smiled. "You were going to do that anyway." Gabe wasn't ever going to be the poster child for PDA, but Dante got a public cheek kiss for making playoffs. He was pretty sure he could get first base for a Cup win.

"With *tongue*," Gabe added seriously.

Laughing, Dante curled their fingers together. "Deal. Just make sure I take my mouth guard out first."

Gabe grimaced. "Ew."

"My thoughts exactly." Dante closed his eyes and breathed deeply. His body couldn't stave off the bone-deep exhaustion of the season any longer. "Next year, then."

Gabe kissed the back of his hand. "Next year."

Anyway, in a handful of weeks Dante would be lying with his boyfriend on a beautiful secluded beach, eating his weight in poke and getting sand in inconvenient places.

It wasn't a deep Cup run, but as consolation prizes went, it didn't suck.

They fell asleep.

DANTE'S INSTAGRAM post didn't so much go viral as take over social media for the next week. Apparently he was loud even when he was trying to be subtle. Gabe probably shouldn't be surprised.

For the first day and a half, Dante let him hide in the house and play with Mario.

Then he booked them a four-day golf package in a place with shitty cell phone reception while their agents and the PR firm handled the media requests.

Dante got six hundred mosquito bites and lost half a dozen golf balls. Gabe slathered him in calamine lotion every night and fell even more stupidly in love.

The day after they got home, he let himself read the single article Erika had forwarded.

Dekes' Baltierra and Martin: Parents of World's Cutest Cat?
By Kevin McIntyre

This week Quebec City forward Dante Baltierra took the internet by storm when he posted a collection of pictures, including one of teammate Gabriel Martin and an adorable kitten snoozing together with the hashtag "catdads."

Since then social media has been abuzz with speculation as to whether the revelation that they are coparenting a feline was intended to indicate Martin and Baltierra are in a romantic relationship. Reporters at less free-thinking outlets have implied anything beyond a platonic friendship would negatively impact the team's performance. Requests for my opinion and insider knowledge on the subject have flooded my inbox. My editor insists I address the issue. So here goes.

Are Martin and Baltierra in a romantic relationship?

I mean, probably. Why else would Baltierra post a picture of them kissing, even if it was on the cheek?

Are you going to ask about their relationship next time they have media availability?

No. My job is to talk about hockey, and if I ask about it, neither of them will give me an interview ever again.

Don't you think this will impact the team's performance?

For better or for worse? The Nordiques made it to the second round of the playoffs after trading one of their top defensemen and losing Fillion to a season-ending injury, and to cap it off, they had just named Martin as their captain. I think they're fine. If they're not fine, it will be front office's job to handle it, not anyone in the media's.

How cute is that cat, though?

So cute. Do the Dekes sell cat-size jerseys? What number do you think she wears? Can Baltierra get me her autograph?

Gabe smiled and closed the article. He made a mental note to be extra nice to Kevin this year.

Then he went downstairs to find out if they had any food in the house or if Dante wanted to go out to dinner.

POSTGAME

"WOW." DANTE wobbled unsteadily as he looked up at the enormous photograph framed over their mantel. "How'd you get it done so fast?"

Gabe was feeling a little light-headed himself. He blamed the champagne. "I paid the photographer. Like. A lot."

As soon as he realized he'd have the chance to keep that promise, he'd made sure the moment would be commemorated. He wanted to look at it every day for the rest of his life—a photograph of Dante taking the Cup from his hands while Gabe kissed him on home ice in front of twenty-eight thousand ecstatic fans.

Dante leaned heavily into his chest. Gabe compensated by sitting on—falling onto—the couch and dragging Dante with him. "You should've had her edit out my beard."

"No! It was *lucky*." Last year Dante hadn't grown one, and they'd exited playoffs early. They hadn't taken any chances this year.

"That doesn't mean we should have to look at it." Dante hated how it looked so much he'd shaved before he finished his second celebratory beer.

"I love your ugly beard."

"Oh God, I'm going to throw up in my mouth."

Gabe turned to see Slimer standing in the doorway. He had a bottle of premixed margarita taped to his hand.

"You have *never* just thrown up in your mouth," Dante said. "It's always on someone's patio, or in a potted plant, or *in the hot tub*—"

"The potted plant was Yorkie," Slimer protested. He hiccupped. "Which is why I came in."

Gabe blinked. "Because Yorkie threw up in a plant?"

Slimer shook his head, then quickly stopped, his face turning the same shade as his margarita. "'Cause he and Jenna are putting Gabby in the Cup."

Dante scrambled upright so abruptly that he elbowed Gabe in the stomach, and Gabe almost pulled a Slimer. "Adorable! I have to see it."

As usual, Gabe could do nothing but follow helplessly after him. Honestly, it was a pretty sweet place to be.

The backyard was in chaos. They probably owed their neighbors about a zillion apologies. Under a sunshade at the far side of the property was the Stanley Cup, a big shiny trophy that would soon have Gabe's name engraved on it forever.

Gabe's namesake was sitting in it… kind of. At almost two years old, Gabrielle Yorkshire didn't really fit. But that wasn't stopping Yorkie from holding her so that it *looked* like she was sitting in it.

Gabe couldn't blame Yorkie. He and Dante already tried the same thing with Mario, who wanted none of it. At least Gabby seemed reasonably content with the idea.

Until she spotted her favorite uncle, at least. Then she waved her hands and squirmed until Yorkie laughed and put her down. She raced across the yard and straight into Dante's arms.

He swung her up into the air and propped her on his hip. "Hey, squirt. What do you think of Daddy's new toy?"

Gabby thought about this for a second. "Shiny," she concluded. "Big."

According to Yorkie, she had entered the magpie phase. "That it is," he agreed.

"Shiny," she repeated, this time flailing toward Gabe, the only person who could give Dante a run for the title of favorite uncle. Her chubby fingers caught on the chain around his neck.

"Careful," Dante cautioned, but he handed her over so she could look at it more closely.

Gabby tugged on the ring a few times before she let it fall flat against Gabe's chest. "Small."

At Dante's offended expression, Gabe couldn't help but snort.

Then Dante said, "Well, don't worry, squirt. We'll get him a bigger, shinier one soon."

Cup rings were obnoxiously large and gaudy. Gabe couldn't wait.

And if Dante meant something else… well. That would be pretty great too.

Keep Reading for an excerpt from
Scoring Position
by Ashlyn Kane and Morgan James

PREGAME

STILL STICKY with sweat from his morning run, Ryan Wright sat at the kitchen table in his parents' Vancouver home and dug into his bowl of Magic Spoon. His sister Tara would roll her eyes and call him a child for eating knockoff Cocoa Puffs—which she would be wrong about, because eating a high-protein, low-carb cereal that tasted like childhood was absolutely an adult decision—but Tara wasn't here. Even the nutritionists wouldn't complain.

Mostly because Ryan didn't tell the Voyageurs' trainers about his breakfast choices.

But he had texted his sister when the first boxes of cereal arrived in the mail. *You're an idiot*, she texted back. *Also, maybe you wouldn't have to defend your adulthood if you didn't crash at our parents' house all summer, every summer.*

That was rude and hurtful on top of being incorrect. It was a month, max—the last of his off-season training and a visit with his parents before his return to Montreal for camp. Besides, plenty of hockey players spent large portions of their summers where they grew up. *Staying with family isn't childish, it's practical. Mom and Dad are so busy, I'd never see them if I didn't, he'd responded. Don't be jealous because Mom loves me best.*

This was a blatant lie—Tara was the favorite, having split the difference between following in Mom's footsteps as a doctor and Dad's as a therapist by getting a master's in genetic counseling—but Ryan preferred to pretend he didn't know that. The truth was Vancouver was an overpriced metropolis with a housing crisis, and Ryan wasn't going to make it worse by buying a house he wouldn't even live in for most of the year.

And seriously, his parents? Never home. If it wasn't regular office hours or emergencies, it was out-of-town professional development seminars.

Speaking of… he'd almost forgotten that Tara was supposed to be presenting at a fancy conference this week. Ryan pulled out his phone to text her some vague chirping encouragement… and realized his notifications had blown up while he was out on his run.

His heart sank. That many unread text messages, WhatsApp alerts, and pushes from *theScore* could only mean one thing—a trade.

Ryan didn't want to believe it was him… but he knew it was. However much a team appreciated the way he could get the locker room fired up, that wasn't enough to keep him. Ryan was a middling center on a good day, and there was no loyalty in professional sports.

Even Gretzky had been traded. Ryan just hadn't expected he'd be eating breakfast alone at his parents' kitchen table the first time it happened to him.

He tried to set aside the sinking feeling in his stomach and the way his skin had suddenly gone cold. Then he opened theScore to view the damage. It would be easier than getting the news from a teammate. Still, a piece of cereal seemed to have lodged in his throat.

Fuel Sends Lundström, Second-Round Pick to Montreal for Ryan Wright

Fuck.

Ryan's head swam and he sagged in his chair. He'd thought he had at least another year with the Voyageurs—that was when his current contract expired, and his agent seemed to think they were making good progress negotiating an extension.

But that trade? That was like offering up a brand-new Ferrari and a road bike for a three-year-old Toyota Corolla. Montreal would've been stupid to pass that up.

Through uncooperative, disbelieving eyes, he skimmed the article, but the content didn't magically make sense of the headline. Traded to the Fuel for a young, cheap, talented right-handed defenseman and a second-round pick.

Did the Fuel just *like* losing? Tanking for a better draft position didn't make a lot of sense if they were also giving up picks.

What did you think was going to happen, Ryan?

He dropped the phone and scrubbed his hands over his face in hopes of silencing that nagging internal voice, but it was no use. He'd been living with Josh's parting words in his head for the past four and a half years, and he'd probably be hearing them for the rest of his life.

Josh had been headed for Silicon Valley, backed by his trust fund, his bachelor's degree, and a determination to make his own mark on the world. If the timing had been different, Ryan might have followed. At twenty-one, he'd almost given up on the idea of hockey as a career. And then a scout showed up at his last college game to check out the goaltender on the other team, and Ryan was invited to a tryout in Montreal, and....

And obviously it had been stupid of him to think that just because Josh *could* do software engineering anywhere in the world, he'd want to do it where Ryan was.

What am I supposed to do, huh? Pack my shit and make new connections every time you get traded?

Ryan ran his hands through his hair and pulled at it until it stung. Getting traded was bad enough. He didn't need to relive heartbreak on top of it.

He swallowed as he thumbed out of the app and into his texts. Several teammates—*former* teammates—had sent unhappy messages filled with *Fuck!* and *What?!* and crying emojis. Bobby's was a gif of a toddler throwing a tantrum.

Ryan had been traded. To fucking Indianapolis, of all places.

He thought of Montreal, with its crowded streets and tightly packed buildings, and the neighborhood he'd settled into, with the eclectic inhabitants who spilled out onto the streets in any weather and poked their noses into Ryan's business because he lived in the neighborhood, not because he was a hockey player. He thought of the campus grounds and the coffeehouses nearby that were always crowded with students, and of his apartment near Metro Centre with the metal steps to the front door that conspired with ice to try to kill him every January, and the cozy living room where he liked to cuddle with his hookup on his days off.

Nice knowing you, Mathieu. But hey, at least he'd learned his lesson with Josh. Ryan's life was not conducive to having a boyfriend. Mathieu would understand.

He was still stunned, staring at his phone and the unanswered texts, trying to process just what had happened, when his agent called.

Maybe she had good news. Maybe this was all some kind of bizarre press-office fuckup. He hit the screen so hard it hurt his thumb.

"Tell me I'm dreaming," he said instead of hello.

To her credit, Diane didn't sigh. "I'm sorry, Ryan."

Fuck. He squeezed his eyes shut and pinched the skin between his brows. "The Fuel?"

They played in the Western Conference, so Ryan had only played them twice a year. Three years ago they'd drafted Nico Kirschbaum, a first-round pick who was supposed to be the new Hockey Jesus or something, but so far it hadn't done them any good. Other than the fact that they were terrible, he didn't know much about the team.

"On the plus side," Diane said, "real estate is cheap?"

Fuck, he was going to have to sell his apartment.

Fuck, he was going to have to find a *new* apartment—with training camp starting in a week.

He pushed away his bowl of cereal, his appetite gone. "Can you… I mean, I'm obviously a little blindsided. You would've told me, right? If you'd known this was coming?"

"That *is* my job." She had a real way of conveying meaning with tone, Ryan thought. It was just pointed enough to put him in his place for questioning her competence, but gentle enough to make him aware she understood he was hurting. Management didn't always tell guys or their reps up front. "I didn't find out until a few minutes ago. I just got off the phone with the Fuel's GM."

That seemed promising. Ryan was good at his job, but his job was solid third-liner and penalty-killer. He was never going to be the guy who rated a lot of personal attention from GMs. "And? What's the situation?" He snorted. "Don't tell me Indianapolis suddenly discovered a desperate need for some sandpaper." Ryan wouldn't exactly call himself a grit player, but that was mainly because he was too short. Still, he was a pest—good for drawing penalties by pissing off the other team—but there were plenty of other annoying forwards in the league, and most of them were better at scoring goals than he was.

"I didn't get that impression, no," Diane said smoothly. There was a rhythmic, muffled tapping—ballpoint pen on a legal pad. "It was weird."

Okay, not so promising. Ryan's heart sank further. "Weird how?"

"Just *weird*. He wanted to verify what school you went to, asked about your major, that kind of thing." Maybe the guy was a college sports fan. Ryan had gone to the University of Michigan. Their fans were on a whole other level. Weirder things had happened. "Listen, I don't know what's going on, but you saw the details," she continued. "There's more to this than meets the eye."

Ryan had hoped he was only being paranoid. He'd heard a few rumors, but gossip from Indianapolis didn't filter reliably all the way to Montreal. "Locker room problems?" The Fuel wouldn't be the first team to struggle with developing a winning culture, and while Ryan might not be the most knowledgeable man on the team about how to *win*, he was a pretty good hype guy. Morale he could do.

At least, he had in Ann Arbor and Montreal. Though from the outside, the Fuel resembled the Pit of Despair. So maybe not.

"Maybe." More tapping. "I'm not sure. I just don't want you going into this unprepared."

Just heartsick and bitter.

He let out a long breath. He had to get used to it. Sure, this was the first time he'd been traded, but he was twenty-six. It wouldn't be the last. It probably wouldn't even be the most painful. Having his home ripped out from under him was just never not going to suck. "Thanks, I guess. I appreciate it."

"Hey, just doing my job." There was the sound of paper shuffling. "With that out of the way, I want to give you a few details about the transition. They're going to want you to come in for entry interviews, PR, all that stuff. Most of it should be scheduled during training camp, but you might want to think about getting to town a couple days early. You know anybody on the team?"

"Kind of. I played at Shattuck with Tom Yorkshire, but he was younger than me. We didn't exactly keep in touch." Boarding school was almost a decade ago. Yorkie had had to grow up fast when he became a dad at nineteen. Looking after a bunch of sweaty players was probably child's play after that.

Heh. Child's play.

"The captain's not a bad guy to know, though, if you only get to know one person."

"Yeah, I guess. I'll track down his number."

"Good," Diane said approvingly. "Okay, I'm going to let you go. Expect front office to call sooner rather than later. Keep your eyes open for shenanigans and call me if something smells weird."

Despite himself, Ryan smiled weakly. Knowing Diane had his back was cold comfort, but it was better than no comfort at all. "I will. Thanks, Diane."

They hung up, and Ryan gingerly pulled the phone away from his ear and glanced at the notifications.

Twenty-seven.

He hadn't gotten that many since he signed his first contract—a one-year, two-way deal that saw him play the first half of the season with Montreal's AHL affiliate. But there was no time to get nostalgic now.

He needed to pack.

ASHLYN KANE is a world-traveling homebody who defines herself by her contradictions: she loves chaos but craves order, and writes the most when she has the least free time to do it. Her house is as full of half-finished projects as her writing folder. With the help of her ADHD meds, she gets by.

An early reader and talker, Ashlyn has always had a flair for language and storytelling. She attended her first writers' workshop as an eight-year-old, won an amateur poetry competition as a teenager, and—the crowning achievement of her adulthood—received a starred review in *Publishers Weekly* for her novel *Fake Dating the Prince*.

Her hobbies include DIY home decor, container gardening (no pulling weeds), music, and spending time with her enormous chocolate lapdog. She is the fortunate wife of a wonderful man, the daughter of two sets of great parents, and the proud older sister/sister-in-law of the world's biggest nerds.

Sign up for her newsletter at www.ashlynkane.ca/newsletter/

Website: www.ashlynkane.ca

MORGAN JAMES is a clueless (older) millennial who's still trying to figure out what they'll be when they grow up and enjoying the journey to get there. Now, with a couple of degrees, a few stints in Europe, and more than one false start to a career, they eagerly wait to see what's next. James started writing fiction before they could spell and wrote their first (unpublished) novel in middle school. They haven't stopped since. Geek, artist, archer, and fanatic, Morgan passes their free hours in imaginary worlds, with people on pages and screens—it's an addiction, as is their love of coffee and tea. They live in Canada with their massive collection of unread books and where they are the personal servant of too many four-legged creatures.

Twitter: @MorganJames71
Facebook: www.facebook.com/morganjames007

HOCKEY EVER AFTER · BOOK TWO

SCORING POSITION

You miss
100 percent of
the shots you
don't take.

ASHLYN KANE
MORGAN JAMES

Hockey Ever After: Book Two

Ryan Wright's new hockey team is a dumpster fire. He expects to lose games—not his heart.

Ryan's laid-back attitude should be an advantage in Indianapolis. Even if he doesn't accomplish much on the ice, he can help his burned-out teammates off it. And no one needs a friend—or a hug—more than Nico Kirschbaum, the team's struggling would-be superstar.

Nico doesn't appreciate that management traded for another openly gay player and told them to make friends. Maybe he doesn't know what his problem is, but he'll solve it with hard work, not by bonding with the class clown.

It's obvious to Ryan that Nico's lonely, gifted, and cracking under pressure. No amount of physical practice will fix his mental game. But convincing Nico to let Ryan help means getting closer than is wise for Ryan's heart—especially once he unearths Nico's sense of humor.

Will Nico and Ryan risk making a pass, or will they keep missing 100 percent of the shots they don't take?

www.dreamspinnerpress.com

For Jax Hall, all-but-dissertation in mathematics, slinging drinks and serenading patrons at a piano bar is the perfect remedy for months of pandemic anxiety. He doesn't expect to end up improvising on stage with pop violinist Aria Darvish, but the attraction that sparks between them? That's a mathematical certainty. If he can get Ari to act on it, even better.

Ari hasn't written a note, and his album deadline is looming. Then he meets Jax, and suddenly he can't stop the music. But Ari doesn't know how to interpret Jax's flirting—is making him a drink called Sex with the Bartender a serious overture?

Jax jumps in with both feet, the only way he knows how. Ari is wonderful, and Jax loves having a partner who's on the same page. But Ari's struggles with his parents' expectations, and Jax's with the wounds of his past, threaten to unbalance an otherwise perfect equation. Can they prove their double act has merit, or does it only work in theory?

www.dreamspinnerpress.com